READS LIKE MURDER

IN HONOLULU

By

G Donovan

To Lynette

My Good Friend. — We Have so much fun talking. So glad you are a <u>Reader</u>.

Mahalo & Aloha,

Dream Books LLC
www.dreambooksllc.com

Dream Books LLC

www.dreambooksllc.com

Published by Dream Books LLC

www.dreambooksllc.com

ISBN: 978-1-61584-150-9

Printed In the USA

Acknowledgements

Mahalo nui loa to my Ohana – family. Ds, Martins, Herles. Donovans -- all. Those of you who have read my works and those who haven't. Mahalo for all the years of believing in me. Especially Uncle Joe, who instilled in me the love of mysteries. And mom and dad, who encouraged my imagination and reading, that lead to my love of writing.

Linda, Maura, Jane, Barb, Anna – all my friends – aikane – peers and editors. You know who you are. Mahalo for your faith and hard work to help me get here. You always believed in me.

Mahalo to the people of paradise – Hawaii and the aloha spirit.

Thanks Jacob Morris and Dream Books LLC for giving me the break of a lifetime! And making my dreams come true.

Ha'i mo'olelo malama kamali'i ike akua
Story caretaker of god's children

Table of Contents

GLOSSARY

Mo'opuna kane -- Grandson

Ka nai'a   mokuaina – dolphin island

Kahuna – holy man, religious leader

keiki -- child

malihini – newcomer

kanaka -- man

kauhale – home

wa'a – canoe

kahana – turning point

hou – new

makani – wind

e komo mai -- welcome

hanai – adopt

pau - finish

CHAPTER ONE

I think these mysteries are rubbing off on
you.

Perfection is underrated. A perfect day is simple.

The languid thoughts sifted easily through Haley Wyndham's mind like the gentle, coastal breeze brushing against her face. To her, perfection happened on a daily basis.

"Whoa!" she gasped, narrowly avoiding a little girl who opened a car door without checking the bike lane!

She wheeled back around to make sure the little girl had not been frightened out of her wits. No, bike incident was invisible to the minor. Good. Haley didn't want to mar her perfect day with smashing into a kid. Sighing with relief she turned back on her way. Okay, less daydreaming, more attention to the road if she wanted to live long enough to reach her shop.

She increased her speed cycling alongside the vehicles at the curb, anticipating the open space of a NO PARKING zone just ahead --

Suddenly she was catapulted onto the hood of a car and rolled to the pavement with her bike atop her legs. Haley fought to catch her breath. On the asphalt, staring up at the gray-tinted sky, confused and dazed at her abrupt position on the ground, she gasped until her lungs filled and emptied in normal rhythm.

"That car hit you!"

"Call an ambulance!"

"Don't move. It's safer to stay where you are."

As best she could, Haley sorted through the cacophony of confusing observations and well-intentioned instructions from the crowd.

Someone had hit her!

Slowly disentangling herself from the bike, she assured the chorus of spectators that she felt fine. Despite more advice to remain on the pavement, she carefully came to her feet, trying to ignore the pains vying for attention up and down her body. It was an instinctive show of stoicism to achieve an upright position, because she had no intention of lying on the street under her bike.

The crowd gathered in sympathetic concern, but most onlookers soon dispersed when she assured she was not injured seriously. Despising the attention, she brushed off their anxieties and her clothes while ignoring the bumps and bruises she knew she would feel more distinctly and persistently later in the day, and straightened, cringing at the myriad hurts. This was not her first wipeout and she felt lucky to walk away from the crash; collisions between bikes and cars notoriously went in favor of the autos. She groaned while attempting to take a step toward the curb. Her right pant leg was ripped, and scrapes along her right leg and arm were annoying, but little more than burning scratches. Her cap was torn beyond repair, and her headache testified to the practicality of a helmet -- in the future -- over a fashion statement. The greatest casualty seemed her bike: totaled.

Haley rubbed her head. "Did anybody see what happened?"

A dark-haired man in a suit lingered, seemingly more genuinely interested in her health than the various, curious on-lookers who had been drawn to the accident site. He helped her carry the wrecked bike to the curb.

"What's important is what you saw." He picked up the shattered pieces of her CD player.

"A green car was racing from that corner and swerved right into you." An elderly lady appeared out of nowhere and seemed certain of her facts. "It was deliberate. I've seen enough of these things on TV to tell that it was a murder attempt!"

Dark-haired Suitman countered with his own absolutes. "It was a blue Honda."

He perched with a hand on Haley's elbow and she had to step aside to steer clear of the unwelcome grasp.

"You're injured. It's important that we get the facts clear before the police arrive," he said almost to himself. "Hit and run, multiple injuries. This will mean a hospital stay. Back injuries. Oh, and a head injury. Do you know how serious this is? I do. I deal in this line of work."

"Hit and runs?" She must be dazed from the surprise or the knock to the head because he was confusing her. He was also annoying with his unwanted hovering.

Haley asked the group, "Did anyone get a license plate number or a good description of the driver?"

Both helpers chimed in again, but when pressed for details admitted they could not be certain of any opinion strong enough to be considered a fact about the driver or the car. The lady, however, was standing by her color as green for the vehicle, while aggressive Suitman insisted it was a new blue Japanese import. Probably a rich driver, he speculated.

The older woman became fed up with the overbearing businessman. "Can't you leave her alone? She's hurt, skinny little thing. Where is that ambulance?"

Taller than the lady, Haley did not consider herself too thin, either. Trim, not skinny, she silently corrected, but offered, "I'm fine. I don't need an ambulance." She edged away from the interfering group. "If you could just settle on a description for the police it would help."

"Say, you sound like you're a lawyer." Suitman seemed suddenly suspicious.

"Must be the headache. No, I just read too many cop books."

"I watch them on TV," the elder lady reminded, "and you're right to want this crazy driver caught."

"And prosecuted," Suitman insisted. "There's money in this case, I promise."

Now it was Haley who suspiciously regarded the overly helpful stranger in the suit. While he appeared, and dressed, like a well stuffed businessman, he was as pushy as a used car salesman. His hovering manner, though, and the incisive cut of his conversation labeled him as someone with an agenda.

A San Diego squad car pulled up at the curb. The tall, ginger-haired policeman approached and introduced himself as Patrolman Cross.

"You all right?" he asked first, still assessing her.

"Just a few scrapes. This isn't my first tumble. First time I've been hit, though."

"Report said a hit and run. What did you see?"

"The pavement."

His only reaction to the truthful quip was a nod. He whipped out a notebook to take her statement. His next comment was stern and businesslike as he looked down on her from a height well over six feet. "Where's your helmet?"

An accusation. Both knew the inevitable reply.

"Left it at home." She resisted the urge to hold her throbbing head lest he send for an ambulance. Ending up in an overcrowded California ER would turn this nasty incident into a disaster. She would monitor her headache and if it didn't go away in a few days she would go see a doctor. By then she would be in Hawaii.

Cross, built solidly, his freckled, muscled arms tanned under the white uniform shirt, just shook his head in exaggerated tolerance. Undoubtedly he had heard it all before. The law-enforcement issue sun glasses obscured his eyes, but from the crinkle at the edge of the crows' feet, and in the dry, superior, long-suffering tone, she read the condemnation with complete clarity.

"Try and obey the traffic laws," he advised. "Ready to go to the hospital for a check-up?"

"No way! I'm fine."

Suitman stepped forward with aggressive advice. "You don't know what injuries you might have. When they catch this guy he'll have to pay for this big time. Hit and run, that's serious, ask this officer. Car versus bike, always a winner for the cyclist if you let me help."

Feeling shaky, achy and the onset of a queasy stomach, she just wanted to get going. She assured them all her injuries were minor and that she needed to get to work. The thought of things falling apart at the shop clarified her anxiety to a new priority. There was nothing she could do about the accident and total write-off of her bike, but she had responsibilities at the store that needed tending before she left for Honolulu.

Patrolman Cross waved his sun-burned arm toward his vehicle. With the ease of his muscled fitness, he effortlessly hefted her mangled cycle in one hand and into the roomy trunk of the patrol car.

Suitman approached her again. "Give me a call later and I'll work on this with you."

Reading the business card, the errant little clues all came together in hindsight. Lawyer. She folded the card and handed it back to him. What luck that her accident was witnessed by an ambulance chaser. Only in California. Such a perfect end to her perfect morning. Not!

"Come on," Cross told her, opening the passenger door and shouldering between her and the lawyer. "You sure you don't want to go –"

"No."

"Okay, your choice. I'll take you to your job. Where we going?"

"Merchant's Harbor."

He gave a nod toward the ocean. "The tourist trap. A couple more blocks and you would have made it."

Almost. The old hand grenades and horseshoes thing. Her days were usually more perfect than almost.

The morning sun started to gleam through the anemic clouds with a soft, golden glow. Most mornings she loved the overcast weather on the temperate California coast. Clammy vapor shrouded the world nearly every misty dawn, clinging to the ground and the water – the ethereal fog insubstantial, the sun a promise of brightness and warmth. The mild day, invigorating and fresh, filled with promise, encompassed everything she needed in way of excellence.

The misty weather calmed her. She was not going to let an annoying and painful incident like an accident get her down, she vowed, limping toward the row of intimate cottage shops along the waterfront.

Accompanied by Patrolman Cross and bike, Haley led the way along cobblestone sidewalk that wound around the shops skirting the waterfront. Joining them was Amy Shimimoto, the bookkeeper, when they reached the shop.

Cross seemed amused as he read the front sign. "Reads Like Murder. Mystery bookstore. So you work here, huh?"

A dry cough emerged as Amy observed Haley. "This is going to be some story!"

"I can explain everything!" Haley promised, already gearing up for another debate with her friend on the safety issue of bike riding.

At approximately four feet ten inches, Amy cast a formidable presence far beyond her physical stature and her seventy-ish age. Surveying the arrival of Haley, Cross, and the bike, her expression was a mix of concern and irritation. With her terminally amused slant on life, this time with a dash of concern, she patiently awaited an explanation as she unlocked the front door of the bookshop.

Incongruous with the casual left-coast shopping center perched on the cusp of the harbor, the broad front windows of Reads Like Murder reflected a macabre theme of mayhem and homicide. Novels of foul deeds rested next to ornate daggers, a noose, a pair of old fashioned derbies, and a varied selection of other trinkets and props associated with malice aforethought. Rounding out the mystery motif were pictures of various incarnations of Sherlocks, Poirots and Charlie Chans.

12

Cross came to Haley's defense. "Your employee's late but it's not her fault."

Amy's eyes narrowed, "Miss Wyndham owns the store. I'm the bookkeeper."

The officer's eyebrows raised and he appraised the accident victim with an interested expression. "Owner. Okay." He said to her, "You need to be more careful, miss."

The quaint shop was next to the seaside walkway edging the waterfront, nestled scenically close to the bay. A famous local shopping destination, the area was built with individual little shops styled after a New England coastal town. The trendy, unique stores were scattered around cobbled walkways and old fashioned lamp posts, each business reflecting individual wares, most with excellent views of the ocean.

Here customers could ramble from shop to shop, exploring varied goods from custom chocolates to nautical art. Eateries ranging from the casual menu of burgers and drinks competed with four-star sea food restaurants and a café specializing in French cuisine. All these quaint establishments were enhanced by a curving promenade snaking along the water's edge. The popular spot took advantage of the natural ambiance of the glittering azure of San Diego harbor, with the Coronado Bridge in the distance arching gently across the cloud-dotted Southern California sky. Fresh breezes cooled the tender heat of the days, while the nocturnal drifts off the ocean gave a romantic nip to the evening air.

The policeman admired the shop and offered an approving comment. "Business must be great if you can afford the rent here."

"Killer prices." Amy smiled at her own pun.

The cop chuckled. "Killer, I get it."

13

CHAPTER TWO

There s nothing I can do now.

Cross carried the bike up to the front alcove that set the stage for entry into the mystery store. The porch was shaped like a Victorian England front step, with a replica plaque of Baker Street's most famous address.

Haley unlocked the dead bolt. When the door swung open Amy paused on the threshold like a character out of an old pantomime skit. Her foot hovered in mid-air and she balanced there for what seemed like long moments, finally stepping back to the sidewalk. Swinging the door wide, she gestured with a sweep of her hand at the scene inside.

Books and overturned display tables jumbled the floor. Some of the shelves along the walls had been swept clear of merchandise. Over Amy's shoulder, Haley studied the mess with delayed surprise. Either from the recent accident, or the shock of vandals striking her property, or both, the younger woman felt weak, leaning on the doorframe and shaking her head.

"What are you waiting for?"

Haley stood aside and nodded for Cross to look for himself. Instinct held her fast to her rooted spot in the doorway. She had never been the victim of any crime before. Two in one morning rocked her to a complete standstill.

"We've been robbed!" Amy gasped.

Years of vicarious investigations between the covers of myriad novels did not prepare Haley her for the wreckage of her shop. Not one to panic, she found she could not react at all.

Cross gave her a blank look for a beat. Then he dropped the bike on the pavement and shouldered his way into the doorway to glance around the store. Taking a half step in, he did a graceful, if belated pirouette and spun around to face the women again.

Running fingers through his wavy hair, tentatively he commented, "I guess this is not the way you left it yesterday?" On Amy's glare he amended his question. "Let me check this out."

Cross entered the shop with his weapon drawn and carefully stepped around or over the clutter as he snaked his way to the back of the main aisle. Senses jolted back into place, Haley's mind raced, clicking into gear and thinking along the well-trod path of literary sleuths that were as familiar to her as her own family. She ached to follow the officer, to inspect the damage, to see if the creeps who vandalized her store were still there. She leaned in and assessed the damage without entering the room. Cross returned, picking his way back to the entrance.

"No one's around. Cash register looks okay. Can you see anything missing off the bat?"

Haley combed back the shoulder-length sandy hair that had fallen in her eyes. Shaking her head, she stared from one area to the other trying to take it all in and come up with something brilliant to say. Chief Detective Inspector Sloan would have had a good come back at this point. Although Sloan didn't own a bookstore and he didn't have anyone running him off the road, either.

"All the books trashed are average, current mysteries," she explained to Cross. "Some first editions, but of no special value. The

15

collectibles are kept in the back room near the office." The impact of the message sank in. "Oh! Oh -- the Holmes room!"

"Don't disturb anything! I'll call robbery,"

Squeezing past the crouching officer, Haley dashed past the mess. To the side of the main rows of books a small nook brimmed with merchandize and memorabilia. In the center of the cubby hole was a genuine nineteenth-century sofa and chair, and a mantle depicting period decor. The chamber was a miniaturized replica of a Sherlockian-styled sitting room. The glass-fronted Victorian shelves held many valuable mystery collectibles available for sale. The walls, tables and shelves held books related to Homes, and colorful accessories associated with the Great Detective and his contemporaries.

"Oh, no." Haley shook with dread.

Most of the rare tomes were scattered across the floor or furniture. Thankfully, the Holmes bust atop the case was intact. Without waiting for official permission, Haley knelt down to assess the damage. The books seemed unharmed and mostly accounted for at first glance. The knick-knacks, ranging from curved pipes to deerstalker caps, were out of place, but appeared undamaged.

"Hey!" Cross's rebuke echoed through the store.

"Did they get the Sherlocks?" Amy scooted in and knelt on the floor next to her boss.

The patrolman joined them and warned sharply, "Don't touch anything!" Assured his command was obeyed, he added, "Hey, looks like this back door has been jimmied."

Haley and Amy joined him at the rear of the shop where a door led to the narrow service alley between stores. While they studied the damage, they agreed the manual lock was scarred and certainly not the way they had left things the night before. The electronic keypad seemed intact.

"That doesn't make sense," the policeman sighed as he closely examined the door. "This is electronic . . . hmmm."

"What happened to the alarm?" Amy asked no one in particular.

Cross wondered the same thing. Haley informed him the whole shopping complex, as well as her own condo, were protected by Cabrillo Alarms, a mega-security company. If the keypad was damaged, the alarm should have sounded, which obviously, it had not. Bypassing the electronics, without a key, the intruder would have to break the old fashioned dead bolt. The damage to the door clearly testified to that secondary step.

While the officer checked the area and ushered them away from the back, they slipped into the Holmes room. Here it smelled like an old library, the scent of leather and the indefinable, but distinctive odor of pages and bindings that had lived through many years in protected spaces. Since most were aged, well-worn books, they would remain open if someone rifled through them. That was exactly what it looked like to Haley.

"As far as I can tell, all the Holmes books are here. These are the most expensive volumes in the shop. Why didn't they take any of them?"

"Maybe that's not what they were looking for." The bookkeeper shrugged. "Be thankful for small favors. No theft, no problem. The thief probably won't come back. He must have been looking for a quick fix."

Hiding the smile at the hard boiled detective lingo coming from the senior citizen, Haley stepped over to Amy's domain, the office. With a groan, she studied the wrecked room with papers scattered on

17

the floor and desk. It would be tough to figure out if anything was missing from here.

Amy angled past to survey the damage from a closer perspective. Confident the bookkeeper would do a better job of assessing things in there than she could, Haley returned to the main room of the store.

The officer went to the patrol car and retrieved a camera. He took shots of the interior and exterior of the shop. When he returned Haley related what she had been pondering as she investigated the disarray.

"This has got to be connected to my hit and run," she told Cross. The officer's look was long-suffering irritation, but Haley continued. "I'm nearly killed this morning and my shop is robbed! It's too much of a coincidence!"

"Yeah, everything's a conspiracy," was his sarcastic response.

"Not everything!" she countered. "What happened to me and my store has to be connected!"

Wandering the area, making notes along with the pictures, Cross stopped near her and stared down with a stern glare. "Do you know how many bikers get hit by cars every day in San Diego? Do you know how many break-ins we have?"

She stood her ground even though her head felt like it was splitting from the raised volume of the argument. "To the same person on the same day?"

"You're absorbing too much from these shelves, Miss Wyndham. Relax and let the police handle this, please."

Miserable, she gingerly folded her legs beneath her to sit in a clear space on the floor and surveyed the mess. Reads Like Murder was her livelihood, but more than that it was her passion. As much as she tried to keep up the brave façade, the vandalism was disturbing on a number of levels. Not to mention her aching head, legs and ribs that were now throbbing persistently.

Worse than her physical ache was the inner fear creeping through her system. Someone tried to kill her! With the vandalism here at the shop she was convinced she was a target! Why? She was a bookseller! How innocuous was that? Why would anyone want to kill her or damage her shop?

Her imagination leaped to various, grim possibilities. Everything from being mistaken for a drug dealer to being a look-alike for a mobster's girlfriend swirled in her overactive imagination. Calming, she knew wild theories would only feed panic. Despite the skepticism of the police she was convinced she was a target. What should she do now? Flee to Hawaii as originally planned for today, came the immediate, calming directive.

Cross interrupted her thoughts as he stopped on the threshold. "Have you discovered anything missing?"

Slowly, pressing her lips together to keep from groaning, Haley climbed awkwardly to her feet. "I can't tell yet." Sweeping the hair out of her eyes she shook her head, nearly losing herself in the enormity of the crime. This was no entertaining fiction being read from a comfortable beach chair. This was her life! Someone had vandalized and desecrated her private zone! "We won't know until we can check out everything."

Amy joined them. "We'll have the shop spic and span in no time," she said briskly. She looked pointedly at Officer Cross. "When we're allowed to, that is."

He had the grace to blush. "If you find out that anything is missing, please let me know. I'll file the initial report, and you can add to it when you know more about what's been taken."

Haley's spunk returned in a snap. "What do you mean? No CSI? No detectives? What about dusting for prints and DNA and checking for witnesses?"

Cross shrugged. "Sorry." He gestured to the ruined books on the floor. "This isn't some mystery book, you know. We have too many petty robberies to send lab teams for every little incident. Call me with a list of the missing items and I'll file a report. I'll give you the necessary information for your insurance company."

"Thanks," Haley shot back, a bullet of contempt. "Meanwhile some sinister thug is out to get me and you're going to file paperwork!" She managed to sound more angry than afraid, and finished with, "We appreciate our tax dollars at work!"

Cross offered a sympathetic sigh. "Listen, we don't have the manpower for a more thorough investigation. Without evidence of a threat to life or the proof that some pricey books were stolen, there's not much more we can do."

"Right." Haley's voice dripped sarcasm.

As if ashamed that he couldn't do more, Cross turned abruptly and left. Almost immediately, he opened the door again. "Where do you want this?" He hefted the mangled bike with one hand.

Amy pointed toward the back of the shop and huffed. "In the store room." Belatedly, she added, "Please."

Coursing through the narrow aisle between displays and bookshelves, Cross managed to avoid stepping on the scattered books. He deposited the bike in the back, managing a deft dance through the haphazard clutter and back.

"Good luck," he awkwardly concluded, as if wanting to offer more assistance, but constrained by the legalities of the system. "I hope your insurance company comes through or something."

Amy muttered indignantly as she followed him to the door. "You come back before you go off duty young man! Walk us to the parking lot! That's the least you can do!"

Cross's civilly polite nod seemed standard-issue, especially formulated for a demanding public. "Yes, ma'am." With an easy, off-handed sigh, he waved at the bookkeeper, then the owner. He closed the door with a sturdy slam.

"Amy!" Haley knew exactly what her bookkeeper was doing.

"Hey, you aren't aggressive enough. Over thirty and not married? I have to watch out for you."

Haley sat in the Sherlock nook and started brushing off the books and replacing them on the shelves. "If you're such an expert on matchmaking, then why haven't you married Max?"

"I've been married, had kids, grandkids, been widowed. Now I'm going to savor some time to myself. When I get lonely, I know where Max is."

For months, the persistent Latino next door had badgered Amy with proposals. Secretly suspecting her bookkeeper had a soft spot for the engaging and overt Max, she kept pushing for her friend to accept a date. Her subtle hints were no different from Amy's manifest pushing, she realized.

"I didn't notice any ring on Officer Cross's finger."

"Amy! No policemen."

"They're more stable than beach boys."

"No beach boys. I date surfers --"

"And millionaire bookstore owners who take you out on their yachts-"

"If you tell me again that Sam Simon is my match-"

"He was the best catch you'll ever have." Amy shook her head. "And you let that one get away! You should have done serious fishing when he took you out on his boat!"

"He's a bore!"

"A rich bore. Now, policemen have steady jobs, good health plans. Cross is cute."

"He doesn't believe me."

Amy's response was hesitant. "I don't doubt what happened to you this morning, but you really think this and your accident is connected?"

"Yes." The response lacked her earlier conviction to the policeman. Sitting here amid the ruined store, it seemed less like a plot. "Sherlock does not believe in coincidence," she spoke her thoughts aloud to reaffirm her theory. "It defies the laws of statistics or something that I would be hit and my shop would be hit on the same morning."

Amy shrugged. "True enough. But Cross is right, too. This is a big city and we've got crime."

Ticking off points on her fingers, Haley reiterated that no money was kept in the shop, so none was stolen. No books, as far as they could tell, had been taken. The vandal -- or burglar -- had been looking for something he hadn't found.

The older woman nodded. "So why do we lack faith in the police? Because all these mysteries we read are rubbing off on us. In fiction the police are never as clever as the talented amateur detective who makes sense of the clues and solves the crime."

"Crimes. I think someone deliberately tried to run me down this morning. Why? Why break into the shop and wreck it?

"They wanted to kill you and destroy what you own." Amy's eyes gleamed as her imagination ran free. "Could be there are some secret plans here that a spy courier left in one of the bindings of a book."

Haley glanced at the intrigue section covering the latest best seller by Amelia Hunter, to old and hard-to-find classics like UNCLE paperbacks. A cardboard standee of the notorious Hunter was trampled on the floor, but otherwise the spy corner seemed intact.

Amy was a great fiction-talker, but Haley decided, "This has got to be simpler than some international conspiracy."

"Maybe it was Mister Simon, the zillionaire. He wants to get back at you for dumping him. Or he wants to merge stores. Maybe that's why he asked you out. He doesn't like us 'cause we have style. He has only wholesale books by the trainload." Fired up now, the older woman's eyes were alight with excitement not at all sympathetic to the fearful events. Her phraseology slipped from normal English to something she might see on a TV show. "Think like Perry Mason! This is connected! The big man is gonna try to wipe us out!"

Haley laughed at the usual condemnation. The big discount bookstore chain had a monster franchise just a few blocks away in the old, tourist-oriented Gas Lamp Quarter. Their shadow, however, cast itself much farther than mere geography.

"I thought you wanted me to marry Sam Simon, the legendary date-that-got-away."

"No argument, he was a good catch." Amy scowled. "Doesn't mean I like him or his methods. He has no taste."

"Because he'd like to price us out of business?"

"Right. He's still the good catch that got away. If you and Sam would have hooked up it would have been a nice merger."

Secretly Haley wanted to believe Sam Simon, the local-born Fortune 500 competitor, was responsible for the vandalism. It would confirm her suspicions that, yes, this little, but stylish genre shop was a thorn in the side of the giant megastore. It would cement her theory that Simon was a rotter of the first order. It would confirm that she had good taste and better sense when she cut off his social advances.

"This is a bookstore dealing in fiction. You're imbibing too much in our products."

Satisfied the Sherlock shelves were back in shape, she returned to the main room and then stopped, backing up to study the fantasy section. At the insistence of her parents, she had a bookshelf dedicated to speculative fiction – fantasy. She justified that by leaning heavily on old favorites like Jules Verne and HG Wells. Those authors and a few others muddled into several genres, including mystery. The locale was adorned with crystals and colorful fantasy prints depicting Atlantis, mer-people and various fringe icons. How could she argue with parents who had provided some of the capital for her to open this shop? She couldn't, of course, so she'd bowed to the eccentric tastes of loved ones.

Several of the legend and myth books were out of sequence, two on the floor. Replacing them, she wondered what had caught her attention. Something was missing. Which book? It had a blue binding, she recollected. Not certain, but thinking it was related with Atlantis, she called to Amy, but the bookkeeper was back in the office. She would contact Cross and let him know that so far, the burglary consisted of one missing blue book, but she couldn't remember the title. Wouldn't that look great on the police report!

Haley ignored her injuries and aches as she worked to get the place ready for opening. Already gathered outside were concerned fellow merchants, tourists, curious spectators, and, she hoped, paying customers. In a lurid way, maybe a crime in a mystery bookstore would be good for business.

"Hey, wikiwiki" Amy gently urged as she gave her boss a little nudge. "We should be open already!"

"I know."

Staring out at the faces of the lurkers, she felt a shiver of unease. What if one of them was the burglar coming back? Returning to the scene of the crime? Unfinished business? There was a pervading strain of suspicion within. Well, she felt she deserved it after an attempt on her life and the vandalizing of her business!

"I'm hurrying. Good thing I'm already packed."

"You sure you want to go to Honolulu after this?"

In a few hours she had to catch a flight to Hawaii. She could justify the trip as business -- Kana had insisted she come as soon as possible to share some fantastic find. Should she cancel the trip because of this mess with her store? A more practical person would be tempted, but she knew her business would be left in good hands with her relatives and friends. With this creepy little crime wave this morning she deemed it essential to escape to Hawaii and her mentor, Kana. Wise and caring, she knew his calm acumen would center her. Even better, he would side with her; maybe even solve this strange mystery surrounding her.

"Kana says he has a real treasure for me." The little intrigue created by her mentor made her anxious to return to the island where she spent some of her favorite childhood adventures.

Haley slipped into the office and sliced off the torn leg of her jeans, then did the same to the left pant leg to have matching cut-offs that were uneven and ragged, hardly stylish, but good enough until she could get home. Replacing the scissors, she studied the trashed desktop. Amy had not found anything missing so far, but the place was such a mess a thorough search was going to take some time.

"That will have to do." Amy accepted her with an unenthusiastic seal of approval when Haley returned to the front and gave the go ahead to admit the waiting customers.

Just about a half-hour behind schedule, Amy turned around the OPEN sign and officially declared the shop ready for business. The throng spread out, scanning the books with casual interest and the rest of the store with more scrutiny, as if searching for clues so they could solve the real life mystery of the break-in. They were, for the most part, of course, avid readers of the puzzle genre, so wanting to solve the offense was second nature for them. Tourists, regulars, and curious neighbor merchants crowded inside. The sensational break-in created more business than usual, drawing the nosy, the concerned, and those interested in the genre. Much initial commotion was expressed with drawn-out chit-chat and well wishing, but gradually the guests wandered the shop, absorbing a real crime scene. Most likely, few customers tasted anything this sensational in their mundane lives, and the novelty attracted high curiosity.

Haley's cousin, Garvin Wyndham, arrived with his dog, Nacho. Both slipped behind the counter. The dog curled up in the corner, while Garvin, nicknamed Gar or Gav depending on the mood of the

26

labeler, went to work bagging purchases for the customers he charmed. Like many local college students, Haley's twin cousins, Gar and his sister Skye, worked most evenings at a job, in this case the family shop. That left days open for classes or surfing, whichever came first.

"Hey, you better hurry up if you're going to catch your flight."

Haley glanced at the clock and back at the crowds of customers. She was crazy to leave her business after the crisis and during the rush. But Kana insisted he had something important for her. Trusting that Gar and Amy could handle everything, she stuck with her resolve to leave.

Gar had few ambitions beyond his life as a part-time clerk, part-time PHD-candidate, and part-time surfer. Making enough money from surf competitions and bookshop work to support his beach habit, Nacho, his beach house, and his car, his life was complete. Not that he needed any more income than the healthy inheritance he was already spending.

Tall, sun-bleached blond, a deep blue in the eyes and more tanned than his sister, the family resemblance was still obvious. Despite the brainless blond connotations, both the twins were as smart as they were good looking, an advantage they had used many times for their own ends. The brainy intellect was especially deceptive for Skye, who was expected to act – and could act – like a stereotypical blond.

Moving out of the way, Gar took over and Haley made her way to the back of the shop. She had tempted Fate with her cavalier musings about perfection this morning. Interacting with the elbow-to-elbow customers, who fervently, happily, discussed mayhem and murder in a whole new, personal light; it became a strange experience

27

of almost third-person acceptance that violence had preyed on her twice this morning. For the patrons the reality and fantasy were now melded; the crime scene linked to the mysteries she was selling across the counter at a brisk pace.

The store was a haven for aficionados of the thrilling tales of crime and detection. The very atmosphere promoted colorful insight into the lives of Doctor Thorndike and Fu Man Chu. Treading these paths along the canyons of reading material offered the smell of old books, the close feel of rooms crowded with undiscovered adventures, and the small knick-knacks that made it seem Simon Templar and John Watson were alive within these walls along with many favored colleagues.

She cautioned Gar, "If you need me to come home –"

"There's cell coverage in Hawaii." He offered a quirky, lopsided grin. "We'll stay in touch."

Nacho's furry mass rubbed against her leg, followed immediately by a wet tongue on her knee. She crouched down, wincing as sore muscles and scuffed skin stretched in discomfort, but she still hugged the affectionate Golden Retriever/Yellow Labrador mix.

Breaking a trail to the rear office, Haley sat down at the desk and studied the cubicle that had been partially restored to a semblance of order. The desk and cubby hole were still disarrayed, seemingly main targets for the burglar, who had been looking for something in a book and at the desks; here and at the apartment. So far, the only missing items were a blue fantasy book that she had yet to identify.

Sifting through the papers, Haley found her e-ticket for the plane. She had set aside a new paperback to read on the flight – where was it? Righting the knocked-over Rolodex, she stopped.

28

There was a page hanging out. Quickly she thumbed through, alarmed to find several card sections missing. The F through O pages.

Chilled at the personal attack on her property and, vicariously, on the customers, friends and family members in her files, she sat back and studied the desk, the room. What would Watson see here? What questions would he ask Holmes to spark a flare in the flint-like intellect of the Master Detective?

What had the unknown intruder been looking for in this simple shop? Why had he hit her this morning? That thought sent chills along her skin. She was a target! Insane! Why?

Glancing at her watch she groaned. The stupid timepiece had stopped. Shaking her arm, she checked the desk clock. Yikes! She should have been on the road to the airport twenty minutes ago! Dashing to the front, she raced through an explanation of the Rolodex and missing addresses to Amy and Gar. Nacho came around and barked in sympathy with her agitation. Petting the dog, she continued to issue orders to her cousin to call Cross about the missing address pages.

With a wave, she dashed off hoping the lunch hour traffic would not be too bad on the roads and freeways. At least the rush to make up lost time gave her a more immediate crisis to think about, effectively shoving the concerns over the break-ins to the back of her mind.

CHAPTER THREE

"Trying to spy on the opposition?"

When the flight attendant announced preparations for landing, Haley strained to see a glimpse of her beloved islands out the small window. Flying high over the distant blue sheet of ocean, through the wispy tufts of clouds, she could identify the dark blue land forms of Molokai and Maui. These isolated islands seemed so small in the vastness of the Pacific; it was amazing they had ever been discovered. She was grateful that they had been found by good old Captain Cook. She couldn't imagine a life without visiting here.

Walking through the debarkation tunnel at Honolulu International, she barely appreciated the warm humidity. It was subtly richer and deeper than San Diego's weather, and it enveloped her instantly.

She paused by a lei stand in the terminal and allowed the waves of Hawaii's gifts to sweep over her senses. From the airport window, she could see Diamond Head far across the city, a dark and dramatic backdrop to the perfect blue sky and the boldly azure ocean. In between, the glittering towers of hotels and high rises dotted the terrain. The exotic scents of a plethora of flowers wafted through the sea-brine air and blended with the jet fuel and diesel exhaust to make each aloha a unique signature on her impressions. No place else in the world looked, smelled, felt and tasted like Hawaii.

As she walked toward baggage claim her phone rang. Checking the ID, she answered the call from her cousin Skye. She punched the button and a voice was already yelling at her.

"Haley, we've had a robbery! Our apartment has been robbed!"

For a moment Haley's mind went blank. Break-in. That was the shop. How did Skye hear about the crime? Why was she mixing it up with their shared condo? Unless the blond -- usually rational against stereotype -- was reporting another crime.

"A break-in. You mean the shop."

"What? Not a shop! Haley, our condo has been broken into!"

A second burglary? At her home? A chill of creepy disturbance snaked along her spine and shivered the back of her neck. Crime. Three criminal acts against her this morning. It was unbelievable. Unreal – no – this was reality, not the stories in her books. No fictional detective hero was going to come sweeping through the front door and make it all go away.

"There's nothing I can do now," she told her cousin, distressed. "I'm in Honolulu!"

"I know, I know, but I wanted to tell you!"

Haley calmed. This was all past tense. So Skye was all right. "What happened?"

"I came home after class and the front door was open. The whole place was wrecked!"

While waiting for her luggage she pulled the story from Skye, who had finished dealing with Officer Cross and was at Reads Like Murder. It was hard for the college student to know what was stolen, but Haley asked her to double check for address books.

"And I'll be home as soon as I can. Maybe tomorrow."

"No rush, Haley, everything's okay," Skye assured. Now that the initial excitement was over she was more herself. "Officer Cross is helping. He asked me out, too." Yeah, just like Skye.

"Skye, no dating cops!"

"I think he's cute. Call you later."

Haley claimed her bags and collected her Jeep at the rental car counter. The bright Hawaiian sun felt good on her skin and the fresh trade wind blew her hair in swirls of tawny clouds as she reveled in the freedom of the moment. The anxiety from the morning peeled away with each mile she drove on the familiar path toward her landmark, Diamond Head. Like a beacon of hope radiating right to her senses, she calmed as she drew closer to her goal.

Skye called back and told her their address books had indeed been vandalized and pages torn out. The cops were on the case. It didn't make Haley feel better.

By the time she arrived at her hotel in the center of Waikiki, it was late afternoon. She called Kana as soon as she tossed her bags atop the bed in the room. Anxious to meet with him, she tried to order her thoughts into a coherent list so she would make sense when she related the nerve-wracking events in San Diego. She valued his calm, philosophical approach to problems and knew he would help get her back on track. Then there was the mystery of what special treasure he had for her. The anticipation of a valuable book sweetened her expectations. Three, four, five rings. She opened the lanai doors and paced outside to breath in the salty breeze. Leaning on the railing, then pacing some more, impatiently, she was irritated that he was not home. Frustratingly, Kana still needed to catch up with Twentieth Century technology because he owned neither a cell phone nor an answering machine.

The first order of business would be to go shopping, she decided; first a hat and then a watch. Luckily she was here in the heart of bright, aloha fashions, so it would be easy to replace the Hawaiian print baseball cap that was destroyed in the accident.

32

Maybe she should wear a helmet from now on? Okay, replacement cap and luau print helmet, and a watch.

Then she could kick back and relax while she waited for Kana to return. Maybe the relaxation would help her puzzle out what was happening to her formerly perfect life.

***

Walking along Kalakaua Avenue became a dual experience of past memories mingled with real-time enjoyment. The city had changed in the many years since she initially visited here, but core elements always remained the same. Countless trips around the world came to mind as only brief stabs of distracted recollection. The most distinct recollections were from Hawaii; before, during, and after visiting various ports around the globe. While not her hometown, Honolulu still felt like home.

Only child of Dale and Lissa Wyndham; two academics who graduated from Stanford, married, traveled the world on various projects and study tours, and at one point gave birth to Haley. The main base was always San Diego, where her grandparents – only one set still living when she came around – were mundanely normal. Then the small family landed here in Hawaii when she was ten years old. Instantly, Hawaii became the home of her soul. The natural beauty and the aura of its native vibrancy captivated her in her youth and retained an anchor in her heart.

Instinctively aiming toward the sea, she took in the sights, smells and feeling of bustling Waikiki this late afternoon. Strolling toward Diamond Head, she sauntered through the surf until she reached the pink landmark of the Royal Hawaiian Hotel.

Immediately striking because of its bold hue and regal structure, it was one of the first hotels on Waikiki beach. It had survived the Pearl Harbor attack and the invasion of the tourist industry. Brushing the sand from her feet, she replaced her shoes and walked up to the nearby mall.

This had been intended as a working holiday and she was determined to see that through. The miles separating her from the intrigue and bookstore in San Diego had dissipated the anxiety over the crimes. She was on Hawaiian time now. No worries. Let SDPD handle things. Time to squeeze the holiday bit ahead of the working part of the trip.

Stopping at a snack stand, she took a plate of sushi to the sand and sat on the beach to watch the surfers. The sinking sun on the mango-hued horizon was warm on her face and the fresh fish and seaweed nourishing after the tasteless airline food. She called Kana's house again and there was no answer.

At International Marketplace she found the surf apparel store -- where she bought her old hat -- was still there, she noted with satisfaction. Hastily straight past the shockingly bold aloha print wear, she went right for the caps. She studied the choices, debating whether she should buy something she could live with or keep shopping for just the right replacement.

Beyond the hat rack, out the window of the shop, Haley snagged sight of someone staring at her. She zeroed in to identify the dark-haired, perfectly coifed Carrie Kahunui watching her. Haley waved and Carrie jumped as if startled she was noticed. Haley didn't really want to visit with the aggressive rare-book dealer and competitor, but it would be rude not to at least make some social polite-talk.

34

Carrie was walking away when Haley exited the shop and called to her. Carrie stopped and turned in her usual graceful manner seemingly right off a fashion runway, her flowing aloha print dress floating in the air with the sudden motion.

"Aloha, Carrie!"

"Haley, is that you? Why I didn't recognize you."

Why was Carrie lying and trying to avoid her? Their eye contact through the window was unmistakable.

The short woman crossed the distance and stopped a few feet from Haley, assessing the younger woman with clear disdain. "My, you look like you've been in an accident. What have you been doing? Your appearance is worse than usual."

She rushed through the amenities so fast she was nearly breathless when she completed the superficial, typically tactless sentences.

"My bike argued with a car and lost," Haley shrugged, wearying of the explanations of her scrapes. "What are you up to?"

"Just – just -- window shopping. As if it's any of your business!"

Flinching at the rebuke, Haley didn't know how to respond. Their relationship had always been competitive, sometimes prickly, but never openly hostile. Had she caught Carrie on a really bad day? Then it wasn't a bad hair day. Carrie made the most of her visual assets.

Haley made a final attempt at being civil. "Shopping at the children's store? Are you -- uh – expecting?"

What amused her most was the thought of prim and proper Carrie having anything as messy and undisciplined as a baby! A little person would jumble up hair, jewelry, and clothes, and would take focus away from Carrie's attention to Carrie. That did not sound like the self-centered competitor Haley had come to know and dislike.

"Oh -- oh no!" Carrie squeaked. "No, I'm shopping for my new little niece." She smiled falsely. "So, what brings you to town?"

Her mood at least thawed from angry confrontation to cool disdain. Struggling with small talk. That was some improvement.

"Business and pleasure. You know, get away from the grind and all that. Catch some sun and sand."

Kahunui's lip twitched. She possibly caught the irony that the sun and sand in San Diego hardly seemed different from Hawaii. "Business. I suppose Kana is going to give you some kind of scoop like he always does? You know the two of you aren't always going to come out ahead of me." Her tone crept into wicked jealousy. Realizing her raised voice was attracting attention from other shoppers, she plastered a smile on her face. "Well, I must run. Aloha."

Puzzled by the encounter with the she-shark, Haley watched after her for a moment, then turned away, not letting it bother her. Right now her stomach was grumbling that it was after dinnertime; her system still running on California time. The sushi snack had stayed the tide of hunger for a while, but she was ready for a real meal now. She headed in the direction of Kana's shop, hoping he would be there when she arrived. Then she could grab him and they could head over to the plate-lunch counter together.

Slanted sun baked the concrete canyon of tourism along Waikiki's main strip. Burned-red beachgoers who had been worshiping Sol all day were sweeping off the seared, golden sands and heading for their hotels. Dodging the escapees armed with towels, books, and wide hats, she had to duck into a doorway to avoid a large man wielding the straw beach mat under his arm like a sword.

The amusing moment was spoiled when she realized she was standing at the entrance of a Super Simon Bookstore right there on the main street! There was a gaudy sign depicting the CEO Sam Simon of Super Simon. The guy was a nut for alliteration and corny advertising, but no one could argue with the multi-million dollar success. Miffed that her mega-giant competitor rented, or probably owned, half a block in Waikiki, she peered in the store, appraising the rival company.

"Trying to spy on the opposition? It's better from inside the store, deary."

Haley turned in surprise at the arrival of the dreaded Sam Simon, who materialized next to her. Tall, athletic, tanned, pale blond hair, blue eyes, he was the archetypal California playboy. Born and bred in La Jolla, Sam yachted, played polo, tennis and the stock market. From old money, he invested his inheritance in a superstore for books and was the public's new hero for reading material. Despite all the money, fame and looks, Sam remained annoyingly in touch with the commoners. It was just like him to pop in and visit one of his stores somewhere in the world and see how the displays looked, if the staff was friendly, and if the profit margin was wide.

"Hi, Sam. Hawaii certainly seems popular these days."

"They let anyone come over. If you wanted to check up on me, you could have just stayed at home and dropped by on your bike." Glancing at her scraped leg, his face crinkled in sympathy. "Sorry to hear about your shop, by-the-by. Terrible thing about crime these days, isn't it? And too bad about the little accident."

"How did you find out?"

"Bad news travels fast in our little circle, deary."

Sadly, the bibliophile cliques on the Pacific Rim, not to mention the social register of successful business people, were a small group. She rubbed elbows with Carrie and Sam all too often at auctions or estate sales where they were inescapable. Unfortunately, they seemed unavoidable during her working holiday as well.

Sam grabbed onto her wrist to study the broken watch crystal. He gestured to his own timepiece, and then stuttered, hastily removing his arm from sight. The glimpse was long enough for her to notice his usual, ultra-expensive gold watch had been replaced by a common department store purchase. "At least you didn't damage a good watch. Still like shopping off the rack, I see."

Wondering why he had fallen to the common ranks in timepieces, but not caring enough to ask, she reclaimed her hand and fabricated a smile. "Thanks for your touching concern, Sam."

"Really, Haley, when are you going to grow up and join the adult world?"

Fingers combed hair away from her face in annoyance. "What is that supposed to mean?"

She had heard his complaints before. His line was almost a quote from their last meeting when she -- again -- refused to go out on a date with him. He could be a fun, athletic companion for a good sail, but anything beyond that was just not worth the time investment. Time, his attitude toward it, was the problem.

"How about dinner? Two San Diegans adrift in the wilds of Honolulu? I have reservations for a table at --"

"No thanks."

Date one had been nearly two years ago. Still he did not get the
hint that date two would never happen in his lifetime. As he took
hold of her arm to guide her through the crowd, she dropped back,
suddenly distrustful. She blamed it on the new shadow of paranoia
plaguing her on this bad day.

"You have reservations for one or two?" she wondered
suspiciously. "You knew I was in town?"

"You know the book business is a close-knit family."

From behind a book display Haley caught the flash of Carrie
peaking at her. Was Carrie trying to hide? It was like something out
of Charlie Chaplin! That she had been spotted was obvious!

Sneering at the hated endearment Sam always used, and the
ridiculous games Carrie was playing, Haley shook her head in
disgust. "You can tell Carrie to come out of hiding now," she
announced in a voice loud enough to reach the ears of everyone at the
front of the store, including Carrie.

The concealed bookseller crept from her refuge and stood
behind Sam Simon. "Why would I hide from you? You think that
crazy old man is going to give you – "

"That's enough!" Sam hissed. "No need to be uncivil. We're
all in the same game, girls. I'll see you at dinner, Haley."

"Sorry, I have plans, Sam."

His thin smile disappeared. "Not meeting with that old fossil,
Kana, are you? Haley, there's a whole life out here beyond your
musty old collectable books! You need to live a little. Get out from
under the old people."

There was his hang-up again with age. Sam was in great shape
for a guy in his forties -- late forties. If he spent more of his precious
time enjoying life, and relationships, he might be worth some

attention. Instead he was obsessed with his looks, his fitness, his age, using all possible enhancements to cheat Old Father Time.

Amy had jokingly wondered if Sam was behind the vandalism of the shop. As much as Haley disliked him, she knew the suspicion was ridiculous. Nice thought, though.

"Thanks, I think I'm already living." She briskly slipped away.

"I'm in town until tomorrow, deary."

She ground her teeth at the overused *en-dear-ment*. In her haste to make a dramatic exit, she made a clumsy spectacle when she ran into a cardboard standee advertising a book signing. The picture on the ad did not do justice to the guest author. The spry, mischievous personality of the most amazing woman she had ever met; Amelia Hunter managed to leap right out of the cardboard picture. Smiling at the image of the extreme novelty of the writer, to use a pun, she turned and ploughed right into – Amelia Hunter!

"Amelia!"

"Haley," the weathered, older woman cooed. She gave a wink. "I couldn't help but overhear your very correct refusal of dinner with Sam." She hooked an aged hand in the crook of her arm. "Very good taste on your part. One of the many things I've always liked about you."

Age never disclosed exactly, Hunter was guessed to be about eighty. Still fit, incisive, shrewd, she was a notorious character in Honolulu. The younger woman noted, with sadness, though, that Amelia's posture was a little stooped and her color was not as good as it usually was for a woman of reasonable health living in the tropics.

The mature hazel eyes assessed her with the skill of a diamond cutter appraising a gem. The elderly woman's expressions were usually mild, but the keen gaze gave away the sharpness and intellect still sizzling in the over-active brain.

"I can give you some of my better rejection lines."

The woman had to have been a mighty catch in her day. Amelia, and maybe even Hunter, were not her real names. The pseudonyms were as colorful and metaphoric as the local celebrity and author. A former war criminal/spy hunter during an era when such fields were dominated by men, she made an incredible mark in the covert world, and retired from the OSS/CIA to make killer investments. After buying up much of Honolulu's choice property after the war, she retired a few decades back, then started writing autobiographical books. After that series finished, she worked her way to spy thrillers set in the Pacific during World War II. The books, as with everything else she did in life, were a smash success.

"What brings you to Honolulu this time? My signing? I'm flattered."

"Oh, the usual stuff."

Still clinging, Ms Hunter wondered, "If I wrote my true memoirs, darling, would you like the exclusive sales rights?" Well read and traveled, it seemed Amelia had done almost everything and continued to do so at an amazing pace for her age. "You are one of my favorite people."

"Why would you do that and miss all the money you would bring in from the Simon bookstores?" Haley's tone held more aggravation than she intended. Amelia was tough and crusty around the edges, an amazingly shrewd businesswoman, but underneath, a loyal friend.

For a moment the lined face grew somber. "There are much more important things in life than money, Haley. Things you can't buy. Love, health, longevity." Her arms gestured around them. "Paradise." She scowled at something over Haley's shoulder.

From the reflection in the big bookstore window, Haley saw Sam Simon and Carrie were watching them. "I feel like I'm in a spy movie," the bookstore owner quipped.

"If only." Hunter sighed. "Having worked with the real thing, I much prefer the movie spies. " She leaned close and dropped her voice to a whisper. "I used to have the worst crush on Illya."

Haley scanned her knowledge of the spy fiction lining the shelves of her store. This reference harkened back to the Sixties. "Ah, the Russian heart-throb."

Hunter rolled her eyes. "They belong to your fictional cloak and dagger world, not mine, Mores the pity. I think you would have fallen for Napoleon."

The energetic senior must have been pretty saucy in her day. Still was, apparently. Fictional spy boyfriend. Funny how a lot of things seemed better in fiction than in reality. More interesting than Haley's last few dates, certainly.

"Do you ever enter into conspiracies?" the older woman asked.

"Occasionally."

"Why don't you live here?" Hunter continued in a pleasant, slightly loud voice. "The magic of the islands is something Kana and I have tried to share with you for years, but you've never made the jump."

"Business," Haley shrugged. "My family, such as they are, and my shop, are in San Diego." A little wistfully, she sighed as she glanced across the street at the burning, amber sun glittering on the waves curling onto the golden sand. "It would be nice."

"When I die I'll leave you an inheritance so you can open a shop here." Amelia winked. "And maybe that memoir for you to publish posthumously."

Haley laughed at the absurd joke. "I don't want you to die. I want you to keep writing best sellers to boost my sales. And shower me with your flattery," she added truthfully.

After sharing a hearty laugh, the older woman admitted, "I overheard you tell the odious Simon you are already committed with our friend Kana for this evening." She gave her a quick hug, during which, she whispered, "I can't talk now. Call me later. I have something important to tell you." When she drew away, she announced with more volume, "Drop by when you have time. And if you wish, I will sign some books for you to take back to San Diego."

"Thanks, Amelia. I'll call before I leave."

She held onto the smaller hand and read in the bright, hazel eyes a prompting to go along with the secret. From the reflection in the glass she noted Sam was still staring at them. So there was some little intrigue going on with Simon and Hunter. She would go along with it for now and get an explanation later, but this was so frustrating! Did everything have to be layered in intrigue today?

"But I might not forgive you for giving Sam such an exclusive this time," she teased, happy to see Simon scowl at the comment.

"Nothing personal, dear, just marketing."

Nodding, she agreed she did know it was business. Amelia scurried away across the street and when Haley waved, she checked the sidewalk behind her. Sam Simon was still watching Amelia. What was going on? Haley pondered it as she continued strolling.

Making her way through the colorful and crowded International Marketplace was like an adventure in shopping. It was commercialism at the top, with hawkers yelling out from their gaudy carts, with merchants waving their bright aloha shirts at the passersby The pervasive scent of sun tan oil and a myriad of tropical flowers layered the atmosphere with local color.

She emerged from the shops as the reflected sun was beaming off windows along Kuhio Street. Here the stores were less garish, the merchants friendlier, and the trees old and knotted, folding over some of the venerable buildings. It was like dropping back to a quieter time and place.

The afternoon was slipping by and still no response from Kana. The latent paranoia from her violent misadventures of this morning surfaced. She quickened her pace as she walked for a few blocks on the serene back avenue of Waikiki. When she came to the weathered neighborhood of quaint stores where Kana Hagoth kept his beloved rare-book haven, she breathed a shallow sigh of relief. She paused next to the flower shop on the corner, gazing fondly down the crooked, cracked, lava-stone path leading to the familiar door and affectionately took her time touching the hibiscus plants as she passed.

The title over the door was Magic Island Books. Carved in the weather-painted wood was an enchanted scene of a tropical isle and two dolphins arching through faded blue waves. To the commoner it was the entrance to a bookstore. To those with vision, touched by the magical dust of Pacific pixies, Kana called it his time and travel machine.

"When you walk through these doors, you enter an enchanted dimension," she recited quietly, his voice echoing in her mind as she spoke one of his oft-mentioned quotes.

To her, every bookstore, especially this one, was magical. The tomes, the atmosphere, the way the shop smelled with the musty lingering of old pages, the trace of weathered leather, were all enchanting. The faint scent of hibiscus drifting in, and the subtle bouquet of misty plumeria blooming near the open windows facing the yard, made it seem a world removed from reality.

Surprised the door was closed, she tried the knob. Startled it was locked, she knocked. "Kana!" she called, rapping her knuckles several times on the square panes of glass inset into the old wood. She was certain he would have returned by now. "Kana!"

What was he doing leaving his shop all afternoon and into the evening? Did he forget she was coming? Was he out on a mad hunt for priceless volumes? Had he lost track of time? Not unheard of for him. He should have called. But he had no cell phone. Should she just enter the code on the security keypad and let herself in? That seemed a little intrusive, even for a good friend.

Automatically she glanced at her watch and noted, with difficulty through the broken crystal, that it was no longer working at all! She had to make this a priority: watch, then cap. Hawaiian time was one thing, but running a business in California demanded she live by schedules and appointments.

Flipping out her cell phone she checked the time, worried about the lateness. Kana had been out of contact all day! This was so unlike him to skip an appointment. Well, not really, she had to admit as she strolled around to check out the upper apartment over the store. Like all avid readers, Kana had a tendency to lose track of time and be absentminded about anything outside the covers of a book. Still, it was unusual for him to forget her, particularly since she was here today at his urgent demand.

Stopping in next door at Emma's Flower's, Haley asked if Kana had gone out. The lady behind the counter, Mrs. Emma Kahuku, was an old resident of the area. Haley had known her as long as she had known Kana. Emma beamed happily when Haley entered. Rushing around to hug her, the friendly woman drew her into the shop.

"So good to see you again, Haley. Kana didn't mention you were coming! I could have a big dinner for you tonight!"

Kana hadn't mentioned she was coming? Emma was an old friend and a bit of a busybody. She knew everything about the neighborhood. "I guess he forgot," she struggled for an explanation. "He has some great find to show me. I'm surprised he's not here."

Emma seemed puzzled. "He hasn't been here since he closed shop early on Monday."

Nonplussed, Haley listened as Kahuku explained she had accepted three packages for him over the last few days. She thought he was on one of his many buying trips.

About the same age as Kana, somewhere in the seventies, Mrs. Kahuku liked to keep tabs on her next-door neighbor. Haley always thought Mrs. Kahuku wanted to be more than a friend. Did everyone in her acquaintance have romance and matchmaking on their minds but her? Was she the only single person content with her life?

A little disconcerted at her mentor's absence, Haley went around to the back of the shop. Now she was getting spooked. What had happened to Kana? What if whoever was after her was after Kana now, too? No! He was like family! He was her mentor!

Kana had introduced her to the magic of books, but not as symbols of prestige and accolades, as her parents considered their scholarly, erudite academic works. He taught her that books were enchanted keys, opening journeys to wherever imagination roamed.

Treasures were found, not in pots of gold at the bottoms of rainbows, but in tales. He had presented fantasy worlds about ancient gods, mystical kingdoms and charmed beings that lived in the sea. He was a dreamer, just like Haley. He would not forsake a reunion with her.

Returning to the shop, she walked around to the side door, knocking firmly, then tested the knob. To her utter surprise, it turned in her hand! The door was unlocked. There, he was home! He simply hadn't heard her. Or was something wrong? Concerned, knocking and calling, she warily entered, her heart pounding with anxiety, her nerves straining with dread. Kana was in his seventies, and he lived alone. What if something had happened to him?

Standing in the doorway of the storeroom she froze in her tracks. The small office area was completely ransacked -- papers, books, drawers and shelves disarrayed. Stepping close to the desk she saw dark, dried-liquid smears on the surface and splashed around the furniture. Her stomach curdled; for she was convinced the marks were bloodstains.

Carefully peering into the main, large room of the shop, she cringed at the now familiar scene of chaos with books scattered everywhere. Dreading what she might find, she made a quick, jogging tour of the shop and didn't stop until she returned to the back door, exhaling a huge sigh of relief. Okay, no body. That was good.

Where was Kana? Obviously he did not know about the ransacking so that had to mean he was safe. No, just that he might not have stayed here. What about the bloodstains? She was finding it hard to think straight. What should she do next? Go check upstairs at his apartment and find out if he was there. Could he have been injured and returned to his home? Was he being held hostage? She should call the police.

Shivering with dread, instincts impelled her to go upstairs to Kana's apartment over the shop and see if he -- or his body -- was there. The thought terrified her -- but what else could she do? Experiencing traces of trepidation at this solo mission, feeling that it was probably a mistake, she jogged out the back door, dismissing premonitions of warning.

CHAPTER FOUR

"Sounds like it should be exciting."

Distraught, she raced around the back of the building, trotted up the old wooden stairs and paused on the landing to catch her breath. Incongruous with the worn, faded structure that probably dated back to the war years, was a new, metal security screen door at the entrance to Kana's apartment over the shop. The lock was intact. No break-in up here. She pounded on the door, and after a moment, felt too jittery to wait for a response.

Scrambling for her keys, she unlocked the doors and instantly ducked around to the left to reach the electronic security key-pad lock. Punching in the appropriate code -- 0221 -- the security pad beeped, indicating the code was accepted, the house secure, and no police would respond. The logo on the keypad gave her a momentary start: Cabrillo Security. One of Sam Simon's many companies! She'd never noticed that before. Of course, until today she never gave security measures a second thought. They were supposed to work!

Standing with her back to the open doorway, the streams of dying Hawaiian sunlight beaming into the musty apartment, her panic receded enough for rational thought. Don't blunder into a crime scene like so many rash amateurs in novels.

"Kana! Are you home?"

A moment's pause, then she inched forward. The place was neat and clean, tinged with the stuffiness of a closed library. Circumspectly stepping further into the small kitchen, she proceeded into the living room. Every wall was lined with bookshelves, so many she'd always wondered why the floor didn't cave in upon the shop below. The furnishings were extra-comfortable; plush couches and chairs neatly arranged for optimum comfort in reading. No sign of foul play. No sign of Kana Hagoth.

Encroaching farther into the room, she searched for anything obviously amiss, but all seemed tidy and in order, consistent with Kana's personality. Irrelevantly she wondered how he had ever gotten mixed up with her zany parents. Everything about him was so obvious, deep and creative.

"Kana! Are you here?" She glanced inside the bedrooms in a quick perusal. Empty. Windows closed. "Kana?" Another pause, then she wandered back to the kitchen.

Relieved that unlike her recent unpleasant experience, Kana's home was not violated, she knew the inevitable next step. This was becoming an unfortunate habit! She used her cell to dial the operator and ask for the Honolulu Police Department.

As soon as she hung up she strayed toward the door leading to the living room, and then stopped. Wandering around seemed like an infringement. She had only been here, upon invitation from Kana, into the kitchen and living room. She had a key and knew the code precisely for . . . for this purpose. In case she came and Kana was not here she could come into the shop, or apartment, and make herself at home. Okay, now she was feeling reactionary. Kana really could be away on a business-trip-gone-long.

No, the tossing of the shop was real. And what about the blood stains? Her own experiences this morning in San Diego were not imagined. Something was going on – something bad – and it now included Kana!

Then why was the apartment untouched? Maybe the burglar didn't know about this place? Too many questions. Too much confusion. She needed help to sort this out. Kana would be the perfect sounding board, of course, but his disappearance was part of the mystery, wasn't it?

Locking up again she trotted downstairs to wait in front of the shop. She wouldn't want some over-eager patrolman mistaking her for a burglar. Just what kind of policemen would she encounter here in Honolulu? The image of Officer Cross flew into her mind, and she wondered if he had asked Skye out on a date yet. The not-so-simple life in San Diego seemed a dimension and a world apart, shattered by the same intrigue now stalking her here in Hawaii.

Knowing it might take a long time for the officials to respond to the call; Haley visited Mrs. Kahuku to inform her about the crime and pressed her a little more strongly about what had been going on in the last few days. She wanted some details resolved before the police arrived.

"Break in! But this is such a good neighborhood!" Emma Kahuku, properly shocked at the crime, shook her head in dismay. "Kana gonna be so upset. He loves them books like his children." She gave a wink to her guest. "Maybe more."

The florist shop had no customers and Emma waited with her in front for the police. From here there was a clear view of the bookshop next door, but when Haley paced to the end of the room she realized the view of the bookstore was obscured by the refrigerators

filled with leis and flowers. Emma would not have seen anyone
sneaking around or breaking into Kana's place from this side. When
the intruder broke into the shop Emma did not see him.

"And you can't remember where he was going?"

"He likes to keep to himself." There was the slightest hint of a
pout. "You know how he likes to just take off. I invite him for dinner
when I see him, but he doesn't always come over. Even the delivery
man know when Kana not answer he bring the boxes here, yeah?"

"Yeah," Haley sighed.

Everyone knew how Kana liked to disappear on the trail of book
treasure. This time, though, she was afraid his absence was more
sinister than a shopping trip.

A blue and white HPD squad car pulled up in the driveway of
the bookstore. Impressed at the speedy response, Haley went out to
meet the officer, deducing that since this area was the tourist mecca
of Honolulu, it was probably well patrolled, and infractions were
dealt with swiftly.

Policemen seemed to be about the same build on both sides of
the Pacific. Bulky, well muscled Officer Dean, as he introduced
himself, shared a general stamp of commonality with Cross in San
Diego – and how cops everywhere should look -- the physically fit,
good-looking elements of law enforcement personnel. Dean was a
tall, tan, broad, surf-bleached sandy blond in his late twenties. He
took out a notebook and politely nodded in appropriate places while
she offered her statement. Knowing this sounded, and was received
as, routine in the extreme, she tried to stress her concern about her
friend.

"It's not like Kana to miss an appointment with me," she insisted, trying not to sound like a typical complaining tourist. "Look, there's been violence –"

"Take it easy, lady," the officer cautioned.

"There's blood in the back room, and you have to do something!"

The mention of blood triggered an alert in his so-far mellow, green eyes. "Violence and blood, huh? We got it covered."

She paused in her recitation when an unmarked, chromed-up, late-model, white Mustang convertible -- with an HPD revolving blue police light on the dash -- angled into the drive. HPD officers were supplemented for using personal cars in their work and were issued the siren and light to identify them as official police cars. Part of the status of driving a private vehicle was that it was a noticeable status symbol. Even for the flashy rides she'd seen, this one was over-the-top cool.

Smoothly emerging from the driver's side was a medium-height, lean Polynesian/ Asian man with close cropped dark hair and a nifty Aloha-print shirt. The only evidence of his office was a revolver tucked in a waist holster and a badge visible from a belt case. Casually adjusting his wrap-around sunglasses – a fashion affectation, or perhaps to hide his eyes -- since the sun was nearly down and the shadows were deep on this back side of Waikiki. He glanced at her and the store with laser-sharp scrutiny, which shifted quickly to an expression of apprehension.

"Are you the person who reported the break-in at Kana's shop?"

"Yes."

"Lieutenant Chase." He firmly shook her hand.

53

The concerned demeanor calmed her, while the sincere tone further encouraged her. That he addressed her mentor in the personal meant this was not just another cop, and Kana was not just a faceless missing person.

"Hi. My name is Haley Wyndham. Kana's not here at the store and it's been vandalized. You know Kana then."

The non-question got his attention. "What makes you say that?"

"You called him Kana. Denotes familiarity."

"So it does. Yeah, I know him." Even through the sunglasses she felt he held her gaze for a penetrating moment. "My – uh -- mother sends me here all the time. Collects Charlie Chan." Straight faced easy delivery. It was not a joke. "Did you have an appointment with Kana?"

"Yes. I came in from the mainland a little while ago." She paused, trying to gauge how much would be interesting information and when it would reach the point of nonessential, but his pleasant face stayed focused on her and she took that as a positive that she had his attention. Already she liked dealing with Hawaii cops better than San Diego cops. "I was meeting Kana about some books he had for me and when I entered the shop from the back door I saw the place was tossed -- searched."

Noncommittally he nodded. "And you called HPD."

"Well, no, then I went upstairs to his apartment he keeps above the shop --"

"You just walked in?"

"Yeah – no – it was unlocked. The shop was unlocked – did I say that already? But the apartment was locked. I have a key and I know the code."

"The security code?"

"Yeah. I told you, Kana is an old friend."

The lieutenant's face was unreadable when he responded, "Kana's casual about keeping his commitments."

"Not with me."

"Did he forget to set his alarm? He can get absentminded when he's focused on books."

"The locks were fine. Anyway, his place is untouched, but I saw what might be bloodstains in his office at the rear of the shop."

Flustered, she knew she was sounding blond and she knew it, but this unexpected break-in after similar twin events in California, was unnerving her.

Chase's concern was piqued at the mention of blood. Giving a nod to Dean, he walked the perimeter of the store. Checking the front door, confirming it was locked; he peered in the windows and saw a portion of the destruction. Marching around the corner, Haley trailed behind. Reaching the rear door Chase paused briefly to check for evidence of forced entry, and then looked inside the store, then back at her.

Removing his glasses, his eyes narrowed. "How do you know the apartment was not disturbed?"

"I went in. I told you, I know the code."

Again, a neutral nod. "When was your appointment?"

"He called me Monday and we arranged for me to meet him here this afternoon."

"And you haven't talked to him since?"

"No. Mrs. Kahuku has been holding mail for him since Monday, though. You'll have to talk to her."

He smirked. "Thanks, I'll make a note."

She forgave the sarcasm under the circumstances. "After the trouble I had this morning, I was worried." Before he had a chance to voice the question she continued. "I own a bookshop in San Diego. It was broken into last night and so was my condo. So naturally I thought Kana's was too."

"Really?" Not only did this get his attention, he actually seemed interested. More than Cross. Score another point for HPD! "This morning you say?"

"Yeah."

"You've had a busy day." He scanned the immediate area. "We'll take it from here."

With a nod he cautiously entered the shop; Dean, a hand on the revolver tucked in his holster, followed. Carefully trailing behind, Haley silently tracked in their footsteps. At the office, Chase tossed her a brief, irritated glance, but said nothing. Continuing into the main room of the shop, he stood there assessing the damage.

This was the first time Haley was coherent enough to study the scene of the crime, borrowing strength and security from the police presence. The store was torn apart, books and shelves on the floor, in some cases pages even torn from bindings. Not just the fictional mystery section, either, but many genres of books seemed to have suffered. Aching, she wanted to sweep the ruined volumes of history, fantasy and suspense in her arms and repair them. At the same time, her wrath stirred at the monster that devastated such prized material. More pressing than either misery or revenge was her escalating fear for Kana's safety.

"Are you all right?" The tone was compassionate, even understanding. Lieutenant Chase placed a hand on her elbow. "Why don't you go back to your hotel and --"

She stood her ground. "No, I'd rather stay here and help!"

Now that his shades were perched at the top of his head, his earnest, yet stern brown eyes made her want to take a step backwards. They were disapproving, but kind and she found it hard to reconcile both reactions coming from a civil servant. Dealings in her past had given her a healthy diffidence toward representatives of the law: patrolmen, lawyers and security guards. Chase, however, confused her. Not knowing how to respond, exactly, she decided honesty was her best companion in this circumstance.

"Please. Kana means a lot to me. And his belongings. If you know him you know he loves the books as if they were his family."

"Ohana," he quietly corrected. A wry smile wrinkled the corner of his mouth. "In Hawaiian that means family. Yes, I know exactly what you mean. Haven't you had a rough enough time today? I can give you a report."

She believed he really would, but that was not good enough. "Maybe I can help -- let you know if anything is missing. He's an old friend. I know this place pretty well."

"Maybe," he agreed in an unreadable tone.

Dean cautiously wandered the room while trying to look like he was not listening to the conversation. He stopped to examine a ripped book. Haley moved forward, instinctively reaching to rescue the damaged merchandise.

Chase stepped in front of her, bodily blocking her interference, and gave her a long-suffering sigh. "Please, no civilians. Just stay back and let us handle this."

With a slight nod she gave silent assent. Crossing her arms lest she be tempted to touch anything, she watched the detective study the room he made his way to the stain on the floor. Haley followed behind at a good distance and cringed when Chase examined the gruesome evidence of dark stains splattering the desktop, the papers, and the floor, from the desk to the door. Crouching alongside the officer, striving to think like the many detectives she loved to read about, she noted only splatters and smears on the floor. On the desk there were several big splotches, even -- yuck! -- a large puddle that tightened her stomach.

Chase glanced at her, clearly annoyed. Then, incongruously, he smiled. "Mahalo for your concern, Miss Wyndham. That means thanks. You will be happy to know this is not blood."

Relieved, but skeptical, a little irritated to be so wrong, especially to this very human cop, she edged closer to the deep burgundy stain. Daring to sniff, she embarrassingly felt her assessment of the color might have been a subconscious reaction. An honest mistake from several feet away she excused.

"Liquor?"

Seeming relieved, he chuckled. "Yeah. Some kind of wine I'm guessing from the color and scent."

"Kana doesn't drink," they both stated in unison.

For a moment they stared at each other.

"You do know him well," he commented as he came to his feet.

"I told you."

The sound of a crunch startled them both and Chase carefully stepped away from the desk. "Interesting. Glass. Clear," he concluded as he studied the floor. She crouched down next to him, careful not to scrape her tender knees on the carpet. Only inches from his face, she held his gaze momentarily, then turned back to the mysterious find.

"Clear glass. What does that mean?"

"Someone brought wine to Kana, who doesn't drink. Then this mystery visitor breaks a glass, not a bottle, and then cleans up and," he glanced around the area, "seems to have taken the bottle with him. Hmm."

He left the room to do a more thorough search. Without touching anything she examined the papers scattered in disarray. Most were shipping and phone orders; a few were scribbled memos. Since the mess was so atypical of Kana she was certain that foul play had preyed here.

Studying the manifests she deduced that only orders received last week were here. Moving over to the doorway she leaned out to check the inside front of the store and noted envelopes lying on the floor under the slot. A hefty stack of mail cluttered the entry mat. She did the math: Kana had called her on Monday morning. Mrs. Kahuku had received packages for Kana the last few days and had last seen him on Monday, so that had to be the starting point. Kana had been gone -- missing or otherwise -- since Monday afternoon.

She quickly and covertly snooped until the crime scene photographer and lab techs arrived in what she thought was record time. Impressed at the interest in a burglary – she didn't get crime scene techs in San Diego this morning! – she folded inconspicuously into a corner of the store as the policemen went to work.

Chase sidled into the not very large room, made smaller by the clutter of people, plus the books layering the floor instead of crowding the wall-to-wall shelves looming over them like the shadow of Diamond Head. Issuing orders, occasionally casting annoyed glances her way, but mostly ignoring her, Chase ran the operation with calm efficiency.

After the crew gave him the all clear the lieutenant started examining the papers on the desk. Without being asked Haley joined him, volunteering her observations about what the paperwork meant; shipping orders, phone orders and some personal notations scrawled in what looked like an alien tongue, but passed as Kana's handwriting. She also reminded Chase about Emma's account of Kana's last known appearance on Monday, and the boxes at the flower shop.

Chase stiffened during his search of a basket stuffed with outgoing packages and envelopes. He drew out a small box sealed with tape. "This is yours."

He handed it to Haley. Taking it, she was uncharacteristically speechless.

"It is addressed to you," he gestured to the scrunched printing; the address of her home in San Diego.

Why would Kana send her something to her home? He always sent books directly to her store. "Can I open it?"

"In a minute."

Chase called over a short, Asian/Polynesian man wearing an HPD Crime Unit vest over a bright aloha shirt. The man with an easy smile introduced himself as Danny Cho. With efficient professionalism Cho quickly processed the box.

"CSI to the rescue," he finished with a flourish. "Anything else, Keoni?"

"No. Mahalo, Cho. See you back at the station." At her questioning look he translated, "Mahalo means thanks."

"Right." She grew uncomfortable under his stare. "What?"

"Nothing. Go ahead and see what it is."

Ripping the tape off the brown covering she opened the end and pulled out a tissue wrapped bundle. Carefully unfolding the thin paper, she gasped out. "Oh, wow. This is incredible!"

A native necklace of what looked like rough-hewn coconut beads unwound as she drew it into her hands. At the end of the pendant were twin wooden dolphins arching above a crystal. "Beautiful," she whispered. She looked up to meet the frowning expression of the cop. He puzzled her -- the way he continually altered from disapproval to concern, compassion to cool efficiency. "What?"

His countenance was wiped clean of anything but placid curiosity. "Is this significant to you in some way?"

"The dolphins or the necklace? No. Why?"

"Does Kana always give you jewelry?"

"Never. I don't know why he would want to send this to me." She glanced around the desk, wishing answers to all the questions piling up would magically appear. "I don't understand it." She examined the beauty of he craftsmanship and the lovely detail in the etched dolphins. "They remind me of the dolphins in the sign."

"The sign?"

"Over the shop. You must have noticed it every time you came in here to buy Earl Derr Biggers."

"Who?"

"He wrote the Charlie Chan books."

"Oh. Yeah." His smirk was refreshingly self-effacing. "I don't remember dolphins in the sign."

"They see but they do not observe, Watson," she muttered under her breath."

"What was that?"

He was much better than Lestrade. Better looking, too. She would cut him a break. "Just quoting a book. Nothing important. This is the coolest necklace I've ever seen." Just holding it in her hand made her feel a tingle of emotion. With amazing creativity some talented craftsman had put unique skill into this pendant. "I love it. Just because I don't understand it doesn't mean I'm going to give it up. That's a double negative. Never mind. I can keep it, right?"

"It's addressed to you," he conceded, but seemed reluctant. "He meant to send it. I wonder why he didn't."

"Yeah, I don't get that either. Why would he send it to me?" She pondered the question aloud. "He knew I was coming to see him today. And why a necklace?"

"So this isn't why he would have you come over?"

"For a necklace? Even if it is cool, which it is, no." She pondered the question for a moment.

"What did he tell you?"

She thought back to the conversation so long ago in experiences more so than time. "He said he had a treasure for me."

"A treasure."

"Yeah. I guessed a rare book."

Chase studied the box. Unsatisfied, he paced around the desk. "Kana loves dolphins." He fingered the amulet. "This is very nice workmanship. Kana supports local artisans. Maybe it's the treasure. A gift. With nothing mysterious about it." He shrugged. "To use a pun, maybe there's nothing sinister to read into this."

"Funny."

"As a detective I often read suspicious circumstances into commonplace life."

Liking him more and more, she matched his grin. "Yeah. Same here. Occupational hazard." At his questioning look she pointed to herself. "Mystery bookstore owner."

"Right. Well, what then? Is it your birthday?"

"Not for a few months."

Chase was silent for a moment. "Maybe he just wants you to appreciate something of the culture while you're here. You could use some of that."

It was not exactly a condemning tone, nor condescending, but she recognized it as a mild censure. "What do you mean?"

"You claim you're a friend of Kana's," he began, leaning on the desk, but committing his entire attention to her.

"I am!"

"You've come here often."

"For years!"

"Yet you know nothing about Hawaii. Even the simplest words are foreign to you."

She defended, "Not all. Wikiwiki. Means quick. Amy, my friend, uses that all the time."

He waved away the burgeoning argument with a gesture of his hand. "Never mind. The important thing is that there is a crime, but not so serious. I don't think it's a reason to worry about Kana. He'll show up."

"How can you be so sure?"

"For one, no body," he countered, mellowing. His voice was optimistic. "And no more wine," he delivered with a smile. "Whoever brought the wine, and presumably ransacked the place, left without doing serious damage. Kana wasn't even here, I'm thinking.

So we don't really know what happened, and while his whereabouts is cause for concern, Kana should be fine."

"He would not have ditched out on me. And his place being tossed after mine was tossed this morning, well that is beyond coincidence!"

Amused, he repeated, "Beyond coincidence, huh? I've seen coincidences before in my line of work. Did it ever occur to you that someone broke into your store and found your home address there? Then, knowing you would be gone and tied up this morning with the burglary, they went to burglarize your empty home?"

No, that had not occurred to her! Nor to good old Officer Cross, either, apparently. If it did he had not mentioned it. Hmm. Was her imagination running amok with crime conspiracies when this was simple burglary?

She told him with decreased conviction, "It's connected. It has to be."

He countered firmly, "Kana's eccentric, loses track of time and will go anywhere on a whim if it has to do with a rare book. And as far as the break-in goes, we have crime here in Waikiki. Just like there must be crime in San Diego."

"You can't dismiss this." He seemed unconvinced so she pressed her case. "I know enough about Hawaii to know things are way casual here. Don't be too casual about his disappearance."

Chase was irritatingly calm and reasonable. "I'll go upstairs and check out his apartment."

Haley led the way and typed in the numbers on the keypad -- 0221 -- what other code would a bibliophile and mystery fanatic use? Then she stood back, anticipating Chase's MO of suggesting she stay out of the way. A rumble in her stomach reminded her it had been a while since her inadequate meal on the plane and the sushi snack on Kalakaua. Self-consciously, she held onto her mid-section.

"Hungry?" Chase smiled.

"It's been a while since my last snack."

"We'll have you out of here soon."

The sun had disappeared below the buildings of Waikiki and Kuhio Avenue was plunged in deep shadows. The sky darkened with fingers of purple clouds streaked with the pale tangerine of the coming sunset.

Glasses still propped atop Chase's head, his eyes were unshielded and accentuated his laid-back attitude. They entered the small apartment and the cop switched on the light. The bright illumination from a cluster of bulbs – Kana believed in adequate brightness for reading at the chipped and worn wooden table -- bathed the tiny kitchen in an unnatural hue of yellow, reflecting the old, worn enamel of the saffron shaded pre-WWII appliances. The tile counters were tinged from years of cleanings, while the gray linoleum on the floor seemed as dated as the building. It was homey and cozy, a place she felt comfortable. The smell of pineapple and some kind of fresh flower in a vase by the sink lent a lived-in atmosphere, rimmed on the edges by the musty, closed smell of books shut indoors with no ventilation.

"It is not like Kana to vanish without word to me. I should know, I've known him since I was ten."

While the detective wandered further into the apartment, she lingered in the doorway. Chase stopped an examination of the computer desk in the small living room and stared at her.

"I didn't realize it was so long."

"I'm not that old!"

"No, that's not what I meant —"He sputtered into laughter at her mock indignation. "Really. I just . . . ." He stared at her for a moment. Again he seemed on the brink of saying something, then gave a mysterious nod and looked away to examine the room. Over his shoulder he said, "Time has a way of getting by us, I guess."

Curious comment. "I'm not vain about my age. I have too many relatives reminding me how old I am and how unmarried I am."

He stopped to look back at her. His smile wide, he gave a nod. "I know exactly what you mean."

"Really? You're single with a nagging family I take it?"

"Yeah."

That he would be included in her much-maligned status of persecution for the unmarried, she felt another thread of connectivity to this charming stranger. Perhaps this sudden kinship urged her to confessions she would not normally make to people she just met. Or policemen.

"Kana's a friend of the family, but like my grandfather really."

"Yes." His strong jaw flexed and his dark eyes squinted with perplexity. He seemed about to comment, again, then moved to study the cubbyholes in a small desk. "Your ohana, your family, don't live here in Hawaii, do they?"

"No, California, but we visited almost every summer." He shot her another puzzled glance and she decided to give him the condensed rather than the encyclopedic version of her family history. "My parents are professors. I spent my childhood pursuing various cultures, including, fortunately, Hawaii. Now, they teach in Northern California at the College of the Pacific. They've known Kana forever."

Stopping to study her, he cocked his head in assessment. "Sounds like you've moved around a lot."

"I guess it could get tiring."

"Yeah," she agreed quietly, amazed at his acuity. She placed the jewelry around her neck, still admiring the craftsmanship.

Walking through the apartment, ending in the doorway of the small bedroom that was simply furnished with a bed, a desk and a nightstand, she declared everything to appear normal. This was the only room with no books, she noted immediately.

Joining her, the policeman paused to admire the canvases on the wall. The vividly colorful paintings cast a spell, freezing both observers into a moment of timeless admiration of beauty and wonder. Chase relaxed, his expression appreciative, serene, even. Haley could only agree; breath taken away by the stunning visual scenes.

"Those are amazing!" She had never been in Kana's bedroom, but knew instantly how very fitting these paintings were for the occupant. They were everything Hawaii in a frame. She fingered the dolphins on her necklace. "Yeah, he does love dolphins."

Incredible how she was finding Kana had hidden secrets. She considered him family – ohana – yet, was discovering how little she knew about him as a person. Their shared passion for books had excluded everything else surrounding his life. No, not exactly. He had always wanted to teach her about his culture and she had never bothered, never had the time for the culture he loved. That didn't make her much of a friend.

"Commissioned by an anonymous local artist," Chase explained, raking the canvases with an appreciating eye, drinking in the rich detail of the art.

Focusing back on the paintings, she examined them with the inexpert eye of an art class drop out, but with the inner soaring of a soul thriving on tropical beauty. In each seascape, the brightly hued landscapes of stark, emerald cliffs plunging into the cobalt sea were enchanting. White clouds billowed in a brilliant blue sky, and sleek dolphins seemed alive in the roiling surf. Like depictions of a mystical Bali Hai where magic would be as commonplace as the stunning views, these complimentary paintings seemed like nature's bookends, capturing some ethereal land of dreams.

Chase drew in a deep, satisfied sigh. "Magnificent, aren't they?"

The four, large paintings, one on each wall, dominated the room that was strangely devoid of bookshelves, as if Kana came here for contemplation of paradise instead of the pursuit of knowledge. This room represented one part of Kana's life that had been relegated to an escape from the literary, with a twist into the realm of fantasy. No one else she knew owned amazing art like this. Stepping closer, she gravitated toward her favorite, a stunningly cerulean ocean back dropped by a perfect sapphire sky. Neon, triple rainbows arched between fluted cliffs of Ireland-green, and all shrouded a cove where outriggers large enough to sport sails drifted in the bay. Two dolphins played in the waves curving into a pristine-sand bay. Two dolphins in each painting. Definitely a theme.

"I've never seen anything like these." She breathed it in a whisper as she stared at the scribble in the right bottom corner.

"Nani," Chase barely breathed, studying them closely. "Beautiful," he translated. "You know, it reminds me of the stories Kana always tells about the old Hawaiians. They lived on the sea.

They navigated to these islands by the stars and the waves. We are part of the sea."

"That's lovely," she smiled at him, finally drawing her eyes from his strong face and back o the painting. She tried to decipher the signature. "K-A-M – something."

Moving closer, Chase studied the canvas. "Style looks familiar. Some local who's in the shops, I guess."

"Kana just loves mysteries." She smiled, never tiring of staring at the otherworldly realms. "Why does he keep them hidden in the bedroom?"

"He likes mysteries," he quoted, then grinned. "They're like talk-story I've heard about. The hidden island of the ancients." He half-smiled in a nostalgic air.

"Talk-story?"

"Telling stories Hawaiian style." This time he laughed. "Surrounded by books and I'm going to have to invest in a Hawaiian dictionary for you."

"I've done fine without one all these years." Her words concluded with a little huff.

"Then you haven't met enough Hawaiians."

"Maybe," she conceded. "What about this mystery island?"

"Oh, just old tales." He signed almost nostalgically. "A refuge. An old myth," he dismissed. "Pu'uhonua. Refuge."

The most striking painting, and largest, was a superlative canvas done in aggressive colors of blues and greens, depicting an amazing island in the background – the same one represented in the other artwork – with two double-hulled, sailed canoes in the sculptured bay. Two dolphins were in mid air, leaping from the water across the bows of the canoes. Haley recognized the craft as the kind ancient Hawaiian's used to sail across the Pacific as Chase had mentioned.

"You know if you're going to keep coming to Hawaii, you should really learn more about the richness of our heritage," he told her, staring into her eyes.

"I think I'd like that. Maybe you can recommend a good tutor?"

"I – uh – yeah – I can." He smiled, then straightened, and without looking directly at her again, nodded toward the door.

"After we find Kana," she stipulated.

"If he's missing," Chase corrected. "I think we've finished here."

Double-checking all the rooms as they exited, Chase offered her a lift to her hotel. After the exhausting day she readily agreed, not up to walking, even if it was only a few blocks away.

The short night drive with the top down was reviving. The warm wind snaking through the tall buildings of Waikiki whipped around the busses and people to fluff her hair. The tangle of traffic and sub-level of fumes did not diminish the feel of humid sea breeze, or the hint of plumeria and ginger in the air. She had never had trouble finding the little bits of paradise amid the crush of civilization weaving through Hawaii.

"So did I convince you yet that Kana is missing?"

"I'm trying to be open minded and consider all the facts before I form any theories."

She couldn't argue with the Sherlock-like technique.

Pulling up in the hotel driveway off of Kalakaua Avenue, Chase promised to keep in touch with any leads in the case. Unique in her experience with the police, Haley believed he would not only keep

her apprised, but that he would find out something worthy of
reporting to her.

***

After grabbing a candy bar from the hotel gift shop on the way
up to her room, Haley locked the door and immediately opened the
glass doors of the lanai. Taking a seat at the little outside table, she
breathed in the evening air and tried to relax while she punched in the
number of her shop in San Diego.

From her vantage point she had a fair view of the glow of sun
rays on the watery western horizon -- just through the towering high
rise hotels strangling this back little corner of Waikiki. Angling to
look toward the mountains, a wedge of the Ala Wai Canal was visible
and she could spot thin outrigger canoes coursing through the water
for evening practice. The small craft reminded her of the paintings in
Kana's room and she watched them with piqued interest as they
trailed their way along the thin strip of water backing the high rise
canyons of Waikiki.

Garvin answered the call as she settled back in the plastic chair
on the narrow lanai. "How's paradise?"

"Could be better, Gar. How's things there?"

"Fine. Business is great."

"Don't let Skye go home by herself."

"Not a chance. Nacho and I are taking her to our place. That
dweeb Cross promised to escort her home tonight, but I nixed that.
Just to be safe, he says."

"Cross." It was a growl of exasperation. "I don't want my
cousin dating a cop."

71

"I already warned her. She is not going to date a cop! I'll have Nacho lick him to death or something first!"

In her weary mind, Haley had trouble processing the crazy information blasting her way. The entire world really did revolve around matchmaking, she was deciding. Patrolman Cross after her cousin? The possibility of a cop in the family? No way!

"Look, Gar, I need you guys to be really careful. Something bad is going on here."

"Ah, tremors in the Force?"

She sighed, wondering if her cousin would ever grow up. "Get serious, not Jedi. Kana's shop was vandalized -- even worse than mine -- and Kana is missing!"

"Oh, man. That's heavy."

"Hey, Cross could prove useful as long as I don't leave him alone with Skye. Might scare away the bad guys or something."

"Just please be careful, okay?"

"Got it. I'll tell Cross. He promised to come tonight just to check up on us, but he meant Skye. Maybe a conspiracy will give him something to think about besides my sister."

Haley didn't know if she liked his plan or not. Nor did she appreciate being included in something dramatically intense like an unknown plot. Secret schemes were part of the world of alien abductions, JFK theorists or Ripperologists. Not bookstore owners. Yet, how could she refute his categorizing?

"This is getting pretty bizarre," he concluded. "And here's one more quirky factoid. The book stolen from the fantasy section. Get this, it's about mystical islands. Atlantis and Beyond or something like that."

She vaguely remembered the book. A dust collector in a mystery store. Why would the robber steal that?

"Okay, thanks."

"Yeah. Good luck. Careful. I'll call tomorrow to check in."

"Careful yourself, cuz. I don't like the vibes swirling around the Force."

"Right. 'Night, Gar."

Haley sighed, staring at the dark background of night and the little lights from hotel windows in the high-rises around her. The stress of the day had kept her from even one decent meal. Forcing her weary body to move, she showered, changed and walked to the nearest shopping center. She treated herself to a scrumptious dinner at a Waikiki seafood restaurant overlooking the ocean. Grilled mahi-mahi with mango sauce, seasoned rice with seaweed, a side of poke – raw fish seasoned in shoyu sauce and crispy seaweed -- all downed with a soda filled with energizing caffeine.

Soaking in the luscious ambiance of the deep, velvety waves washing the white sand of Waikiki, she leaned back in her chair with a sigh of contentment. Hypnotized by the undulating colors of orange, red and burgundy, the dancing sunset bleeding dying rays into the ocean, she allowed the tension to drift away on the tide.

Feeling remarkably better with decent food in her stomach and the calm night surf to sooth her nerves, she felt capable of handling life now. As she walked the strand of damp sand, slowly making her way back to the hotel via the beach, she called Amelia Hunter. The elderly woman's cryptic words from this afternoon were puzzling.

There was no answer on the phone and with disappointment she folded up the cell. Apparently she would not get answers to any of her questions tonight.

With the last of the orange sun-echo dripping into the indigo night-sea, the scenery and the meal reviving her, she removed her sandals and ambled into the gentle, bath-temperature sea. She found a core of peace she had been lacking since early that morning. Aware enough, and coached enough by her parents about cosmic centers and spiritual meaning, she knew what she was feeling was her own personal balance with nature, with herself. This was where she drew her serenity and strength -- the sea.

Walking along the night-bustling Kalakaua Avenue, she meandered through the shops, still looking for a good watch and the right cap. At an expensive jewelry shop on the corner she paused to consider crossing the street for dessert – a shave ice or maybe an ice cream cone. Her eye was caught by a display of glittering baubles designed by local artists. As she wandered she fingered the artistic coconut necklace that felt warm and natural, as if it had always been hers. Not a huge fan of lots of adornments, she was already attached to her dolphin amulet.

Dazzling silver caught her attention through the glass and she did a double-take at a delicate and beautiful watch with linked dolphins as the band. It was amazing. The colors and arcs of the dolphins reminded her of the paintings at Kana's, and her new necklace.

Glancing at the entrance she was disappointed to see the shop was closed. Moving nearer to find out when the shop opened, she started in surprise at the flash of a face in the reflection of the glass. Turning, she peered into the crowd, but saw no one familiar. Who had she seen? It had reminded her of Carrie Kahunui, but now the competitive bookseller was not in sight now. Spooky.

Strolling on, she found herself on the doorstep of the enemy where she could spy on the competition. She paused in front of the Super Simon Bookstore. Someone inside suddenly thrust their face right up against the window and she jumped back. The wrinkled, mischievous visage of an overgrown Leprechaun smiled back at her and winked. Then the imp pulled back and Amelia Hunter waved at her, then in an instant she was outside enthusiastically hugging her.

"Checking out the competition again?" Amelia Hunter accused with a smile.

Haley gave her a warm polite smile, shouldering out of the embrace. She wondered if the old girl had nothing better to do than hang out and try to give out autographed copies of her book. The thought was poignantly painful, but why else would Amelia be here at Simons? She was over eighty, or at least that was public speculation because the spy-writer had never revealed her exact age. Amelia's life may have been an amazing adventure, but now advanced years might have left her feeling empty. Perhaps this was a way to stave off the loneliness and disintegration of old age.

"Are you all right?"

Amelia tensed, but in counterpoint gave her a broad smile. "Of course. So, what brings you here this time?"

There was no way to keep a secret about Kana's disappearance, but Haley hesitated to share the heavy news with the older woman who did not look well. "I need to talk to you."

The hazel eyes scrutinized her. In a non-response, she said, "Haley, you look done in. Maybe a hearty meal after all the traveling today? That would give us a chance to catch up."

"No. I just came from Kana's —"

In a theatrically loud tone she asked, "So, did Kana save some wonderful little tidbit for you? Anything you can share?"

Haley managed to squeeze them into a not-so-busy corner of a doorway. "I didn't meet with Kana. He wasn't at the shop. And his place has been tossed!"

Amelia offered a brittle smile. "You know how he loves to forage for good buys." She shrugged off the concern. "Tossed. That's very dramatic. Maybe he has a new inventory –"

"No, the place was vandalized, Amelia, it was a mess. I tried calling you to let you know."

The elderly woman stiffened and kept the false smile plastered on her wrinkled visage. "I'm sure it will be fine. Why don't you drop by and see me tomorrow? Don't tell anyone you're coming. Let's keep it a secret," she finished with a whisper as she hugged Haley, and then released her embrace.

Amelia's attention was riveted by something behind Haley and turning, she drew in a sharp breath as Sam Simon joined them. "Ah, two of my favorite ladies." He bowed his pleasure as counterfeit as his tone. "Come to surrender to the superior force, Haley?"

"Hardly, Sam. I'm just catching up with Amelia."

Simon placed an arm around the thin ex-spy. "She knows where the money is, Haley. Not in quaint little specialty shops like yours. So, what did Kana have for you this trip?"

Did everyone know her business? It was annoying that her competition could track her every move. Irked at his seeming omniscience with her life, and the coup at cornering Amelia, she decided to question Amelia tomorrow.

As soon as civilly possible, she bid them good night and slipped away. Completely exhausted, she walked back to her hotel, checking behind her, still spooked by the memory of the reflected face in the window. Utterly paranoid, feeling absurd for thinking she was being watched or tailed, she was irritated at all her excursions and busy work. She should have been in bed hours ago after the grueling trials she'd faced.

Thumbing through her cell numbers, she started calling a few mutual friends of Kana's as she strolled Kalakaua Avenue. None knew where he was, none had talked to him this week. No one said much to alleviate her concerns when they all calmly conjectured that he was off on an impulsive buying trip.

Sitting on her lanai watching the dark strip of smooth ribbon that was the snippet of dark ocean, she admitted, in the comfort and calm of her hotel room, that Kana was known for impulsive spending sprees.

Perhaps Kana had stumbled on some incredible find of the literary variety, forgotten to inform her, and flew off to some far quarter of the world.

It was time to go to bed and put this frustrating day behind her. Thumb moving to shut off the phone she stopped. Numbers. Addresses. She didn't check the addresses at Kana's shop! What if some pages had been taken out of Kana's address books, too? Tempted to go back to Kuhio Avenue and check tonight, she was too exhausted. Admitting only in a bleak, sideways kind of notion, she was also too scared to go back there on her own, at night. She could tell Chase. Tomorrow. She wished she had asked for his number. Hmm, that would be a switch, her asking a guy for his number. She would resolve all that in the morning, she decided, curling down on the pillow, staring out at the night sky peaking through the slit in the lanai door blinds.

CHAPTER FIVE

"You know, there are easier ways to get my
attention."

Haley awoke early. The aches and pains from her accident had
not seemed so prevalent yesterday, but this morning they slowed her
pace to a sedate walk to the beach at Waikiki. The sand was raked by
hotel beach boys preparatory to the day's invasion of sun worshipers.
The diffused dawn breaking over Koko Head was muted by the
hulking, dark mass of Diamond Head dominating everything in
Waikiki, even the concrete towers.

Instead of renting a bike, flinching at the thought of getting back
on a cycle and working her knees or bending her ribs, she walked the
strip of sand from the beach access path up to Kapiolani Park, then
back. The relaxing scenery and the crisp, warm, morning air breezed
in from the ocean, the fellow fitness walkers and joggers, gradually
receded to background distractions as her mind sank into the currents
of mystery surrounding her life. Not the kind of intrigue bound into
neat volumes found on the shelves of her store, the events of
yesterday were both repulsive and intriguing, disturbing, yet curious.
Occupational hazard; so steeped in mysteries, she found she could not
tear herself away from working to find why she had been singled out
for mayhem.

What was her next step? Chase should know about the address
book pages. She also needed to find out if Amy found anything else
missing?

78

Stopping at a beachside café, Haley sat at one of the tables on the open-air lanai. The buffet was too tempting to resist, and she indulged in treats like mango bread, macadamia nut bread pudding, and an assorted fruit bowl served in a half-pineapple. One of the greatest things about Hawaii was the amazing varieties of luscious tasting treats. At home she could find fresh tropical fruit like papaya and mangos, but some of the more exotic selections like lilikoi and star fruit were hard to find anywhere but here.

Leaving unfinished the last of her tropical fruit (even though it was so amazing!) she coursed around the tables to make her way to the street. She stopped, then turned back, when she thought she spotted the immaculate Carrie Kahunui at a row of shops just outside the restaurant. The petite bookseller was gone now, if she had been there at all.

Was it just a trick of the light? Was this personal crime wave getting to her nerves and making her paranoid? While Haley strolled back to her hotel she called Chase. The HPD switchboard was a slow and tedious process, finally leaving her disappointed that the officer was not at his desk. She left a message on his machine that she would appreciate a call back, and then she walked to Kana's shop.

The police tape across the shop door caused her to hesitate. She was not the type to break the law or ignore rules. Pausing on the front step of Magic Island Books, the sun peaked out from behind a billowy cloud and shone like a spot light on the dolphins over the door, and on the amulet around her neck. Fiddling with the trinket, she chose to not risk crossing the local PD. Instead she went up the old wooden stairs to Kana's private apartment. When she reached the top landing, she saw the lock had been forced and the door was slightly open.

Amazement registered in slow motion.

Danger! Run!

Fear set her into instinctive survival motion. She turned to run down the stairs. Falling head first, she closed her eyes as her head propelled toward the wooden steps. Someone had slammed into her shoulder blade to give her a mighty shove.

***

". . . and I'll tell him again. Soon as your boss cop gets here!"

Mrs. Kahuku's sharp and demanding voice, Haley identified, wincing as the effort of blinking her eyes open brought on incredible explosions inside her brain. Her groaning attracted the attention of the tall, shadowy forms around her. Shading her eyes from the glare of the sun, she recognized Mrs. Kahuku, Patrolman Dean and behind him a new officer. It seemed her week for getting to know the police of two states.

"I was pushed," she blurted out, trying to sit up.

Dean held a hand on her shoulder. "I think you should wait for the ambulance --"

"No!" She shoved him away. That was all she needed to make her week complete -- a visit to an ER! "No, I'm fine, really. I get these little injuries a lot. But this time I was pushed!"

Bending her knees to sit cross-legged, and then abandoning that painful position for the sake of her torn knees, she hissed in a sharp breath at new pains taking her mind off the head damage. Both knees were covered with paper towels, improvised bandages from Emma Kahuku, she guessed. Great, her injuries from yesterday exacerbated. New mutilation acquired. When would the fun end?

"I told him I saw a man running away. Through the alley," Mrs. Kahuku assured helpfully. "You sure you don't want no doctor, sweetie?"

"No, really." Haley looked at Dean, but he was still too tall and too enveloped in bright sunlight. "Kana's apartment was broken into. The lock was damaged. I heard someone inside and I turned to run and he pushed me."

Dean reasonably, even sympathetically, explained he had discovered those facts already and he didn't expect a full statement at this time.

Another shadow crossed her field of vision and Lieutenant Chase crouched down beside her within easy sight. His face was filled with concern. Not needing to look into the sun anymore eased some of the strain within her skull. Having an ally there that she could trust made the pain in her head move to the back of her focus.

His eyes arrested her attention, taking the sting out of the physical hurts and touching her heart. His face was creased with deep distress, transferred to the dark eyes that were intensely worried. His anxiety was as sincere as if he was a member of her family, and that warmed her even more than the tropic rays baking her skin.

"You know, there are easier ways to get my attention." His apprehensive smile kept the remark considerate instead of seeping into flippancy. "So you surprised your serial burglar I understand. I was just up there, and I don't know what's missing. After you're back from the hospital --"

"I'm not going to the hospital." She struggled to stand and Chase helped her.

"You got a nasty knock on the head --"

"Believe me when I say these accidents happen."

81

The bloodied paper towels were sticking to her knees and she tore off the excess, knowing she should at least get herself cleaned up. Maybe there would be something she could use at Kana's.

"I'm going upstairs to check out Kana's apartment."

Walking as carefully as possible, hoping she didn't sway as her perception indicated, she took slow, tentative steps. Grateful to hold onto the old wooden railing, climbing was slow as she cringed and resisted moaning every time her knees bent on every painful step up the stairs. Chase was close behind, carefully holding onto her arm, probably expecting her to fall at any moment.

"Lab boys are on the way," Chase supplied when they reached the threshold.

"I know, don't touch anything," she recited.

He stopped her with a gentle touch on her elbow. "You're sure you're up to this?"

"Yeah. Thanks." She gave him a smile that she didn't have to fake. His compassion bolstered her quavering nerves and helped her ignore the sting of the injuries.

Expecting the worst from her overwrought imagination, Haley was pleasantly astonished to see very little vandalism and no dead body. The neat apartment had barely been ransacked. The office and living room were hardly messed up, a few books and papers on the floor. Only then did she realize her subconscious must have expected to find Kana's body. Relieved, she felt stronger, able to cope with a search of the apartment.

"You must have disturbed him in the act," Chase supplied quietly; solicitously still holding onto her arm in one of the few spots it was not scraped. "I can't tell if anything's been taken. Do you want to take a look later?"

82

"I can check now."

As she perused the apartment it all started to fall into place in her head. The books here were categorized, just like at her home, and her shop in San Diego; she had learned her craft from her mentor. Everything was divided by sections. She had copied the technique of cataloging from Kana. Here, at her home, at her shop and Kana's shop -- all the same. The area of most disturbance in all locations -- the fantasy section. The intruder was looking for something very specific.

"The robber was after a book that he didn't get the first time."

"And what makes you say that, Sherlock?"

"No need for sarcasm."

He laughed a pleasant ripple of enjoyment. "That wasn't my sarcastic voice."

"Sorry. I haven't figured that out yet."

"Guess that will take more study."

It was no trick of her dizzy vision that his eyes were alight with invitation. Pleased, confused, feeling a little warm, she sat down on the arm of an over-stuffed chair. Focus. She was trying to make a point about the crime . . . .

"The guy has hit several places. The criminal is willing to commit assault to find whatever he is looking for. What is he doing?" she wondered.

"Looking for something specific." Chase's voice deepened. "If he didn't find it, he is still a threat."

Haley hobbled over to check the office. Kana's personal address book was mangled -- C through H sections torn out -- just like at her place and her shop. She pointed it out to Chase. She sat down at the desk to search for a piece of paper. Just in time she remembered not to disturb anything, so she scrambled around in her pocket billfold for some scrap to write on. Finding an old receipt, she started scribbling on the margins. In very tiny letters she made four lists: inventory of books rifled at her shop and home, Kana's shop and Kana's home. Then she made a list of address book pages stolen at the four locations.

Sensing someone standing over her shoulder, she glanced at Chase, who was reading her list, squinting due to the small printing. When she explained what she was doing he withdrew a notebook from his back pocket and asked her to copy the lists for him.

"I don't know what it means," she admitted as her nearly illegible scrawls flew across the paper, "but there is a pattern. The burglar is looking for someone with a name from C to H. And something tied in with fantasy books."

"Fantasy? Kana specializes in mysteries, doesn't he?"

"Mostly, yes, so do I, but we also have crossover sections of genres that overlap into mystery. That includes books on historical crimes or fantasy books dealing in some kind of detective theme or mystery. For instance H. G. Wells, or the old Lord Darcy series."

Crouching down beside her, he scanned the lists, thoughtfully nodding. "I think you might be right." Glancing at her with a speculative look, he concluded, "And maybe only you can figure out the connection. Mind if I pick your brain?"

"As jumbled as it is? What an offer. How can I refuse?"

He smiled an easy, natural inclination that lit up his face all the way to his dark, exotic eyes. "Okay, how about I make it tactful. Shall we discuss the case over lunch? My expense account."

"If you don't mind me detouring to Emma's place for a quick clean up and a dose of extra strength Advil?"

"Deal."

***

"You know the barbeque plate lunch place down the street?" she wondered as they walked to his car. "It's good food and cheap if you're on a budget."

"Who isn't," he asked, followed by a smile.

She was getting used to the lopsided grin that was kind of cute on him.

"Thanks for the consideration, but I can afford to treat you to a nice lunch. Barbeque plate lunch, huh?" he laughed as he started the car. "I've never been there."

That surprised her. He was the native. "I'll take you there sometime. What about Fong's Sushi? You know that one, right?"

As they cruised along the street, she learned there were local hangouts he had never heard of, places she loved to frequent on her visits. Like most Kamaaina – locals – Chase shunned the tourist trap of Waikiki, he informed.

The internationally renowned Hawaiian chef Wo Fong owned several restaurants, two that Haley knew of were in San Diego and two in Honolulu, none of which she had ever managed to visit. Lieutenant Chase took her to Fong's on Kalakaua, for her introductory treat and her first delightful surprise was the casual Hawaiian atmosphere. Blended so perfectly with the feel of a local hang-out, while still catering to the heavy tourist trade of Honolulu, the eatery was not as pricy as expected, but looked elegantly extravagant. It wasn't an easy balance to achieve favor with both locals and vacationers -- as she knew from her own shop in the touristy San Diego -- but Fong's managed nicely.

Feeling self-conscious about her battered knees, Haley kept them tucked under the table. Her head bumps at least were covered by her hair, and while it might be tough to find a comfortable position to sleep tonight, she was grateful she did not look as bad as she felt.

Chase recommended the macadamia crusted mahi-mahi and she readily agreed to try Fong's version of her favorite fish. He ordered a soda to drink, explaining, that like his uncle he did not drink. That added a few more points to the tally she was taking of his character, because she didn't drink either. A few times she had given alcohol a try and ended up doing and saying things that were fuel for ridicule from her friends. Coke made life so much simpler.

"While we're coming clean, I hope you won't mind if I confess that I had you checked out with those cops you don't give very high marks."

Haley wasn't insulted at the procedure. Munching on her salad, she agreed it made sense, really, and she didn't blame him for taking the logical step. It gave her more confidence and underscored her impression of his thoroughness and talent as a cop.

When the mahi-mahi arrived they concentrated on the exceptional meal, discussing Hawaiian cuisine before business. Both born and bread by the Pacific, their tastes were remarkably similar, and she interrogated him on local favorites of his for anything ranging from sushi to cheesecake. Longing to learn more, feel more about this magical paradise, she turned investigator and questioned Chase about his roots.

"Hawaii is changing more every day." His expression darkened, and he let slip a grumble about progress not being a good thing sometimes. Shaking his head, he visibly shifted out of his deep thoughts, obviously uncomfortable about where they had strayed. "Now, let's talk about your habit of attracting crime," he directed with a quirk of his lip.

"I probably seemed a little suspicious when we first met. No wonder you had me checked out."

Clearing a spot on the table, he took out his notebook and studied her lists, while she did the same with her scribbled notes.

"Shall we start with the obvious?" There was a wry glint in his eyes matching his tone. "Someone is looking for an address, or a client, that is common to both you and Kana."

"And a book."

"Okay, a book, too. So, what can you tell me about mutual acquaintances of you and Kana? I mean, you don't have to get personal or anything with details about your relationships -- just, you know -- just -- uh -- relationships --"

His embarrassment was charming and she laughed. "Am I dating any of the contacts? No."

"Oh. I mean -- not what I meant," he corrected, tracing lines through the condensation on his soda glass. "I mean, who do you both know?"

"A number of people, but all it would take would be someone to have our client lists. That must be what he is after."

"He? Is it a he?"

Frowning, she played with the bits of macadamia nuts crumbled around her plate. "I don't know." She closed her eyes, flinching at the memory of the push down the stairs. A gentle touch on her hand gave her reassurance. "I didn't see him. Or her. But it was a strong shove." She opened her eyes, startled at the concern in his.

He did not remove his hand. "Sorry. This is too troubling–"

"No, let's keep at it. I want to find Kana and this is the only way. I don't know where to start. We know a lot of people."

"Anyone – uh – exclusive. Some prized client that is a secret? Or a real find that has an item others would want?"

Slowly shaking her head, she drew a blank on those possibilities. "No enemies, if you're going to ask that obvious question. But there are rivalries like crazy. Carrie Kahunui and Sam Simon are two examples. Carrie lives here. Sam is from San Diego, but travels all over the world. He happens to be in town. I saw him last night."

He gave a tight nod. "What is your take on this business with the books and the addresses?"

"Well, you said it -- someone is looking for a place or a person that is common to both Kana and me. What it has to do with our fantasy collections I have no idea. I still have to check to see what's missing from Kana's collection. And only one book was taken that I know of from my store. Arrgg, I still have to call Amy. That's my bookkeeper. She was supposed to find out more about that book."

The detective nodded thoughtfully. "Okay. After my lab people are done getting prints, we'll go over Kana's clients and yours and see what you have in common. Maybe something will come to mind. "

"Hmm, negatives will occasionally give you answers instead of positives?"

"Sometimes."

"I think I've heard that before from Nancy Drew." At his confused expression she reiterated that she agreed, and wondered if there was anything else on his mind.

He offered a smile. "We can pool our findings, uh, shall we say, at dinner?"

Refusing to admit how charming he was, she chose to focus on the more practical aspects of the casual meetings. "I like the way you operate in Honolulu, detective. I like being a police consultant. At this rate, I won't be paying for many meals."

"Mahalo." His smile faltered, and he went back to concentrating on his glass. "So, you never answered the question. Are you dating anyone?"

"Not on either side of the Pacific," she responded, intrigued where this might be going. The interplay reminded her of a practical, and now a desired item of business. "By the way, would you mind if I get your cell number? Just in case I need to get in touch?"

"My pleasure."

CHAPTER SIX

Are you impugning the character of your local police department?

Returning to the scene of the crime always held significance in her favorite mystery books, but Haley didn't know what to expect — how she would feel -- when she and Chase arrived back at Kana's shop. The lab team had left and managed a hasty, but incomplete job of cleaning up. She expected more efficiency from the cops since this was a personal case for Chase.

In movies, TV shows and books, Haley always saw the mechanics of an investigation without any of the real life depth and substance she was experiencing now. That included the high-end unpleasantness of nasty surprises like break-ins, hits on the head and an underlying apprehension for her safety and that of her loved ones.

In Kana's apartment the dread was under control when she confronted the terrible mess. She felt it was her responsibility to replace the books, reestablish his orderly quarters and business. No one on Dragnet ever mentioned this minor detail of crime's aftermath, she sighed. She was calling in a service to handle cleaning up the wine stains and debris, though.

"Let's check out the addresses first," Chase suggested.

They placed the rolodex on the kitchen table where they could sit side by side and read out the names. Chase also brought over some of the recent mail order forms and in a separate stack placed correspondence.

"This would be so much simpler if Kana believed in Twenty-First Century technology," he grumbled, sorting through the pages.

"I'd buy him a PDA for Christmas if he'd use it."

"Which he wouldn't." They both completed the thought and smiled at the shared knowledge of the missing mentor.

They started with the missing C through H sections, then ran down the list of phone orders, mail orders and recent shipping receipts. The work was interrupted by a call on Haley's cell. The ring was a current pop favorite, the custom signal of her cousin, Gar.

"Hey, Gar," she answered.

"Hey, we just got a box from Hawaii and I thought you'd want to know. It's heavy, like books."

"Books?"

"Yeah."

"From Kana? Did you open it?"

"Here's the kicker, cuz. It's not from Kana, it's from Amelia Hunter."

"Oh," she replied, deflated. "Yeah, she's got a new book out. She promised autograph copies for the store."

"Oh," Gar sighed, sounding disappointed it was not a juicy piece to the puzzle. There was the sound of paper crunched at the other end. "She's a funny old bird. Has a kitchy Hawaiian post card in here. It says, 'Haley, wish you were here. Aloha, Amelia.' Hey, this is no new book, Haley; this is an old, musty book. All worn and – and old."

Curious, confused, she asked the title.

"Can't read it, the lettering is too faint. Something about a ship's log. The writing is all ancient and everything."

Was it some kind of cryptic mystery being played out by the former spy? Or a valuable gift? "See what you can find out about it and call me back. Did Amy figure out anything more the missing book yet?"

"No. Haven't had time. We're swamped, cuz. Being a crime scene is good for the crime bookstore."

"Okay. Let me know when she does. And Gar, make sure you put Amelia's book in a really safe place."

"A safe place?"

"Right. I know you can find one."

"Uh – sure."

Hanging up, she called Amelia, but received no answer. Then she reported the details of the conversation to a curious Chase. She was certain the box was a link to Kana's disappearance, but did not know how or why. Chase agreed – with less enthusiasm – that it might be important.

He did concede, "You could be right. Maybe your cousin should take the book over to SDPD –"

"Oh no, I think it's better off in our hands."

"You said yourself it could be a link to Kana –"

"Or not. You don't know the SDPD like I do."

Amusement surfaced easily in the Hawaiian detective. "Are you impugning the character of your local police department?"

"I guess I am," she admitted lightly matching his tone. "But you're –"she couldn't help the smile. "Nicer."

"I'm not sure I can condone that, Miss." Then he smirked and winked. "But I'll let it pass for now."

Haley stood, stretching aching muscles while trying not to stress the bruises and scrapes all over her body. She dialed Amelia's number again and after a few rings hung up. "We should stop by Amelia's. She's not answering the phone, but maybe she's outside or something."

Soberly, he told her, "I can't let you go with me to talk to Hunter."

"What?"

"You're a civilian and you're far more involved already than I should have allowed."

"She's connected to Kana; she's one of his oldest friends. And we don't – "

"And I'll find out everything I can," he promised. "If possible I'll let you know if anything turns up, but this is an official police investigation –"he held up his hand to stave off her protests. "I'll be in touch. I have your number," he held up his own cell phone. "Try to get some rest."

"Rest!"

"This is official," he reminded, standing at the door. "I'll drive you back to the hotel." Cutting off another protest, he overrode, "I will not leave you alone at a crime scene."

"I'll walk back."

He offered a gentle grin. "Come on. You've been wincing around all day. Give your muscles a break. Let me drive you. It's the least I can do."

Reluctantly accepting, she appreciated the style and comfort of the Mustang as they cruised back to her hotel. It was a brilliantly pleasant day in paradise, with the sun warm, the sea breeze refreshing, and the hint of flowers and salt in the humid air.

Dropping her at the curb, she ambled toward the lobby, noting he was already on his phone, and she overheard him request information on Amelia Hunter. Well, two could play at this game, or at Chase's game, actually. This concerned her friend Kana, her family, and who knew how many others in her circle.

Until now, Haley had always thought of the tales in Amelia's books as quasi-biographical, but mostly boastful exaggerations. Amelia's adventure tales were playful and gaudy yarns that sold books and enhanced sales at Reads Like Murder. As a person, Amelia was over-the-top and overwhelming . . . and maybe not above slipping into her old spy habits.

Was Haley being paranoid? Even turning on Amelia, from worry over Kana? What else was she going to uncover? Something menacing about Amelia or Kana? She hoped not. With more questions creeping from the shadows, and few answers, she had to find out for herself.

On the positive side, she was also getting to know a nice cop. And right now he was speeding in his way cool Mustang over to interrogate Amelia Hunter.

***

Haley noted Chase's eyebrows arc above his sunglasses when he pulled the convertible into the curved driveway. The Black Point estate built on the expensive and scenic lava edge near Oahu's eastern rim was framed in tall palms and crusty rocks. Hiding her smile, she exited her rented red Jeep parked in front of the palatial grounds and ornate gardens alongside the elegant mansion.

Perched on a crag overlooking the ragged, black lava coastline off of Diamond Head, the house had a million dollar view and a multi-multi-million dollar price tag. Not that anyone here relocated much. This was old money territory that stretched from the cliffs of the dormant volcano, around the narrow strip of beach at Kahala, Oahu's equivalent of Beverly Hills.

"What took you so long?"

His scowl was readable around the sunglasses. "Silly me, I stopped at the station for a minute. I didn't know it was a race."

Before he could object, she scurried up to the large, double red doors, taking in at a glance the details of how the rich-rich lived. Her family was well off, using money to live comfortably, travel, and enjoy the good things in life. This estate spoke of a more rarified level of wealth and revered money that the former-car-dealer-Wyndhams could only dream about. The awesome estate and all it represented brought home how little she knew Amelia. They were buddies in book collecting and literary notions. They were storytellers and addicts of the mysterious printed word. Haley, however, had never been out here to the elderly woman's house and never guessed at the level of prosperity and comfort afforded the sensational writer.

Hidden discoveries. Just like Kana's Hawaiian paintings and native loyalties, she pondered, fingering the dolphin amulet that she had not removed since receiving it. How many new angles to her friends would she uncover because of the unexpected crime? As in the beginning of her favorite fictional novels, she had a feeling this was only the beginning of unforeseen and unpleasant revelations.

"Nice car," Chase wryly quipped, shaking his head.

"I like it," she smiled. "Gets me to places I need to go."

"Like beating an official law enforcement rep to interview someone who might have information about Kana?"

95

"I know Amelia, Officer Chase. I can make this a little easier. Help you get information. Besides, I have an open invitation to visit Amelia any time."

"Amelia. So you're on a first name basis –"

"I've known her for years. She's a regular author for my store. Don't we need Amelia's permission to search the house?"

"Something like that," Chase sighed, "but we're not going to search her house. We are going to knock – I mean – I am going be official about this. I will knock on the front door –"

"And I'll just happen to join you?" She gave him a unyielding smile.

Haley crowded next to the detective, and gasped when he tapped and the door swung open. Because of her recent experience with unsecured entries this gave her instant jitters. Inside the house the deep and distant bark of a big dog rumbled.

Chase, stepping ahead of her, called for the owner several times, receiving no response. Trading a look of concern with him, he gave a silent nod, as if understanding her probably-not-so-subtle alarm. Reaching his hand back to rest on the stock of the .38 on his belt holster, he held a restraining hold on her arm as he took a step inside.

"Ms Hunter?"

Trepidation swept over Haley as she crept onto the tile entranceway, staying tight behind the detective. Nothing seemed disturbed in the immaculate foyer and Haley took a breath of relief, feeling a little ridiculous for feeling so paranoid. Amelia was probably in a back room of the enormous house. Not every place she entered was a crime scene these days!

Concern tempered, she attuned her senses to the scene, absorbing every detail. She was impressed with the quality of tasteful furnishings. Twin, tall, Oriental vases filled with lush, overflowing tropical shrubbery flowed nicely into the T shaped short hallway ahead. Stepping to the right, toward the sound of the dog, they quickly entered into the sunken living room. The wood and wicker furnishings served as understated foreground to the magnificent view of the Pacific just out the panoramic, open glass doors that took up the entire ocean side wall of the room.

In front of the stunning cerulean of the sea stretched a spacious, verdant-green lawn beside a tropical-decorated deck sided by palm trees and flowered bushes. The briny/sweet scent of the ocean and the flora permeated the room with refreshing air embraced with plumeria and ginger. The faint sound of wind chimes accentuated the gentle background brush of the surf on the rocks.

"Ms Hunter?" Chase called.

The whining of the dog was close, maybe in the next room.

"In here," came the frail voice of Hunter from around the corner.

Chase lightly trod through the big, comfortable living room, to the other side of a partition made of art deco bubbled glass that shielded a small office. When he stopped abruptly, Haley adroitly veered around him to note books and papers strewn around the floor and furniture of the office. The glass door leading out to a back lanai stood open. Fresh ocean wind swept in, fluttering the litter, kissing the room with the misty sea breeze. The amazing view served as a surreal backdrop; the wide grass, the black rocks, the deep blue ocean beyond.

In the foreground was the shocker. Atop the clutter of the room was the body of an attractive Hawaiian woman in a beautiful, pastel, aloha print dress marred with splattered blood. There was no question that the deep burgundy stain on the hardwood floor, was not wine this time, but blood.

Drawing a sharp gasp, Haley snapped, "Carrie!"

Chase kept his eyes and weapon on Amelia, but demanded of Haley, "You know her?"

"Carrie Kahunui! Yeah I – I know her – knew her. We're – were – competitors."

Swaying, Haley caught herself on the doorframe, then hastily stepped back, her shocked mind tilting sideways as it tried to take in the grisly view of her first murder victim in real flesh and blood. Holding her stomach, she could not take her eyes away from the queasy sight of the deceased. Heretofore she had read countless murders between the pages of mystery novels. She surrounded herself with and made a living from mayhem, torture and death. On a daily basis, she passed by the shelves of her store crowded with sinister villains and destruction. Every volume of intrigue and conspiracy touched only skin deep, only as a subjective representation of fiction.

This incongruous sight -- the limp body flung amid the clutter -- rocked her. The vivid scarlet blood was splashed erratically on the expensive dress. Most disturbing of all, the head turned toward her with the blankly glazed eyes gazing, without sight, at the doorway. Making the tableau more grotesque was the embodiment of the ultimate violence in the same scene as the blooming hibiscus hedge rimming the access to the sea and bordering the lanai. It could have been the end of an act to a play; the people were shocked into stillness as frozen as the corpse, while the gentle wind blew the papers, the cast waiting for the curtain to drop. It was too strange to be real, but too tragic to be fiction.

At the side of the room, the elderly, thin form of Amelia Hunter hunched, silent, her aged hands shaking as she stared at the corpse. In her loose jeans and oversized aloha shirt Amelia looked weak – frail and shrunken -- no longer an image of the spy she had been in her prime. Maturity and tragedy marred her and perhaps the weight of sorrow -- or guilt -- seemed to curve her into a shattered ghost of her former life. A large, black Labrador crouched at her side, softly whining, mistrustfully watching the new intruders.

"Amelia," Haley finally gasped. "Are you all right?" Haley's voice sounded strange to her own ears – distant and raspy.

With his left hand, Chase took a firm grip on Haley's arm and only then did she realize she was slanting off-center, her chilled body drifting with a mind disconnected from reality. With his right hand, the officer still leveled his .38 weapon at Hunter.

Haley shook her head, disoriented and appalled that she was now enacting a scene she had imagined myriad times in her familiar mysteries. Living it; experiencing the horror of death. She felt an unexpected creeping dread that someone she knew was murdered; smelling the incongruous air and surf and blood, seeing the glistening crimson wash spread on the bright material and dark floor – it was all surreal.

"Keep your hands in sight, Hunter."

Chase's stern command took Haley's attention from the body to the old woman. Suspect. To the cop, the elderly spy was now a suspect? Think. What would Joe Friday do? No – too old. Stone – too East Coast. Magnum. McGarrett – yeah -- what would he do? Yeah, he would have his weapon trained on the obvious suspect.

Amelia's voice was thin. "She was dead when I came in –"

"Is there anyone else in the house?'

"I don't know."

Dialing his cell with one hand, the policeman called in the report of the body, requesting back up and a full crime team. Ordering the elderly woman to stand clear of the desk, he searched her quickly. Then he moved to check for a pulse on the victim, while reciting a caution that anything Amelia said would go on record.

"I did not kill her," the former spy testily repeated, her usual spunk resurfacing. "I came in and discovered her just like this. I didn't touch anything either," was her salty rebuke. "I know better."

"I'm sure you do."

The ex-spy's face twisted with a tart snarl. "Someone broke into the house with Carrie and they killed her. I did not."

"I'm not arresting you," Chase countered tightly. He made a sour face at Haley, shook his head with irritation and asked. "Do you feel comfortable with her?"

The odd question took her a moment to assimilate. "Yeah."

"Stay here both of you."

While Chase searched the rest of the house Haley studied Hunter, trying to ignore the body on the floor. The old woman seemed pretty calm for having a murder victim in her house. Well, of course if half the things in Amelia's books were true a body in the study would be no big deal to the one-time Mata Hari. So why was the older woman so upset? It was unnerving to come face to face with a body in the den, that's why!

What about the mess – so familiar to her over the last few days? Here, in the magnificent paradise of Hawaii the vandalism had ended in murder. With a chill, she knew such a fate could have befallen her or her family and friends in San Diego.

Like trying to ignore a pink elephant in the room -- the corpse -- she could not keep her eyes from the macabre fascination of staring at the lifeless body. Flinching while she studied the victim, years of crime reading surfaced. The placement of the body seemed as if Carrie had been flung onto the floor. Pooled blood around the head area splatters on the dress, the floor, the papers, and no other visible wounds, spoke of a fatal blow to the back of the skull . . . .

Appalled and sickened at her sudden objectivity over someone she knew being murdered – and seeing the body! – she forced her gaze to the other person in the room. Transfixed, she stared at old woman who was upset, and that irritated her. This was the spy master! Shouldn't the veteran be the calm one, reassuring the novice? Why was the bookstore owner calm and the spy reacting to a dead body?

"What happened?" Her voice sounded shaky and low, but breaking the silence eased nerves that were prickly with reaction to the stunning find. Maybe she wasn't so objective after all, she decided, as her stomach rippled. "What was Carrie doing here?"

"I came home a little while ago. Carrie -- I found her like this. I don't know why she was here."

The distraught emotions struck at Haley's heart. Could Amelia really be a clever killer? Shame started surfacing that she could doubt a friend's sincerity. Amelia was elderly and had sustained an incredible shock. There was no way the older woman could murder a healthy, active younger opponent like Carrie.

Moving over to comfort the woman, in direct denial of her betraying thoughts, she was interrupted by Chase returning and questioning Hunter's statement. She requested her facts be recorded immediately, with the officer countering that anything of such an official nature had to be handled at the police station. When Haley followed along to join the meeting, Chase ordered her to leave. Looking to the elderly woman to counter the command, she was disappointed when the offer to tag along as moral support was refused by both of them. Cliché comments about lawyers and rights flitted through her mind, but Haley read the compassion in the officer's eyes – a trait she was beginning to translate readily in his expressions – and watched them exit the crime scene without debate.

CHAPTER SEVEN

Under other circumstances I would think
that was a great pick up line."

From the garden bench at the rear of the estate, the idyllic picture of paradise -- ocean, beach, sky, palms – spread out to her left. Eden was ignored as Wyndham watched through the window in macabre fascination as the HPD crime team worked through the details of investigating a murder site and body and preparing the corpse for removal.

The process was an observation in detached reality for the avid mystery reader. So often she had lived this scene vicariously in the pages of favorite books, yet now she was plunged into the adventure, a first hand witness of the aftermath of ultimate violence.

Despite her past, Amelia seemed to be taking this murder hard. When carted off to the police station to make a statement, the old girl did not act like a seasoned killer and who-knew-what-else from the old days. The woman looked her frail age, presenting every bit of the innocent-coming-upon-a-murder-victim.

Pacing along the side of the house by the garden with the black Lab trailing behind her, Haley gazed through the wide windows. The crime techs were packing their gear, and she turned away with a shiver that vibrated up from the inside. The scenario she was living through now was a common twist in mystery novels: the murder, the suspicion of who could be responsible for the heinous act, the shifted perception of some unknown element to cast light on the guilty.

How did any of this connect with Haley's bad experiences from yesterday, and possibly Kana's mysterious disappearance? It was too much to think these extreme and unusual events being separate coincidences. What it all meant, who was responsible, what was the big picture – and most importantly where Kana was – had yet to be answered. The mysteries were piling up faster than the solutions.

Bypassing the rooms where the crime lab teams were still working, she ducked in the back door and around some rear hallways. Curiosity caused her to pause at each room and study the rich style and numerous books peppered everywhere. The main entry hall led to a living room decorated with teak antiques, Oriental art, and treasures from around the globe no doubt acquired during Hunter's many travels. The majority of the collectables seemed to favor the Pacific cultures, mostly island themed tiki and nautical regalia. Elegant rooms decorated with tasteful, rich furnishing were appreciated momentarily, then Haley moved on to find the most important place in the house.

The black Lab padded at her heels as she coursed through the big house. At last, the stunning library. Always her favorite room in any home, this held one of the most superlative collections she had ever seen. The furniture was British colonial-era leather and wicker, with an antique roll top desk that was probably a century old. She could imagine Rudyard Kipling sitting there scribbling out his lines for Gunga Din with parchment and ink.

There was a magnificent painting of a sailing ship in the lusty sea above the mantle. On the shelf behind the desk were photos of Amelia with friends in various places around the world; Hawaii,

Hong Kong, an unnamed, exotic tropical beach. There was a picture of Kana and Amelia aboard the ex-spy's boat.

Despite the obvious tropical scents just outside the door, this room pervaded the telltale mustiness of paper, bindings, leather and books. Reminiscent of libraries, it was a combination of odors that could not be bottled or imitated, and could only be accumulated with the original ingredients. For a moment she stood in the center of the room and drew in deep, invigorating breaths, feeling the goofy smile on her face at the pleasure of absorbing such a wealth of true treasure – books. First editions of famous fiction and non-fiction stocked the shelves. The matching-set collections from Twain, Kipling, Hemingway and many other famous authors rested behind glass fronted bookshelves that were probably as old as the original books inside. Strewn, tattered, well-worn leather tomes scattered the tops of several cases and tables, as if Hunter had been interrupted in a read-through of the favorite friends.

Idly scratching the dog on the head as she perused the volumes on the open shelves, she was surprised to find some cheap, new books with paper covers that seemed out of place and outside Amelia's interest level. Those anomalies sported the all-too-familiar gold seal on the binding that denoted it a Super Simon Book Club Edition. Curious, she was tempted to take a look – her hand hovering close to the brightly colored inch-wide picture of an anonymous South Seas scene on the paper spine. She better get Chase's permission before she touched anything, she reconsidered. Memorizing the title; Treasure Hunts of the Pacific -- Volumes One through Four -- she reluctantly left the bibliophile's haven and explored her way out of the house to the kitchen door.

"This estate is amazing." Surprised by Chase's stealthy appearance, she hoped he didn't notice her startled jump. "I take it you've been wandering?"

It lacked the tone of accusation she expected and she gave him a hopeful smile. "The dog needed a walk."

Chuckling, he countered, "Care to show me around?"

"I'd like that. How's Amelia?"

"Fine. She's still at the station." He held up his hands in surrender. "But, I didn't arrest her."

From the kitchen they ambled on a garden path winding through bushes exploding with tropical flowers. To the side of the huge yard were broad-leafed banana trees that gave a natural barrier covering to the lava-block wall separating the property from the neighboring estate. The dog followed along quietly, shadowing their path, completely accepting their company in lieu of her owner.

"Amelia doesn't look well."

"No," he agreed thoughtfully. "Don't worry; I didn't give her the third degree."

Within a few steps they were in the back of the grounds and next to an extended lanai that merged with the lawn. Through the window they could see the crime scene techs leaving the far end of the living room. Instead of returning to the house, Chase led them to a low lava wall overlooking the jagged black rocks along the beach.

He leaned a foot atop the porous blocks. "Did you know Carrie Kahunui well?"

"No, just as a competitor." She tore her eyes away from the calming lapis waves curling to shore and studied him. "I hope that doesn't make me a suspect."

"Do you feel like one?" He almost smiled.

"NO!"

"The ME's assistant put her death within the last few hours and you have an excellent alibi."

"You? I guess that is pretty good."

"About as good as you can get."

"What about Amelia? Will you arrest her?"

"Questioning, I told you," he reminded, irked.

"She's an old friend of Kana's. I think this murder is connected to Kana's disappearance."

"Not enough facts yet." His eyes narrowed. "You've got a suspicious mind. We have no proof that Kana is missing."

"He missed his appointment with me –"

"And he's been known to miss more than that –"

"He's been gone for days –"

"Not unusual because of his obsession for books," he countered with a tone sharper than usual. Taking a breath, he returned to his usual, easy demeanor and asked with a wry tease, "Maybe you can't see it because you're obsessed with books, too?"

Not sure how to handle Chase's irritation with Kana, his gentle humor during a murder investigation, she nodded. "All these weird things going on are not coincidences. Do you think Carrie was the one searching Amelia's study? Or was she here for another reason?"

The disapproving frown seemed to seep all the way to his brown eyes. "We don't have enough facts to know anything. Unlike my popular fictional counterparts, I have seen coincidences. I can't discount them."

"Whatever. At least wish Amelia good luck for me."

"I will. Are you – uh – leaving?"

Did she imagine a hint of – some undertone of disappointment -- in his voice? "I'll be at Kana's cleaning things up." At the kitchen door she stopped to look into his eyes. "What?"

"What do you mean, what?"

"Nothing," she covered quickly.

Afraid now her imagination was forcing her to read too much into relationship subtleties that were probably not there. About Sherlock Holmes, Charlie Chan and Judge Dee, she was an expert. Getting along with the opposite sex - total failure so far in her life. Best that she stayed with what she knew.

"Just watch out, okay?" he warned.

"Sure."

"I'll walk you to the car."

As they strolled, with the Lab trotting behind, she asked the lieutenant about gunshot residue, blood stains and fingerprints – questions he refused to answer. She tried a more subtle approach. Something from the pages of Sherlock Holmes. "What about the dog?" she wondered, genuinely worried for the old woman's faithful companion if Amelia was arrested. Not much of a watchdog, but obviously a loyal friend to the elderly woman.

"I'll see she's all right," the officer assured, scratching the overweight beast behind the ears.

Friend to crime victims and dogs, she smiled as she climbed into the jeep. Lieutenant Chase was a pretty good guy. "Then you are going to arrest Amelia?"

"That's not what I said," he cagily replied. "Have fun at Kana's."

CHAPTER EIGHT

You're a civilian, remember?"

Haley started the clean up first, then the cataloging of books and papers. The task proved to be quicker and easier than expected. With a little help from Mrs. Kahuku, they were able to tidy everything, including the stains on the floor. Review of evidence was in a holding pattern, and it would take time for results from the wine, fingerprints and DNA tested.

What if the wine stain was covering up a bloodstain? It was a flash of suspicious conspiracy stemming from Haley's years of absorbing fictional intrigue. It was possible Kana had been hurt in some kind of struggle. If so, the lieutenant would tell her. Not wanting to be ridiculed, she decided she would let Chase bring that up first. It sounded wild even to her over-active imagination.

Chase was reluctant – even stubborn -- to list Kana as a missing person. Why? Paperwork? If this became official, would he be taken off the case because he was a friend of Kana's? By tomorrow, if Kana hadn't shown up and Chase still dragged his feet about the disappearance, she would do something. Not sure what that would be, she knew it would be time to act instead of waiting around for the officials to solve the disappearance. Even if Chase was a cute and nice cop.

Why was Kana's property ransacked? Someone was looking for something. They had not found it, she concluded with a chill. After failure at Kana's downstairs shop the intruder searched the apartment. How had the burglar gained entrance? She forgot to ask Chase if the electronic lock had been damaged. And which came first, the crimes in Hawaii or San Diego? She guessed the first place had been Kana's on Monday. When the perpetrator did not find what he wanted he thought she might have it in California. Had the criminal then followed her here? That was some long distance traveler. What a lot of trouble! Was he hoping she would lead him to Kana? Maybe she should be a little more careful; she shivered, freaking out at being back here without Chase, without police protection, not just Chase. But Chase was nice . . . .

Solve the crime and you will find Kana. How did the criminal break-into all these places that were secured by Sam Simon's ultra sophisticated Cabrillo Security? Had Chase checked into that? A scary thought shot into her mind -- did the assailant get the code from Kana? Was her friend being held captive by some insane criminal? That was absurd. Why? What could Kana possibly have to inspire such violence? What did she have that included her as a fellow victim? What was the fiend looking for at Amelia's that led to murdering Carrie? That all this was connected seemed completely clear to her.

Ready to scream at the frustration, she determined to lose herself in her work. Among the familiar, the old books, she felt at home, if not at ease, but the activity helped settle her nerves. Mrs. Kahuku labored away with cleaning and filing, humming tunes and chatting from her various locations. When she drifted into the main shop again, she delivered a glass of water to Haley.

"Keoni, he good, yeah?" Her companion laughed as she gathered her cleaning supplies together.

"Keoni?"

"Keoni. Chase. Policeman. Steady job. Good retirement. Something to think about, yeah? Book selling, not so steady for you and Kana. He's always running off, no steady life. Good thing his mo'opuna kane[1] taking care of the case."

Haley was completely confused. "Who?"

"Mo'opuna kane. Grandson."

"Who's that?"

"Keoni is Kana's daughter's son. Kana's grandson, yeah?"

"Keoni," she softly repeated, stopping her work and staring at the older woman. "Keoni. Chase. Keoni . . ." Hazy, long forgotten memories surfaced in a patchwork of a scattered past. "Keoni. Kana talks about him sometimes. One of his grandsons. He's proud of him." The reference confused her. "What about him?"

Emma looked at her as if she was a lunatic. "Keoni is mo'opuna! Grandson of Kana! Keoni Chase!

"Keoni . . . Keoni Chase?" she squeaked. Kana Hagoth. Keoni Chase. Different last names. Daughter's line . . . . "No," she slowly burned in irritation. Grandson! How could he deceiver her like that! "I – I had no idea – Keoni Chase! He never said anything!"

"Maybe he thought you already knew, yeah? You and Kana friends, he probably thought it old news. Maybe he too shy to ask if you know he's ohana."

Ohana. Family. Grandson. That sneak!

Steamed at the newfound family connection – no – angry that Keoni -- Lieutenant Chase -- had lied – well – had not given full disclosure of his relationship with Kana -- she told Emma she could

---

[1] Grandson

leave. Haley would finish the rest of the clean up on her own. As soon as she kicked something!

Straightening shelves, reorganizing books, she vented her frustration in activity. Kana had children and grandchildren, she had met several of them, and yes, years ago, she had met Keoni – as a teen!

Pausing in her work to go to the living room and check out the pictures on the end table near the sofa, she examined them carefully, amazed to find Keoni in two of the family candid shots. Both were set at the beach, at some kind of ohana luau. He was younger in these photos, more carefree. The innocent face of a man before he stooped to deceive a fellow victim of Kana's!

Stalking back to the library, she gathered up a stack of old books on Hawaiian history and mythology, scanning the shelves, trying to find where they should be placed. Familiar with her mentor's mystery collection, she had never really paid much attention to the non-fiction books. The past of the islands were of interest to her, but only fleetingly, never as compelling as the reality of the sand and surf of the present. Her passion had always been who-done-it-fiction, not reality.

Shoving the oversized volumes into a shelf she thought was tall enough, the biggest, heaviest tome smashed into the top wood and flew out of her hands, crashing to the floor. When she bent to retrieve it, she was horrified the binding had broken and the pages had fallen apart. Gasping, grieving for damaging an obviously valuable possession, she tried to put it back together. To her amazement, it was not an injury that separated the book! it was two books! One volume was large and wrapped in an old paper cover! The other book inside was only two-thirds the size and thinner.

112

Taking the two manuscripts apart, she was stunned to find the hidden book was a series of loosely bound, old, faded pages tied together with leather strips, sandwiched between two slender leather covers. On the front of the cover was a tooled design of twin dolphins. Bringing her necklace up to stare at the pattern, she was astounded that the arching cetaceans were an amazingly similar design. Strange. Slowly placing the jewelry against her shirt she focused on the book. Familiar with ancient editions of rare works, she had never seen anything quite like this before.

Wary of her knee injuries and numerous bruises and scrapes, she sat on the floor, carefully turning the fragile pages. This was delicate; Nineteenth Century parchment with faded ink lettering. What was this? It seemed a chronicle with words, numbers, dates, ink splotches and archaic phraseology. There were some thin, sketched drawings of a ship, a wharf, and men loading cargo. Many of the pages were torn, some tattered, some falling out, some pieces missing. The lettering in spots was so faint she could hardly read it, but the readable messages clearly recorded the adventures of a sailing ship plying the South Seas over a hundred years before.

Eyes aching from the difficulty of reading the text, she studied the drawings. They nicely detailed various ports of call in the Pacific, with plentiful representations of Polynesians, palm lined shores, and sea life. It was an amazing collection that any historian or naturalist would love to see, touch, or own. These were outstanding finds! No wonder Kana kept them cleverly concealed behind fake covers. Why didn't he keep them in locked shelves like his first editions? She looked at the cleaned up room and scoffed. A lot of good the glass locked cases did with this criminal. With a last look at the seascapes, she wondered why they seemed familiar, but couldn't take the time right now to study them at length. Instead, she dove into the written account, reading what she could from the damaged and ancient text.

SHIP'S LOG
The Pacific Star
Under the command of Captain Patrick Ryan

Setting sail from Hong Kong in the year of our Lord Eighteen Hundred and Ninety-One. Under special commission from her Majesty Queen Lilioukalani. Bound for home port with Hawaiian Emissary, Iosepa Kalakaua Hagoth

Hagoth! The family name of Kana! She thumbed through what she could read, frustrated that the passages were mostly about the weather, the various passengers, the cargo. There had to be some clue to what this Hagoth had been doing under a special mission for the queen of Hawaii. Lilioukalani. Wasn't she the only and last queen of these islands? A controversy about the monarchy tickled at the back of her memory, but she couldn't grasp the details. She didn't remember too much of her Pacific history, but she knew somewhere around the turn of the Nineteenth to the Twentieth Century, the queen of these islands had been deposed in a coup led by Americans. Sugar barons came to mind, but she couldn't be sure. Gingerly turning a few more frail pages she scanned another paragraph.

Hagoth has turned over to me a document with the queen's own seal imbedded in the wax. At noon today I am instructed to open the secret packet and learn of Her Majesty's wishes. This is not the first

114

confidential commission she has entrusted me with, nor the first time I have collaborated with her Kahuna[2] Hagoth. The holy man and the queen have something cooked up, I'm thinking, and are hoping to include me in on the bargain. As long as the payment is as generous as before, Her Majesty's gold is as easy to spend as anyone else's on these fair seas.

Secret commission! Kahuna Hagoth – kahuna was a Hawaiian holy man – and Hagoth – some distant relation to Kana! What kind of covert and possibly illegal business had gone on over a century ago? And why was it so important to be hidden away in a book within a book?

The sound of the front door opening made her jump and she hastily shoved the log inside the incongruous, large outer binding titled Hawaii Flora and Fauna. She slid that onto a bottom shelf just before she spun around to see Lieutenant Chase give her a slight wave.

"Hi."

She stepped aside with feigned innocence. "More questions?"

"Yes – uh – no – just one." Leery, he walked in, but stayed close to the open door. "Actually, I was hoping I could talk to you. In a less official capacity. Like over dinner?"

"All right," she acquiesced with a scowl. "Mo'opuna kane."

***

"Okay, I haven't been completely honest with you."

---

[2] Religious Leader, Holy Man

"Tell me something new," she snapped back.

"What is that supposed to mean?"

"Guys find it hard being truthful is what it means."

"I did not lie. I neglected to disclose everything about my relationship with tutukane." His frustrated scoff seemed loud even against the hubbub of Waikiki at night with the top down. "I'm a cop," he responded. "I tell the truth."

"When it suits you."

"I withheld complete information until an appropriate time!"

She stared at his reflection through the windshield. Time to chance tack a little to keep him guessing and on the defensive. He deserved it. "Tutukane?"

"Grandfather."

"Hmmm," she responded in a noncommittal huff.

"Kana Hagoth is not just a bookseller to my mother, okay? He's her father. So that makes him my grandfather. Tutukane."

"He's like a tutukane to me, too." The explanation was too little too late. She wasn't really mad at him – yeah, maybe she was -- but not volcanic. She was more disappointed that he had deceived her. Or perhaps the disillusionment was more about her discovering he was falling short of expectations just like every other guy she knew. "Why didn't you say something?"

"I meant to tell you."

"Sure," she agreed acidly as she simmered.

Gazing at the evening's busy pedestrian traffic on Kuhio as they drove, her temper cooled. Hot dance joints with bright neon lights flashed by in dizzying counterpoint to the swaying palms and the sultry twilight. The islands were blessed, or cursed, with offerings for every age and lifestyle. Honolulu had a night life that was as sizzling as the tropic rays baking the beach by day. It was a dizzying contrast to the laid-back sun-worshipers crowding the sand under the sun.

In truth she wanted to be mad at Chase, but his sincere contrition and her personality quirk that made it alien for her to hold a grudge dissipated her irritation. She didn't tell him that, though, and allowed him to explain.

"It never seemed the right time. And, I admit, I had to get the situation down first. You know you and what you were up to – I mean – well – you know what I mean."

"I was a suspect?"

"No! I just had to find out more."

"About what?"

"You. Besides, you didn't tell me you and Carrie had a big fight --"

"Not a big one!"

"Right in Waikiki with all kinds of witnesses!"

"So I am a suspect!"

"Not really, but you didn't tell me!"

Vexed again she crossed her arms and stared at the bright lights of the stores. The night air was cooler than the day's trade wind – marginally. Pedestrians mostly traded swimwear for casual clothes. Restaurants were crowding with the dinner masses and the sidewalks were jammed with tourists wandering to find a suitable eatery.

She would forgive him of course. He was too nice not to, besides, he was Kana's grandson. Chase seemed by nature sincere, but could she trust him? He had not lied exactly, but he had concealed. And what was she doing about the log within the book mystery? Concealing it from him. Everybody had secrets – Kana,

Amelia, Carrie Kahunui, Chase – her. Was it time to cut him a little slack?

Her tone mixed sarcasm and speculation just to keep him guessing for a little longer. "Just when I thought you were different from the usual cop type."

"I hope I am."

"Then why not tell me up front?"

The silence got her attention and she finally looked at him. Staring straight ahead, his expression seemed vulnerable and regretful. "When I heard your name, I didn't know how to approach you."

He had missed her wry angle altogether and was so serious she regretted her flippancy.

"Kana talks about you all the time." He gave her a quick glance, then his eyes were back on the road. "Do you remember we've met?"

"Yeah. A long time ago." It was a pleasant memory, like most of them about the Hawaii of her childhood. Sunny days and beach luaus and lots of fun. From his tone, he did not share in the positive nostalgia. "Is that a problem?"

At the next red light, he stared at her. "No. Not now," he admitted, followed by a grimace. "I always wondered why my tutukane had a haole helping him with the books."

"Haole?"

"Caucasian. He always seemed to have time for you, but not for my family."

He was jealous? Of her? Astounding!

"Then I grew up and just accepted that Kana and you were pupule in the same way about books. Crazy," he translated at her confusion.

Pupule about books. It had bonded her to Kana when she had weak familial ties with her own parents. How mixed up! Chase felt a similar alienation with his grandfather because of her!

"That's why you're not taking this case seriously," she deduced.

"Because of you? No, because of Kana. I told you I don't feel that way anymore about you, but I know my tutukane. He's missed a whole lot of luaus and birthdays and ho'olaulea – parties – because of his pupule books. It's his way. That's why I'm not so worried about him. I still want to find him, though, and make sure he's all right."

It was a lot to process. She had to push aside her surprise and stay on track with priorities. "All right, then prove it."

They parked at the curb of a small sushi restaurant and refrained from arguing until they had selected several scrumptious looking plates from the unique rolling assembly-line of dishes passing along the counter. They took their dinner to a table in the corner and settled in after Chase ordered two sodas from the waitress.

"What if I wanted wine with my sushi?" she wondered with a spark of asperity at his take-command attitude. Not that she would drink alcohol just to spite him, but she was vexed enough to snipe.

"Then I would make you pay for it yourself. Something I share with Kana. No drinking."

Well, she couldn't fault his high moral standards, but chose not to compliment him. He was bringing out all kinds of emotions and revelations and it confused her. She wasn't sure what she felt about all of it so she remained silent. Let him keep talking, maybe more surprises would surface.

"Okay, you wanted me to prove I was nicer than the other cops you know." He almost smiled at the challenge. "Without asking for lurid details of your past encounters, let me ask you this. How can I prove myself?"

"Help me find Kana."

"That's what I'm trying to do."

"Then why not officially list him as missing and get the full resources of your department on the case?"

"How do you know I haven't?"

He was playing her again and she managed to not show her anger when rising to the bait. "Have you?"

"Yes."

"Why didn't you tell me?"

"Because it's not your case." He pushed the rolled sushi around the plate with his chopsticks, dipping it into the shoyu sauce with abrupt jabs. "And maybe I was being a little petty about your attitude."

"My attitude?"

"A civilian, flying in here from California, thinking you know everything and trying to run an investigation."

"I was worried."

"And that's one of the reasons I like you."

That sounded sincere. The conversation could have been a condemnation if not for the glint in his eyes and the twitch of a smile on his lips. She could have taken it as an insult had it not been for the endearing tone that cooled her escalating temper. There was just too much to like about this guy and not enough rancor in her system to fight the charm. He meant well, and this was a chance for him to show if he could also forgive and forget like she could.

120

"Then prove it."

Chuckling, he asked how he could.

"Include me on the case. I want to help."

"I can't do that. Officially."

Her suspicion decreasing, she grinned, "All right, then unofficially, did you get any specifics on the wine? The time of death on Carrie? What did Amelia have to say?"

Laughing, starting to eat now that the tension was diffused, he replied after consuming the California roll in his mouth, "Even if the Coroner's Office worked this fast, I wouldn't let you know. You're a civilian, remember?"

"Who is personally involved in the case? Remember?"

A subdued trill interrupted his next comment. Checking his cell, he blinked at the number I.D. "Excuse me." He growled into the phone. "Palani, this is a bad time, bruddah." A brief burst of conversation from the caller. Chase scowled. "Kamala? Not again!" he snapped loudly. Wincing, glancing at Haley, then the others around them, he ran a hand through his thick, dark hair. "What is wrong with you, man? Don't you have any respect for me or my job?" He drew in a breath. "Okay, don't answer that. But you should at least have some respect for our ohana! This is the last time. I promise you, Palani. Understood?"

Closing the phone, he waved for the waitress to bring the check. "Sorry I have to skip out. I'll drive you back --"

"I can walk --"

"I asked you out and it's my responsibility to see to your safety," came his curt response.

"Chivalrous. You think there's some danger to me?"

His eyes shaded in the familiar expression she was coming to read as deep, inner anxiety. "I don't know. Just to be on the safe side, it wouldn't hurt for you to be seen in the company of a cop, would it?"

Amused, she smirked. "Under other circumstances, I would think that was a great pick up line."

His smile proved again he could be as charming as he was exasperating. "I'd think so, too. Let's finish our meal and then I'll take you back."

"I don't mind being seen with you. Not adverse to the idea," she initiated. "And there's no reason you can't take me along on your police work. So I guess I'm going with you."

"This is not about Kana."

"You said ohana. Isn't that a relation?"

"Family."

"And Kana is your ohana –"

"Not the only one who likes to get into trouble."

Muttering a few not-completely-distinct words that her argumentative nature was probably the reason she didn't get along with previous cops, he denied her request. She badgered him as they finished the yellow tail and ahi until he finally surrendered with an exasperated chuckle.

"Kamala is my sister-in-law."

"Okay. And Palani?"

"My brother."

Paying the bill, he escorted her out to the car, staying a little behind so she could conveniently carry on a conversation. He was gentlemanly enough to open the door to the Mustang for her and she was gracious enough to not dispute the very old-fashioned gesture.

"Well, ohana means you stick together in good or bad and right now my brother and his wife are putting me through some bad," he explained as they navigated the crowded streets of Waikiki toward her hotel. "I've got to pull some strings and get her out of lock up."

"Your sister-in-law is in jail?"

"Again."

After she forced away her smile, she wondered, "So why do you help her if she's breaking the law?"

"Ohana –"

She had her own quirky relations. "Okay, I get it."

After a deep sigh he explained, "She's a member of the Hawaiian Restoration Cause. All too frequently she's arrested for protesting, making trouble. The rest of the family is not happy. I'm angry. My brother supports her radical causes." She must have worn her dubious expression with obvious disdain, because he clarified, "Ohana means obligations." At her puzzlement, he questioned, "Wouldn't you do the same thing?"

Her snort was derisive. "Family and obligations are not usually used in the same sentence with my relations."

"What about Kana?"

"Kana is my literary kahuna," she labeled, slipping into the Hawaiian vernacular.

Her family ties were not issues she wanted to think about in these turbulent times. She steered back to the conversation, happy to think about other family problems than her own.

"So you're close to your brother I guess?"

Chase laughed. "Yeah. We live in the same house. That's one reason it would be hard not to help his wife."

He explained that he still lived in his parent's big house on the windward coast because expenses were too high for him to live alone in Honolulu. For economic reasons, many singles roomed with others, frequently ohana. If married, most Hawaiian couples needed both partners working in the average household.

She had lived in Hawaii during her youth and visited often as an adult. How could she be so unaware of the social and economic climate? Kana never said anything – no – he wouldn't. His role had always been mentor and his world of books. Their visits had been about escaping reality to bury themselves in the fantasy realms of fiction. Their dominion centered on the page, the content, the magic of literary works, hardly ever beyond the covers of their treasures. For the remainder of the drive she listened attentively to the rest of Keoni's story, striving not to put her foot in her mouth again tonight.

"Whenever I get married, my wife will have to work if we expect to rent a house or apartment of our own. Which, of course, I would want. And buying a house is pretty much out of the question these days."

"Yeah, real estate is expensive if you live near the beach."

"I'm sure you have a similar problem in San Diego."

"Yeah, actually, I share a condo with my cousin."

"Ah," he nodded in understanding. "Here, we live on an island. Limited room to expand into suburbs. Hawaii will always have a finite area for living conditions while the population expands."

"I see the problem." He was giving her a lot to think about and her mind wandered into unexpected areas. "So," she casually asked, not sure she wanted to know, or why, "is there a candidate in mind for Mrs. Keoni Chase?"

His smirk was just a bit self-conscious. "Not yet."

They drove around some side streets and finally pulled up to the curb in front of her hotel. Before she exited a figure near the front of a nearby café caught her attention. Sam Simon! They traded eye contact and he stepped forward, reluctant, as if he was sorry they had to acknowledge each other.

"Haley, still here?"

"I could say the same to you. I thought you were going back home yesterday."

"Yes, but I found a few things to keep my interest here, deary." He looked to Chase. "Lieutenant."

Surprised, she looked from Simon to Chase. "You know each other?"

"We met. Officially," Chase informed curtly. "He was a business associate of Carrie Kahunui."

"Right."

"Well, have a fun evening, you two." He squeezed Haley's hand that rested atop the car door. "Amusing to see you're sliding downscale," he whispered as a parting shot.

Pulling out into the traffic lane, Keoni kept glancing back in his rearview mirror. "So, you know him well?"

"We traveled in the same circle for a while. He wasn't my taste."

"Oh. So you dated."

Everybody was too interested in her lack-of-love-life. "Yes. My family and friends consider him the one that got away. That was when they wrote me off as hopeless and I became their official target for matchmaking. They're convinced I have no ability to run my social life."

A sputtered laugh exploded from the driver. "Tell me about it! Over thirty and single. It's like you're considered a flake and the ohana is willing to accept anyone for you!"

They traded knowing looks and both laughed. "Exactly," she finished. "So, is Sam a suspect in Carrie's murder?"

"I'm not saying. This is an official investigation for as long as I can keep it that way, Miss Unofficial Investigator."

"But you talked to him."

"As an associate of Kahunui's. Just like you."

"He's the one who told you I had an argument with Carrie, isn't he?"

"My sources are confidential."

"He exaggerated the scene."

"Duly noted."

About to chide him more, she held back. His actions of letting her stay in the car were in counterpoint to his earlier words. Amused that he did not stay at the curb long enough for her to exit, she wryly wondered, "So you're taking me with you."

Frowning, he kept his eyes on the road. "I didn't want to leave you back there with Simon. He could turn out to be a suspect."

"Great. I can be pretty good moral support for sticky family situations. Lots of experience in that category."

"Well, I feel better knowing where you are and you're not getting into any more trouble," he considered.

Liking the idea of sticking with him, for safety, of course, she agreed.

***

Never stepping foot inside a police station before this, Wyndham had no idea what to expect. The buildings around them were old stucco, wedged between weathered neighborhoods and crisply new mirrored-glass and steel high-rise offices. From the outside the Honolulu Police Department was styled with a modern, yet tropical architecture. Large glass windows fronted the deep, multi-storied facility that was edged with palm trees and flowering bushes. Chase swung the Mustang into the reserved parking lot accessed by a touch pad at the security gate. Haley thought of the security at her business and home, hoping the cops here had better luck with their system.

"Did you ever check with Cabrillo Security about Kana's locks?"

"No tampering," he responded as he angled through the lot to find the first empty space. The area was sparely dotted with cars; the entrance well lit. "Someone had the code or could break it."

They walked the short distance to the building in silence. Haley scanned the area with relaxed curiosity, feeling safe at the heart of law enforcement for the islands. Automatic doors swept aside as the lieutenant and she entered.

Checking in at the foyer desk, receiving a visitor's pass and raised eyebrows from Chase's friend, the duty sergeant, the lieutenant led Haley to the back of the building. Passing through large rooms crowded with desks that were meagerly populated by uniformed and plainclothes officers, Chase was waved at and greeted with friendly chat. By the time they reached the holding cell area, Haley felt accepted in the shadow of the respected and well-liked detective.

A taller, broader, bulkier version of Keoni, with longer hair and scruffier clothes, greeted her escort. Giving his brother a quick hug, the cop introduced him as Palani, the younger brother. Palani gave her an engaging smile and elbowed his brother in the ribs, whispering something in Hawaiian that obviously embarrassed the older sibling.

"Stay here," Keoni requested of her. He showed his ID to an officer inside a cage, and he was admitted into a locked wing.

At the other side of the waiting area was a large Hawaiian man who traded disdainful glances with Chase as the detective left. Palani introduced her to the formidable Islander, Teo Kalapana, who did not shake when she proffered the gesture. Good thing, she considered when she got a good look at his meaty limbs. There were scratches on the backs of his hands and wrists. Yuck. Tall and broad in all directions, a brown and cream colored native wrap adorned his shoulders, adding to his distinctive appearance.

The third man in the room was the opposite of the ominous Teo in demeanor if not in physique. His smile beamed from his bronzed face like the sun breaking through morning clouds over Koko Head. He stepped forward, moving smoothly for a man who weighed in at what had to be well over three hundred pounds. He held out a chunky hand first and enveloped hers in a firm shake.

"Kai Watanabi. Party time for da bail out. We gonna go have some kau kau afta dis. You gonna come along?"

"Uh – thanks. No, I'm just tagging along with Detective Chase."

"Dats cool, sistah. He good people. Comes helps Kamala all da time."

Teo snorted from the other side of the room. "Keoni is only skin-deep Hawaiian. Underneath he pure haole. A betrayer to his people," he spat. With a long, unholy glare at her, the big man turned to slump against the wall.

128

"Don't mind him. He always in a bad mood at the cop shop, yeah." Kai gave a shrug, then drifted back over to the sour-mood guy.

"Kai's cool," Chase's brother offered with a smile. "Teo, that's Kamala's kahuna," Palani explained quietly as they took seats across the room. "He's one tough pineapple."

From under long, wavy hair tinged with gray, the subject's frosty scrutiny made her shiver. She had read that word only this evening in the ship's log. "Kahuna. Holy man. A religious leader, right?"

"Holy man," Palani snickered. "You real malihini[3], huh?" At her questioning look he supplied, "Newcomer."

She could argue the point and tell him she had been here every summer, and more, for years, but decided against making herself look worse. She hadn't even remembered the simplest Hawaiian words. Mahalo – it was on the cover of every trash can in the city. A lot of the uninformed thought it meant 'trash', but she was reminded by Chase that it meant thanks. No point in advertising her ignorance.

"Yeah, total tourist," she admitted to speed along the interrogation. Palani's stare was not as easy to ignore as Keoni Chase's. She felt the little brother – and Teo – studying her. To ease the tension of the intense silence, she asked if he would explain what was happening.

"Teo's the kahuna for Hawaiian Restoration Cause," Palani told her. "HRC we call it. Kalama believes in it like nothin' else. So, how long you been dating my bro? He's said nothing 'bout you."

---

[3] Newcomer

"We just met," she replied, a little uncomfortable with the friendly, but blunt interrogation. Maybe it could play to her advantage. "I'm the one who reported Kana missing."

"Ah, right, the wahine from the mainland, yeah?"

Wahine. She knew that meant girl. "Yeah. Did Kana mention anything to you about leaving town? You would have said something to your brother, I guess."

"Kana leaves all de time. None of us worried, yeah? He gonna show up." The younger man smiled. "You gonna stay here a while? The ohana gonna like you."

Irked at the dismissal of Kana's disappearance, and the overt matchmaking comments, she reminded him in a low voice, "His house was broken into. The place was searched. Maybe there was a struggle. He could be hurt or kidnapped!" More information than she wanted to share while Teo was staring at them, but it might help to get family members involved in this.

"Kana is missing!"

"He show up. He out chasin' books. No worries."

Books! That's all Kana's relatives thought about when she mentioned the revered grandfather, or tutukane, as they called him. No concerns for his safety? No speculation about where he could be or what might have happened to him! And scoffing about his life's work! She couldn't believe anyone could dismiss such treasures like that! Didn't the rest of the family care about their grandfather?

After Keoni's speech of ohana and duty, she was amazed at the ready dismissal of blood relations. She cared more about this disappearance – and all that Kana loved – than his Island ohana. Was her mentor as isolated from his family as she was from hers? She had never considered such a possibility.

130

The metal gate clicked open and a tall, lean, Hawaiian woman emerged, followed closely by Keoni. The woman's chiseled, well-defined face, shrouded by clouds of thick, black hair, made her eye-catchingly beautiful. Wearing a t-shirt splashed with bold, bright colors proclaiming 'Hawaiian Rights!' made her entrance striking. She ran into Palani's arms and they exchanged a passionate kiss and embrace. Chase and Haley traded an embarrassed glance at the extended reunion. When the couple separated, arms still around each other, the woman gave a nod toward Teo, but zeroed in on Haley with an amazingly astute gaze.

"Keoni said he brought a friend of Kana's. Aloha, I'm Kamala."

Attention snagged between the wearer and the attire, Haley kind of flubbed through the introduction. "Hi. Haley Wyndham."

Kamala's smile was bright and unexpectedly cheerful for someone who had just been in jail. "Mahalo for letting Keoni come and spring me," she thanked with a solid handshake.

"I didn't let him," she popped back, quick to sever any connection between the cop and her. "I'm just helping him with the case."

Kamala smiled. "Nice."

Her voice trailed away for moments while she stared at Haley's shirt. Wondering if she had spilled soy sauce on the aloha print, uncomfortable with everyone else staring at her, she looked down, noted nothing unusual with her shirt, and followed Kamala's eyes to the dolphin amulet.

"Where did you get that?" Kamala asked in a hushed voice. She started to reach for it, then pulled back. "I've seen that before."

"Kana gave it to me," she shrugged.

Teo gasped and crossed the room to stand right next to her. Kamala's eyes grew wide. Chase shot her a puzzled glance, clearly confused at the reaction. Uncomfortable at the intimidating, pressing crowd of strangers, Haley stepped closer to Chase. What was the significance of this necklace? A very artistic and creative piece, yes, but not valuable or elegant. It was only a crystal after all, not some priceless gem, merged with nicely carved dolphins.

"What is it?" she asked them, avoiding a direct look at the looming Teo and Kai, focusing on the less intimidating Kamala.

The woman looked back at Haley as if there had never been a weird moment. "Nothing. Just a nice necklace that's all." Smiling, the tall Hawaiian woman looped her arm in Haley's and set out in front of the men. "I'm looking forward to getting to know you, Haley. My brother-in-law has made a good choice."

"Not a choice," she corrected wryly. "We're friends."

"Maybe that's just what he needed." Kamala followed her speculation with a wink.

So much for the typical idea of a criminal, Haley considered as they wound their way back out of the police station. Officers they met in the exit gave various comments or head shakes to the lieutenant, who accepted the reactions with stoic silence, but it was obvious he was embarrassed at the ordeal. Some were meant to convey the sympathy over distasteful ohana obligations, but clearly Chase would rather not be the object of pity.

Kai and Teo had silently followed them out, now the kahuna stopped them with his ample body blocking the hallway. "I see you tomorrow," he told Kamala.

"Sure. Mahalo for staying, Teo, Kai."

With a nod the big man ducked away without looking at Keoni. Kai gave a friendly farewell and followed the kahuna.

The tension between the cop and the kahuna sizzled, but Kalama and Palani seemed unaffected by the wariness. The woman disengaged her hold of Haley and they all walked out the front of the building to visitor parking. Mister and Mrs. Chase walked ahead with the couple discussing the recent rally and how Kamala managed to get arrested this time. Several paces behind, Haley asked Keoni about the HRC.

"A local political group. Hawaiian rights. I consider them radicals. Kamala, unfortunately, believes in their cause."

Overhearing, Kamala explained further as they veered toward their car. She had been at a protest at the Capitol building for most of the day. The movement to give land back to Hawaiians in reparation for the illegal coup of the Nineteenth Century was a strong and passionate cause. Her employers, at a media graphics design center, supported her cause to returning Hawaii to the people. She finished with a comment directed at Haley.

"You don't understand Hawaii unless you know about our past."

Strange to hear about the politics of the coup over a hundred years after it happened – and only a few hours after Haley had been reading about the deposed queen in the ship's log. Interesting. If she believed in kismet she would be really impressed.

When they reached Palani's car, he stepped next to Haley to ask, "So how much you like my big bro?"

Haley coughed, but her protest was ignored.

Kamala quickly joined in. "Good to see Keoni dating someone nice. I like you already, Haley. Kana talks about you all the time. Like you're ohana. Just what Keoni needs."

Keoni sputtered a protest but Haley beat him to the denial. "We're not together – I mean – we were but just having dinner – not on an actual date . . . . Taking about finding Kana --"

The woman drew in a sharp breath and looked to Keoni. "Kana is missing?"

"He missed his appointment with Haley, that's all."

"Yesterday," Haley reminded. "He hasn't been seen in days. And his shop and apartment were burglarized!"

Now deadly serious, Kamala seemed desperate to know what was stolen from Kana. When Haley assured there was nothing taken that she could discover yet, the Hawaiian woman breathed a sigh of relief. Taking Haley's hand, she fingered Haley's dolphin amulet for an instant, then locked onto Haley's eyes with an intensity that made her want to flinch.

"I promise to do everything possible to help you find Kana."

Haley felt an instant connection to the candid and outgoing young woman. Not usually one to immediately fall into friendship, she felt an unusually deep understanding of this stranger who did not seem a stranger.

"Do you know anything about Kana that could help us?" Haley asked, wishing Kana had been more open and giving about his ohana. They were all proving to be very interesting. "Where he was going this week? What was he doing? Who was he meeting?"

Releasing the necklace and taking a step back, Kamala answered, "He didn't mention anything." Kamala shrugged. "We haven't talked in a while. He never approves of my arrests, but he supports the movement."

"He does not," Keoni interrupted. "He understands, but he doesn't agree with civil disobedience."

134

"Okay, he would never get arrested, I know, but he works for it in his own way." She stared at Haley. "Kana is the ohana kahuna. Handed down for generations. He knows more than any of us ever will about Hawaiian blood and tradition. I only married into the line, but these boys are part of it."

"Bloodlines goin' back to Kamehameha don' help get good jobs, yeah?" Palani countered with a bitter snap. "You and Kana dreamers," he dismissed his wife. He shoved Keoni on the arm. "Big bruddah, he right to get good work." He gave a toothy, joking grin. "Even if his friends arrest my woman."

"Come up to the North Shore and visit, yeah?" Kamala told Haley as she squeezed her hand good-bye. "Aloha."

As they walked back to the building Keoni apologized, "Sorry about my pupule ohana. My crazy relations," he translated after a beat.

"No, I like them. Really interesting. It's that big hulky Teo who's weird."

"Yeah, he's pupule. Nuts."

"What's his problem with you? He was saying some nasty things while you went to spring Kamala."

"I'm not in line with his radical cause. He thinks all Hawaiians should rally around the old monarchy system. It's complicated, but basically he's an extremist. We have enough of them in this world without Hawaiians joining in."

"Well Kamala and Palani and Kai are nice. I'd like to meet with them again sometime."

"You would?" He seemed genuinely perplexed. "They don't seem your type."

She stopped in front of the doors and wondered, "And what exactly is my type? If you say Sam Simon, I might hit you."

"That would be assault on a police officer," he shot back, matching her wry tone. "Right in front of the police station that would be very dangerous. My friends are cops, remember?"

"I noticed. I'd risk it. Maybe it will surprise you to know I have the ability to converse with all manner of people with a modicum of intelligence. I don't trap myself inside the walls of my bookstore. Not always, anyway."

"No, but you date people like Sam Simon –"

"Once –"

"Okay, once. That it was only one time shows you do have good taste. But he's your kind, isn't he? Rich, a worldly traveler, smart –"

"I can't figure out if you're giving me a back-handed compliment or insult."

"Never an insult."

His appealing grin mollified any irritation. Although miffed at being classified with a stereotype matching her parent's crowd, she resisted the urge to be insulted and switched the conversational track. "Since we're already here, why don't we go check on those test results from the spill in Kana's apartment?" Not waiting for a response, she sped up to be the first inside.

The Hawaiian caught up with her in a couple of strides. "You can't get this involved in the investigation –"

"Too late, I'm already part of it."

She wondered what kind of a lab set up they had and hoped it was more modern than the headquarters.

Keoni sighed, "Bringing you was a mistake." But he was grinning.

CHAPTER NINE

So do you usually date women you just met
at a crime scene?

Walking back into the HPD reception area brought mild amusement to desk duty officer Sergeant Kamekona. The broad-faced Hawaiian smiled at Wyndham as she received another visitor's pass and logged in again.

"Big night on the town, huh, Keoni? Can't get enough of us so you bring your date here?"

"Right," the lieutenant snapped. He looked about to say something else, and both observers waited, then exchanged a wry look when he did not. "This is the last time you'll be seeing us tonight, Kam."

"Whatever you say, Keoni. Have a fun time during this visit, Miss Wyndham." He winked at her and smiled at Chase, who rolled his eyes.

"Mahalo," she grinned as she followed her escort down the hall to the escalator. "You work with a nice bunch of cops," she told him as they ascended to the second floor. "So far better than your colleagues in San Diego."

"There you go bashing my counterparts again," he tsked in a dry reprimand. "What are you going to say about HPD when you get back home?"

"I guess I won't know that until we're done with this investigation."

"Until I'm done," he corrected absently. "This way." He directed to the right when they reached the top and veered down a long hallway.

Chase's long strides made the walk quick, and she read the wall signs as they passed, noting the laboratories were ahead of them. Entering the section marked Forensics was like stepping into another world. Like everything else at HPD, she expected the scientific department to be a pleasant extension of the tropical styled, modern building that reflected the island heritage. Instead, the high-tech lab was filled with state of the art computers, equipment and office furnishings. Polished surfaces, glass and chrome marked the whole department as completely up to date.

A thin, short, Oriental woman in a white coat stood at a table straight ahead. Turning at their arrival, she gave them a wave with a hand gloved in latex. Removing her safety glasses, she put aside her work.

"Hi, Keoni," she greeted soberly. "Any word on your grandfather?"

"That's what I'm hoping you can tell me, Melia. This is a friend of Kana's. Melia Kwon, Haley Wyndham."

When they firmly shook hands, Haley's immediately favorable impression about Kwon elevated. She had an open, cooperative manner and did not question an interloper. It was amusing that his colleagues were more open than the lieutenant about her lurking at the edges of the investigation.

"Melia's one of our top lab rats," he continued. "We're lucky to have her."

"Second shift pays better," she admitted with a slight smile. "And free babysitting. My husband stays home with my daughter."

138

Her demeanor lightened slightly at the thought of her family, but immediately returned to the present. "You're here for a report."

"Have anything on the wine at Kana's place?"

"It just came through," she responded with a tilt of curiosity in her tone. "The wine is an expensive California merlot. I checked the Five-0 database on where it can be purchased here in Honolulu, but so far it is only the high-end stores that have been tagged. You'll have to get someone to do legwork on that." She moved to another area. "The broken glass was from an expensive cut of crystal that we are narrowing down. And there were shards of another kind of crystal, a watch crystal. We're still working on a make on that. DNA results on the blood sample aren't in yet."

Chase exchanged a glance with Wyndham. "Broken glass and watch. A struggle, maybe."

Kwon added, "And underneath the wine was a very small amount of blood."

Haley felt like her insides just plunged to her feet, and noted Chase flinched in distress. It confirmed to her that Kana was attacked and removed against his will from the apartment.

"Hey, don't read too much into that," Kwon warned them both. "It was minor. Less than what you might get from a cut or a nosebleed. My team is looking over crime scene evidence now to see if we can find anything else. It might tie into the anomaly of the watch crystal."

"How minor? Like someone scraping their wrist on an edge of a table or something? Maybe breaking the watch and getting a scratch?" Keoni pondered. "Or a cut from the broken glass?"

"Either one." Melia Kwon turned to Haley, to include her in the delivery. "Not much to start with, but we've built cases on less, that's the good news. Nothing left at the scene to indicate a serious injury, that's more good news." To the policeman, she concluded, "You're the detective, though, so you would know more about the crime scene conclusions from the evidence we uncover."

Haley liked Kwon more all the time. The specialist was friendly, smart, and intimate with the details of the case. Most of all, the tech was sympathetic and did not offer any censures about what she was doing here. Counting herself fortunate to be on the inside of this investigation, Haley remained quiet and not interfering to the proceedings. Such an unofficial position would allow her to aid Chase, even prod him a little, while helping.

Kwon's dark eyes steadily observed Chase. "Are they going to let you stay on the case?"

"Ruffner knows better than to pull me off."

Shaking her head, she told Haley, "Captain Ruffner is the head of the major crime squad. He can be a mongoose about the rules sometimes. Tenacious."

"His bark is worse than his bite," Keoni assured.

"What's important is that a mongoose never gives up. So don't cross his line, Keoni."

The detective seemed to speed into a change in conversation. "What about the murder victim, Carrie Kahunui?"

"I've gone over the blood found at the scene of the crime. All consistent with the victim. Blow to the head was the COD. Cause of death," she interpreted for Haley."

"Yeah, I got that."

At Melia's raised eyebrows, Keoni clarified. "She owns a mystery bookstore. She's a friend of Kana's and kind of – uh -- tracking the case."

140

"Ahhh." The tech smiled. "Anyway, you know the fatal blow was on the back, right side of the skull, consistent with a left-handed killer with above average strength."

"Not a right hander striking from behind?" Chase asked.

"No, not from the angle of the wound," Kwon clarified. "One heavy blow fractured the skull. There would have been a lot of tissue matter splashed onto the killer and murder weapon. If you find either, we can do more DNA tests. So far we've found only her blood type at the scene."

"Don't worry, I'll find the guy."

"And you have a pretty good record on that," Kwon admitted. She had delivered the information to both, but concluded by zeroing in on the detective. "Are the two cases related?"

"We're not sure. Maybe you can tell us."

"I'll let you know."

"Mahalo, Melia."

"Just doing my job, Keoni. Hope to see you again, Haley."

"I hope so, too. Nice meeting you, Melia."

Out in the hall, Wyndham and Chase met up with several other officers who tried to appear casual, but seemed gathered for an introduction to Keoni's guest. While the lieutenant found it annoying, Haley was amused. HPD appeared a close-knit club and bringing a fresh face into the mix meant a lot of attention. She sympathized all too well knowing the scrutiny family and friends showered on any new friends she brought around the bookstore.

Quick to command the conversation once they were out of the building, Keoni directed that she must be ready to return to her hotel. Not anxious to go back to her room alone, she asked if they could go out for drinks. He reminded he didn't drink. Annoyed she had forgotten that tidbit, he smoothly transitioned for her. Most of the dancing and nightclubs would be overcrowded at this hour, so he suggested they make it a dessert stop close to her hotel.

Readily, she agreed, still wary of being on her own, but not ready to admit that concern, nor admit the opposite. She felt safe in his company and liked being around someone so nice and comfortable. She also saw it as a good chance to continue picking his brain about Kana's disappearance.

Parking the Mustang in the hotel garage, he walked her to a beachside café. Sheepishly admitting he did not feel they had time to have much of a dinner with their interrupted sushi meal, he admitted he was hungry and asked if she wanted a decent meal, then dessert. Surprised her stomach was growling at the mention of food, she hoped Chase had not heard the noise.

***

Over mahi-mahi, teriyaki chicken, rice and Hawaiian macaroni salad, she teased Chase about his side order of spam musubi, all washed down with soda. The Waikiki restaurant encouraged casual camaraderie with its laid-back aloha atmosphere and surf-flavored themes. The tables and chairs were constructed with thick bamboo, accessories of surfboards and beach regalia matched everything from the condiment trays to the decorated, exposed beams. While the food ranged in the middle to high-end prices, the fare was upper-grade American-tropical with plenty of meats and sandwiches touched up with pineapple and teriyaki twists. Not far from her hotel, it seemed the perfect place for strangers who were thrown together in a mysterious adventure to get to know each other better. Not that it

142

was a date – this was far from it! This was a merging of practicality - eating and talking for two people trying to move forward in the same direction.

"So tell me why spam is on every menu."

"Long story. All the times you've visited and you never asked Kana?"

It was a valid question, one that she didn't really know how to answer. "Hmm. I guess I was never very curious about these things when I visited him. It was always about books. Being with you, well, you say or do things that make me think or make me want to learn more. Like ordering spam."

His face brightened. "I've never thought about myself as a teacher. Maybe I should lecture you on more of my Island heritage," he joked, leading the conversation wildly off topic with the history of surfing.

The obscure, but entertaining angle on the past reminded her of the ship's log she had discovered at Kana's. Gently, she steered the discussion to more background on the history of the islands. She asked for details about the deposed queen and how that involved Kamala Chase.

It was fascinating to hear Kamala's cause was deeply rooted in the foundation of the past. For hundreds of years, Hawaiians had lived their own caste and monarchy system. The death of Kamehameha, the first king to unite the islands, coincided with Captain Cook's arrival to the archipelago. The advent of Western explorers, whalers, merchants and missionaries marked a time of change for this Pacific society. Many of the old gods, represented in statues and forces of nature, were swept away. Western values were adopted. Then in the late Twentieth Century, a cultural renaissance swept the globe, Hawaii included. The native language returned to schools, dance, song and fashion. The old ways warred side-by-side with the tourist trade and the military, the two major economical incomes for the islands. Hawaii today was a mixture of cultures and desires swirling in an emotional symbolism of the melting pot society it had become in the modern age.

"This is Kamala's purpose, bringing back the old ways?"

Irritated, he admitted that was the surface slogan of Kamala's movement. "Teo is the driving force behind it if you ask me. They want to give Hawaii back to Hawaiians. So what do we do if we drive out the tourists and the military and the US government? Not a good thing. Not everyone who is part Hawaiian wants to go back to native ways or even native cultures. How would we support ourselves? The economy is complex here. Poverty conditions and unemployment are high. State and Federal welfare is commonly used. We are an entitlement heavy society. Politics is about more than just restitution of sovereign land. Don't get me started."

At least he was not bitter. His matter-of-fact comments were sincere and gave her something to think about besides Kana. Not wanting to bring up old gripes that would spoil the pleasant evening, she veered back to socializing. Hanging out with Keoni was turning out to be both educational and fun.

"I think you are evading my question, officer. The truth, now. What is the attraction to spam?" Haley wrinkled her nose as she watched him down a huge bite of the rice/seaweed/spam roll.

Wisely, he caught onto what she was doing and switched to join her on a casual tack. "You think it's more than the salty, greasy taste?"

"Yuck, it has to be!"

144

"Okay. Part of a Hawaii from the old days during the war."

"Tradition."

"Yeah. The grandparents learned to eat it during the war, passed it on to the kids, now we all love it."

"Ohana," she summed up in quiet reflection. A concept of family and more that she was barely starting to glimpse through her new friend. Although she condemned Chase at first for his cavalier attitude about Kana's disappearance, she was learning he had deep feelings of attachment to her mentor, to his very different brother and wayward sister-in-law. Commitments she appreciated and respected and hoped to understand more fully. "I think I'm getting it."

His smile was warm. "If you think you understand ohana, then you're starting to understand Hawaii. That's the center of everything. Love, tradition and aloha. Kind of all mixed together, that's ohana." At her nodded acceptance, he finished. "You feel that for Kana."

"Yeah." She stared out the window lined with raffia and little wooden surfboards. Beyond the sidewalk, over the top of the buildings across the street, she could see the murky expanse of the ocean rimmed by lights from the marina. "I'm worried about him." She stared into Chase's dark eyes, hoping to read his true reaction when she asked. "Maybe he doesn't want to be found. You don't think he's hiding out, do you?"

"Why would he do that?"

"Someone is after him."

"Then why not come to me? I'm the cop in the family."

"I don't know," she pondered, frustrated at their lack of success, confused at what could have happened to Kana. She hated to hurt his feelings, but wanted to explore one of the enigmas connected with her mentor and his relations. "Do you get along with him? You and your ohana seem to think he's eccentric."

"That's a good thing," Chase countered quickly. "If you can't tell from my brother and his wife, and my tutukane, this family encourages individuality."

"That's a good thing," she threw in with enthusiasm. She had never been afraid to strike out on her own path. It was almost a matter of survival to get through her childhood with parents who were not anything like her. "You didn't answer me, though. You don't get along with Kana, do you?"

"He's my grandfather, of course I love him." His sheepish expression quickly melded into chagrin. "Okay, enough of the interrogation. I don't follow Kana's ideas about the old Hawaiian ways. I favor reason and the modern life. That's why I'm a cop."

"Who drives a hot Mustang convertible?"

"Yeah."

This new side of Kana and Hawaii intrigued her. "What do you mean about Kana's beliefs?"

"I know the history and the language and it's part of who I am, but I live in the now. Kana can't see that. Maybe that's why he's so comfortable with old books."

It reminded her of the famous discussion between Sherlock Holmes and Watson when the Master Detective admitted he didn't know anything about the planets or the universe. He knew about the science, but didn't care about details because it did not concern his career or help solve crimes.

"Kamala thinks Kana believes in her cause, but you disagreed. I've never heard him say anything political. Maybe it's just Kamala's wishful thinking."

146

Chase's frown was quickly born and gone. He leaned forward with intensity. "Kana does not break the law. He is a kahuna, though, and has deep spiritual roots in the history of Hawaii. Obviously, that never spread to his obsession with books, which is the side of him that you are familiar with. We all have angles, Haley, and yours with Kana is books. He shares that with you. History of the islands he shares with Kamala." Studying her in silence for a moment, he revealed, "I think you and I have some things in common."

"How is that?" It was not an obvious connection for her to grasp.

"You've visited a lot and you know nothing about Kana's roots. You only know about his work with books. So how much do you live? And how much is your life limited?"

"Is that a confession?" she asked without answering the question.

"I think so. I know all about my tutukane's heritage and don't involve myself with it. So you and I have both closed out something maybe we should learn more about."

Hmm. Live life outside her books -- something Amy lectured constantly. She lived in the near perfect San Diego; often visited here in paradise. How much did she appreciate either location? And Keoni -- he lived in paradise and he didn't want to be part of it! Maybe they were more alike than she appreciated.

"Okay. Point taken."

"Yours, too." With his signature wry smile, he offered another observation. "Families don't always have to be the same. Makes it more interesting when they aren't."

"True." She wondered how much he knew about his family past. Thinking about the logbook with Kana's far-back relative on the ship, she asked, "So tell me about Kana's past. Kamala makes it sounds like you come from a very important background. Kahunas and chiefs?"

With a deep sigh he replied, "Kamala believes so. I think that is why Teo is using her. The Hagoth family was known for being staunch loyalists in the last few centuries. Close supporters of the royal family."

"Really. Sounds like there are some great stories there." At his shrug of dismissal she encouraged by reminding, "Come on, I love a good tale."

To her delight, Chase started with the Hagoth family Hawaiian history during the time period of the ship's log, the late Nineteenth Century. He recounted the tragic overthrow of the queen of Hawaii and her imprisonment in her own palace. Bringing back the old ways and giving restitution to Hawaiians was the core of Kamala's radical cause. Kana agreed in spirit with the idea, but did not support Kamala's radical politics, nor did he like Teo.

"Why do you object to the guy?" Her tone was neutral, concealing her own repulsion at the ominous kahuna.

"I dislike him because he claims to be a holy man but advocates aggressive law breaking. A bad habit he's influenced Kamala to adopt. Which causes me a lot of headaches."

Thinking about the logbook she asked, "What about the queen?" she wondered. "Kana mentioned her sometimes," she hedged.

"A sad time in our history."

"Kana agreed, but he never gave more than an odd comment once in a while," Haley admitted, memories surfacing now that she

148

had not thought of for many years. "Yeah, sometimes he would tell me a few legends, about Pele and Maui and some god of war."

"Ku," he supplied. "Every culture has a god of war I think, but Ku is a mighty legend here in the islands."

She nodded, youthful emotions recollected in the speaking aloud of the exotic and mysterious names. Then came some sobering memories. "Kana hasn't shared so much about the legends in the last few years."

"No, he hasn't," Keoni admitted curiously. "He's stopped that kind of longing for the old ways. I wonder why," he mused almost to himself. Taking a bite of the huge musubi -- rice, and slices of spam wrapped in seaweed-- the whole giant wad fell apart in his chopsticks and both of them laughed, the serious mood broken. "Maybe we stopped listening."

"Maybe because we were always bad students," she pondered. "And Kamala isn't."

His thoughtful agreement brought the interchange to a pause. To lighten the mood, she grinned and pointed at the pieces of meat he had dropped on his colorful aloha shirt. "Next time we're at such a nice beachside place with a great view like this, maybe you can order something you're not going to wear."

"Spam is great!" His smile faltered slightly. "That means they'll be a next time."

Sensing the mood was altered, and liking the feel of a friendly, non-adversarial tête-à-tête, she teased. "So do you usually date women you met at a crime scene?" Did she really ask that? What was she thinking?

The joke was taken a bit more seriously than she intended, but his eyes sparkled when he glibly returned. "No, you're my first." He winked. "And so far I have to admit it's not bad."

***

Sitting cross-legged on her bed, Haley surfed the Internet when she returned to the hotel. Staying up way too late, she discovered amazing facts about Hawaii's history, plus some cool myths. In the historic accounts of the fall of the kingdom, Queen Lilioukalani was archived with great detail. Haley felt a deep sympathy for the deposed monarch who was imprisoned in her own palace following the coup. No mention of a Hagoth surfaced, but several rebellious, even violent, protests were documented following the queen's arrest. Local emotions ran hot about the fall of the monarchy.

Linked to the history blogs were several websites devoted to HRC. Pictures, statements, impassioned goals and boldly colored tropical graphics made her ponder about Kamala. The activist group made it clear they were serious about their commitment to free Hawaii from a government they blamed for the overthrow of their native land. Kamala Chase and Teo were prominently featured in bios and articles. Even on the two-dimensional computer screen, the bulky Hawaiian she met at HPD gave her the creeps.

Not wanting to fall asleep with that foreboding image in her mind, she switched to a search of the traits, myths and habits of dolphins as she fingered her necklace. She dozed off with the laptop propped on her knees, dreaming about sleek silver dolphins leaping circles around a white Mustang, while mysterious shadows edged around them in a dark sea.

CHAPTER TEN

Arranging all these crimes to make
yourself look busy?"

Hope more than logic drove her to dial Kana's number after she awoke. No answer. Not surprised, it dulled the optimism of the fresh new day. Where was he? If only she could channel Sherlock and come up with some brilliant deductions!

Next Haley called Amelia, but there was no answer at her house, either. The old girl did not have a cell phone or the internet – living in the dinosaur ages like Kana -- so Haley would have to check on her at home later in the morning. After the grueling ordeal of finding a body in her home, then being grilled by the police, the elderly woman deserved to sleep in late, but Haley was anxious to discuss Kana's disappearance. If anyone could help her find her mentor, it would be the ex-spy. Haley was also worried about Amelia and wanted to see if the older lady was all right.

To allay her disquiet, she started the morning with a beach walk. Her attitude perceptibly brightened with the stunning beauty of the day. Baking sun on her skin reminded her she needed to find a new hat, but the warmth and brightness felt good, connecting her with the morning sprays of surf and the crisp cleanness of the ocean air.

Her night had not been restful. The Internet search distracted dark memories of danger until she came to Teo's ominous countenance. Falling asleep with her computer had been temporary, and once settled in bed every little sound startling her into numerous spikes of fear. A chair, then the writing table, had been placed in front of the glass door, and her luggage placed in a pyramid at the front door in response to her paranoia.

The walk, followed by the solid breakfast she was about to indulge in, and her innate optimism served to elevate her mood. She didn't want to admit it, but had to vaguely acknowledge, her pleasant evening with Keoni put her in a good mood.

She called California as she reached the café. Skye and Garvin were both at Reads Like Murder, and reported no more break-ins or problems. That was a relief.

Munching on her Hawaiian bread pudding, she stared out at the sparkling, azure waves of Waikiki. Watching the surfers, locals and tourists cavorting in the sea and sun, feeling the rays comfortingly toasting her skin was a pleasant difference from the typical foggy mornings in San Diego. On a wondrous day like this, it was hard to believe the violence and death were surrounding her world. When she stepped away from this idyllic spot, though, reality would be back in her face, demanding she unravel the puzzle of mayhem conspiring against her.

Last night Amelia should have been released from questioning. Should Haley call Chase and confirm that? Maybe she should go visit the older woman today. A return to Kana's place was definitely on the list. Then she needed to call home and find out more about the mysterious book that had arrived at the shop.

Strolling back to her hotel, she diverted through a few shops to search for the elusive ball cap still on her shopping quest. At International Marketplace, she found a store selling goods from toothpaste, to magazines, to Aloha shirts. Not considering herself a tourist, she was surprised to find several relevant items. Stocking her bag with a couple of carved, wooden tiki gods, a cheap, thin paperback offering an overview on Hawaiian history, and more suntan lotion, she returned to Kuhio Avenue.

Warily checking Kana's apartment as she left the door open behind her, she saw she was alone and breathed a sigh of relief. Giving a wave to Mrs. Kahuku, she ducked in, locked the door and went immediately to the secret book hidden away inside the large coffee table volume. Settling down on the sofa she started reading the Ship's Log, and more about the mysterious vessel, The Pacific Star.

Perusing the journal the first time was difficult and quickly led to eyestrain and a headache. There were typical comments about nautical positions, squalls, warm weather, whale sightings, dolphin pods, and storms. The passengers were listed, most merchants, or families, with only Hagoth named as the official representative of the Crown. When she spotted Iosepa Hagoth's name jotted in the faded ink, she stopped to read it carefully.

T-e H--aiian --ph Ha—th reminded me this morn--g of t—Q--en's ord-rs. We—re to sa— No-th-Nor—wes- an- aw—t furth—ord—s.

Haley grabbed a pencil and paper and started translating the difficult-to-read handwriting. After transcribing the paragraphs talking about Hagoth, she put away the secret journal and studied the strange message. Certain these mysterious passages about the Hagoth ancestor were the reason the log was kept hidden, she wondered why it was so important to Kana. Excelling at word puzzles, it didn't take Haley long to figure out the cryptic sentences.

The Hawaiian Iosepa Hagoth reminded me this morning of the
Queen's orders. We are to sail North-Northwest and find pu'uhonua.
That is all the old man will tell me. There are squalls in the distance
at that setting, but for now I will follow the wishes of the grand lady
who has hired myself and my ship. I must make a living, and carry
on the odd request for that purpose, but am glad to fulfill the wishes
of an honorable lady who has been mistreated.

What did pu'uhonua mean? What mysterious mission was a
deposed queen secretly sending this Hagoth ancestor and a whole
ship to accomplish? Appreciating mysteries most of her life, this was
an intriguing real historical intrigue involving Kana's distant family.
What did it all mean?

There was no computer so obviously no Internet availability
here so she could not find an on line Hawaiian dictionary. Stretching
sore muscles she replaced the book in it's hidden location and
pocketed the note; then she stopped cold.

Retrieving the log again she stared at it, running her hands over
the tattered leather as if a tactile osmosis would bring clarity of
thought or a needed revelation. Leather. Old, musty leather and a
worn binding – Kana's find in Maui! Last year when they were
scouring the ancient second-hand store! This was what he had been
so excited to find! Not sure what to make of that suddenly surfaced
memory; she carefully replaced the log in the clever hiding spot.
Smiling at the Poe-like cunning of Kana's ploy to hide a book in plain
sight with – and within – books, she stepped back to make sure the
line of volumes were as normal-looking as before she started her
search.

154

Scanning the shelves she looked for a Hawaiian dictionary and was not surprised to come up empty – hardly a tome to be found in a native's store.

Taking a break, she paced to the kitchen to work out her stiff limbs and rummage through the refrigerator. She cried out in startled surprise when she heard the back door knob jiggle. Gulping down the fear that rose tight enough to nearly strangle her air she dropped behind the cabinets under the kitchen window. Hoping not to be seen she wondered if the unknown intruder outside could hear if she called for help on her cell phone. How fast could Keoni get here? Grabbing the small unit in her hand she edged toward the corner by the sink as the knob was jiggled again, followed by shaking and hitting on the metal security door. Patrol units responded pretty quickly here in Waikiki. Fast enough to stop someone who was trying to break-in here? What if the intruder heard her calling for help? Would it send them away in a panic, or enrage them enough to break-in and attack her? Still feeling the aches of her bike accident and the tumble down the stairs, she cringed at the thought of any more abuse.

The metal door echoed from a resounding kick so hard it seemed to shake the wall. Angry at being literally cornered, berated herself for such wimpiness. What would Watson do in this instance? Sherlock was brave and brilliant. Watson was the every-man she related to more easily. In the Hound, he had shown his usual pluck in the face of danger. Could she do less?

Noiselessly she reached into the nearest drawer, pulled out a long spatula, snorted in disgust, and then gained enough courage to sit up and peer at selection of utensils. There had to be something more menacing in here than a spatula! Grabbing a long meat fork, she took several deep breaths for luck and courage. The best defense was a

155

good offense. Ulysses S. Grant, Duke of Wellington or Shakespeare? Right now she couldn't think straight enough to remember who was buried in Napoleon's Tomb let alone who gave the quote! All she knew was that she was going to melt from her own dread if she didn't act to get rid of the threat out there.

One more breath and she leaped up, wielding the meat fork like a dagger and waved it toward the kitchen window accompanied by a screeching yell! She didn't know who was more surprised – Teo the kahuna -- or her. The huge activist jumped back, so startled he was momentarily frozen. The shock turned quickly to irritation, then swiftly morphed into anger. With a brawny fist, he slammed the security door so hard it bent. Snarling something in Hawaiian, that fortunately she could not understand, he stalked away.

Shaky with relief she slid down against the cupboards to collapse on the floor. What was she, an idiot? What made her think she could scare away a vicious criminal with a fork? Holding her head in her hand she got her breathing under control enough to where she didn't sound like she had just run a marathon -- uphill. Still trembling, but feeling she could speak, she punched Keoni's speed dial.

The unwelcome message that he was out of range did not conclude before she hung up. Should she call nine-one-one? And look like a complete coward to Officer Dean or whoever would respond to the emergency – which was no longer an emergency? Who was she to accuse a local, if infamous, celebrity, of what – warping a security door? Get a grip!

Cautiously standing, she checked the view out all the windows – and the locks on any possible entry or exit – then sat down at the table. Not more than an instant later she was on her feet again. Too wound up to relax, or think, she walked. Nerves still too jangled to allow her to think, she tried Keoni again, noting she was thinking of him on a first name basis.

She had to get out of here! If she wouldn't call the police, it was madness to stay. Collecting all her gear she carefully checked all around before she emerged from the building, rapidly closed the door behind her, secured the locks and ran to the sidewalk. There were plenty of people ambling along Kuhio, but she still scanned every doorway, alley and possible lurking spot for the menacing Teo.

Checking Mrs. Kahuku's shop, she was not happy to see it was closed for the day. So the florist would not be a witness to the assault. No, if someone as plucky as Emma would have seen Teo skulking around she would have called the police. So it was only her word against a Robin Hood type character. She knew at least one local who would believe her.

Scurrying down the street she whipped out her phone again and tried Keoni's number. Again, no response. Where was he? Checking the time she excitedly realized her cousins would not only be up, but would be at the store by now. Connecting on her cell phone, she smiled when the laid-back voice of Skye answered.

"Reads Like Murder. How can I help your plotting today?"

"Hey, Skye, Haley."

"Oh, Haley, how's things going? Find Kana yet?"

"Not yet. Listen, I need you or Gar to read that journal and tell me what it says."

"Gar was doing that last night. I don't have time. Did I tell you that wacko prof of my Lit class decided to give us a unit test tomorrow? Like I don't have enough to do."

"I'm sure you'll do great. Let me talk to Gar, please."

"Yeah, hang on."

California, college, the minor blips of rough currents revolving around her daily life back there seemed light years away from the drama here. Viewed from this new and disturbing perspective, the simplicity sounded so mundane. She also realized that the shop was getting along just fine without her, as were her friends and family. Instead of making her feel left out or diminished, it offered a sense of freedom. For years, that life in San Diego had consumed her and kept her focused in a finite little universe. Maybe that was why she always escaped to Hawaii, to distance herself from the pressure. She loved her bookstore, loved her life, but from this new perspective acknowledged that there was something missing, too. Perhaps the sudden intimacy of life and death was pushing her to wax philosophical, but amid this danger and exotic intrigue, and desperate worry for Kana, she found a vibrancy of highs and lows she had never felt before.

"Hey, cuz, whatsup?"

She was on the middle of the sidewalk in busy Waikiki. She feared Teo jumping out of an alley and attacking her. Safety was in public, but it lacked privacy and confidentiality she needed to discuss things with her cousin. She ducked into a clothing shop and scurried to the corner with matching men's and women's aloha wear.

"Gar, go in the back room and close the door, I don't want anyone to hear you talking."

"Right. You want me to get my secret decoder ring? Shall I set my communicator to Channel D and sit under the cone of silence, too?"

"Not funny."

"Hey, you're getting all double-oh-seven on us. Chill."

"Somebody is serious about finding something and did it ever occur to you it could be a book? A book that I have or that Kana had? Maybe the bad guys thought Carrie had it, or she wanted it. Maybe we have it!"

As she spoke them aloud the accusations made her sound nuts! Gar cracked another joke about her turning spy on them, but she ignored the jibe. Why hadn't she told Chase about the book delivery? Full disclosure was a good idea from her, even if he refused on his end.

"What does it say, Gar?"

"You want me to read the whole thing to you? Good thing we're on the family plan, cuz, but I'm gonna meet Doug in two hours —"

She could tell from the tone he was goading her in his own irritating way. "Okay, give me the highlights."

"It's hard to read. The writing is longhand and faded and —"

"Gar!"

"Okay. It's about a trip that this ship makes in the Nineteenth Century. It's heading for California and diverts to Kauai. There's some royal jewels aboard or something. They drop some people off at Kauai and then head east. Then the journal stops."

"Does it give coordinates?"

"Yeah, but I can't read them. Too faded"

"Okay, how about names of people?"

"Yeah. Maybe. Listen, I can't read them let alone speak them. I'll text it to you."

"Good. Now remember to keep it in a safe place and don't tell anyone you have it. No one but you and Skye should know, got that? This is for your own safety."

"Right, Napoleon Solo. Does that make me Illya? We get a secret password, too?"

"Not yet."

"Oh, there's some sketches, too."

"What of?"

"An island. You want me to scan those and email 'em?"

"Uh, yeah. I'll find a fax place you can send them to 'cause I want them in hard copies. Kana is not technologically wired."

"Gottcha. I'll copy them and send them out whenever you give the word. The secret codeword, of course."

"Right. Take care. And, oh, Gar, where are you keeping the journal? Is it safe?"

"Safest place I know of."

"Good. Thanks."

She dashed half a block down to a drug store that offered copy services and faxing. Calling Gar again, she gave him the number and in a matter of minutes, she was praising modern technology while checking out the intriguing sketches from the journal. Needing to get connected with the Internet, she diverted to her hotel. Safety conscious, she rode the elevator with a crowd of tourists, then ran to her room and threw the bolts on the door. Feeling secure for the moment she booted up her laptop.

The few names and words Gar had jotted down on the fax were confusing. The jumble of letters would require serious puzzle assembly that she didn't have patience for now. Instead she studied the drawings. They were amazing! Two of the black and white sketches faintly resembled the paintings at Kana's. Less detail, and lacking the dimension given full and vibrant color, still, they depicted the same island scene she was sure. She was chilled from the eerie coincidence. A subliminal warning clicked in the far reaches of her brain – no fictional detectives she knew about accepted coincidence. Was she blending reality with fiction again? This time she felt all those literary investigators might be right.

Pictures of a bay steeped by hills on two sides, with dolphins and double hulled canoes in the water. The painter took inspiration from these sketches or ones also representing the same island? Which wasn't sinister in any way. Kana owned the book, and wanted the sketches to come to life in full color paintings. Why hide them? They depicted a place similar to Kauai, but she couldn't be sure, she had never seen anything quite like these settings. He must have had the paintings commissioned based on these drawings.

The third sketch was of a grand sailing ship. It looked familiar. A ship she had seen before, but in full color . . . she gasped. Amelia Hunter's library! A ship just like this, but in color. By the same bold, sweeping artist who had painted Kana's pictures! This was beyond coincidence!

A niggling in the back of her mind stirred again, something she knew about the paintings, but it wouldn't surface. Maybe more investigation would help. She had to get over to Kana's now and compare them. And check the other books in the library.

Oh – Oh! – she gasped. Library! The ship painting on the wall in Amelia's library! It was the same artist who drew Kana's islands! And it was a painting of the Pacific Star, she was sure. Yeah – the library at Amelia's estate! The Simon Book Club oversized books! Big enough to hide a ship's log! Maybe Amelia knew more details about the ship's logs or the artwork and the connection with Kana! She had to get back to Kana's! She should go see Amelia. No, first Kana's, just to double check her facts, look at the pictures again, and then to Amelia's. Calling Chase, then Amelia, snarling in frustration that no one was answering her calls today, she folded the phone away and summoned her courage.

Racing to gather her things she made a scan of the hallway before dashing to the elevators. As she was crossing the street she spotted Sam Simon, and after a double take, couldn't spy him again. Was it her imagination? Had paranoia melted her brain? Hoping her instincts were not shredded she dipped into a different hotel on Kuhio and scanned post cards in the little gift shop for a few minutes. Was she completely around the bend on this suspicion thing? She had almost expected to catch Teo lurking somewhere out here. Was she imagining being followed by an ex-date? Did she think Simon involved in something sinister, or was her dislike of him personally fueling suspicions? The millionaire did not excite fear like Teo.

Wishing Chase was with her, she pushed that errant desire aside. Since when did she need a guy to make her felt safe? Since a maniac kahuna tried to break-into Kana's apartment! Not to mention the hit-and-run in San Diego and the unscheduled trip down the stairs. She was a responsible, capable adult and didn't need to be protected by a policeman normally, but it would sure be nice to have her new friend hanging around.

About to leave the hotel gift shop she spotted Sam Simon ordering a shave ice from a stand across the street. What was he doing still in town? Sam. He knew all of them. He dealt in books. She was paranoid, yes. Did she have reason? Was he following her? Feeling vulnerable with the goods – the sketches – in her possession, she slipped out the side of the hotel that lead to a parking garage that abutted International Marketplace.

Stopping at the first kiosk, a glittering mecca of gold necklaces, she searched for the bookstore owner trailing her, but did not spot him. Fingering the jewelry, she was antsy to get going, but held back a few more moments to see if her paranoia was justified. When Simon ambled around the corner casually scanning the shops, her temper flared. Whether he was following her or not this was going to stop!

Keeping a tight hold on the shopping bag containing the pictures – her hopefully clever effort to make important items seem like casual purchases -- she stalked up to the bookstore owner and confronted him.

"I thought you were heading home?" she asked with an edge.

Startled, he studied her, and the bag, before replying. "Detained again on some business." He hefted the shave ice in his hand. "Stepped out for a treat. Care to join me?"

"No, I'm busy."

"Playing cops and robbers?"

The leer in his tone was unmistakable and she ignored it, but appreciated it sounded like jealousy. Maybe Chase was right that Sam was stalking her for amorous reasons and not anything to do with kidnappings and murder.

"I'm still trying to find Kana, yes. Any insight you want to share?"

"Good luck, deary" he coolly replied and walked around her.

He turned a corner in the maze of shops and she waited to see if he reappeared. He didn't and she walked away at a quick pace. The encounter didn't make her feel any better. She was as creeped out about Sam being a stalker as she was of him being a criminal. Once again she wished Chase was with her and felt justified in the desire to have a solid back up. Just like any of her favorite fictional detectives, she was entitled to a sidekick – and hers came with a badge and a gun. Yea team!

Feeling vulnerable with the sketches, despite her bravado with Sam, she lingered at the jewelry counter and pondered her next move. Go to Kana's or back to her hotel? She was burning to do research on the mystery of the journals, but what about safety? Not just hers, but whatever secret was buried in the journals. Frustrated, she tried again to call in her reinforcement.

Taking an escalator to the big hotel next door, she found a corner of the lobby, in full view of the entrance, and called Chase. She breathed a sigh of relief when he answered.

"Oh – hey – you're there!"

"Haley. Hi." Did she imagine the smile in his voice? "I haven't heard anything yet about Kana if that's what you want to know."

The smug amusement in his tone irritated her. Was he expecting her calls now? Could he anticipate her actions? Or was he arrogant enough to think she was chasing him? Chasing Chase? The pun did not lighten her vexation at being predictable to the cop that she liked, but did not want to admit she liked . . . Never mind. There were more important issues to deal with this morning, and she kept on track. "I need to talk to you. Teo came by Kana's place and tried to break-in."

"Are you all right?

"Yeah, I -"

"Did you call HPD?"

"No."

"Why not?"

Was there more outrage or exasperation in his tone? Maybe both. She kind of liked that he was so worked up about it – her. She didn't like feeling dumb about her actions. Or him thinking she was daft or incompetent. Calling the police was the smart thing to do – to a cop at least.

"It's kind of a long story. He didn't get in or anything, and well, he really just tried the door knob and then hit the screen," she admitted. It sounded pretty lame in hindsight. Not something to call the cops about. Satisfied she made the right choice in the heat of fear she concluded that nothing was really damaged and he had departed without further incident.

"You're sure you're all right?"

"Really, I am." It was nice to know he really did care. "Mahalo for asking."

"You're welcome. I'm finding out I need to keep tabs on you, malihini pilikia."

"What?"

"You're a magnet for trouble."

"Funny. You won't want to insult me so much when you find out I've got a lead on the case."

"Really?"

"Yeah. I think I might have a tie in with all of us. Kana, Carrie, Amelia and me."

"Really. You all like books?"

"Do you want to know or not?" she snapped back, too keyed up to take any teasing.

"When I asked you –"

"This is something that just came to light. I'm at the Surfside Hotel. In the lobby. Can you meet me?"

"Sure. I'll leave right now."

She could have waited in the valet parking area along Kalakaua, but the lobby seemed safer. Embarrassed at her paranoia, and freaked out about the craziness spinning out of control around her, she decided to lean on the side of caution. Still suffering mild headaches and myriad aches and pains from the accident and the knock on the head, she had no desire to confront her violent adversaries again. If she had that misfortune, she wanted to make sure she was in the presence of a competent, armed cop, like Keoni Chase.

When she spotted the lieutenant rising up on the escalator to the second floor lobby, she smiled with relief. As was his custom, the cop assessed the area as he strode across the tiled floor and around the rattan chairs, but the gait and demeanor swelled with tension. His scrutiny seemed especially acute when directed at her.

"You sure you're all right?" he asked as he took her by the elbow.

"Fine." Glancing behind him -- just to make sure -- she was further calmed that neither Teo or Sam were anywhere in sight. "Mahalo for coming," she replied, steering him toward an unoccupied area of the reception desk.

Feeling secure with the detective at her side and a reception desk at her back, she went through the now-embarrassing attack-on-the-door episode in detail. Chagrined at her well-remembered fear, she was warmed that Keoni found no humor in the tale, but rather, his strain seemed more noticeable than ever.

"If you can handle it, I'd like you to press charges against Teo."

Not thrilled with the idea of accusing the behemoth holy man, she appreciated that the cop wanted to bring Teo to justice. The motivation had to be personal and while she didn't mind their reasons coming together, she doubted they had much of a case.

"What can you arrest him for, bending a door?"

"Yeah. Attempting to break and enter," he seethed. Her doubt must have bled into her expression because he shot out. "Being a nuisance! Loitering on private property! How 'bout being as ugly as a mahi-mahi?" he finished.

"They're ugly?"

"Before they're filleted on a plate, very," he confirmed, his expression still sour, his responses sharp and annoyed. "Too bad being a pain in my neck isn't a criminal offence the D.A. will support. Otherwise Teo would be in lock up now!"

"You really don't like him."

"No. I'm serious about the charges, though. It will give me enough to bring him in. I can put another line on his record."

"And keep him away from Kamala?"

"That, too."

"Okay." Finally the elusive item in the back of her mind surfaced with the link of jail and Teo. "Hey, did you notice Teo's hands were all scratched when we met him at the jail? Do you think that could have been from a fight? Maybe at Kana's?"

The theory gave him pause. His reaction gave her pause. The thought of the giant, angry kahuna attacking poor, old, frail Kana was sickening. After mentioning it only as a passing theory, she now regretted bringing the possibility to mind.

His frown sobered his whole face. "We'll find out as soon as I bring him in. Which I'll put into motion as soon as we get out of here. Now what were you telling me about some connection with all of you?'

"I had my cousin fax the sketches from the journal I was sent."
His dark eyes narrowed. "What journal?"

"Amelia mailed me an old ship's log, but I think it was from Kana. Maybe he mailed it to me but used Amelia's address to keep his identity out of it." She stopped at his perplexed expression. "Sounds crazy, I know."

"I thought you liked mysteries not spy stories."

Ignoring the sarcasm she continued. "It arrived at my shop after I came here. The drawings are just like the pictures in Kana's apartment, well not just like, these are black and white sketches, and the ones at his place are more recent paintings. Can you remember how long he's had them?"

"I hardly went up to his apartment. We always met in the shop because that's where he really lived," he shot out quickly. "Why didn't you tell me about the journal –"

"Must be the headache." At his censuring glare, she corrected, "I wasn't sure what it meant –"

"Your place was searched; his place was searched; Amelia's house was searched. You were attacked; Kana is missing; Kahunui was murdered," his voice was escalating in intensity and volume until she shushed him. "You didn't think this might be important?" he finished in a quieter tone.

"Okay, okay, it's pretty important. Much too valuable to risk shipping back over here for you to take a look at right now. It's in a safe place."

"That's debatable," he huffed.

Was this the point for full disclosure? Did she tell him Kana had a few pages of another ship's journal hidden away in oversized

Super Simon books? "Look, maybe we don't have to have the journal in our hands. If Amelia will tell us what's going on –"

"All right, on the phone you said there was a connection. What is it?"

She glanced around, making sure they were not being overheard or watched.

"Why do you keep looking around?"

"Besides Teo –"

"He's not going to bother you while I'm around."

The fear suddenly whooshed out of her like a gust of Trade wind blew away all her cares. She felt completely safe as long as he was close. "Mahalo." This might be a good time for complete disclosure. Chase was sympathetic and would not think her weird, or vying for attention. She hoped. "Sam was following me."

Expression darkening, he did a quick scan of the lobby. It was an open air, second story level, with a quaint café on the ocean side overlooking the busy boulevard. Several curio shops lined the outer wall. Help desks for tour agencies backed the cove of elevators, and the reception counter was at the far wall, commanding a good view of the entire floor. Tropical trees and plants rimmed the rails of the seating areas dotted with comfortable, tropical-styled rattan chairs.

"Let's hit the road," he ordered, taking her by the elbow and escorting her downstairs.

"Where are we going?"

"To talk to Amelia."

"Oh." He was taking her along! "Oh! Cool!"

On the quick escalator trip down, she noted his heightened level of awareness. Casual repartee and irritated questioning was swept aside by a professional aura of guarded guardedness. Every face was quickly scanned, every corner scrutinized in a glance while he kept a protective hold on her with his left hand. His right hand had strayed to lightly rest on the revolver in his waist holster.

When they reached the garage entrance, he nearly pushed her into the Mustang. Not insulted by his commanding attitude, she felt secure and protected now to have someone who did not doubt her and was willing to support her without question. After a quick word to the valet, he screeched them away from the crowded alley, past huge tour busses, and through another hotel's parking garage. By the time they reached Kuhio, they had picked up speed and zoomed away. If anyone tried to follow them, and Chase was watching for that eventuality, they would have a hard time catching up to the hot sports car.

"Mahalo."

"For what?" he wondered quizzically, his eyes darting from the rearview mirror, to her, then to the road.

"For believing me."

"That Simon is following you?"

"Yeah."

"You're welcome." His smile was dazzling. "Nice to hear you speaking Hawaiian."

"Mahalo. Again. I think I can get the hang of it after a while."

The sunglasses were, as usual, in place to protect against the blazing rays of the tropical sun, but she was learning to read him with or without the shades. The tension of their exit at the hotel was replaced by a wariness that eased into a casual camaraderie. Feeling comfortable in his company was becoming as natural as the perfect blue sky above and the breezy ocean surrounding her.

170

"The more you hear it the more you'll pick up." It was an open invitation – the lilt in his voice -- the expression on his speculative face as he shot assessing glances her way.

He was just too engaging. "Then I guess I should hang out with a native."

The amazing grin was back. "I can handle that."

Traffic at the back of Waikiki was nearly as congested as on the main drag of the tourist center. She knew she did not have his entire attention as they snaked along the crowded streets, whipping past the Ala Wai, then up some residential streets, then steering toward Diamond Head and the beautiful paths of Black Point.

As they pulled up to a red light, his phone rang. Answering it, he stiffened, glanced at her, and then gave a curt acknowledgement before ending the call.

"What?"

"Teo's been spotted downtown. I think he's going to the rally at the capitol."

He spun around at the next intersection, zooming through the backstreets, then rocketing onto Ala Wai and racing toward the downtown area of Honolulu. Away from her hotel and away from Black Point. He was taking her with him! A thanks might jinx the whole trip so she remained silent in her pleasant surprise.

Chase flexed his fists on the steering wheel. "You know, I shouldn't tell you this, but Simon has an alibi for Carrie's murder. He was clubbing in Waikiki the night before and slept in late. Hotel staff vouches that the Do Not Disturb sign showed on his suite door until Eleven a.m. Security did not spot him in or out all night."

She wasn't sure she trusted security measures anymore after the failures this week in San Diego and here. Did the hotel use Cabrillo

171

Security? Too much investigative work on her part might disrupt the delicate balance of their new relationship, so she gave her response some deep thought. The question kept bugging her, though, and she plunged ahead, even though she might be stepping on his investigative toes.

"The security system for the hotel is entirely digital. And yes, I thought to check. It is owned by Cabrillo Security. Yes, owned by your ex. And Sam Simon even owns a piece of the hotel chain." At her raised eyebrows, he laughed. "So I managed to find out something you didn't think to ask about?"

She liked his teasing sarcasm. It was an appealing aspect of his good sense of humor. "I've always maintained you are a great cop."

"Mahalo."

He shouldn't tell her but he did. She hid the triumphant smile flickering at her lips. So, she was getting under his skin – in an investigative sort of way of course. He was used to her hanging around and helping to find Kana. All good for her cause.

She responded with a tone of mild curiosity that belayed her victory. "What kind of an alibi is that? Don't you think it's suspicious that he showed up here when I did? That this trail of violence has followed him? Or preceded him? Me?" At his frown, she pressed her lips together, knowing what she knew, but unable to articulate it past the raw memory of the attacks and the constant concern about Kana. "You know what I mean."

"Did it occur to you that Sam Simon could be following you because he likes you?" he returned sharply. "You mentioned he wanted to take you out when you arrived."

"Did I?"

172

She didn't remember revealing anything that personal to Chase. On the other hand, that tumultuous and emotional day was now a blur of rollercoaster feelings and events. Hard to believe this was her third day in Hawaii.

"You said Simon wanted to take you to dinner." He glanced at her with a raised brow. "I remember."

"Hey, who am I to argue with a policeman?"

His laugh, then voice, carried the sarcasm. "Right."

Pleased that he recollected so much of what she told him – paying attention to her -- and that their time together was so—so easy – to just hang with, she drifted into silence. The rest of the ride was spent in mute appreciation of the sun and wind rustling her hair, the refreshing scent of brine off the ocean, the mellow bake of the Hawaiian heat on her skin. The comfort of having a bodyguard eased her mind enough to value all those little details of paradise. It was a nice feeling to be free of worry about her safety.

***

"Kamala should be at the Capitol again for today's demonstration."

"And Teo is there, too."

"Right. And you are sticking close to me. I don't know if I can trust you on your own."

"Teo's not a threat anymore. Not with you around. Why do you think he wanted to sneak into Kana's?" There had been no time to toss around suspicions about the creepy kahuna. And the cop still seemed a little suspicious of Amelia, but Haley couldn't give them credence. "Teo had been working with Carrie," she surmised aloud. "After a thief's falling out he killed Carrie."

"At Amelia Hunter's house?"

"Uh – okay, I'm still working on that. Hey, hey, maybe they were searching for the ship's logs!"

He glanced at her and gave an approving nod. "All right. These mysterious logs would be important then."

"And Teo came back today and tried to break into Kana's . . . uh . . . because . . ." her brilliant theory was starting to unravel.

"Maybe he knew Kana had a log."

With little margin for safety he yanked the Mustang to the curb and screeched to a halt. He shifted so he stared at her with full attention. "What?"

"I found an ancient ship's log at Kana's. It was hidden inside some oversized books. Kind of an old spy trick. The log is similar to the one Amelia sent to me."

"And you didn't tell me all these details before because?"

"I – uh – really wasn't sure how they all fit in. I was kind of hoping to figure that out and – uh – have a working theory for you before I – uh – clouded the issue." At his tight-lipped frown of disapproval she rushed on, "I thought the main focus of everything was finding Kana! Now there are all kinds of subplots going on that I'm trying to understand –"

"That's my job! I'm the cop, not you, remember?"

"And you're a great one. And you're super to let me help and I'll let you see the log as soon as we catch Teo," she raced out in one breath. "Maybe he'll explain everything." She forced herself to silence as he stared at her, the classy sunglasses taking on an ominous cant, shielding the eyes that she could not read, leaving only a taut facial expression to relay his irritation.

With a snort he turned back to the wheel and screeched into the traffic lane again.

***

Driving along Ala Moana Boulevard with the top down, Haley appreciated the cottony clouds bunching against the emerald of the gouged mountains behind the city. The perfect day must have had a tempering affect on Chase, because he soon transitioned to a tour guide, pointing out some points of interest as they traveled. All tension from their conflict forgotten, her opinion of him elevated again. He didn't hold grudges, or display a bad temper. He was turning out to be a real cool guy.

In the lofty, reflective shimmer of high-rise windows she watched the rippled manifestations of sky and sea, of historic edifices, of boats in the harbor. A huge cruise ship was docked by Aloha Tower and small figures scurried around busses or wandered in groups as the passengers spilled out discover the wonders of Oahu.

Downtown Honolulu contained fascinating paradoxes that symbolized the rest of Hawaii. Old stone buildings used when this land was still an independent kingdom, nestled within the same block of the new steel and glass skyscrapers towering into the azure sky. The ancient and the modern clashing in a strangely elegant and profound statement of co-existence personified the islands. Known as the melting pot of the Pacific, Hawaii was an example to the world of how cultures, races, religions and creeds blended together to make a thriving, enticing society.

As the Mustang pulled onto a quiet side street, they cruised past an imposingly elegant structure she had seen many times in post cards and magazines but never stopped to explore. A three-story palace, the white-washed columns sparkling in the bright tropical sun, stood out like a beacon amid the lush trees and lawns surrounding the huge block. Literally, it was a palace, she remembered, and for the first time had an interest in the building; its history and its significance to Hawaii, but specifically, to Kana's logs.

"That's the king's palace."

"Iolani Palace," he identified, slowing the car to pull into the front drive.

She felt a little like a commoner coming for an audience to royalty. In travels to Europe and the British Isles she had visited castles and cathedrals. Fun for sightseeing, but she never felt any connection to them. After reading some of those ship logs, she knew there was a personal history with the Hagoth family to this monarchy. Perhaps Kana's ancestors walked these sparkling white steps and met with the king right there on the front lanai overlooking a charming bandstand on the lawn. The past was alive for her now through the mysterious chronicles of a long-dead sea captain and his puzzling commission to the royalty of Hawaii.

Chase pulled the sports car over to an open parking spot near a majestically giant banyan tree. Walking around to the rear of the palace she was curious that the front and rear had the same design. It was an imposing structure and she strolled the length, checking out the palm-frond design on the pillars, the elegant dark wood on the doors and windows, the ornate carvings in the steps.

"When we have more time, I'll take you on the tour," Chase offered as the strolled past. "It's a pretty cool place. Lotsa history."

176

"This is where the queen lived and was imprisoned, wasn't it?" she asked.

"Right. Regrettable part of our history."

Following him to a walking mall beyond the banyan tree she was surprised they were now at the back of the Capitol building. She had no idea the old palace and the modern seat of government were next to each other. They paused at a statue of Queen Lilioukalani. Gazing from the elegantly portrayed monarch, to her royal residence beyond, it was easy to imagine the queen had walked these grounds on a day, much like this one, over a century before. She had ruled a nation, endured a coup, and in between instigated a mystery for a long gone Hagoth, and Kana. Not to mention Kana's grandson and a bookstore owner from San Diego.

"The demonstration is in front of the Capitol," Chase told her as they walked up the steps to the unique state structure.

The Capitol building was impressive; the open ground floor ringed by a mote. The center of the volcano-shaped roof opened to the sky. Chase explained it was a symbolic shape that personified Hawaii as an island state, with origins in the molten upheaval beneath the sea, still surrounded by the sea, which still signified the life of the people. Lacking walls on the sides of the first level, they walked across a finely tiled circle-mosaic of swirling flows of green, blue and white centered exactly under the skylight in the top of the building over five stories above.

"Again, the ocean, the sky and the clouds," he gestured to the round artwork. "Hawaii."

Walking through the large building they headed toward the bright front steps where a crowd was gathered against the backdrop of the sun-drenched green mountains and cerulean sky. Scattered around a statue that Chase said represented Father Damien, the Catholic priest who served in a leper colony here in the islands, were a collection of protester/demonstrators. In their shorts, t-shirts, sandals, with the high humidity and temperature, they seemed a quiet, even slack crowd. A few signs declared they were from HRC, a few more defined statements of opinion – *Hawaii for Hawaiians! Native means us!*

As long as she could remember, Haley had been regaled by tales of the wild and revolutionary sit-ins at Stanford, the walk-outs at UCLA, the lay-downs at UC Davis. Those had been her parent's defining years and were never far from sentimentalizing the turbulent Sixties and their part in the cultural turmoil. Her generation, particularly in San Diego, had been reared in times of peace, prosperity and luxury. She had no connection to this kind of political activism and had never held an interest in it. Knowing Kamala and Kana's ancestor-Hagoth with the mysterious connection to royalty, she had an interest now.

A low-key, but nonetheless sincere political gathering on the steps of the State Capitol was something new for Haley and she watched with interest that turned to disappointment when nothing happened. Was everything in Hawaii nonchalant even down to civil unrest? Yeah, it seemed tough to envision disruption of paradise. The beach-city attitude was prevalent in her home of San Diego, too. Not a bad thing; fitting her personality, certainly. It gave her a moment of sympathy for the protesters. Only a moment, though. She was far more interested in Chase arresting Teo than in political causes.

Various people dressed in business attire, tourists with cameras, city workers, all skirted the protesters with a little attention to the activity. A few photos were snapped, a few double takes, but the civic gathering went mostly unnoticed. Kai – she forgot his last name – was impossible to miss. The huge, but affable Hawaiian was dressed in a bright red and white aloha shirt. Standing in the sun like a monument for local clothing stores, Kai was talking to an HPD man over by the statue. Scanning the crowd, Haley was almost relieved there was no sign of Teo. Even with Chase there to protect her, she was a little apprehensive about facing the threatening kahuna again.

Spotting Kamala was easy. The artistic woman was dressed in a vibrantly colored t-shirt with rainbows and political slogans. She was trying to hand out pamphlets to passersby. Angling through the dozen-odd participants, Chase came up alongside his brother's wife.

"Hey," she greeted him with a laugh, "are you here to talk me into leaving before we get arrested?"

It made Haley wonder what Kamala did to warrant the continued arrests, since this was anything but a violent or confrontational event. The Hawaiian woman brightened when Haley came around to Keoni's side, and Kamala gave her a hug.

"Thank you for coming! I'm so glad to see you again."

The effusive and friendly attitude was sobering under the circumstances. Fortunately, Chase steered Kamala through the people and over to an alcove by some metal-plated elevators. She couldn't hear what he was saying, but by the time they stopped Kamala was sober and anxious.

"What is it?"

"We're looking for Teo."

"You're not going to arrest him again are you?" She glared at her brother-in-law.

"He tried to break into Kana's," he informed curtly. "I want to talk to him."

Kamala bit her lip. "Why would he do that?"

"You tell me." At her silence, he pressed. "He's here, isn't he? Why are you protecting him?"

Haley moved closer. "What if he had something to do with Kana's disappearance?"

"He couldn't!" the sister-in-law insisted, but her face revealed doubt.

Chase's attention strayed from Kamala to the knot of protesters. His stare zeroed in on a man holding a sign. The big poster was visible, not face, but from the shape and bulk Haley could guess who was hiding behind the placard.

"Teo!"

The sign was flung to the ground and the kahuna spun around, pushing through the crowd to make a run.

"Stop!"

Keoni ran forward and straight into a human wall of protesters. As the policeman pushed one way, then the other, the mass moved to block his progress. No such obstructions prevented her from assisting him and she pivoted around the nearest activist and through a gap in bodies to dash out in pursuit of the wanted kahuna.

She heard Chase yell after her but she kept running as the surprisingly fast, bulky Teo raced across the tiled floor of the capitol. Down the steps and across the walkway she dashed knees and head aching from the exertion and pounding on the pavement. A quick glance behind clued her that Chase was – yes – chasing her now – followed by a few protesters who were vociferously protesting the cop's interest in their leader.

Under the huge banyan tree, Teo zipped around the multiple branches driven into the soil and switched sharply to the back steps of the palace. Haley was losing ground now, the twists, turns and brutal pace sending shock waves of pain through her limbs and brain. She would not give up, though, more determined than ever to lay her hands on her chief suspect. This crazy activist had to be the one responsible for the break-ins and Kana's disappearance.

Winding around the old former royal residence, beating along the immaculate white walkway to the front of the old Palace, she was gaining ground. What was she going to do if she caught up with him? Hitting the lush green lawn her knees appreciated the cushioned ground and she closed the distance between them, now a little worried she would catch him! What would she do if he suddenly turned and confronted her? What if he had been after her at Kana's? Was she playing into his maniacal plan even now?

From the left a blur flashed into her vision. Keoni! At an intercept course for the kahuna! The cop's dead run cut across the lawn and on target for the Hawaiian. As Teo reached the impressive, crest-emblazoned gates of the square, he glanced around and spotted Chase. The broad activist hardly hesitated, but trotted off the sidewalk and onto the four-lane, high-speed King Street! Yikes! This was like some insane reenactment from Magnum or something!

Haley slowed, then stopped in horror as the large, lumbering figure dodged two cars! Chase was right behind him until a driver panicked, skidding to a halt at an angle that flipped the detective onto the hood of the car.

"Keoni!"

Fear knotting her throat, Haley watched as Teo continued his suicidal escape; barely missing a tourist van! He threw himself at the

181

feet of the King Kamehameha statue across the street just in time to avoid a head-on with a bus!

Haley used the confusion to make her own dash through the now stalled traffic. The policeman, thankfully, was in one piece and on his feet continuing the pursuit before she reached him. Following Chase to the other side as soon as the bus moved, they stared at the tourist attraction of Hawaii's first king.

Visitors with cameras milled around the impressive sculpture. Some even clicked a few snapshots of the cop and his companion who were panting with fatigue. Of Teo there was no sign. Chase jogged through the old courthouse behind Kamehameha. He asked a few onlookers if they had seen Teo. Haley trailed along behind, worn out and lacking the energy to do more than keep her friend in sight. After several negative responses from eyewitnesses he returned, shaking his head.

"He's gone."

"How can a guy that big move so fast?" she wondered, her pace slow. She actively worked at not limping but her right leg really hurt.

"How could you?" he shot back, eyeing her legs. "And what were you thinking chasing him?" He stopped and held her shoulder. "That was pupule!" As she opened her mouth he supplied, "Crazy!"

"Yeah, it was."

They stopped at the crosswalk to return to the palace square legally. After safely reaching the grounds Chase called HPD and reported Teo's escape. Chase led her to the impressive white steps at the front of the old building and plopped down next to her. She leaned over, catching her breath, noticing pain in her back and ribs now that she was off her feet. She was going to be so sore tomorrow.

Hearing a noise behind them she turned, caught by the beautiful, glass-inlaid doors at the entrance, momentarily distracted her from her physical pain. From around the corner, on the white lanai, Kamala and Kai appeared, the woman giving her a wave. With an unreadable expression the sister-in-law approached. Chase followed Haley's focus and stood when Kamala joined them.

"I guess you didn't get him," she began.

"No."

"Teo's in big pilikia again," the rotund Kai shook his head.

"You don't seem outraged or surprised," Chase accused his sister-in-law.

Kamala's dark eyes glanced away from Keoni's, took in Haley, then back to briefly brush with her relative's. Gazing out at the long stretch of verdant grass, she leaned on the white railing of the palace. "When he showed up today, there was something up with him. He wouldn't talk to me. I thought he was mad." She shrugged, then sighed. It sounded a lot like a surrender of regret. "Like he was guilty or something."

"Dead right," the cop snapped back. "He tried to break into Kana's while Haley was there!"

Kamala placed an arm around Haley. "Are you all right?"

"Fine. He couldn't get in." Kamala's reaction was puzzling. Not what she expected from a staunch follower, from the kahuna supporter who was jailed for her convictions.

Kai patted her back. "You don't be scared of Teo, little sistah. He can get pupule about our rights, but he not lolo enough to hurt anyone."

183

Chase opened his mouth to supply a translation, she guessed, but Haley beat him to the punch. "Crazy and stupid. Yeah, I'm memorizing those words."

Chase corrected, "He's crazy but not stupid, Kai. He's up to something involving Kana and he could have hurt Haley if he had gotten inside the shop. I'm not going to let him get away with that."

Biting her lip, the artist confessed, "It's his temper. He can't control it sometimes. I wouldn't say this to just anyone, but you're ohana," she told Keoni, but also included Haley. "You're good people, Haley, and Keoni's friend. I'm not going to protect Teo from his bad habits at your expense."

"Mahalo, Kamala. This might be hard, but I have some questions to ask you, too." Chase showed as much compassion as she displayed reason and her estimate of both, fine people skyrocketed. "If you'll excuse us, Kai?" It was not a question or a request.

"Sure ting. See you later, Kamala. Aloha." The big man walked away around the corner of the palace.

The strikingly beautiful native gave a nod for the others to follow and Kamala stared across the lawn to the quaint bandstand. Streams of afternoon sun bathed the sharply painted wood, the tall palms surrounding the ancient square filtered the sparkling brightness to dapple the lanai with fluid shadow and light. The heat and humid air kissed with a taint of salty ocean breezed across their faces, sweeping with it the flowery scent of plumeria. On this very spot was ground zero for the coup that deposed the monarchy and the mysteries of the Hagoth ohana. The moment was pure Hawaiian, and leaning on the rail where the great queen herself might have stood, it seemed the appropriate place to talk of kahunas and intrigue.

"We think Teo might be connected to Carrie Kahunui's murder and Kana's disappearance," Haley revealed, and was gratified when Keoni did not object or refute the theory, or the 'we' including him in her speculations.

The trade winds blew Kamala's long hair across her face. Wiping the dark strands out of her eyes, she addressed Haley first. "Teo has always been obsessed with reclaiming Hawaiian's sovereignty. He believes Kana has records about mokuaina pu'uhonua. People forget, Kana is a kahuna, too. He knows more about Hawaii's past than all of us put together." She was adamant. "Teo respects that! He would never hurt Kana!"

The detective was skeptical. "What about Carrie Kahunui?"

"I doubt that he even knew her."

Too confused to take in everything, Haley asked Kamala to explain about the kahuna stuff. When she noted Keoni's expression denoted less perplexity and more of the aha-I-get-it-now attitude, she asked for them to let her in on the latest secret. Another hidden surprise – like Keoni being Kana's grandson – felt like it was about to dawn on the horizon. And there was that word again – pu'uhonua – the one mentioned in the log

"There's an ancient Hawaiian legend about a mythical island where those seeking perfection and purity will be safe. Some believe that was what the original Polynesians were after when they stumbled onto Hawaii," Kamala related.

"A myth," Keoni scoffed.

"Many want to believe it," the protester snapped back. Facing Haley, she continued. "When Lilioukalani was overthrown and imprisoned there are stories that some of her followers sought out mokuaina pu'uhonua. Dolphin Island; an island of refuge. A place where they could find their perfect paradise without the influence of westerners or non-Hawaiians." She glared at her brother-in-law. "Don't you remember those stories when we were growing up? There was an island hidden by the gods and preserved for those pure in heart."

"Kana used to talk about it when he was fed up with local politics," Chase admitted. "But they are stale talk-story. Old men trade those kinds of tales over beers. Teo is educated –"

"He is a kahuna who believes in the ancient ways," she corrected sharply. "He often hopes for . . . "her voice trailed away as her expression lit with alarm. "Teo believes Kana knows about mokuaina pu'uhonua. But he wouldn't hurt Kana. No one would. Kana is too kind and full of old wisdom!"

"But someone killed Carrie, and Kana is gone," Haley pointed out with desperate fear.

"Do you think Teo went to Carrie for information on his mythical island?" he asked Kamala. "Kana and colleagues. With Kana missing, maybe Carrie got in the way –"

"No, Teo would never kill anyone," Kamala refuted, but the tone lacked conviction. After quiet retrospection, she maintained that Teo was obsessively consumed with the old legends about supernatural Hawaii, but only for knowledge. "Why would anyone kill over a legend?"

"Tell me more about the island myth," Haley requested.

"Apparently kahunas in tune with the island could funnel incredible power to use to help Hawaiians. Teo says Kana knows this." Her expression grew tense and her voice lowered. "Teo told me a haole was helping Kana search for more information on the secrets of pu'uhonua, but would not give me a name."

186

Chase blurted out, "Amelia," without hesitation.

"Haole?" Haley questioned.

"Caucasian," Kamala translated. "Like you or Amelia."

"Right." She had to remember that. Haley did not want to think of her friend as a suspect and tried to veer Chase's suspicions away from the old spy. "Teo couldn't kill? Not even to get something he believed would help his cause? Amelia couldn't possibly have hurt Kana or Carrie, we already established that," she reminded."

Kamala shook her head, but it was a slow and unconvincing gesture. "Teo is not a murderer."

"Then why did he run?"

"He had a cop chasing him!" Kamala shot back to her brother-in-law.

Chase insisted the big kahuna had a lot of explaining to do.

Haley asked them both, "And where is Kana?" The crimes and legends were obscuring her single-minded purpose. She needed to find her mentor.

"I don't know, but I promise I'll find him," Keoni assured, squeezing her shoulder.

Satisfied they were back on track Haley followed them back to the Mustang. They promised to keep Kamala in the loop and she gave an oath that she would help any way she could, even turning in Teo if she heard from him. As they drove away from the regal palace, Haley studied it until they turned the corner on the busy street. Up until this visit she had been one of the uninformed tourists, visiting this paradise regularly, but never knowing more than the surface of beaches, books and places to eat. Today she had walked on royal ground, touched part of the past with her own hands. She would have to come back here after Kana came back. She would like to see Hawaiian history through his eyes.

"Where are we going?"

"To Kana's to get that ship's log," Chase responded as the Mustang zipped through the traffic.

She tried calling Amelia again, with no luck.

"Who are you calling?"

"Amelia. Still no answer. Do you think she's okay?"

"Why?"

Concern escalating, she asked if they could swing by the Black Point estate and check on the elderly woman. "I'm worried about her."

"Okay."

They were skirting the gaudy hotels of Waikiki when Chase asked if she was worried something had happened to Amelia. As if the same thought transferred from her mind to his, he voiced her newest anxiety.

"You think Teo might be a threat to her?"

"If he's involved with Carrie's murder and Kana's disappearance and everything else that's happened, yes."

The wind whipped her straw-colored hair into her face and she sighed with irritation that she had yet to buy a new hat. A triviality compared to everything else that had happened to her in the last few days.

"You think he hopped a plane to the mainland and tossed your shop and house –"

"Why not? If he's motivated enough to kill for information on his supernatural island, he could fly over to San Diego for the day."

His nod was slow, but he didn't seem convinced.

"What?"

"Teo just doesn't seem the type to be so – I don't know – stealthy. Kamala said he has a temper and his police record proves that. Get him going on something that impassions him and he can really make trouble. Sneaking around, going to the mainland, all seems – I don't know – out of his character. I'm not discounting it, I just have to think that through."

"So all the pieces don't fit perfectly. Yet. We'll know more when you catch him."

Amelia's house was dark in the late afternoon shadows. Hoku barked from the other side of the door as they rang the bell several times. Again, Haley called on her cell and received no response. Chase checked over the gates to see if there were any doors or windows open, or sign of a break-in, but could detect nothing out of place. He called HPD and ordered extra patrols for the area just in case Teo came looking for Hunter.

"Shouldn't we get in there?"

"Break into her yard or house?" The officer scowled.

"She could be hurt."

Chase scanned the windows, door, and gates visible to him without breaking down anything. He did a walking inventory that everything was intact. There was no sign of a break-in or anything suspicious. They could try her again tomorrow. If there was still no sign of her he might be able to persuade his captain that forced entry was a viable option.

"But something could be wrong," Haley tried again, stubbornly standing on the doorstep, anxiety increasing at Hoku's continued barking.

Sighing, Chase put in a call to his department, but his captain was away. Instead of leaving a message, he hung up and told her he would call back later. With a final look around Haley was persuaded to leave. Their time could be put into better pursuits.

***

As they drove back toward Waikiki Haley tried Amelia's number again. Still no answer. With a sigh of frustration she stared out at the sea buzzing by as they sped along the highway. The gigantic orange sun was slipping closer to the indigo ocean amid a striation of multicolored clouds. Bright sails from catamarans and boats, dinner cruise ships and small private boats dotted the horizon as spectators drifted out to sea to catch another stunning Hawaiian sundown.

"I'll have to take you out to Sunset Beach sometime. Unbelievable sunset, obviously from the name."

"That sounds great," she smiled, thinking it also sounded a lot like a date. A romantic date. That idea was kind of pleasant.

Coursing through the traffic converging to the hotels of the concrete mecca he grumbled at the traffic jam. "Bad time to get back here, all the tourists who have been roaming the island for the day are coming in for the dinner cruises and hotel luaus."

"Dinner time already! I think cop business made us skip lunch again."

"Can I buy you dinner?"

"Again? How about my treat this time? You're working on a cop's salary."

"And you're working on a bookstore owner's salary. I know from Kana that's not very rich."

Evening in the center of the tourist trap was not where he wanted to be, Chase told her, but she assured him she had a few ideas to make it a good outing. Parking at her hotel, they walked down the street, the air balmy and warm. She stopped at a small set of shops not far from Kana's. It was a hole-in-the-wall local hang out with an amazing variety of native dishes blended with the cultural mix of Hawaiian, Portuguese, American, Chinese and Japanese cuisine. The specialty of the house was barbeque, so they agreed to order mixed plates and share the variety of chicken, pork, noodles, rice and manapua.

"No spam this time?" she teased.

"I was tempted, but thought I'd try their other dishes. I can have spam anytime." He dug into the pile of noodles with his chopsticks. "We're making a habit of this you know."

She liked the engaging smile that went along with the comment. "Yeah. Do you mind?"

"No." He took a sip of his soda. "I'm actually impressed. I've lived here in Oahu all my life and never knew about this place. Which is great," he complimented after he swallowed his rice and pork.

"Maybe there are some useful things to learn from a tourist."

"I don't consider you a tourist," he corrected. "You've been here enough to qualify for residence status. But you've never looked any deeper than the surface of the beauty and the vacation spots."

"Too busy with my nose buried in books. That's going to change. When we were at the palace today I felt like I could turn around and Queen Lilioukalani would be standing there over my shoulder. It wasn't history anymore, it was real."

"Kana will be glad to hear that. I'm afraid I wasn't much of a student to him, either." As he pushed the manapua -- a tasty, doughy Chinese treat -- around on the plate he scoffed, "He had to get someone to marry into the family to listen to his talk-story about the old legends like mokuaina pu'uhonua. Then Kamala's politics pushed her away from him, too."

"Tell me about this magic island."

Mokuaina pu'uhonua, he related, was a dream of the wistful yearnings of old men. It was a legend, like Atlantis. A place troubled people could conjure in times of need. An enchanted realm where modern worries were vanquished and life would be perfect. He was too pragmatic to believe in anything that fanciful. He trusted in what he could see – evidence. After all, he was a cop.

It had to be pure fiction, of course, but Haley didn't dismiss the notion of a hidden island so readily. She understood the dream of escaping reality through books. She experienced pu'uhonua every time she opened the cover of a novel. Who was she to discount the myths of those who wanted to believe in magic?

As much as she hated to align with her parents, she was well versed in tales of Atlantis and her sister island in the Pacific, Lemuria. Okay, that was a bad example. Lemuria, was the New Age believer's alien-invasion-magic-world that went along with space invaders building the pyramids and helping primitive humans to evolve. The ill-fated society supposedly matched the fate of its twin and sank at the bottom of the Pacific. Coincidently, not far from Hawaii. But that myth was about the farthest thing in the world from Hawaii.

After dinner they walked down to the beach and strolled in the sand. The ocean was a dark ribbon, the waves crashing in a frothy song to the grainy shore. A silver moon peaked out between clouds over Diamond Head as they took their time crossing the beach. Live bands played in almost every nightclub along the hotel line and they stopped to listen to the free concerts of ukuleles, guitars, bongos and drums. When they sat down at the breakwater they dipped their feet in the cool sea.

Chase released a huge sigh. "I don't think I've ever had a better time in Waikiki. Mahalo."

"You don't get over here to the tourist trap enough."

"I never had the right guide before."

She could say the same thing. And did. The walk back to the hotel was slow, both equally reluctant to end the evening. He didn't stop at her hotel lobby, but followed her into the elevator. Before she could ask any awkward questions about what he had in mind, he apologized for not receiving authorization from his boss to provide her with protective custody.

She had grown accustomed to having Chase at her side. Now that would have to end. About to ask him if he could spend the night on the chair in her room, she hesitated when he gave her a piece of paper.

"I'm staying with a buddy who lives down on Kalakaua," he explained. "Just about five minutes away. If you need anything, call me. I'll keep my cell on. That's the address if you need to run down – to see me -- or anything."

Five minutes away. Better than nothing. "Mahalo." She wouldn't admit how much better she felt. "You mean you really asked your boss to protect me – I mean – for protection?"

"Sure. As far as I'm concerned you're still in danger. You have been since San Diego," he told her with certainty. "So I'm keeping my eye on you," he assured, with a twinkle in his eye, as they reached her room.

She felt better all ready.

Once inside, with the door locked and a chair propped up against the knob, she collapsed on the bed and kicked off her shoes. Dialing Amelia's number, she was worried that there was no answer still. Ending the call she realized they had never stopped at Kana's for her to show Chase the ship's log! They had gone to dinner and that fantastic walk long Waikiki's beach at night – and they forgot about the case! Laughing, she nestled against the pillows and wondered if she should call Chase back. As soon as she rested her eyes for a minute. She would call him in a minute. He would still be walking to his car . . . .

***

When the morning sun broke through the slit in the curtains Haley was surprised she had slept through the whole night still in her clothes! Knowing police back up was just down the street must have settled into her subconscious like a calming wave lapping onto shore. After her shower she stood on the lanai watching the morning activity on the streets below. The ocean sparkled with the glittering dawn, catching surfers knifing through the waves as a new flow of tourists and locals flooded Waikiki.

The buzz of the cell phone brought her inside. She wasn't surprised at Chase's voice bidding her a good morning and asking if she would like to help him out today. He already knew the answer to the nearly rhetorical question, she was sure, but she agreed anyway for the record. He told her to meet him out in front of the hotel.

While waiting for Chase, she called Amelia. No response. When Keoni arrived she asked if there had been any reports from the patrols, or if he had heard from Hunter. Both answers were negative.

They stopped at a local bakery to buy malasadas, a yummy, doughy, sugar-dusted treat, then stopped at a fruit stand for much healthier pineapple and mangoes. With the top down and the morning breeze whipping her hair it was a perfect start for the day. She almost felt guilty enjoying Hawaii and the company of Chase without knowing Kana's fate. Almost.

"So where are we going?" she asked as they snaked up a narrow road crowded with tall trees overhanging the two-lane highway.

"Carrie's. Ever been there?"

"No. What are we going to do there?"

"You're going to use your expertise as a book person to tell me what I can't see."

"Bibliophile. That's a book person."

"Gottcha."

Savoring the top-down energizing, not to mention the company, she felt like everything was going to be great. They were going to find Kana and he would be just fine. They were going to solve Carrie's murder; Amelia would show up, and paradise would get back on its correct axis. How could anything be seriously amiss on a morning like this?

"Hey, did you realize we forgot to go to Kana's last night?" she told him with a laugh.

His mouth dropped open in surprise. "Wow. We were going to do that after the palace, weren't we?"

"Yeah."

"Hmm. Must have had other things on my mind." The twist of humor made the question abstract and she just smiled.

Not knowing Carrie through anything but their competitive literary relationship, Haley had no expectations about her house. Nestled in a wooded area in the hills behind Honolulu, the Oriental styled, single story manor was tastefully elegant, reflecting the late owner's taste. Inside, the home was decorated with understated luxury in sparse, but expensive furnishings and art consistent with the fussy former occupant. The library was done in dark, modern shelves with feng shui touches on the walls.

Chase's first observation matched her silent thought. "No mess."

Haley smiled with satisfaction as she entered the room that was dominated by books, but was subtle in its comfort.

"Considering your relationship with the murder victim I should be questioning you, you know."

She went along with the joke. "Am I a suspect again?"

His smirk dissipated any concerns. "Let's say I consider you a person of interest."

The wry tone made her laugh, then she felt a little guilty at the inappropriate humor at the expense of a murdered colleague. "Mahalo. I'll take that as a compliment."

A conversation grouping of plush chairs resting on an ornate Oriental rug gave the place a warmth and coziness difficult to define in such a large room. Multi-leveled shelves displayed rare, old books from behind museum quality glass.

"Magnificent."

Lost in the quality of the collection, she grazed past the titles with appreciation and envy. There were amazing books here, of varying ages and restoration, many were collectors' dreams. Only when Chase theatrically cleared his throat did she return to her assignment.

"Here," she pointed to a waist-high shelf where oversized books dominated the row. They were not Simon Book Club editions, and after being granted permission, she reached to pull one out, then stopped.

"What?" he asked, standing next to her shoulder.

In the close, unventilated room, she noted the pleasant scent of his aftershave, then shook off the fanciful distraction. "There's a gap here between the books. A volume is missing." She threw a gesture around the walls. "Note how the other shelves, all of them, are neat. Carrie was a neat freak, you know." She gazed around. "There's a large book missing." She read some of the titles in this section aloud. "Underwater Photography. Explorations Under the Sea. Kingdoms —" she gasped and straightened, grabbing onto his arms. "Keoni! This is like – hey -- there was a book stolen from my shop, from the fantasy section! It was about Atlantis and other mythical, magic kingdoms! Like the book that's missing from this set!"

Clearly confused, he shook his head, scanning the titles on the shelf, then stared at her. Gazing right into her eyes with his dark, brown, deep . . . .

"What does that mean?"

"Uh – I – uh – don't know for sure," she stuttered. Realizing she was still gripping onto him, she let go and backed up a few paces. "I had a missing book, she has a missing book, Amelia has missing ship's logs, and who knows what was stolen from Kana's."

"Which means Amelia could be the one who is trying to collect the books –"

"No. Then why mess up her own library?"

"To fit the pattern of the crimes and throw suspicion away from herself. She's a cunning veteran of the spy craft –"

"She a collector," Haley shot out, practically stamping her foot in adamant support of the elderly woman. "No one who loves books like she does would vandalize a library," she guaranteed, bringing their rapid-fire debate to a standstill. The defense was instinctive and sure. "Besides, she's Kana's friend. Aikane. It means a lot to them."

He chuckled and nodded. "To us, too, I hope, Haley. And I hope Amelia and Kana appreciate what a loyal aikane you are to them. So you think someone is looking for these ship's logs. Amelia and maybe Carrie and maybe Kana had them? That leaves only – who else is there?"

"Teo."

Chase shrugged at the suggestion. "He's never struck me as the literary type. I was thinking of someone else in the book circle."

Ah, she thought she knew. "Sam Simon as the odd man out."

"Sam Simon," he ruminated with pleasure. "I still haven't had my chat with him –"

"We –"

"No, I'm handling him alone."

"I have a right –"

"To do your job and let me do mine. I'm dropping you off at Kana's. We can finally have a look at those logs and then you're going to let me be the detective like I'm supposed to be. I'm interviewing him alone."

The firmness in his tone was absolute. She was not going to get around him this time. As they exited, Haley wasn't sure which she was more pleased about; definitive progress on the case, the inclusion of Simon as a suspect, Keoni including her in the investigation, or the secure hold he had on her arm that he did not seem inclined to release.

They took the freeway across town, toward the dominating hulk of Diamond Head to the crowded stop-and-go-bumper-to-bumper traffic heading into Waikiki. Sailboats bobbed offshore in the azure sea, thready clouds drifted across the blue-blue sky, baking her skin through the Coppertone. Again she was reminded of perfection. She had jinxed herself a few days ago when such thoughts strayed during her bike ride to work. This was better, though, and much closer to flawlessness. Aside from threats and violence, Kana's disappearance and a murder, it was pretty close to an ideal holiday.

Chase escorted her to Kana's shop with wary tension. Inside he made a quick sweep to assure they were alone. She made a check of the logs and they were still safe. She showed them to the officer and asked if she could keep them here to check while he was gone. He agreed, making a point to lock the door behind him when he left. Then she started a much-needed inventory.

Engrossed in scrutinizing every book on the shelves, Haley did not accomplish much before there was a knock at the back door. Startled, fears spiking, her heartbeat regulated when Keoni announced himself and called her name. She went to the door and opened it.

"Next time I'll call you on your cell," he promised. "Are you all right?"

"Just a little jumpy being here alone. That didn't take long."

"I couldn't find Simon. I'll try again later. What are you doing?"

She explained her methods of cataloging the books and trying to determine if anything was missing. She had discovered nothing obvious. Chase took time to go over the desk contents, looking into checkbooks, bank statements, anything else that would provide a clue to where Kana might be or what he had been doing on Monday. Both considered nothing seemed out of order; no big withdrawals from any accounts, no big sales, and no plane reservations to Rio, he joked. It was, as he had theorized, that Kana took off on some adventure and did not bother to notify anyone of his whereabouts.

Dissatisfied with the working hypothesis of the police, Haley could offer no proof to counter the conjecture. Nor could she offer any sinister theft. All the books she was familiar with here were still here. It would take a few more days to replace everything, though, so nothing was conclusive. When he suggested they break for lunch she agreed. While out they could swing by her hotel and pick up her laptop.

The hotel's café with the great view of Waikiki was chosen for convenience. While waiting for their food Haley went up and grabbed her computer. During the meal she shared her findings with Keoni.

An Internet search of Amelia Hunter revealed some things she didn't know. The biography was extensive, mentioning her spy service during the war and her second career as an author. In the Pacific she traveled alone, often out of contact with the Navy for months, yet she succeeded in eluding Japanese efforts to capture her. When she did encounter the enemy, she did not hesitate to do whatever it took to survive. No body count was given in this day and

200

age of political correctness, but Amelia had defeated not only human opponents, but the sea and jungle as well.

The bio brought Chase back to his pet theory about Amelia being involved with the crime spree. "She's got what it takes to take care of business." Chase promoted his case as he munched around fries and a mouthful of mahi-mahi burger.

"She's innocent," Haley maintained. She called Hunter's house again. Still no answer.

"The only way to know for sure is to talk to her face to face," Chase suggested. "As soon as we're done we'll head out there. First, do you want to split a slice of macadamia nut pie?"

"No fair, I haven't exercised most of the week!"

"I'll take you swimming later," he promised as he flagged down the waitress.

***

Pulling up in front of the beautiful manor in the bright morning sun brought out details lost during their evening visit yesterday. The Black Point estate seemed a little rumpled around the edges since it hosted a murder. Some gravel and shrubs from the Oriental garden at the side would never be the same again from foot traffic and what looked like a vehicle backing over bushes and statuary. Yellow police tape stretched across the gate to the backyard as well as the front door. The owner must have used the garage to get in and out since the wild events.

The frantic barking of the dog echoed behind the door before Chase knocked. He repeated his actions several times, each pound louder than the rest. The Labrador barked out at the intrusion, but never came to the door.

"Hoku's not much of a watch dog, but she's good with leftovers, Ms Hunter told me. More likely to lick you to death instead of bite you, so no worries. But she can't open doors."

Worried about the way-too-long lack of response from Hunter, she still had room in her attention span to comment on his observations. "So you like dogs?"

"Sure. You?"

"Yeah. My cousin has a sweetheart of a Retriever mix who's just as vicious as Hoku. What does Hoku mean, anyway?"

"Means star," he translated.

With another knock, and more whining from the dog, she voiced her worry. "Do you think Amelia is all right?"

"You're really worried, aren't you?"

"She hasn't looked well lately. This whole thing with the murder in her house was rough." The correlation between her own experiences and Amelia's made her shiver with empathy. The last few days she had been concerned about the criminal aspect of all this on Hunter. Sympathy for the older woman's health surfaced above all other considerations now. "Maybe she's unconscious or something. She hasn't answered her phone."

A door slammed. The barking intensified in volume and distress.

"Is that from the beachside?" Haley's sense of direction was confused. The background noise of the ocean crashing against the rocks, the brush of wind against her ears, she couldn't sort it all out.

"Stay here!" he ordered and sprang through the back gate, which was unlocked.

Not about to stay by herself she sprinted after him. Crashing through the low bushes at the edge of the lawn, then into the Oriental garden where they dodged statuary and shrubbery, she slid to a stop when the taller, more athletic cop vaulted over the sidewall. Her knees and body were in no shape for extended physical maneuvering, but she hiked one foot on a Chinese figure and lifted to grab onto the top of the lava-block wall that was taller than her average height.

She caught a glimpse of Chase racing down the small side street, then turning the nearest corner. What was he doing? Hoku was still barking like crazy inside the house. What was going on? Another break-in? When she spotted Chase briskly returning while talking on the cell, she knew she had stumbled into trouble again. Carefully sliding down to the ground she kept her back against the rough edges of the solid lava barrier. Was there an intruder inside? Or did one just escape? Chase certainly wasn't chasing Amelia! The image of the ex-spy trying to elude a cop with an appropriate pursuit name was a momentary droll twist to the situation. The fear of confronting the monster-sized Teo sobered her quickly. When Chase jimmied the latch to open the back gate she hurried to stay by his side.

"What is it?"

"There was someone in the house."

"Did you see him?"

"I don't even know if it was a him. I heard someone running, then a car driving away. By the time I reached the corner the car was gone."

"Was it Teo?"

He gave her a stern stare. "I couldn't tell."

"I'm nervous, okay?"

203

Chase took hold of her fingers, keeping his right hand near his revolver. Casting occasional glances at the grounds and the detective, they circled around to the garden. Opening the side gate allowed them both into the rear of the property. When they passed the small cottage behind the house Chase commented that Amelia told him she kept some of her collectables in there. He led the way to the kitchen's back door and pointed to the broken jam.

"Pretty slick to notice that just running by."

"Mahalo. I'm going to check inside. You stay here this time!"

"No way! I'm with you."

His lip twitched with irritation. "Just – just do exactly what I say all right?"

"Absolutely."

Wild scratching and whining from Hoku came from the closed door leading to what was the dining room if she remembered correctly. With expert skill Chase turned the knob and quickly opened the door, keeping his revolver ready for any threat. Then a big mass of black smothered them. Hoku, licking and whining to receive their undivided attention, was jumping all around.

"You stay here with the dog," he ordered, hefting his revolver, then crept into the next room.

Disobeying his instructions, she followed, Hoku at her heels. She was shocked to see books and pictures were strewn on the floor in the dining room. He pushed her back against the wall and whispered for her to stay out of the way. Then he disappeared around the corner, into the next room.

The silence and the solitude unnerved her. This was the part in mystery novels where the perpetrator raced out from some concealed hiding place, eluded the officer and collided with the innocent bystander. Then of course the sidekick was killed! Too nervous to stay alone with only the too-friendly Hoku, she crept through the house, tracking the trail of debris.

The living room was tossed negligently. Books, magazines and cushions were thrown about with no regard to value. Without touching anything, or following in the obvious foot marks of dried mud, she crouched down to study the books so shabbily mishandled.

Books! The library! Knowing the study filled with rich literary works, she only took a few paces before halting, her abrupt stop surprising the dog, who ploughed into her calves. An armed policeman was in the house and this was not a good time to go dashing around on her own. Should she call out and alert him? What if the bad guy was still here? Not anxious to get another hit on the head, or worse, and not relishing stumbling onto Amelia's dead body in the other room, she decided caution was the wise choice. Curbing her impatient curiosity and worry about the books, she took a moment to look over the tomes in this room. She noted that only big books were tossed open, torn or their covers bent back.
So the robber was looking for big books. Big fantasy books about myths.

"Are you all right?" Chase called from somewhere toward he back of the house.

"Yeah."

Hoku took off to track the sound, she supposed. She followed, pleased when the black dog traipsed into the library.

"I told you not to come in!" the peeved voice shouted.

Jumping, she gasped out, "No, you told me to stay out of the way. . . ." her voice fizzled away as she rounded the desk and confronted the inert body on the floor of the elegant library. "Oh no."

Kai – she couldn't even think of his last name. Kai, the big Hawaiian who tagged along with Kamala and Teo in their political aspirations. She knew almost nothing about the nice, pleasant man who had been friendly to her in unconditional aloha.

"Poor guy. He was – was a nice guy." She pressed a fist against her lips so she would stop babbling in a verbal show of her shock.

Poor Kai. How much had he followed Teo in passion against modern Hawaii? How had such an easy-going guy met a brutal end here in this quiet library? Amid books and relics of his ancient homeland, the huge man had fallen to something as elemental as what looked like damage to the back of his head. As with Carrie's body, Haley wanted to look away from the blood and death but just kept staring at the ultimate residue of violence.

Behind her, Hoku slid against the back of her leg and whined. With firm force, Keoni grabbed her arm and pulled her away from the doorway and down the hall. He didn't stop until they were out on the back lanai and he pushed her onto the bench. His arm gently rubbing her shoulder, he encouraged her to take some deep breaths.

"I'm okay," she assured in a voice that was shakier than she thought she could sound. "I'm okay," she repeated.

"Sure? You're pale and cold."

"Fine. I'll be fine. What is he – was he doing here?"

"I don't know –"

"It's so confusing! It doesn't make sense –"

"Haley, Haley, just relax. Don't worry about this, okay, that's my job." Gently he led her away, Hoku trailing behind. He had her sit on the block wall near the ocean. "I'm going to call for back up and forensics and check around. You stay put. Promise?"

"Promise."

"You're sure you're okay for me to leave –"

"Yeah. Go. Do your job. I'm fine."

Staring at the foaming surf crashing against the black lava property line gave her a focus. The fresh air pumping in and out of her lungs surged the purity of the sea breeze and ocean spray into her system. Hoku placed a wet nose on her knee in sympathy and she scratched the mutt's head in appreciation.

With a stick she drew designs in the sand of the nearby garden. Hoku sniffed at her instrument, but soon drew bored following the swirls and lines of the tool. Frustrated and impatient, Haley drew out letters.

WWSD?

What would Sherlock do?

When Keoni emerged from the house, she scribbled through the letters and stood up to meet him. "I don't know how you get used to this."

"What?" Keoni asked quietly.

"Death. It just comes out of nowhere."

"I don't get used to it." He sighed, flustered. "But I get used to handling it. As soon as back up arrives I'll have them take you home."

"I'm afraid the next body we find is going to be Kana's," she barely whispered, the fear that violence had already extended to her mentor alive in her imagination.

Dark knots of dread settled in her stomach with the memory of long-ago anguish. She had not felt this kind of hurt since her beloved grandmother died. The kind of emptiness that was really filled with heartache – a loved one gone -- replaced with pain. She was not ready for that mourning for Kana.

"There's no reason to think that, Haley. Kai wasn't connected to Kana."

"That you know of. Yet."

"You're jumping to conclusion –"

"Amelia is Kana's friend. Kai's dead body – he is dead, right?"

"Very."

"Kai's body is found at Amelia's. Just like Carrie's. Two dead bodies in the same house. Even Inspector Lestrade would figure out they were connected."

"Who?"

"A detective who was never as bright as Sherlock. I'm not insulting you, I'm pointing out the obvious," she told him. Turning from the calming sea to look into his eyes she felt back on her axis. She was only an expert in fictional murder mysteries, but from them she had learned enough to bring the unreal into the reality she was living through now. "Kai's death has to be connected to Carrie's. Her murder's got to be connected to Kana's disappearance. What about Amelia? Is she dead, too?"

"There's no sign of her in the house."

She breathed out a sigh of relief. "Maybe she's disappeared. Or been killed."

"And maybe she left to get some supper and Kai came in here to steal something."

She gave a tentative glance at the house. "Could he be the guy who broke into Kana's? Did he know Carrie? How does this tie into Teo? He's the one who tried to break into Kana's. Maybe they were working –"

208

"Hey, pau[4] already," he insisted, holding up his hands in surrender. "That means the end. We have too many questions. Let's not make guesses. Let's just work with the facts, okay?"

Calmed, pleased, she gave him a wavering smile and nod. "Excellent. Sherlock would be proud."

"Thanks," was his wry retort.

The lab team, headed by the ever pleasant Danny Cho arrived sooner than she expected. Or perhaps it was the timeless mysticism cast by the enchantment of the ocean's lulling waves and the Trade winds' mellow sway that slid her mind into a state of null, non-time. The magic of the ebb and flow of the tide seemed to freeze time itself as the wave remained the only motion.

"Having a rough vacation in paradise, yeah?" The skinny tech, Cho, smiled at her as he toted his equipment into the house.

The rhetorical and all too cheery comment seemed out of place at a murder scene, but typical of the police geek's nature. Perhaps it was a coping mechanism to keep the gruesome profession livable? She suspected Cho was probably effervescent no matter what he was doing or wherever he spent the day.

Chase escorted her through backyard where she was sternly invited to sit on the wicker love seat just beyond the kitchen. She kept calm by petting Hoku and keeping the lovable mutt from pestering the police, while she watched the patrolmen, then the forensics team, gather and move equipment inside. Knowing she was not cleared to go anywhere else, she impatiently waited, biding her time while watching the surf play on the rocky shore, studying the sea

---

[4] Finish

birds swooping near the reef, spying a few dolphins arcing through the undulating ocean, and sorting through her theories.

When police emerged from the back door, Haley scurried to the lanai. When they took the bagged body out she stayed clear, but was close enough to hear the medical examiner. He told Chase, who followed him outside, that further reports on the head wound would be faxed to his office. Then Cho exited with boxes in both hands. He swerved over to smile at her.

"Kinda different seeing Chase's date at crime scenes."

"I'm not his date."

"Whatever."

"Does he – uh date a lot?"

"Not that I've seen. You're an improvement. See you at the next murder, yeah?"

Chase held onto her shoulder and steered her to a padded bench facing the ocean. "Never mind him, Danny has no social skills. How are you doing?"

"Okay. How about you?" She wasn't sure she believed his comment about getting used to the bodies. He seemed too sensitive for that tough-guy attitude.

"This is part of my job, remember. I'm puzzled. Kai. Tough for a sumo wrestler to take him down. Someone, though, managed to crack him on the back of the head, with what looks like a blunt instrument, with enough force to kill him."

"Blunt instrument. That's a rerun. You're not suspecting Amelia –"

"Even though this is her house and her second dead body here this week, no. She wouldn't have the strength for a blow that hard. But who else was in here hanging around in her house? I have to go with the theory Kai was taken by surprise. He's not the type to get into a fight and lose. They – whoever was ransacking the house and searching for something -- closed the dog up in the dining room. Was it someone the dog knew? Locking her in the dining room indicates otherwise.?"

"The dog in the almost night."

"What?"

"A Sherlock quote. Do you think Hoku would have attacked the killer if it was a stranger?"

They both looked at the dog, who mistook curiosity for affection. She trotted over, tail wagging so hard she almost moved sideways. Hoku basked under the petting that doubled for Chase examining her. He reported no evidence that she scratched or bit anything except some nasty smelling dog food.

That made Haley wonder about the dog's care and she headed for the kitchen. Food and water bowls were filled. Hoku was spoiled.

Chase continued. "Or did Kai come with someone – like Teo – to toss the place? Maybe Teo and Kai had a fight and Teo killed him. His killer had to be the person we heard running away." He pinched his lip in thought. "Teo is one of he few people who could get Kai off guard and come up behind him and . . . ." he cleared his throat. "Well, Teo is strong enough."

Dazed that she had so misjudged poor Kai, Haley just shook her head. He didn't' seem like an accomplice. Something else was bothering her. Echoes of Sherlock's great question of the dog in the night. The dog behind the door. She scratched the head of the faithful Lab who seemed upset by all this madness. Haley knew exactly how she felt. Crime was not easy to deal with. Popped off the pages of safe and sedate mysteries, reality death and violence was extremely unpleasant.

"We need to check the library."

Chase's lips set in a grim line, he nodded. "I was waiting for that."

"And we have to find Kana."

"We will." His confidence was absolute. "Let's go look at some books."

Coursing back through the hallways filled with elegant vases and antique treasures, she marveled at the amazing life Hunter must have enjoyed. Rooms filled with impressive, yet tropically understated furnishings. Decor spoke of a personality appreciating the fine things of life, using them to enhance a living space rather than show off wealth.

In the library, she looked automatically to where the body had been. The markings and blood were covered by a tarp now, thankfully, and she could focus her thoughts on the rest of the room with more ease.

He took hold of her hand. "You don't have to do this now," Chase quietly reminded with a whisper in her ear.

The intimate concern warmed her tentative nerves and strengthened her resolve. "No, I can handle this. I was just observing. Sherlock always says we see but do not observe."

Smiling, he asked what she observed and reasoned.

"I don't know about deductions yet. That's your department. Did you notice, though, only the big books are damaged, the others were just thrown around," she ruminated, releasing her hand in his to gesture at the evidence. "The killer was looking for something inside

212

a bigger book. I'm going to guess a ship's log." She glanced around, needing his reassurance on another obvious point. "Is Amelia dead?"

"I don't know."

"What do you think?"

"I don't know yet."

Blowing out a relieved breath, she told him she was not giving up hope. She had to believe Kana and Amelia were alive and all right. She searched the floor, groaning, not in physical pain, but emotional torment at the damage wrecked on such valuable and precious artifacts as the books in Amelia's collection.

"They're ruined. So many ruined," she cringed, flinching at the ripped covers and fragmented pages littering the floor. Most of the multitudes of books were on the ground and she hesitated to step in and further damage the manuscripts.

"It's okay, they can be repaired." He patted her shoulders with encouragement. She could hear the smile in his voice, when he long-sufferingly sighed, "You're as bad as Kana and his reverence for these dusty volumes."

"We have to find out about the books that were on the oversized shelf." She carefully picked her way through the debris on the ground, skipping and hopping at some points to keep from stepping on tomes or torn pages. At the bookshelf in question she stopped and scanned the ground. Two of the volumes she sought were closed. On the shelf, there were bits of parchment. She pointed it out to the detective. "That is the same kind of material used in the old pages of the manuscript. It was here!"

"What?"

"The ship's log that was sent to my shop. Or the one from Kana's, or another journal very much like it."

Her gaze traveled the room, her eyes scanning without seeing as her mind churned on the puzzle. She stared at the wall, the painting of the Pacific Star, when her eyes refocused. Painting. Familiar. Same style and colors as the art at Kana's apartment. She gasped.

"You see it, too," he confirmed her unspoken question, standing next to her, also staring at the framed art.

"Yes! The same artist created this painting and Kana's."

Chase stood close to the picture and Haley joined him. Finally she sighed, frustrated that they were inching their way so slowly to conclusions.

"Not so easy in real life," he relaxed, looking at her with amusement. "If this was one of your mysteries you could skip ahead to the last chapter."

"I never cheat like that. Spoils the suspense."

Hoku was cozy at the base of one of the shelves, stretching atop a first edition of a Dickens novel. Good taste. While not placing a finger on anything, Haley did peer at several of the large books with critical scrutiny, lying down close to the hardwood floor to check inside the coffee table books that were purchased from Super Simon Books. When Chase joined her, she directed his attention to her discovery.

"Just like Kana's. This book has been hollowed out, just like at Kana's! So maybe Amelia had the ship's log in here before she sent it to San Diego."

"Okay."

"Either the murderer discovered it, or he discovered the hiding place. This has to be what the murderer and the kidnapper are after! Whatever is in the book is the key to everything – that is probably why Kai and Carrie were killed! They were searching for the book

214

and never knew that Kana, or Amelia, sent it to me until it was too late! That's why Carrie, or maybe Kai, or accomplices, ransacked my store and my place. But they were too early by a day!"

Seizing her by both shoulders, he ordered her in a calm, but firm tone to take a breath and relax. He insisted she tell him her theories in a rational and sensible manner so he could understand the crazy picture she was weaving.

"You jump to conclusions with no evidence!" he nearly yelled. "Hunter has been out of touch since Carrie's murder. The thing that blows your theory is we don't have a connection between Kai and Carrie or Amelia. Kai is tied to this only because his dead body was found here. He didn't have an interest in books or myths –"

"That we know of –"

"Kamala would have mentioned it yesterday at the palace if Kai was involved with Teo's passion of the old legends. Kai was involved with HRC. Books wouldn't have blipped on his radar."

"He knows Kamala and she could have introduced him to Kana."

Chase shook his head, either in exasperation or a negative. "And what did you mean about kidnapping?"

"Maybe Teo kidnapped him to find out about the book. Maybe he's got Amelia, too."

Scanning the room, pacing around the mess, Chase toured the area and came back to stand next to her. "We're skirting the obvious. The common denominator in all of these people is Kana. Amelia could be responsible, directly or indirectly, to Carrie and Kai's murders, and possibly the murder of Kana—"

"No. He can't be dead. And besides, they were friends –"

"Sometimes that means nothing when measured against other priorities," he scoffed.

She did not – could not -- believe Kana was dead. "You said she couldn't have killed Kai –"

"You pointed out yourself that this is her house where two murders have occurred. Maybe she had help. Maybe she's in collusion with Teo! I don't know yet, but she's very suspicious."

"She couldn't have killed anyone," she defended, but knew Amelia had killed during the war. Did those skills ever – to use a pun – die? Could you really forget how to kill?

"Are these books valuable? The one sent to you?"

Haley was still upset with his attitude. "You're being cynical."

"Realistic, I'm a cop."

Admitting it only to herself, there were grounds for suspicion of the former spy. Haley hated to think Kana's old friend had betrayed him and was capable of murder, or misleading all of them, and getting away. Anything was possible, though. "Amelia is an old woman –"

"An ex-spy who knows how to kill, lie, evade and steal. She's looking like a prime suspect to me. Not alone probably, she needed help with Kai, but I can't ignore her as a person of interest."

Reluctant, but intellectually agreeing with the assessment, she countered, "Why? What's the motive?"

"The mysterious ship's logs?"

"She sent it to me –"

"Someone sent it to you using her name. We won't know the truth until we examine it and you've got that in San Diego!"

If Amelia betrayed Kana, then was there any hope of finding her mentor alive? She could not accept that anything less. "To Kana and

Amelia aikane is important. A trust. Like giving your word. Besides, Kana is an excellent judge of character. He dislikes Teo, right?"

He grinned and agreed. "I won't discount the friendship, but you have to consider that whatever is at the bottom of this string of violence might be more valuable than a friend. its worth a lot of violence and two murders so far."

Miffed at his narrow view of the case, at him thinking realistically -- like a cop -- she refused to believe Amelia would betray Kana. She was too nice of an old lady. There had to be an outsider murdering these people, not someone she knew. Even as she thought the defensive refusals, she knew they were naive and blindly loyal, but hoped they were closer to the mark than Chase's theory.

His cell phone rang and he responded, seemingly happy to have a distraction from the argument. "Cho is back to finish up. I'm going to talk to him."

Again she was left on her own. Walking out to the beach with the dog, she called her bookstore and when Amy answered spent a few minutes catching up on vague summaries of what had been happening here, carefully avoiding spilling too much about any more danger or Lieutenant Chase. When her cousin came on the phone, she asked what news he had on the log.

"It seems legit," Gar told her with uncharacteristic excitement. "Seems there were a number of these ship's logs sold in the last few years. Several at auction. And the cast of suspects who wanted to buy them is going to sound familiar. Sam Simon, Carrie Kahunui, and Amelia Hunter."

Haley released a low whistle. "Wow."

"Yeah. Apparently, this sea captain was known for some rollicking adventures. The logs are entertaining and he's a pretty popular historian if you're into this kinda thing. Anyway, Hunter ended up buying two of these goodies over the last few years at auctions. You know, though, for every book that goes to auction there are private collectors behind the scenes trading a dozen more."

"Right."

Gar might be a surfer with a part time job at a bookstore, but like Haley, he and Skye grew up to inherited money. This generation of Wyndhams came from unassuming paternal grandparents, who owned car dealerships in Southern California in the post World War Two years. The business, known within the family as gold mines on wheels, sprouted fortunes for all the relatives. They weren't filthy rich, but they understood wealth and appreciated it.

Chase joined her as the lab team cleared out.

"Look, Gar, gotta go. Thanks a million. I'll call later."

Hanging up, she stepped over to the door to await the final exit of the techs.

"Trying to make captain this year, huh Chase? Arranging all these crimes to make yourself look busy?" one of the stocky Polynesian men joked.

"If I did that, then I'd make the solution look easy, too, Nephi," he fired back with a wry twist of his lips.

"Yeah, bro, pretty akamai."

"Mahalo." The sarcasm was as thick as lava.

Cleared to go inside again, they returned to the library. Willing to indulge her fantasies, as he labeled them, he looked over her shoulder as she checked one of the Simon oversized books that had

already been examined by the techs. There was an expertly sliced
hole dug out in the center, which would hide another book easily.

"Okay, what can you tell me about Carrie's tie in with you and
Kana and Amelia?"

Instead of a history connection, Haley gave her theories.
"Carrie collected rare books. She wanted the journal. That was
probably what she was looking for when she was killed." She
revealed the information Gar had given her, trying not to sound too
smug about her continued skill at detective work. "So Amelia, Carrie
and Sam all wanted these journals. Did you know Carrie was dating
Sam Simon?"

Chase was making notes. "Great. This keeps getting better.
Why didn't you say so before?" He scowled at her. "I thought he was
stalking you."

"I didn't say that."

"You said he was following you –"

"He was but not stalking – never mind!" she snapped, certain
she could see a glint of humor in his eyes.

Serious, he questioned, "Why didn't Kana go after these logs?
They sound like just the thing he would love. And he had at least one
in his possession. But he didn't bid on any?"

Puzzled, Haley stared at him for a moment, surprised she had
not thought of that. "I don't know. He could have gone after them
anonymously. Happens all the time at auctions. But why?" She had
no answer for that.

Most of the books in the place had been searched. The detective
and bookstore owner deduced from the remaining three carved out
large books that there were three logs missing. While the policeman
was studying other details of the room, Haley started replacing

volumes on the shelves. Not in any order, but getting the fine, expensive collectables lovingly to their proper places.

"Amelia owns a boat." His pleasant voice broke through the silence.

"Right. I remember."

"There's a picture here."

"Hmm."

"It's called the Hoku Moana. In English, that's Ocean star."

"Pacific Star," she whispered.

"No, Hoku Moana. Ocean."

"Yeah, I know. And Hoku. The same name as the dog."

Haley leaped from her spot on the floor to join him at the desk. There was a nice photo of an elegant, blue and white sailing boat. The Hawaiian name was on the hull.

Her breath caught in her throat as excitement escalated. "Pacific Star is the name of the ship in the logs. Kana's ancestor was aboard the Pacific Star."

Things were coming together but she didn't understand the big picture of the puzzle yet.

"Maybe we need to make a more thorough search of Carrie's library?"

Haley sighed as she gazed around the room. "What about this mess?"

"We'll let Amelia deal with it."

"What about Hoku? Amelia might be missing just like Kana. She wouldn't leave her dog behind voluntarily, would she?"

"She doesn't seem the type, does she?"

"No. I can't sneak Hoku into my hotel. We can't let her go to the pound!"

220

"I'll make sure she's taken care of, don't worry. She can stay at my place."

Caring, competent policeman, and compassionate to dogs. This guy was almost too good to be true. "That's nice of you."

"We'll leave her here for now and I'll pick her up on my way home tonight."

They went to the kitchen to make sure Hoku still had enough food and water. Another call on the cell distracted Chase, who made angry noises as he listened. When he hung up he stared at her, the anger clear in his eyes.

"What?"

"Somehow the reporters are onto a sensational scoop. My boss is handling Kai's family and the announcement to the press, but Kamala doesn't know yet."

How did cops sort out all this emotional and professional mess every day? Small crimes, disappearances, murder – all traumatic for everyone involved she was learning. As much as Kai's demise disturbed her, she had started to see him as a statistic in the greater picture of Kana's disappearance.

"What are you going to do?"

"I should tell her personally."

"I can get a taxi back to Waikiki."

"No, come with me." He hesitated, then took a deep breath and plunged ahead. "We're in this together."

In the car, he dialed Kamala's number, but it went to voicemail without an answer. Thinking she might not have come into the city today, he called his home and talked to his brother Palani. Kamala was on her way to work. The hills and valleys of the windward coast were difficult for cell signals. Keoni told his brother he would check in at Kamala's work later.

"You didn't tell Palani," she observed after he clicked off the phone.

"No. Palani and I are both in the non-fan club for Kamala's activities and HCR friends."

"Even Kai?"

"Think about it. Kamala spends a whole lot of her time and energy hanging out with Teo and Kai. How do you think my brother feels?" His eyes narrowed. "And don't even think of including him on the suspect list."

"Who?"

"Palani, my brother!"

Aghast, she cried out, "No! Of course not! It never crossed my mind!"

He gave her a crooked grin. "It crossed mine. Goes with the job to be suspicious."

***

They cruised around the tip of Diamond Head, taking the scenic route past the lighthouse and the old bunkers that secured the rim of the volcano, before she asked where they were headed. The white, choppy curls of the cobalt waves sprinkled with windsurfers were breathtaking. The multitude of tourists snapping pictures and the various locals with surfboards atop cars attested to the weekend spirit. Everyone else seemed to be enjoying amazing resources of Hawaii, while Chase and she searched for a murderer.

Her cell buzzed and she answered the call from her cousin.

"Hey, Gar."

"Hey, cuz, we've been reading your mysterious log. I hate to tell you this but resale, this is not going to sell for as much as it could."

"I may not sell it at all, Gar. Why?"

"Damaged. Some of the pages are ripped out and some have been torn – like someone snagged a corner for a shopping list or something."

A nasty vandal had destroyed parts of the log pages, notably the sections with coordinates. Whatever the story the captain of the Pacific Star had to tell, it was a location the owner of the log wanted concealed.

"When I find out more I'll let you know. Hard reading this old stuff."

"Just keep at it. Thanks, Gar."

She relayed the news to Chase who did not have more of a comment than a shrug. Checking out their current location, she realized she was paying no attention to her own whereabouts.

"Where are we going? Carrie's?"

"We have about a half-hour to kill before we can see Kamala. I think there is a more important place to look over again. Kana's is ground zero. We're missing something there so I thought we'd head back to his place. I don't want you going back to your hotel."

"No argument." She wouldn't confess to her fears about being alone, or how comforting it had been to hang out with a skilled, armed, sensitive cop.

"So you'll stick with me for now."

Behind her hand she smiled. This protective custody was turning out very good on many levels.

Chase's phone rang and he juggled driving with talking – expertly she noted. When he hung up he was frowning. "That was the lab at Five-0. They've been running the in-depth DNA tests."

"I thought your HPD lab was state of the art?"

"It is, but backlogged. Five-0 gets things done faster. Not better, mind you, but faster."

"Do I detect a little rivalry here?"

"Just a little." He surrendered a quick grin. "There were no substances found at Carrie's murder scene that belonged to anyone but her. No blood or skin traces. HPD is still working on elements they vacuumed up from the floor, but that will take a while. Numerous prints. The lab is still sorting."

"And Kai's murder scene?"

"Too soon to tell."

At Kana's shop the cop went through the same routine of searching the rooms first. They settled into their old duties of looking through books and papers, going over the oversized volumes again. The officer even moved a few bookshelves trying to find a hidden safe or false backing. After all their efforts they did not find anything they considered important. It was almost time to leave to meet Kamala, but Chase suggested they go to Kana's apartment once more before they left Waikiki. When they went up, they checked every paper, book and record that might be useful.

Haley returned to the bookshelves in the spare room. Chase leaned against the doorframe watching her, finally asking what she was looking for, and reminding it was almost time to get on the road.

"More logs. In the oversized books. They're all getting a once-over in case there are more secret compartments."

He joined her and after a moment said, "I have a thought."

The announcement made her wary. "That I'm not going to like?"

Standing beside her he offered a wry smile. "You're getting to read me pretty well. What if Kana went off on one of his excursions? Not book buying, but in search of mokuaina pu'uhonua?"

"And not tell anyone?" She scoffed, insulted that the theory was all too possible. It was Kana's nature to strike off on adventures and not tell anyone the details. "What about the break-ins?"

"He inadvertently revealed his intentions and someone is trying to find him to stop the search."

"Then you believe in the legend of a magic island?"

"No," he refuted instantly. "But Kana believes it. Teo believes it. Others must, too."

The situation wasn't unprecedented. The Great Detective himself had faked a death over the falls in Switzerland. She wasn't thinking that Kana had constructed this crime wave – and it certainly didn't explain the things that had happened to her in San Diego. Taking off on a quest, though, that was pure Kana. It hurt to think he trusted no one with his mission; her or Keoni. Without agreeing or disagreeing, she felt it was possible.

"Like a conspiracy of silence?"

"When you put it like that it sounds ridiculous." He frowned in apparent disapproval.

"No, there's all kinds of conspiracies to protect secrets. Think about the Masonic connection to Jack the Ripper." At his blank look she rattled off a number of examples from the aliens at Roswell to the theory that the moon landings were faked. "If the secret is valuable enough, people will kill to keep it safe. What if moku pu'u – uh – whatever -- what if the refuge of Dolphin Island really existed?" His scowl made her quickly recant. "What if they believed it was real? If they thought they were protecting a sacred trust to save it from detection, then they would go to any lengths to preserve the secret!" He didn't seem quite on board with her ramblings. "Well you're the one who brought it up."

"What if Teo believed it?" he countered with such solemnity it sent chills along her skin. "What if he was trying to silence Kana –"

"No!"

"Maybe Kana went into hiding to save his life."

"And Teo killed Carrie and Kai and maybe Amelia to find Kana?" Slowly nodding, she thought through the theory. "Chilling. But still, pretty good, officer."

"Mahalo. Now we better get going."

"Just one more spot I need to check."

She went into the bedroom, Chase following, where they studied the artwork placed in four directions. Such imaginative, colorful work . . . . She gasped as the answer snapped into her memory. "The artwork, Keoni! The style and strokes and use of color – it's Kamala's!"

"What?"

"The shirts she wears!"

"Yeah, those loud ones. She designs all that stuff for her group . . . ." his voice faded away. His eyes widened. He stared at the painting on the wall in front of them. "You're right. It's hers. She knows a lot more than she told us." Anger bubbled on his expression

226

before he pushed it aside. Teeth clenched, he considered. "It's about time to go talk to her anyway."

He took her by the arm and rushed them through the small residence.

"Are you sure you want me with you?"

"This killer is still out there. Probably interested in these logs. And you are right in the middle of it, Haley. I think you'll be safer with me."

That's what she thought. She didn't argue with his authoritative command. He was not giving her a choice and for once she didn't mind being bossed around by a guy. He was a nice guy, and knew what he was doing as a cop. Keeping company with him was no sacrifice, either.

"Besides, I'm going to ask for your expertise to help me."

"Really?" To be consulted by a policeman, this policeman, was pretty cool. That it was becoming a habit was extra cool.

CHAPTER ELEVEN

"I should put you into police custody."

Calling his sister-in-law as they zoomed makai -- toward the ocean he explained -- in the Mustang, he was pleased to find Kamala in the office and told her to wait for them. Racing out to Hawaii Kai, they rocketed past some amazingly picturesque beachfront scenics. Haley was caught up in the incredible artistry of nature, reminding her of the paintings. The environmental canvas of blue sky, azure ocean, green palms, emerald mountains, spectrum rainbows, cottony clouds, all served to make for a breathtaking drive.

Kamala's small studio was located in the quaint shopping center fronting the Koko Head Marina. With the dramatic, fluted Koolau mountains beyond, the sparkling, crystal blue water, the dark wood of the shops, the colorful hulls and pristine sails, it had to be a creative artist's dream to work here. Wouldn't be bad for a mystery bookstore, either. Hmmm, something to think about for the future.

The shop, Hawaii Kai Graphics, was next to a hair salon on the corner of the building that overlooked a stretch of dock. Entering the small business was a shock, the senses transformed from tropical Hawaii to worlds seen only in imagination. A mural of planets and stars, complete with strange spacecraft, covered the wall nearest the door. Several ultra-modern, ergonomic computer desks were set up at angles facing the window.

Before arriving, she had not inquired what kind of work Kamala did, but now it was obvious. Her art was her life, and she was lucky enough to be able to earn a living doing what she loved. Liking Keoni's sister-in-law initially, she now felt a kind of kindred sprit in the vibrant young woman. It made her stomach ripple with anxiety thinking she might be a murder suspect. She prayed that nothing so sinister would come to light. Such a discovery would be so wounding for Keoni.

Kamala spotted them and waved. Smiling, she dashed over and hugged Keoni, planting a kiss on his cheek, and hugged Haley, to her surprise. Not from a family or circle of huggers, the open aloha spirit was unexpected, but not unwelcome.

"What's going on?" she asked, looking from one to the other. "Did you find Teo?"

With a compassion Haley had seen before, Keoni quietly told of Kai's demise. Arms around his relation, he gave her his regrets and offered silent support. There was nothing to say at a moment like this, so Haley hung back and tried not to watch as Kamala struggled to hide her tears of grief. Several of the stages of mourning paced through her; denial, confusion, disorientation.

After a surprisingly short interlude, Kamala composed herself and asked if she could inform her friends. Chase gave her permission to do so since his close relatives had already been notified.

"How did he die?" Kamala wondered. "Was it a heart attack?" A broken-hearted smile wisped across her lips as she explained to Haley. "Kai loved his kalua pig. Plenty of it. Always with lots of poi and rice."

Keoni placed a steadying hand on her arm. "He was murdered." Before she could react with anything more than a gasp the cop continued. "He had broken into Amelia Hunter's house and we found him there. The place had been ransacked. Maybe he came back and was searching for what he missed when Carrie was murdered. Did they know each other?"

Speechless, Kamala stared from one to the other as her brother-in-law continued. She shrugged her shoulders, but couldn't talk. After a few more tears were shed, Keoni offered to take her home.

"No, no, I'm okay. He was the easy one to get along with, yeah? The butterball aikane who loved to be included in everything we did," she smiled as tears rolled down to her lips. "He was big bruddah, we used to say." She took a breath and her composure stabilized. "And before you ask, he had no enemies. He treated everyone good. Even when we got arrested." She shook her head. "Not like Teo. He makes pilikia all the time."

"And enemies?"

She stared at him in silence.

"Who?"

She continued to look at her brother-in-law for a moment, indecisive.

"This is murder, Kamala."

"There are a lot of political enemies." She shrugged, then reached over to the nearest desk and plucked some tissues into her hand. Dabbing at her eyes, she answered, "People who oppose HRC. They want us to go away. To shut up. Teo always argues with them. But never Kai. Kai is – was – always in the background."

"Who doesn't like Teo?" Chase pressed.

"Government people, developers, real estate reps, hotel owners. The list goes on." She bit her lip and glanced from one to the other, settling on Keoni again. "Within HRC, he makes waves with his obsession to find pu'uhonua."

"Did he argue with Kai about it?"

"No. Kai went along with Teo . . . ." her voice trailed to an uncomfortable silence. "They argued sometimes cause Teo could be so hard line. But then Kai would just walk away. Teo would never hurt him. No one who knew him would hurt him."

Haley thought, but did not vocalize, that maybe it was someone who didn't know and like Kai that killed him. As much as she disliked letting Teo off the hook for something, maybe he didn't' kill his aikane.

"People were lining up to get Teo out of the way," Chase concluded. "But not Kai?"

"No," Kamala whispered.

The dead man was loyal to HRC and his aikane. He wouldn't go along with anything really illegal, Kamala was sure. Not burglary or theft or murder. Kai just cared about their Hawaiian rights. Not enough for violence.

"Let's get back to Teo. He's still a fugitive. So who hates him enough to confront him?"

Kamala sighed, then said, "Kana."

Haley was the first to defend her mentor and was well into the tirade when she realized no one objected to her ravings. Backing away from the passionate defense, she surrendered that she was just letting them know her stance.

Chase asked Kamala if Kai had any connections with Amelia Hunter. She did not know of any, she told them. Keoni had not made any notes and, as the questioning wound down, his attention was held by Kamala's t-shirt.

231

Haley noted that the woman's shirt sported the name of her company; Hawaii Kai Graphics. The signature style of bold color and design was unmistakable.

"Your art," Keoni began without preamble. "You painted the pictures in Kana's apartment. And the painting in Amelia Hunter' study."

"Yeah," she admitted proudly. "I wasn't supposed to tell. They wanted it a secret, but to me it was pretty obvious. All modesty aside, my stuff is getting pretty well known thanks to the HRC."

"Why the mystery?" Keoni wondered.

"They didn't want anyone to know about the island."

"They?" Haley asked.

"Kana and Amelia. I painted the pictures for them both. Kana wanted the four paintings of the island and Amelia wanted the old sailing ship."

"What island?" Clearly the officer was losing his patience.

Kamala pondered for so long Haley thoughts she wouldn't answers. Finally she responded by suggesting, "Let's take a walk."

Leading them out the door they strolled down the quaint, wooden sidewalk to a shave ice shop. Kamala ordered some of the luscious icy treats and they sat down at a table.

They were overlooking the heartbreakingly stunning view of the marina's indigo water and the wooden docks enhanced by the pristine lines of the boats, masts and sails. Storm-kissed, blue/gray afternoon clouds drifted over the jade, ragged cliffs at the far side of the bay. Columns of rain misted the distant scene like veils of silver glitter, and the blue of the sea was so rich it defied a name or description to Haley's dazzled brain. Could there ever be a more perfect day than this? The weather, the view, the sculptured facets of nature's infinite

232

colors and beauty -- all breathtaking. Yet, Kamala spoke of a mythical island even more rarified than this! A myth indeed. How could someone as pragmatic as Kana, or life-worn as Amelia, believe in such tales?

"Ka nai'a mokuaina," Kamala told them. "Dolphin Island," she repeated in English.

Chase shook his head in irritation. "So what is so mysterious about that?" he scoffed. "What does that old story have to do with anything?"

"Haole ears," Kamala smiled and gestured to Haley. "That means Caucasian," she defined. "Ka nai'a mokuaina. Dolphin Island. An old legend in Polynesia. Like Bali Hai."

"Shangri La," Chase translated. "More like Fantasy Island. It's a myth."

"Yeah, I know. Lemuria," Haley swallowed the smooth, refreshing, fruit-flavored shave ice melting on her tongue. "A lost island that was sister to Atlantis here in the Pacific."

"Right," Kamala agreed.

Haley supplied aloud, "A place of perfection; no illness, no discord, everyone lives there in peace and harmony. Supposedly, a magical realm where old world herbs and advanced technology created a supernatural society. It was also suspected, according to the new age stories, to have possible connections to other worlds, other portals and dimensions. Every culture has such tales, but many myths and legends have a seed of truth in them."

"This just gets better." Chase sighed, using the straw as a weapon and digging savagely into his blue shave ice. "You're not seriously suggesting Kana and Amelia believe in pu'uhonua for real, are you? They love the legend, that's all!" He looked at Haley.

"Earlier, when I was speculating that Kana might have run off on a search for the place I was just theorizing. I don't believe it!"

The possibilities were pondered for a moment by his sister-in-law before she nodded in the affirmative. "We might not believe it, and we know it doesn't exist, but that doesn't stop a kahuna and his old friend, and Teo, from their wishes. Maybe their beliefs."

The conversation was astounding, bringing her imagination to life, and Wyndham could hardly catch onto one thought when another, even more outrageous idea, popped into her mind. What Kamala said could be true. The more Haley thought of her adopted tutukane - his attitudes, the things said and not said over the years, the mysterious friendship with the former spy, Hunter - it all started to make a kind of chilling, bizarre kind of sense.

What if Kana and Amelia, who seemed to be in poor health lately, had gone seeking pu'uhonua? To escape not just the modern world, but the ills of mortality? What if Amelia sent the ship's log to Reads Like Murder as a guidepost, a clue, well knowing Haley's curiosity could not resist solving the disappearances? Deciphering a personal and emotional puzzle would be Kana's gift to her so she could understand what he had done – so she would not worry. And Haley, above all others, including his ohana, would be able to read such a clue. To understand his motivations? Didn't he anticipate that she would want to find him? How could he believe she could let this mystery drop when her life was dedicated to solving them on the written page?

Was this a conspiracy between the old friends? It sounded fantastic, but was it outside the realm of their beliefs? Of Kana taking off on a hair-brained adventure with Hunter? Why? Fulfill Amelia's dying wish to find refuge? Or to save Kana's life because he knew Teo was after him? Was Teo after proof of the magical island to further his political causes for native Hawaiians? Did Kana long to explore and discover the secret island of his ancestors? The various possibilities and motivations sent her heart plunging like an icy ball of cold dread.

"What if he went there to die?" she blurted aloud without realizing what she was saying. It was tactless and she instantly regretted allowing her own fears to be verbalized. "Sorry."

Chase's scowl told her he did not appreciate the comment any more than she liked thinking such a slap of reality. Kamala's face, though, turned from distress, to sadness, to a strange kind of calm understanding.

"I think you might know him better than any of us, Haley." She stared at Keoni. "He always had a love of the ancient and magical. As sad as it might be, that could be correct."

She reached across the table to touch her hand, and Haley's skin, basking in the tropical splendor of the Hawaiian afternoon, heated from baking in the Oahu sun, chilled as she realized Kamala was touching her with her left hand. She had eaten her shave ice with her left hand. Kamala was left handed! No – stop thinking like that! Kamala could not be a suspect in having anything sinister to do with Kana's disappearance. She loved Kana.

Keoni refuted the theory. "Kana hasn't been sick in as long as I can remember! If someone is guilty, it's got to be Amelia. She killed Kai and Carrie Kahunui and left the country."

No, Haley shook her head in silent refute. Not the kindly old lady who was clever and brilliant and funny and weak. She could not be a murderer.

Kamala gave a low groan of refusal. "No, I don't think so, either," agreeing with Haley's silent rejection. "She would never betray Kana. And she would never leave her dog."

Did it come down to the dog in the night? What kind of a person would abandon a loyal dog? Someone who was desperate? Did Amelia leave to follow Kana? In her weak health, Amelia would never survive an ocean voyage alone. Kana had to be helping her; to die out at sea? What did any of this have to do with the magical island of dolphins and the evil Teo, she wondered, fingering the amulet around her neck.

"I don't like it any more than you do!" she snapped back. "The only way we're going to find out is if we can find Kana!" Haley told them, refocusing on her main goal.

Snapping to his feet, Keoni threw the rest of his shave ice in the trash and grabbed Haley by the hand. "Come on, then, we're going to find him."

With a wave to Kamala, who gave her a sign of crossed fingers for luck, she practically jogged to keep up with the rushing detective. When they jumped into the Mustang, Chase had the engine running and the machine rolling before the doors closed.

"Where are we going?"

"I wish I could drop you off at your hotel."

"Why?"

"Why do you think? Maybe I should put you into police custody."

"I hope that's a joke."

"Not far off. I've never met anyone who needed a keeper more than you."

"I've led a normal life up until this week! Well, not normal, but not like this!" The words finally penetrated. "But you're not taking me to the hotel," she evaluated, hanging onto the dash as the car whipped around a corner, peeling through the quiet lanes interlaced through the shopping center along the waterway. "We're heading to the marina office?" she guessed, as the Mustang targeted the end of the street that dead-ended into the boat dock administrative building.

"Amelia keeps her boat here. We don't have a warrant to search it yet. If it's here."

"What are you thinking?" she asked, but it was a guess. "That Amelia took Kana to find this Dolphin Island?"

"That would make some kind of wacky sense. They're aikane. She's got a boat. Kana doesn't. I can't tell you how many times they've taken off on fishing trips. And mysteriously, they never come back with any fish! What if they've been searching for pu'uhonua all this time?"

Ripping through an intersection, Chase turned the car down a driveway leading to the marina offices. How were they going to find Kana? It was a big ocean. And this theory might make sense in explaining the behavior of two old, desperate, fanciful aikane, but what did it have to do with the violence and the searches? She posed the question to the lieutenant as they screeched toward the main building, then answered it herself.

"The key is in the ship's log that Kana sent me, I'm sure of it. It was vitally important that I get that book and figure out the mystery. And Teo wanted it, too. He killed Carrie and Kai over the books. He tried to kill me in San Diego and find the log! The answer is there! We have to examine the sketches more carefully."

"You're not a detective," he countered sharply, "so it's not up to you to find out. You're a civilian."

"I've managed to do some detective work."

"Yeah." His laugh was worn. "I'm always just a little behind you."

"That's the way I like my relationships."

Pulling the car into a parking slot, shutting off the engine, he leaped out, watching her as they jogged up the steps of the rustic styled building. His voice was hopeful. "Does that mean we have a relationship?"

With a little tingle of delight the possibility made her feel happy. "I think we do. I'm not sure what kind, but, yeah, we do."

He opened the door for her. "Yeah, I'll buy that."

Chase's police badge, proffered to the harbor master, gained him access to the needed data. That included the slip number of Amelia Hunter' boat. They also learned the disappointing information that the boat had been taken out yesterday morning. Always out early in the morning and sometimes not coming back for days.

"The old girl's been taking it out a lot, lately," the gray haired, sun-wrinkled master named Herley admitted, showing them the log. Accent placing him as a transplant from Down Under, he continued. "We all like Amelia, that's why we keep an eye on her. She hasn't been looking too good, lately. We're worried about her out on the ocean with no one around in case of an emergency."

That he did not seem much younger than Amelia and Kana made his remarks charming and touching. They were all watching out for each other here in a way that she had never experienced before. Aikane. Ohana, even the non-blood-relations kind, seemed to matter here. It meant something to be a friend, to be family.

What would detectives and unofficial investigators do without the busy-bodies of the world? "Does that mean you keep an eye on where she's going?" she wondered.

The trim man in the polo shirt with the logo of the marina gave her a smile and a wink. "You got it right." He showed them past logs.

"Look at the dates," Keoni told her.

"The day of Kana's disappearance."

Gazing out the window, watching the masts bob with the undulating water, the clouds sailing across the crystal sky, the policeman seemed deep in thought. Haley followed his gaze, admiring the brilliant Hawaiian sun on the sparkling blue of the bay, the contrasting nautical wood architecture of the marina center, the sculptured line of the distant mountains.

"Does Teo, the kahuna, have a boat here?" Haley wondered to the master.

Herley's eyes narrowed while his lips curled upward. "Not hardly, mate. The prices we charge here separate the riff from the raff."

"Does Sam Simon have a boat here?" Chase asked when he turned back to the older man.

"He does," the manager assured. He accommodatingly gave over the information, adding that the boat was in port.

***

Walking out to the quays, Haley resisted as long as she could from questioning the cop, lest her friend banish her from this phase of the investigation. "So why are we going to talk to Sam?"

"He's a party of interest."

"I know him better than you. I can help," she volunteered to preclude any doubts he might have about her sticking around.

"That's what I had in mind."

"Really?"

"Yeah. I guess I'm getting used to having you around."

Simon's impressive, sleek boat was tied at the far slip along a quay near the end of the marina. The magnificent craft with a sheltered pilot's cabin and at least three deck levels was clean and crisp in its blue and white trim. Simon's yacht was in San Diego, so this must be a rental, or perhaps he owned a boat in every port. He was rich enough to manage that.

As they approached, Haley watched the business magnate emerge from the lower cabin to the main deck as he prepped the vessel to sail. He spotted them and gave them a sour nod.

"Permission to come aboard?" Chase asked tersely.

"Fine," he disagreeably accepted and stood aside as they climbed up the ladder to the deck.

"Where you were this morning?"

"So much for pleasantries." Sam's eyes narrowed at the policeman, ignoring Haley. "The same non-alibi, as you called it, the last time we chatted," he shrugged, continuing with his work at coiling a rope on the deck. "I slept in. Never left my room at the hotel. What crime spree has occurred now? Don't you have any other suspects in this town? Or any other crimes to keep you busy?"

240

"This is connected. Amelia Hunter' house was ransacked. We haven't been able to find her. Any idea where she might be?"

He continued his duties on deck as they talked, "I'm not her keeper."

"Her house was searched. Isn't she one of your star writers?"

"She's also a celebrity to Haley." He stopped and glared at her. "She needs the publicity more than my store. Maybe you should ask her. Maybe this manufactured crime wave is something she and the old man Kana cooked up to attract attention."

The cold stare and the opening gave her a chance to jump in. "What's your interest in all this, Sam? Why are you still hanging out in Hawaii when you were supposed to be going back home?"

"Junior detectives have no authority here," he growled at her. He gave his attention to the officer. "I was about to call you. My boat has been searched. I wanted to file a report with my favorite Five-0."

"HPD," the younger man corrected.

Chase exchanged a glance with Haley, and she was sure he was thinking the same as she was, that this was an unexpected development. Simon's boat searched. That veered her suspicions back to Amelia despite her willingness to believe in the older woman.

"Here, I'll show you." Simon gestured to the door leading to the lower deck, and included her. "You're invited, too, Haley. Even though this isn't my yacht, I'm sure you remember the way below decks," he insinuated with a drawn out, suggestive tone.

Simon opened the door and waved for her to enter. As she set foot on the first step, she saw something from the corner of her eye, but it did not register with any identification. Just a blur of someone lunging from behind.

"Hey!"

"Ohhh!"

"No!"

Then she was falling, amid grunts and groans, the all too familiar sensation of tumbling. Next came the well-remembered pain of hitting the steps, and finally smashing to the deck.

***

Dark. It was too black and her head was ringing, hurting badly from all sides including the inner one, her breathing tight. The motors revving, the floor vibrating under body, she realized she must have lost consciousness. The slap of water on the hull, the swaying motion testified they were out on the ocean. Trying to move, she knew that the lack of air and the pains coursing through her body were from a weight smashing her.

"Keoni?" she whispered, hardly able to get that out of her compressed lungs.

She wiggled her shoulders, slowly edging her way out from under the burden as the boat jolted. Slowly sitting up, she confirmed that Chase was her companion in the hold and he was starting to stir. Gently shaking his arm, she tried to determine if he was badly injured, but the narrow strip of light seeping through the hold doors afforded her little visibility. They must be in the lower deck, the one used for storage or bunking extra guests.

"Keoni. Are you all right?"

"Not sure," he groaned. "Did he just hit us and lock us in the hold?"

"Yeah, but you have a gun," she reminded. "Are you okay?"

242

"Head. Ouch. Everything else is just sore." He groaned as he slowly sat up. "You?"

"Okay. But good thing I have a hard head." She helped him prop against the bed and leaned on his shoulder to study his head. "I don't see any bleeding. That's good."

"Yeah. Mahalo."

"Just shoot the lock off the door and we can get out of here. And you can arrest him." She rubbed her temple. "Was it Sam who hit you?"

"Well who do you think . . . ." he squinted at her. "There was someone else, wasn't there?"

"I had that impression, yeah."

A second assailant? Or had someone caught all of them by surprise? Then where was Sam? "Did you see who actually hit you?"

"No, all I was seeing was stars," he snapped back sharply. "Sorry. I'm angry at myself."

"It's not your fault!"

"Yeah, HPD looks unkindly at officers who let the bad guys get the drop on them."

She rubbed his shoulder. "Then let's go back up there and get Sam or whoever attacked us. Then we can find out about what he did with Kana."

"Great plan." He patted his belt. "Might go better against the bad guys if I had a weapon. He took my revolver."

Fear crept in and she stared at the slit of light up at the entrance. It had been so nice to depend on the solid tenacity and security of an armed cop at her side for the last few days. While the concern never left her, it decreased remarkably when she as with him. Now they were together in common vulnerability.

Fumbling in the small cabin, Haley found a switch and the uncovered bulb splashed the confined space with stark white light. She scrambled up to one of the bunks and uncovered a second porthole, adding even more light to the dingy lower deck. He reached across the narrow aisle and did the same on the starboard side.

"What about your cold piece?"

He stared at her for a moment, nonplussed. "My cold piece?"

"You know, your extra weapon that's hidden in an ankle holster or at your back."

Snickering, he shook his head. "You really do read too many novels, wahine. It's not the wild west, you know; this is Hawaii."

"Does that mean you don't have a spare piece?"

"Yeah, that's right. I never thought I needed one."

She didn't even try to keep the sarcasm from her tone. "Guess you know better now."

"I'm already reconsidering."

"Who attacked us?" The blur seemed like a large shadow – "Teo! He's killed Sam already and he'll come for us next! He's going to kill us and dump us in the ocean. That's probably what he did with Kana and Amelia and –"

"Haley," he barked, wincing at his elevated tone.

She rubbed her head in her own reaction to the loud response.

"Calm down. We're smart. There's two of us. We can handle this." He waited until she obeyed him then asked. "What makes you think it was Teo?"

"Big. He was big." There was something else, more elusive and elemental than the impression of a shadow. "Big hands. Like

when I was shoved down the stairs at Kana's apartment," she
decided.

"Okay. So Teo has made the same connections we have. Why
didn't he kill us?"

"Well, I'm glad he didn't!"

He gave her a quick hug. "I am too. But if you're right then he
is our chief suspect. Then he's killed before. Why not kill us and
make this easy?"

Fear made her voice a low whisper. "Because he wants
something from us?"

He placed a hand on her shoulder. He blew out a long breath
and stared at her for a moment. "I know this is frightening. We're in
a real jam, here, but we're alive and we're not helpless. Okay?"

She nodded, absorbing his confidence and courage. "Okay."

"Now first, we're going to see what we're up against."

Chase, with Wyndham close behind climbed the short stairs to
the door. He took a deep breath and squeezed her shoulder again.
Then he carefully reached up and rattled the wood. There was no
handle on this side of the door. He squeezed his fingers in the narrow
slit space and tried to pry it open. It was firmly locked. Slamming
his shoulder into the door, she joined him as they stood together on
the narrow steps. The actions were ineffective and painful to body
and brain. He backed down a few steps, telling her they should kick
it, when two gunshots plowed through the wood.

"Stay away from the door!" Teo shouted.

The officer looked ready to argue, but she pulled him down to
the deck, repeatedly assuring him he did not want to fight someone
who had a gun.

"Well, we know its Teo."

The fear was escalating, and she did not want to imagine what would happen if the mad kahuna shot Keoni. They were shark bait anyway, right? Yet, in the corner of her mind there was the hope that somehow they could get out of this.

Leaning on the top bunk, Chase dug his cell phone out of his pocket. She did the same. Both were crestfallen when their respective instruments would not register a signal. Again, the sense of panicked isolation and impending doom threatened to driver her into paralyzing fear, but she turned to her strong friend for moral support.

In a low voice, Chase told her to start searching the cabin. Find anything that could serve as a weapon or possibly a tool of escape or another way out of the small space. There was no other doorway, of course, but they looked anyway, as well as testing the wood around the small portholes. The construction of the ship was solid and in the tiny quarters they frequently bumping into each other as they tossed the bunk mattresses, linens, and pillows. After a few jokes about throwing pillows at Teo, Chase gave an exclamation of excitement at a new discovery. Emergency supplies. A few small boxes of extra canned food were the only items under the lower bunks. No knives or even can openers, he griped under his breath, but he elicited a triumphant snort as he emerged from his excavation with a flat metal object.

"For reflecting off the sun."

"That will be great to use when he throws us to the sharks. We can blind them," she snapped back acidly. Picking up a can of tuna she tossed it back in the box. "How about we pummel him with fish food?"

Snickering, the sarcasm did not dull his optimism. "Go ahead and sulk, but this is actually useful."

"I'm not pouting. I'm an idiot." She wiped the hair out of her face as she sputtered out a derisive laugh that lacked humor. "Sam. He was following me. He knows everyone who is missing or was murdered. Teo knows them all too, apparently. And they both know about this mysterious island." She slammed a fist on the bunk. "I'm an idiot! Sam owns Cabrillo Security!" Before he could voice whatever comment he was forming she explained. "The company that provides security for my condo, my shop, and Kana's! He owns the hotel he's been staying in! He could manipulate the security tapes for an alibi!"

"That's how he got in and out of everywhere."

"Yeah. And he must have been in it with Teo to get information on this mystic island."

"But Teo double crossed him?" the cop considered.

"I guess. Sam supplied the money and the means. Teo got ideas from Kana and Amelia and wanted those logs. But I bet Teo wants the fame for discovering the island for himself. To further his cause."

Chase gave a slow nod while holding onto his head. "Yeah. That fits. Can't prove it, but it all fits. Wish we – you – would have figured that out a few minutes earlier, Detective Wyndham."

"Me, too, detective."

There was one metal box left under the bunk and Chase dragged it out. Locked, he jiggled the lid for a moment, then reached into his pocket and withdrew a multi-function knife. Working at prying the lock, he explained, "There might be a weapon in here, or even a flair gun."

It worked in Jaws, she figured, so anything would help at this point. The box, though, seemed large and flat for a flair box.

The lock snapped off and the lid flew up. Inside were waterproof cloths folded around a square almost as big as the box. Carefully, he drew out the object and unwrapped the material. Haley gasped at the big blue book.

"My fantasy book! The one about Lemuria," she whispered. "This is the one taken from my shop!" Opening it up, she was distressed to see paragraphs and pages had been highlighted, notes scribbled in the margins. "Why would Sam want this? Because he had to understand the significance of Kana's interest in a refuge?"

"Pu'uhonua."

Turning another page, small papers cascaded onto the deck. Sorting through them she shook her head. Unbelievable. These were the address pages and rolodex cards from her store and home! Sam had secured them in the stolen book. Why? She reached for another volume wedged in the tight compartment.

"Wow, look at this!"

The next book was almost as much of a surprise. A ship's log. One very similar to the one she had found at Kana's. Kneeling down next to him and grabbing another square of cloth, she lifted the heavy item and tore off the covering. Another log book, and a third. A whole collection.

"These are just like what Kana or Amelia sent me. And what he had at his apartment inside the other book."

"Just like these?" he wondered as he unwrapped the last bundle to reveal another worn, tattered leather-bound book with brittle parchment spilling out of the binding.

"Similar, yes."

248

"You might be handling evidence." Chase gently took the one from her and replaced it in the covering. "If Simon stole this from Amelia and Carrie, then," his voice rang with intensity, "then we've got him for murder. Multiple counts."

"Is there any doubt? Kidnapping us isn't enough?" she scoffed. "He's in on it with Teo!"

"It looks that way, but at this point Simon could be a victim of a double-cross, or even a victim. Maybe he just cleared the way for Teo to murder for him. This has given us a connection to Simon. Evidence always helps tie things together in a neat package," he retorted, then visibly his expression softened and he looked at her with incredible sorrow and sympathy, so powerful her eyes started burning in sympathetic response. "He must have killed Kana and Amelia, too."

She couldn't believe that. "No," her voice trembled.

"It makes sense." He drew her into a comforting hug. "I don't want to believe it, either, but why would he keep them alive? And if they were alive, why haven't they surfaced?"

She shook her head, drawing away from his shoulder, unable to comprehend that her dear friends were dead. Her creative and agile mind quickly made the link to the next level of obvious conclusion. The killers captured the two of them with the same fate in store for them.

He replaced the lid and shoved the box under the bunk again. "Now, let's see if we can do something about being rescued."

"They're going to kill us." The thought of being under the power of the muscled, mean Teo gave her the shivers.

"We are going to be fine. Trust me."

249

He held her by the shoulders, staring into her eyes with his own filled with confidence and determination. He wanted her to believe they could come out of this alive, because he believed it. She wasn't sure she had ever trusted anyone that much – with her life.

"That's what the heroes always say before things go really bad."

"I won't let that happen." He winked. "Besides, things are already bad." His wry tone faded and he offered a reassuring smile. "And I promise to get us out of this."

"Good plan," she agreed with a confidence she didn't quite feel, but wanted to believe. "What is your plan?"

A small window above the top bunk was the largest portal to the rest of the world. Opening the shutter, Chase scanned the sea and sky, leaning on the port hole, the mirror in his hand.

"Could be worse. We could be tied up," Haley offered. When her companion did not respond she continued. "What would Frank and Joe Hardy do? They were always in a fix. Like when they got tied up they always found a convenient nails to untie their ropes. I think that was in The Missing Chums."

"And a dozen others."

She snickered. "You read Hardy Boys books?"

"Didn't everybody?"

"I thought you disapproved of Kana and his books."

"I don't appreciate that he chose his obsession over his ohana, but it doesn't mean I don't like books. Or mysteries." He gave her a lopsided grin. "I am a detective."

"You are always forcing me to reevaluate my opinion of you, officer."

"For the better I hope."

"Always."

250

The boat took a turn and Keoni speculated they had been running southwest, now, according to the angle of the sun, they were heading north. She gave him a slight smile and asked where he learned to read the ocean and sky like that. She had grown up in San Diego, Hawaii, England, the Mediterranean, and had been around boats and oceans all her life. She didn't know anything about them. He assured he had been a Boy Scout and a Sea Scout and knew enough to determine they were headed north. To the North Shore of Oahu, or to Kauai? The tone altered, and he ended with a puzzled frown.

"What?"

He grimaced at her, and gave a strong grip to her arms. "You were right. Teo could dump us in the ocean."

If she had the choice of being strangled by Teo or being thrown into the ocean she would take her chances in the water anytime. A good swimmer, as she was sure Keoni had to be, the sea was better than personal combat with a behemoth!

To avoid the fear she concentrated on fitting the pieces of the mystery together. It all seemed so elementary now that they knew the ending. Like sneaking a peak at the last page of a novel, the ending was clear now. Just like Holmes always told Watson. Simple if you know how to observe and deduce.

"Simon must have taken the wine to Kana's apartment."

"Yeah," the cop approved. "He might have eliminated Kana and Amelia out here. It's the smart way to dispose of bodies in Hawaii." His tone softened. "But he could have done that to us already. What is he waiting for?"

"Taking us somewhere?"

"Could be. Why?" He grinned. "I bet your nimble, akamai mind is already working on that. Why keep dangerous adversaries alive? We're not only inconvenient; as long as we're alive we're dangerous to him."

The conclusion to that question filled her with dread, "Information?"

"Exactly. That would tie in with all the break-ins, wouldn't it?"

There seemed only one possible explanation. "Teo thinks I or we know something."

"Yes."

Turning from the port hole he sighed. "No planes or boats spotted. We have to work out a plan," was his next, somber observation. "Teo has my revolver and could have more weapons." His snarl was suddenly angry. When he noted her – she must have worn the startled distress on her face – he mellowed. "Teo and I have a rivalry as you've noticed. He wants me dead and I want him behind bars. Our only hope is to take him off guard when he comes down to get us. If he's that dumb."

"I hope."

"Or maybe," he nearly laughed, "He IS dumb and has no plan!" Excited, he gripped her arms again, unable to contain his enthusiasm. "I don't think he has a plan to cover this contingency. Our arrival to question Simon scared Teo! It forced him to improvise. He knew we were onto him and he acted impulsively. "

"Do you think he was already here? Or was he coming to kill Sam?"

"I don't know. I'm sure kidnapping us was not in his plan. Maybe killing Simon was not in his plan, either! He might have wanted to nab you to get information out of you, or find the ship's

252

log, but you've been with me for most of two days. He may not have
had the opportunity. So he went to Carrie, and then Amelia. And Kai
must have gotten in the way, too."

She could not see a reason for glee. "So we walked right into
his trap –"

"No, he formulated a hasty and ill-conceived plot after we
confronted him. There's a difference. People are going to miss us –"

"Not for a long time –"

"But he knows they will miss us. With two other high profile
disappearances, he can't afford to be connected, but there is no way
he will be free of suspicion now. My colleagues will find my car.
The harbor guy knows we were checking around for Simon and
Amelia. Simon's boat will be missing. All of this is going to work
on his nerves like when you rub your hand on a sea star. Very rough.
He's going to make more mistakes. And then I will get him!"

It all sounded fine from an analytical point of view, but hardly
helped them now. It also painted Teo as irrational and dangerously
afraid, pushed into a corner. Human and animal nature would react
the same in such an instance; they would fight back. Teo had no
choice but to dump them overboard and hide evidence that they were
there. Once he got back into port there would be nothing tying them
to him.

The kahuna was not the only one cornered. The lieutenant was
also cornered. Who would be the more dangerous? She hoped it was
her friend, the cop.

"Teo is panicked," he was convinced.

Sorting through the clues, irritated she had not put this all
together earlier, more details surfaced. Inconsistencies hit her about
Sam Simon. The missing gold watch was usually on his right wrist

because he was left-handed. She remembered left-handers, like Sam, Kamala, and her cousin Gar, usually wore their timepieces on their right wrists. That was not the only aberration, she concluded. He had been wearing the replacement watch on his left hand. Was Sam the murderer, or was it Teo?

The boat turned in what Chase deduced was a westerly direction. Sure enough, when they looked out the port again, they were headed toward a wall of dark clouds that obscured part of the afternoon sun and the horizon. Around Kauai, he guessed, and remarked a recollection that this area northwest of the Hawaiian chain was known for unusual squalls and sudden storm fronts.

Dolphins raced ahead, now chattering and cavorting in the waves, as if trying, in their own way, to speak to the humans in the boat. One dolphin, with a nick on the right side of his nose, kept leaping so close to the boat Haley was worried he was going to be injured. Chase commented he had never seen the gregarious mammals offer such elusive invitations for sport. She had to agree. Just when it seemed the cetacean would be struck by the bow, he veered off to frolic in the waves and disappear, only to pop up a few moments later.

Increased rocking bumped them into each other and the wall, and they moved away from the window to secure a better position on the bottom bunk. Chase muttered that he couldn't understand why they were heading into a storm, then he grew quiet. Probably formulating theories silently so she would not be so worried, she guessed, which wasn't working because she was beyond worry. Sam – or Teo – whichever madman was at the helm -- was taking them into a storm so there was no chance they could survive once he threw them overboard. Or maybe threw their dead bodies over board . . . .

Think of something else! Think of something else . . . Dragging
out the waterproof box, Haley unwrapped and stacked the logs.
Chase muttered something about evidence but she ignored him. She
had to get her mind off their peril and reading was the best antidote
for fear in this little jail cell on the water. Reading was the best
antidote for anything.

She started sorting through them. Finding the front pages dated
in one form or another, she started with the latest log, dated 189 --
something. There were sticky notes with random scribbles she could
not read attached to several sections of the volume. After turning a
few pages, she found some folded sheets of stationary and graph
paper and removed those.

The notebook paper was scented, with hibiscus flowers
sprinkling the border, and with the printed name and address of the
writer. Chilled, she read Carrie Kahunui's name, realizing this was a
note from the slain book collector. It was addressed to, 'my dear
Sam'. If Keoni was waiting for solid proof to connect Sam to
Carrie's murder, they needed to look no further.

Scanning the letter, her skin chilled.

My dear Sam,
I send this along to you as the first token for our long future together.
One down, three to go.
Aloha nui loa,,
Carrie

The next sheet of paper was less interesting. Coordinates;
latitude and longitude numbers were listed in columns. Some were
crossed out; others circled, denoting a work in progress sheet. The

calculations were beyond her since she was heavy on English studies and barely scraped by in the math department. She knew someone, however, who could make sense of this.

"Well, officer, you wanted proof. Take a look at this."

Chase turned from the perch at the upper window where he had clambered up to again. She handed him the coordinate paper and explained what she had found. Excited, he jumped down and sat on the floor next to her treasure. Haley thumbed through the last log, carefully, mindful to not damage it further than the crumbling parchment was already.

As quickly as she could, she scanned the pages, now eager to find corroboration of a theory bubbling in her mind. The old language of the Nineteenth Century was a little tough, along with the faded, scrawling handwriting, to decipher, but a fascinating picture formed from the script.

The log talked about the Sandwich Islands, the queen who had been deposed, and the underground movement to protect the so called 'magic' of the monarchy. What did that mean? Adding to that mystery, the legend of pu'uhonua as the enchanted island was called in Hawaiian myth. How did it tie in with the logs? Lemuria was not named, but a place of mystery called ka nai'a mokuaina was mentioned several times.

Mokuaina pu'uhonua. Having a connection, starting to make sense of it all, was satisfying. Strangely, that mattered even when they were about to be killed. It must be what detectives felt when they have done all to solve a case and knew they were right.

"Okay, we have motive," he nodded, then handed the log back to her. "What I'm worried about is Simon's opportunity to waste us as soon as we reach our destination." Frustrated, he quietly and

256

slowly jiggled the doorknob. Securely locked, he moved the fitting
back and forth. "Maybe I can loosen it."

It was better than sitting around waiting to be killed. There was
only room for one person in the doorway, though, so there was
nothing she could do to help. "Let me know when you want me to
spell you."

Curling onto the window bench she carefully turned the pages
of the old logs, reading the difficult messages wherever legible
sentences or words were visible.

*Hagoth has --- board with --- people. They seem to def—to him.
In the ways --- natives when –ere is a alii -----. There is gr--- --argo
with Ha---- this time as well. I would guess -- ---ng journey ahead ---
--- insists they are only ------- for the northe—island of Kauai. The
strangest mood --- come with the party. ---- ---- to do with the recent
-- ----- --- of the queen. ---- bloody Americans ---- with things they
don't underst----. The crown ----ced with the mighty fist of money. I
---- seen it happ--- too ofte- --- recall. These beautiful isles --- --ver
be the same.*

A large group of people with lots of supplies boarded the ship
with Hagoth after the queen was deposed. They were on their way to
Kauai, but the captain wondered why they carried so much cargo.
This was one of the sections where sticky notes marked it as
important. Scanning the faded, incomplete messages on the brittle
parchment was tedious and she rubbed her sore eyes, then blinked, to
relax the strained muscles. Then she skipped ahead to the next
bookmarks and focused again on the old handwriting.

Before we came ---- the nor---- tip of the magnificent emerald --
-- of Ka----, Hagoth came -- --- cabin. We shar—a drink of---well. A
dr----- to the fond memo--- of the past. Those day wi-- --ver be seen
again --- the--- isles. He shook --- hand and bid --- aloha. --- --ot
say so but -- --- this is – --nal parting. Wi--- the queen impri---- he
says he --- ---- to his people here – Kauai. He --- no place --- --- go.
Perhaps that –plains the multitude --- animals, baskets of plants and -
--- crates of tools.

--long the way the dolphins --- --- the bow. Hagoth and his
people --- ---- excited about the escort. I have often --- --- silvery
creatures cavorting in --- waves alongside --- ship. I --- surprised
these Hawaiians --- --- in wonderment at the sea ----

So Hagoth and his party were relocating. The Hawaiian was
treated with respect, as if he held some honored position among his
family. She would have to ask Keoni what ali'i meant. So why was
this group fleeing? Driven out by the American planters who usurped
the government? Perhaps supporters of the monarchy had to lay low
for a while. And what was so important about this old Hagoth and his
voyages aboard the Pacific Star?

From what she could make out the next few pages were
comments on the weather and what the captain was reading from the
clouds and the waves. A storm brewed to the north and he was
concerned it was heading toward their destined bay. He ordered the
ship prepared for hard weather, and warned Hagoth they might not be
able to get them to shore if a storm beat them to safe harbor.

258

--goth seemed unconcerned at the turn in --- weather. Many times -- --ve crossed the Pac--- together. He is – mariner with—a ship and --- --ad the waves --- clouds as --- as I.

Hagoth was not worried about the approaching storm. The veteran captain, however, thought it might prevent them from stopping at Kauai. The next page was nearly illegible, but a paragraph at the end caught her attention. She moved the book into the full sunlight from the porthole to be a better view of the words.

sorry to s-- --- last of old Hagoth. What --- --orable way to see him off. --- ---- like the old days when the whalers ---- ---- to these shores. The natives ---- come out in their long canoes and gre— the ships. When we sailed --- ---- bay there were seven out------ rowed by strong men. They took Hagoth's ---- and –ods and struck out to the --- point ---- --, into the dark curtain --- nd and rain. These natives trea-- ---- like a ----- king! Soon the storm clouds swallowed ---. It turned the – ip – the bay to ---- out the weather. The playful ---pins had the sense --- ---appear in the face --- --- storm.

The canoe group from Kauai took Hagoth's party and sailed into the storm, to some secret location in the northern island of the archipelago? They treated Hagoth like – what – a king – was the captain trying to say? Perhaps Hagoth was royalty? Then that would make Kana a descendant of the monarchy. Wow, pretty cool. Kana never said anything! Such connections would explain why Hagoth and his family would flee from the American takeover of the islands. Perhaps they colonized in some remote area of Kauai's rugged and breathtaking shores. What a story! Despite the mortal peril facing Chase and her, the reader inside appreciated the amazing tale.

"This is incredible," she told Keoni.

He turned from his covert attempt at scraping away at the lock with his belt buckle. "What?"

"Do you know anything about your family genealogy? Has Kana ever mentioned that he was related to royalty?"

"No," he scoffed. "He's a kahuna."

"Yeah, but this log is talking about Hagoth being treated like he was really respected. What does ali'i mean?"

"Royalty." He gave her his full attention. "Let me see."

He scanned the pages she turned opened for him, deciphering the most difficult passages.

When the boat stopped both tensed, jumping to their feet. Above the roar of the wind and lashing rain, they heard the incongruous chatter of dolphins. Chase took her by the shoulders and pushed her behind him.

"He's going to expect you to rush him," she hissed, holding onto his arms.

"You going to suggest throwing tuna?"

A much better flash of inspiration nearly blinded her brain with brilliance. "No. Books." She could hardly believe what she was suggesting.

Neither could he. Turning to gaze at her with raised eyebrows of astonishment, he incredulously asked, "What?"

"The logs. They are precious to him. He thinks they'll lead him to mokuaina," she guessed, believing it to be true even as she spoke the flash of inspired supposition. "If we throw those at him he's going to be confused. Even for a moment – a second – he'll hesitate. Kind of the reverse of Scandal in Bohemia."

He touched her cheek. "Whatever that means. You are brilliantly akamai, Haley."

Akamai meant clever. "Mahalo," she thanked him, then grinned.

Grabbing the Lemuria book, she handed it too him, guilty she was going to be damaging priceless, old books to save their lives. "Here, use this on the bottom so maybe it will cushion the blow for the others."

Latches snapped and wood crashed above them, indicating the top deck door was unlocked. Sounds of rain and surf grew louder. Chase seized onto the stack of books. With his other arm he pushed her to the side.

"Stay out of the way, whatever happens," he ordered her.

Grabbing the metal box, she didn't know what she could do but throw this at Sam. Suddenly, any futile actions seemed better than dying helpless and unresisting.

The doors opened, splashing overcast sunlight into the dark space. They were ordered out, and unsteadily they climbed the stairs, Chase holding the books behind his back. He slid his right arm, with the make-shift weapons, along the railing, as if he was hanging on in the rough weather. Haley did the same with steadying herself with her right hand pressing the rail, while holding the handle of the metal box.

"Time to talk, haole! You gonna come on out now!" Teo was shouting above the wind.

Chase held onto her arm and stayed in front of her on the stairs.

"He means me?" she whispered.

Chase yelled, "What do you want with her, Teo?"

"She gonna show me a location. Or I kill her and you right now." He almost growled at the cop. "I gonna kill you haole-lover traitor, anyway!"

"What is he, nuts?" she muttered, then shouted back, "You're a lunatic – a – uh – pupule!" she sputtered, incredulous at his demands. She shouted back, "Where is Kana? Did you kill him? Him and Amelia?"

That was not the kind of confession she was hoping to hear, and crossed her fingers that he did not admit to those murders.

Teo's large form took up the doorway. He leaned in and demanded they come topside. He jabbed the policeman's revolver toward the officer and angrily snapped, "The old kahuna and the old woman, de split before I could find out the secret. But we learned they sent it to dis haole wahine. That's the only reason she's alive, bruddah. And you, too. If you don't tell me what I want, you gonna be fish food next."

Haley's sigh of relief that Kana was safe died in her lungs. Keoni and she were sentenced to death no matter what. Stall, just like Magnum or Travis McGee would do. Stall until Keoni or she could think of how to save their lives!

"You ransacked my place and my store! What did you think I have?" Play dumb. Maybe he'll get made enough to argue and slip up so Keoni could grab the gun! "You ruined by bookstore! And my house! Did you try to kill me, too?"

"I didn't do nothin' to you. Now get up here!"

"The bike accident in San Diego? You needed me out of the way, like Kana and Amelia!"

262

Chase joined in with the interrogation. "Then did Carrie find out? She wanted in on the action? She couldn't find the logs, right, even by tearing apart the shops and apartments. You were looking for the books or aliases or anything that would help in the quest."

"She got in de way! You're next if you don't get up here!" The boat rocked and he held onto the door jam with his hand as he switched his aim to Chase. "The log books not enough. I need de location!" The revolver swung around to zero in on Haley. "Tell me where it is!"

"What are you talking about!" she yelled back in frustration.

"Pu'uhonua!" He yelled against the wind. "You and old Kana know all about it! Kamala didn't. Amelia, maybe, but she's gone, too. That only leave you, wahine!"

She scoffed several times, speechless at the insanity. "You think the magic island really exists!" she finally shouted.

Haley stared at the scratches on the big hands of the kahuna. Her pathetic attempts to solve the crimes had been off target. Teo – she thought he was involved – the left-handed clues – meant nothing. All the intellectual theories meant nothing now that Kana was dead and they were about to be killed! It made her mad!

It was hardly triumphant that they DID have all the pieces. If only she could have made all the theories meld into a solution before! Too late to solve the crimes. Too late to save their lives.

"You tell me where it is! Now get up here! Both of you!"

Following instructions, Chase moved as if to sit on the side of the railing. A precarious spot, she felt, but she was so blind by the change in light, a sudden shaft of sun through the clouds, she could not even see the big assailant. Chase was leaning heavily on her, was it an act or was his head really hurting and debilitating him? No, he was concealing the logs from Teo.

263

Suddenly, the detective lunged, tossing the books at the gunman. The revolver barked out a shot as the kahuna instinctively shielded his face from the assault while trying to grab one of the logs. Chase tackled him and the two went down on the deck, outmatched from injury and sheer muscle-power that favored the criminal. Haley raced forward and slammed the metal box onto Teo's hand, trying to loosen his grip on the weapon.

The boat tilted and dipped in the heavy surf, throwing her away from the struggle. Teo managed to push away from Chase, but the cop scrambled back to slam the huge man. She jumped when, above the rain, a shot echoed, the bullet plowing into the deck. She managed a few jabs of elbows and fists and stomps of her feet to their assailant.

With a vicious twist of strength, Teo knocked Chase overboard and into the sea. She made a grab for him, but only caught a fist full of air as she lost balance, slammed into the railing, then bounced off and plunged into the ocean.

THE MAGIC OF KA NAI A MOKUAINA

The drop into the abyss seemed to last forever. Even through the panic she knew that could not be true, that it could not be endless. The descent into the liquid ink finally slowed, and while her senses remained rooted in shocked terror, her mind ricocheted to strange possibilities and options as she dropped. The water above was an aurora of colors graduated from her level; dark blue, to cerulean, teal, and then gold as the streams of sunlight penetrated the top layers of the sea. There was no sign of any thing beyond her -- no boat -- no Keoni.

The isolation, more than the fear of drowning or physical harm, hit her with an upsurge of primordial terror she had never known before. Shot at, attacked, eaten by sharks, left to bleed to death in the world's largest ocean; it all paled in comparison to the aloneness. In the fractional moments she had to consider it, she wrestled against the horror by kicking and stroking as hard as she could toward the atmosphere, fighting to reach upward for sanity.

Breaking the surface, she spit out water from her mouth and nose, coughing and gasping as her strong paddling kept her barely above the mighty waves. Her head was still spinning from the intensity of the descent and fight to the surface. Weak and terrified, she fought for balance in this alien territory.

Growing up on the Pacific Rim she knew how to swim, but she'd never being this far away from land or in this deep of a region.

The swells were massive, surged to powerful mountains by the grips of the heavy storm. She couldn't see more than a few dips and curls away. Where was Keoni? Where was the boat?

"Keoni? Keoni!" She shouted at the top of her lungs, spitting out the salt water splashing into her mouth. What happened to the boat? "Keoni!"

Although she was in tropical waters, cold was seeping into her skin, penetrating deep into the bones. The dark clouds surrounded her, as if they had dropped to the sea, swirling wind and spray, leaving no space; heaven and ocean merged.

Still light-headed, she started sinking, fighting to stay afloat. A hand splashed above the surface several feet away, appearing suddenly, then abruptly it sank. Calling her friend's name, she swam toward Keoni. He surfaced again, and she grabbed onto his arm, wrapping hers around his waist.

Coughing and sputtering out bitter sea, they wheezed in air, choking and swallowing more ocean. Fighting to keep above the undulating waves, they worked feverishly to maintain any kind of margin above water.

Twisting around, Haley searched for the boat. The fight for survival had taken a long time, apparently, because there was no sign of Simon's craft. Breaking the surface after another crushing swell, she thought she saw white fins. Dolphin or shark? Were the dolphins saving them from sharks?

A huge roller buried her, tearing her companion away. When she came up for air she gasped for breath, frantically calling for Chase. Suddenly a dolphin flipped out of the liquid blue, dipping in and out of the ocean around her. When a second dolphin swam up right next to her, she couldn't have been more amazed. The graceful creature bumped up against her several times, leaning into her shoulder. It seemed the logical next step was to wrap her arm around the slick body.

When the dolphin accepted her weight she grabbed onto the cetacean's fin as she had seen trainers do at Sea World. The stabilizing help gave her enough foundation to scan above the waves for Chase. Yes! There was the detective fighting to keep his head above water. The first dolphin was circling him. About to release her hold on her rescuer, the dolphin swam toward Keoni. When she was close enough she grabbed onto her friend.

"Are you okay?"

The Hawaiian coughed, gulping in air, but nodded. He enveloped her in a tight hug, then released her to hold onto the dolphin.

"Ye—ah. You?"

"Good." Stunned that he was alive, that she was alive, and that they had been saved by dolphins! all she could do was giggle in relief! It was so amazing. Before she could ask him anything else the cetacean's started gliding through the water. "Whoa, what are they doing?"

"We're hitching a ride!"

A few dips into the ocean and her dolphin picked up speed. She hung onto the fin with both hands as he spun off, taking her on a parallel course alongside Keoni's traveler. They had just been saved by dolphins! Daring to stretch her bravery and credulity further, for a moment she stroked the side of the mammal. His skin felt slippery and firm, slick like wet vinyl, and she managed to hold on through the dipping swells.

As the dolphin undulated through the waves, she tightly gripped the fin, muscles aching from her desperate hold. The drag from the water surged against her legs and she felt the rush of kelp and small sea creatures crash into her exposed skin as they rocketed through the sea.

The dolphin under her hand threw back his head and chattered, as if laughing. She noted he had a scar on the right side of his nose and knew he was the one shadowing the boat, cackling to them as he and his friends played tag with the bow.

Laughing in a thrill of joy, dazzled and stunned by the events that were too horrifying and amazing to really comprehend, she released the paralyzing fear ripping her emotions for so long. She focused on the sheer magic of the moment, racing through waves, wind and rain on the back of a dolphin! Being carried to some unknown destiny, but flying as if on water wings to that unseen future.

They dashed into the heart of the scary maelstrom of stormy, dark clouds hugging the surface of the water ahead and obscuring the horizon. The cetacean rescue squad chattered and cackled between themselves. Other dolphins joined in behind, but it was these two in the front who seemed to be the leaders; the fastest, the strongest, the trailblazers.

Weaving in and out of the huge swells and the dark gray storm clouds they had entered offered no orientation for time, direction or a chance to search for the nearest island. Numb from the overwhelming emotions charging through her system, she hung tight to the slick, slippery body of her dolphin rescuer as they sailed briskly through the wet and tumultuous weather.

Her knowledge of the beautiful creatures aiding them was limited. Many believed they were angels of the sea, helping distressed visitors through their watery realm to safety. There were other stories of surfers or swimmers who had been lead astray and far from shore by capricious dolphins. Still more reports circulated that dolphins attacked predators to save humans. Were these guys lifeguards, or jesters playing a practical joke?

As they skimmed along the water, surfing through the massive swells, the rain intensified. The ride was thrilling, propelled fast, as she held tight to the smooth skin that felt like a slippery olive. The clouds thickened and they were enveloped within a gray cocoon of mist and shadow, where even the blue of the ocean tinted to charcoal and the world turned into a sphere of liquid fog. It became a thrilling adventure for most of the ride, but when she lost sight of Keoni and his dolphin, her stomach tightened with fear. Then they would pop up again and she tried to relax and enjoy the ride of a lifetime.

Beyond the rain and rush of wind, she heard something in the distance. A motor? A plane? The boat? A ship? No one would ever see them in this cloudy mist! She shouted to Keoni, but he didn't hear her. The rain tapered off, the fog thinned, and light filtered through the dimness. They broke into the dazzling sun like an explosion, riding a cresting wave to the pristine shore of a spectacular island.

The dolphins dipped down, the humans instinctively releasing their hold as the creatures circled under the water and flipped back behind them. Her knees hit bottom with painful force, the jagged protrusions of coral stinging already damaged skin and bone. Shakily standing, she was amazed they were in shallow water and they could walk to shore. Keoni took her hand, then wrapped an arm around her waist, and smiling through his exhaustion, guided her to the sand.

Plopping down on the perfect, white beach, they took a while to catch their breaths. Before she said anything, she took in the surroundings, noting the amazing beauty around them. No cars, no trash, no noise, no planes, no swimmers. How had they landed in such an isolated and breathtaking cove? Which island was this? Maybe Kauai or Molokai, or any of the smaller, more remote islands less traveled than Oahu or Maui.

"Are you all right?" Keoni lifted himself up on his elbows. Still working on steadying his air intake, he appeared to be fine.

Giddy with relief and fatigue, she could hardly summon the energy to nod. Scanning the horizon, she thought she saw the dolphin pod cavorting in the ocean. Against the dark gray of the clouds hugging close to shore she wasn't sure. She flung out a wave, a message of gratitude for their timely – magical -- appearance.

The absurd comparison came to mind that a few days ago she had thought perfection was overrated! As if in cosmic declaration of her ignorance and smallness in the universe, her world had tipped topsy-turvy since then and she momentarily longed for that boring routine, that smug, day-to-day existence that gave her a mundane perspective on the commonplace of life.

Staring into the concerned chocolate eyes of Keoni, she amended her wish. Maybe it wasn't so bad to be beached on an exotic and secluded island strip of sand with a nice, stable and, yes, cute, guy. Forget the mundane, she smiled, glad she had experienced so much adventure and lived to tell the tale. And shared it with a good man.

"What are you laughing at?"

"Smiling," she corrected, rubbing at the side of her head to dispel the throbbing headache. "Just kind of feeling nutty that we came out of that all right. Did we really swim with dolphins?"

His matching expression was warm and sincere, "More like we tagged along. Quite a rush, huh?"

"Really." She dug her hands into the sun-toasted sand. "No need to hurry, right? We can spend a little time here not moving, right?" She fell back onto the warm beach and regretted that movement when her head reverberated from the landing.

His grin widened. "Love to. When Teo gets to port, I want my guys there to meet him."

"You don't think he'll go back to the marina, do you?"

"Why not? He thinks we're shark bait right now."

It made her fatigued brain ache thinking about it all. "I don't know. He was looking for his magic island, remember?"

"If he survived the storm, I think he would want to get back to port and establish an alibi. Besides, without you, he can't find pu'uhonua." Groaning, he moved to his knees, soppy in his wet clothes -- his nice shirt and trousers ripped from the arduous journey -- then to his feet, reaching out to grab hold of her hand. "Come on."

Sighing wearily, she longed only to relax. Maybe summoning just enough energy to remove her drenched shoes and bury her toes into the baking sand. Then she could indulge in a nice long nap. He tugged her up and she kept on going. His strong hold around her shoulders stopped her from collapse.

"Are you all right?"

The inane question irritated her. "We just survived death by drowning, dearth by gun, and death by bad guy!. Can't we rest?"

"When you get back to your hotel you can sleep for a week."

271

Content with the comforting physical contact, she gripped onto his hold. With her other hand she dug in her pockets for her cell phone, which she always carried in a front pocket. Drawing out the narrow silver instrument, she opened it, groaning at the soppy metal dripping with sea water. It was dead. Chase tried his as well and both returned them to their pockets in frustration. She patted her back pockets, searching for the valuables she kept on her while traveling. License and credit cards were intact.

She showed them to her companion. "At least I can rent a car when we reach civilization."

"Can't be too far," he reassured. "Getting to a phone is our top priority."

They trudged up the unspoiled shore. A chattering from behind caught their attention and they stopped and turned. The dolphins, two of them, were arching in the sunny bay, splashing in and out of the azure sea, cackling. Then one flipped onto his tail and danced backwards, the second following the antics. With a last twist they flew out of the water, gracefully diving back into the deep

"Almost like they were saying aloha," he quietly commented in wonder.

She had been thinking the same thing, but was glad he was the one to voice it. What she did comment on was the ominous cloud bank obscuring the horizon. "That was a nasty storm we passed through."

"Didn't seem that bad from the inside, did it?"

"Maybe the dolphins know how to steer clear of the worst of it."

"Hmm." He laughed. "I think I'm going to take up a new cause, saving dolphins. Returning the favor."

"I like it."

She reveled in the warm sun on her drying skin, the amazingly fresh scent of sea and flowers, with no detection of fuel or exhaust fumes. Removing her squishy wet shoes, she marveled at the hot grit of the golden sand that was almost too perfect to be real.

"Mahalo for saving my life."

"I have to say the same to you." He leaned over and kissed her on the cheek. "I appreciate it. That was very brave of you to fight Teo. And saving my life in the waves."

"I was too afraid to lose you," she admitted. A half a laugh gurgled out. "And I've kind of gotten used to hanging around with you," she admitted obliquely.

His fond smile was touching. "Same to you."

As they walked the white sands, Chase continually cast glances out to sea. When questioned, he admitted he kept the possibility open that Teo had been caught in the storm and run aground. What a scary thought! She did not want to meet up with him again unless she had a half-dozen armed cops between her and the crazy kahuna.

They reached the end of the curved beach, trapped by a craggy, volcanic hill in front of them, and a thick jungle to their left. Leaning on the rocks, Chase's pleasant expression faded as he rubbed at his jaw. "Teo knows how to throw a punch like a truck."

She winced sympathetically. "You'll have a manly bruise by tomorrow." She rubbed her head. "I know what you mean."

Standing in front of her, he blocked her forward momentum. Gently probing the side of her head, she winced, yelped, and he withdrew his hand, wincing as well. "You've got a bump the size of a baseball on that side of your head." Carefully he parted her wet hair. "It's not bleeding. Just let me know if you feel faint or dizzy. As soon as we get to a phone we'll get you to a hospital."

"I'm fine!" She pushed around him.

"Why don't you sit down and wait for me? I can go hike to the highway or the resort that this perfect beach belongs to. Should be close. It can't be stuck out in the middle of nowhere."

Ignoring the solicitude, she glanced around at the incredible scene. "No, developers would never allow this to go untouched. Mahalo, but I need to stick to it. I don't want to be alone even on this isolated beach."

Soberly, he reassured, "Teo isn't going to pop up here. I'm sure of it.

"I'm not. Guess I'll have to tough it out."

Sitting down on the black lava, she dusted the sand from her feet and donned her wet shoes for an easier trek through unknown territory. Chase did the same.

The jungle was close, right off the sand, with tall trees, thick underbrush and matted ferns crowded in the lush rainforest. The sounds of animals and birds grew louder as they approached. Small creatures skittered in the underbrush, unseen, but heard. She shied away, trying to remember the indigenous predators of the islands. They did not have snakes, thankfully. Mongoose, yes. Spiders and bugs and all kinds of creeping, crawling things that gave her chills just thinking about them. Straining to see into the lush jungle, she hoped they spotted a trail before they plunged into the chunky flora.

"Paradise found." Chase gestured around them.

"It's beautiful," she admitted despite her misgivings.

The jungle was cloying and humid. As they tromped through the thick brush they were soon dripping with sweat, sagging from exhaustion after their arduous swim. At a clearing near a cold stream Chase insisted they stop to rest and sip the refreshing, clean water.

274

She drenched her drying hair in the rippling brook, hoping to keep her queasiness at bay. Chase removed his tattered aloha shirt, dipped it in the stream, then wrapped it around his head.

Appreciating this new scenery—a shirt-less cop, she should have guessed he would be in such excellent shape. Probably a surfer who kept his body toned and fit for his job as well as recreation. Hawaii was one of the best places in the world to indulge in all kinds of fitness activities from water sports to tai chi.

"At least I'm prepared." She tugged at the collar of her aloha shirt. "Always wear bright clothing in case you need to be spotted on a deserted beach or in the jungle."

"Hardy Boys again?" he asked, rubbing his forehead. "The Mystery of Fantasy Island?"

"Kidnapped and left to drown is your fantasy?"

"I was thinking of us on the deserted beach part."

"Oh."

Strolling along the line of jungle next to the beach they saw rare sights never experienced in Oahu. A honu, a Hawaiian green sea turtle, flopped along the shore. Out on an outcropping of rocks in the bay they spotted what Chase was sure were Hawaiian monk seals. They were on the endangered species list! He had never seen any except at the aquarium! The amazing tropical splendor was all breathtaking.

Spotting a narrow trail, they hiked away from the beach. As they made their way through the jungle, Chase linked his arm around her and offered supported without asking. She accepted without refusal or thanks. But appreciated the comforting help.

Haley decidedly tried to absorb the enchanted vista around them rather than focus on her aching headache, the uncomfortable sloshing

of the soppy shoes, her sore muscles, and how the dripping clothes
made funny sounds as they walked. The abundant and magnificent
wild flowers blooming everywhere made it seem a botanical melee of
mixed plants. The trees were grand and huge, and so matted into
each other it was hard to distinguish individual species within the
sweeping canopy.

"Funny, I can't hear any planes. We haven't seen a single
boat," Chase puzzled, carefully stepping over a knot of fallen
branches.

"What island do you think we're on?"

"An isolated stretch of Kauai." He looked at the green cliffs
looming beyond the jungle. "Not exactly the Na Pali coast. I'm not
sure where we are."

The curve of the mountains, the verdant emerald canyons, the
dense rainforest, the uncontaminated white sand beach, the cobalt
blue of the ocean and the pure cerulean of the sky. Paradise found
indeed.

Still holding a proprietary arm around her, Chase led them
toward a well-marked path up ahead. The swath was wide and oft
traveled route. There was no fallen vine or errant growth on the
sandy trail, but a grooved avenue maintained as they followed the
path as it wound back to another secret bay. She wondered if it was a
beach access for the nearest resort, but it looked too wide.

Keoni stopped, studying the path from the jungle to the sand, to
the sculptured slope leading to the sea. "This is a canoe launch." He
gestured inland. "Civilization, that-a-way."

"Like from a five-star hotel?" she wondered, dropping her
voice.

"Yeah, one ritzy enough to have outriggers for the guests."

276

Her stomach was telling her it was close to dinner. The risk to life and the swim in the turbulent ocean had churned up quite an appetite.

"What was that?" Chase asked.

"My stomach growling."

"As soon as we get back to Waikiki I'll buy you the best dinner in the best restaurant we can find."

Taking her by the hand, he led her on their continued trek through the jungle. The noises of the native creatures died down, the hushed tone seemed like a reverent, instinctive thing as they entered yet another alien world in the verdant, luxurious greens of a primordial jungle. Like being swallowed by Alice's rabbit hole, they had traversed through an enchanted portal.

The scent here was heady and rich, far more prevalent than what she was accustomed to in Oahu. There was also a subtle feel to the place that lent an aura of raw nature and wonder to the deep, emeralds and vibrant limes of the leaves, vines and plants. Pristine, as if they were untouched – no – unsoiled by humankind.

Walking single file now, Keoni kept a hold of her hand. Occasionally he would pause, look intently into the rainforest, tilt his head as if it would improve his ability to hear, then he would continue.

"You don't think we're lost do you?"

"No." His tone was completely self-assured. Guys hated to admit they were lost or didn't know what they were doing. "It's an island, we can't be lost. Just keep going and eventually we'll find something."

A spear slammed suddenly into the tree just ahead of Keoni! The officer jumped back, instinctively throwing an arm protectively in front of her, and moving to keep her just behind him. Startled, she did not feel the terror until a fierce- expressioned Polynesian man only partially emerged from the matted foliage.

"Are you pupule?" he snapped at the stranger who was broader and taller than the trim cop. You trying to kill somebody?"

Three other men, as broad and sturdily muscled as Samoans and as intimidating as sumo wrestlers, joined the mysterious attacker. These newcomers held spears directed unerringly at the couple. They instilled instant fear, with no semblance to luau entertainers.

The first man spoke in Hawaiian and Haley caught only a few words. Malihini. That was newcomer, usually referring to tourists. Kapu, the Hawaiian word for forbidden. Keoni seemed confused and responded to them in the native tongue. They, in turn, seemed perplexed, and answered him with more Hawaiian. The demeanors of everyone relaxed.

"What is going on? Does the resort know the javelin class is out of control?"

"They said we have disturbed a kapu forest. They're serious."

"What?"

"There's something wrong. Their dialect. Their phrasing and some of their words, it's just, I don't know, weird. Something is off."

"Why don't you just flash your badge and we can get to a phone?"

Smirking, he darted a quick, amused glance at her. "Is that slang from your detective stories for me announcing my presence as a police officer?" Turning back to the others, Chase spoke more Hawaiian to the men, who gave muttered comments amongst themselves.

"Did you tell them you're a cop?"

278

"No, because they could be pakalolo farmers," he hissed in a quiet whisper into her ear. "Or some other kind of low life criminals with spears, while we are unarmed good guys."

"Pakalolo?"

"Marijuana."

"Oh. Yeah." Her dreadful awareness of current affairs and true crime reared its head. "Yeah, that's a big business here, I forgot. Fertile paradise is lush for all manner of delicious fruits. That goes for drugs, too, huh?"

"Exactly."

The strangers' leader, without a spear, came forward, cutting a swath through the tall brush. If Chase was as startled as she was that the warrior was only wearing a modest loincloth and nothing else, he did not show it. She felt the cop's arm across her waist tense, and he backed them up. The warrior yanked his spear out of the tree and motioned with his head toward the jungle. He spoke a few words, then climbed back into the trees.

"He says we should follow."

"They could murder us!" she hissed. "Don't you remember your own safety rules? Never go to a second location with a gunman?"

He snorted what sounded suspiciously like a laugh. "You really do read too much. If they're pakalolo growers, they're going to escort us out of their patch and make sure we don't see anything we're not supposed to see. They wouldn't be lolo enough to kill us." At her questioning look, he translated lolo as stupid.

She was not sure she agreed with his assessment. For drug runners it might be just as easy to kill the intruders and bury the bodies in this vast, unspoiled wilderness. How ironic if the cop and the mystery bookstore owner ended up fertilizing the marijuana! Chase was the one who didn't read enough. Or see enough movies. Didn't he ever see Live and Let Die? A title she wished she hadn't thought about.

Taking her hand, Chase followed the men. As she paced with him through a close, barely discernable trail, she ravaged her memory for any clue that Hawaiians ever practiced sacrifice or cannibalism.

The odor of cooking fish came first to her senses, followed closely by the grumbling of her stomach. Grilled mahi-mahi! They were going to materialize at a beachside café of the resort and max out the soppy cash and credit cards in her pocket for a fantastic dinner. Mahi, rice, some luscious coconut crème pie – where had she thought of that fantasy -- Gilligan's Island? Then she would find some fabulous lomi lomi spa massages and the thickest, plushest mattress at the resort for her bruised body and aching head.

Breaking through the brush, she slid to a halt as her feet hit the golden sand with mud-caked sneakers. What? This was not a Hilton! Not even a quaint, cheap hotel left over from weekend liberties for World War Two soldiers! This was Swiss Family Robinson!

They faced a clearing that was a semi-circle of sand with smoking rocks in the center. She recognized the smolder pit it as an imu, a hollowed crater in the sand used as an oven for cooking luau pigs. What was unexpected was the total native dress and appearance of women in wrap around cloths colored in muted, tapa-style island prints. The men and children were dressed in loincloths. There were probably about thirty people, some fishing in a heart-achingly exquisite bay with sapphire water, edged by swaying, tall palms and craggy black lava rocks. Some men were working on an outrigger canoe that seemed to be part tree trunk still. Women were sitting cross-legged in the sand pounding tapa cloth and some painting designs on the liable material. Most of the men and women were engaged in food preparation; cleaning fish, slicing fruits and pounding what looked to be poi out of solid clumps of taro.

It was a scene from right out of the Polynesian Cultural Center, an educational and entertaining tourist attraction on the northern coast of Oahu. There, various south pacific peoples worked and taught about life in seven different Polynesian cultures. Food, craft and history combined for instruction to interested and entertained visitors.

Were they only at the North Shore of Oahu? No, this was not the Cultural Center. Nothing there or at other luaus she had been to was this rustic.

"What?"

Awed, confused, Chase shook his head. "I don't think we're at a hotel luau," was his hushed reply.

Aloud, the native Chase ruminated that on many places in the Islands, people lived in bucolic, even primitive circumstances. Poor, they survived predominately off the land. They usually did not have electricity, sometimes not even modern transportation. The nearest phone could be quite a hike, or a horseback ride across jungle or hills to the nearest settlement. Kauai? Had they landed in a remote part of the Garden Isle? They might have beached on Niihau, the privately owned island where no visitors were allowed.

To the left, the brush parted and a massive Hawaiian with a lava lava wrapped around his waist, and a sash around his shoulders, parted the ferns on either side of a narrow path. His bearing, his confidence, bespoke a leadership position, and all native heads turned to him in silent esteem. He gave them a short bow of respectful greeting, although his expression was clearly wary.

"My name is Holokai. E komo mai[5] to our village." Deference was underscored as some people backed away as he approached the malihini.

Behind him, came the thinner, shorter form of Kana Hagoth, and the amazingly spry, Amelia Hunter.

"Tutukane!"

Keoni rushed to hug the grandfather who was short and very Hawaiian in comparison to his lean, tall grandson. The younger relation seemed out of place among the crowd who were decidedly strong in their native ancestry. The detective drew the elderly ex-spy into an embrace as well, all unabashedly overwhelmed with tears of joy.

Amelia Hunter moved away from the relatives and gave her a firm hug. "Haley, my dear, are you all right?"

"Fine," she muttered, feeling pretty overwhelmed herself.

When Kana Hagoth strolled over, still holding onto Keoni, he gave her a loving embrace. "Two of my favorite keiki[6]!" He laughed in delight.

"What are you doing on this island?" Keoni wondered aloud as soon as the surprise reunion settled down. The imposing leader, introduced as Holokai, joined them, standing silently behind Kana. "Are we on Niihau?"

"No. What are you doing here?" He directed his question to Haley. "You found us from the ship's log, didn't you?" He glanced at Amelia. "It was enough of a clue. I had hoped it would explain our disappearance. I did not want you to find us! So much is at stake."

---

[5] Welcome
[6] Children

Confused, Keoni explained the kidnapping and Teo's attack, with Haley adding details that the curt cop glossed over. As they relayed their adventures, Kana -- tutukane kahuna -- led them over to a grove of trees where they all sat on the sand, even the physically creaky Amelia.

Kana asked if they thought he had been lost at sea. Their looks must have given them away, and he nodded, sharing a meaningful glance with the old spy. "I was lost at sea in a way," he commented without clarification. "Metaphorically speaking, since your grandmother died, I've focused on a quest. Something secret. No one in the family knew. Only Amelia, my old friend, shared this mission. She is the one who led me to this pu'uhonua."

"Tutuwahine has been gone a long time," Keoni shook his head.

Grandmother, Haley worked out on her own. Tutu – grandparent. Wahine – woman. She was starting to catch on a little with Hawaiian.

Keoni's happiness was tempered with irritation. "Why did you keep this a secret? Where are we? Why did you have to sneak off like this?" His expression and tone hardened as the cop side of his personality asserted itself. "Why were Teo and Sam Simon so desperate to find it? Did you hide here from them?"

"No. We are here because of the magic," Amelia quietly responded. Kana frowned at the fanciful description, but the silent reactions did not deter the older woman. "That is the only explanation."

Haley's skull was throbbing and she dismissed the supernatural implications that had smitten the older people. Magic? Well, there was the adventure with the dolphins, but that was explainable, not mystical.

Fresh fruits and coconut bowls of deliciously clear water were brought and the younger people eagerly snacked. While they ate, Chase gave a full account of their misadventure at sea with Teo.

"What about a radio or a phone? We need to get Teo. HPD can meet him at the dock if we hurry."

"Plenty of time for that later," Kana assured with a disregard so casual it seemed like a dismissal.

"I want to know now!"

"In good time," Kana firmly commanded.

Chase seemed about to argue, but suppressed his anger and just shook his head. "It better be good, tutukane."

"It will, I promise you."

Kana, Amelia and the Polynesian leader who had been hovering nearby during the whole reunion, guided them toward the rear of a camp ringed with similar grass shacks. Built with a thatched roof, the walls were straw mats that could be rolled up to let the air in, but rolled down to keep out rain and excessive wind. The floor was sand, but he was placed on a faded, woven mat made from green lauhala leaves. Three of the four sides were rolled down on this hut, leaving the proceedings to be observed by the rest of the village.

They were offered time to refresh and wash with clean water in bark gourds. She accepted the comfortable spot on a straw mat in a primitive hut. Chase resisted, but Haley accepted, relishing the private time to lay on the hard, cool ground and rest. Not the Marriott, but safe sanctuary and a few moments of peace.

***

The luscious smell of cooking food filtered to her senses and her stomach grumbled. They had eaten some upon their arrival and she hoped they were planning a huge luau because she felt she could eat most of a banquet. She peeked out the open door of the hut and paused to take in the stunning view.

Before her was an incredible postcard scene less than a hundred yards from the doorway. Tall palms edged the encroaching fauna that bordered a sparkling white sand beach. Ferns, gardenia and plumeria plants nestled in with other greenery. The low, afternoon sun shone so brightly on the surf of the nearby blue waves that they seemed to undulate with multi-colored azure hues and the spray glistened with rainbow prisms. Far beyond, at the horizon, gray clouds blurred the line between blue heaven and sea – perhaps the same stormy clouds that caught the boat.

Her stomach rolled again and she turned toward the cooking center of the beach, noting with delight that low wooden planks were over burdened with kalua pig, fruits, vegetables and other delights she thought might be nuts. So many foods that were familiar, yet unique in a raw, fresh cuisine. There even looked like something resembling a coconut milk bread pudding type dish? She usually preferred anything macadamia nut and chocolate for dessert, but would be happy with fried spam right about now! Hmm, coconut pie, though, was Mary Ann's specialty on Gilligan's Island. The thought made her mouth water!

Allowing her to precede him into the clearing, they were warmly greeted by Holokai, Kana, Amelia and many others. Introductions were made, but the Hawaiian names and faces became a blur in her short memory.

She fell more than sat on a rock. Keoni knelt next to her and brushed the hair from her face.

"Are you sure you're okay?"

"Just tired. It's been some adventure." She steered the focus away from herself with humor. "You do this for all your dates?

"Only the ones who like to meddle in police business."

He helped her to her feet and they emerged to find Kana and Amelia outside. In the fading sunlight the strange jungle hues seemed to light the older people with new tints of vigor. They looked amazingly well. Very well, in fact, for an old woman who had not seemed healthy lately, and an old grandfather who was more than double the age of his grandson. Holokai was a silent companion. She asked why the foreboding Hawaiian was joining them.

"He is kahuna," Kana explained in a reverent whisper.

Confused, Haley looked from one to another. "You're a kahuna, right?" she asked Kana. "That's what Kamala calls you."

"Oh, you met the wayward member of the family. Holokai is a spiritual healer, also trained in the arts of herbs and natural medicines. He is the village leader in matters of life and spirit."

They took their places on some rocks. They were given wooden plates and fresh fruit and steaming meat were piled on for them.

"I think it's time for some answers," she politely insisted between bites.

"First a question," Kana insisted. The short, sprite, pixie-faced elder seemed to have a twinkle in his eyes and a sparkle in his smile, as if knowing the answer already. "How did you come to be here?"

"Teo kidnapped us —"

286

"No." Kana corrected his grandson with amusement. "By boat is not what I ask. How did you come to the island?"

"You wouldn't believe it. We were brought here – well – "

"Dolphins," she supplied.

"Ka nai'a," Holokai nodded. Kana and Amelia smiled knowingly as the kahuna explained, "The dolphins. You were in need," was his simple reply. "Makani[7] Hou and Kahana[8] brought you here. They would not do that except for a reason."

"Who?"

"Ka nai'a. Dolphins," Chase translated.

"You name the dolphins?" She named her car, but it wasn't quite the same thing. Maybe it was considering their amazing trip here.

The cetaceans had saved their lives and were obviously known to the people here. They gave the sea creatures names, cute, but a little weird. "Is this Niihau or Kauai?"

"Ka nai'a mokuaina. Dolphin Island," Holokai explained.

She didn't know whether to laugh or scoff. A look at Keoni proved he mirrored her incredulity. She sided with tact. "Where are we? Geographically."

Holokai leaned forward. "Far from the world you know. Few know of our paradise."

She took in the clues from the surroundings, from the imposing figure of Holokai. From the strange welcome that was both polite, yet distant. Holokai's accent suggested that English might not be his first language, but his Hawaiian seemed natural, smooth and

---

[7] Wind
[8] Turning Point

effortless. Kana and Amelia did not find anything amiss about the whole situation, and she found that curious and disturbing.

"Where are we in relation to the other islands?"

"Away, yet not too far," Amelia told them.

"We are separate," Holokai clarified.

Chase made a sour expression that was a clear, outward reflection of his mutual feeling of distaste. "You're not telling us this is pu'uhonua! The mythical ka nai'a mokuaina?" He adamantly shook his head. "I don't believe that," Chase scoffed.

Amelia was also amused. "How would you explain it?"

Haley was confused. Were they trying to sell this part of Hawaii as the legendary magic island Teo was obsessed about? "I don't understand."

"Where are we?" Chase demanded an edge to his tone.

"Ka nai'a mokuaina," Kana supplied matter-of-factly.

This was getting them nowhere. "Really," she insisted.

"You're not on any chart," Chase refuted. "Believe me, I would know. I've been out around Niihau and Kauai a number of times, and been involved with the Coast Guard. I've seen navigational charts of the area. There were no islands. Not even atolls large enough to sustain life. Nothing detected from the masses of water and air traffic around the Islands. You can't hide an island."

The cherubic smile crossing Holokai's face chilled her with suspicion. From Chase's expression, he wasn't impressed, yet Hagoth and Hunter seemed completely at ease.

So the older people believed this was a mythical island. Okay. There were other mysteries to solve. Haley asked Kana to explain what had been happening. Why had he missed their appointment days ago? And what was the mystery with the ship's logs?

Amelia started out with the last question, admitting she had sent the valuable ship's log to Haley's shop as protection. Then she mysteriously commented that everything would be revealed in time. That was no answer. Haley had heard that enough growing up.

Kana broke in. "I knew Sam Simon was close to discovering the location of this pu'uhonua," Kana explained. "I was not aware of Teo's violent intervention. The log was sent to Haley to safeguard the secret location of the refuge. I could not go back to my shop. I had to come here. Amelia was to join me, but after she had warned you. She did not get the chance because Simon was always watching you. And if our disappearance worried you, I thought you would solve the puzzle of where we were. And be content with that knowledge. Not follow us."

"Sam or Carrie," Amelia added. "Sam broke into Kana's shop —"

"Sam? It was Teo!" Haley corrected.

"You knew that?" Chase snapped back at Kana and Amelia.

"I couldn't tell you the truth, we were being watched," Amelia placated.

"You could have told me when I brought you in for questioning after Kahunui's murder."

She placed a gentle hand on Keoni's. "This could not be made public. Sorry."

"You'll understand everything now," Kana promised.

Amelia took over. "Let me explain. You see, Teo, Carrie and Simon have been after the ka nai'a mokuaina secret. Simon and Carrie came to my house. While there they must have had a falling out and Simon murdered her."

"We know about the search for the secret island." Chase shook his head in confusion and irritation. "Simon, or Teo, or both, are responsible for this whole crime wave. They killed Kamala's friend Kai at your house," he told the spy.

"Kai, a gentle, good man." Kana shook his head. "Why kill him?"

"Why break into the shops and where we live?" Haley asked in response. "Teo wanted the secret location of this island and he murdered Carrie and Kai because they got in his way," she reminded the detective.

"That seems too clever for Teo," Hunter shook her head. "He is an impulsive man. Driven by his passions, not a clever, premeditative type."

Haley shrugged and guessed, "Sam must have helped. We think he was an accomplice." She gave the cop a rueful smile. "Well, you can really tie it all up once you get back to Honolulu."

Kana was unhappy with that comment, but respond. In a rush, he placed his hands on the arms of the younger people and urged them not to worry about police work now. He was anxious to show them the wonders of the island. "Come. Are you strong enough to meet my ohana here?"

Allowing the riddles to sink in to her throbbing brain, she agreed. The cop, though, shouldered free of the embrace. Irritation lent purpose and strength to his stride as he strode through the warm, grainy sand. "Where's the nearest phone? Our cells are history."

"No phones." Kana shook his head.

Haley was amazed at that, but recalled rumors of one island that had no modern conveniences because it was privately owned. Were they there? Was that their Dolphin Island?

"Do you have radio communication with Honolulu?" Chase asked.

"We have no contact with anyone beyond the reef."

"Tutukane and Amelia –"

"Are exceptions."

"What about Sam Simon's boat? I know you would have mentioned if Teo had managed to come ashore. Have you seen his boat?"

Haley and Keoni had discussed the outside possibility that Teo had survived the storm, but they had seen no sign of him or evidence of a shipwreck. They assumed the evil killer had managed to escape after he dumped them in the ocean, and he was on his way back to Oahu.

"You are the only ones here," Amelia assured them. "It's going to stay that way."

The younger couple exchanged looks, and it was Haley who asked, "How can you keep people off a Hawaiian island? What happens when someone visits?"

"There are no visitors."

She couldn't believe that. This section of the Pacific was crazy with swimmers, snorkelers, surfers, boaters – the list was huge. They couldn't just hide an island or a part of an island! She played along with the story, though, to get somewhere. "What if someone is shipwrecked, or cast ashore?"

"Few arrive on our beaches," Kana explained gently, but with a maddeningly matter-of-fact tone. "Makani Hou[9] and Kahana bring some here. We hanai[10] – make them as our ohana."

---

[9] New

"Hanai means adopt them into the family," Chase translated with a lilt of confusion.

This was making no sense, she decided. They could not hide out here among the busiest islands of the Pacific! It was not possible. Mentally, she did not want to accept the obvious implications. They weren't really on a hidden island, right? Were they prisoners? Kana and Amelia were not, but they were exceptions, the kahuna said.

"We need to contact Honolulu," she reminded.

It was Hunter who seemed most disturbed by the demand. "You can't, my dear."

Straining to not let her discomfort show, she looked at Chase and her courage was fortified by his wink of compatibility and alliance.

With a squeeze on her arm, Chase joined in her rebellion. "I'm not sure what this all means, and we both thank you for your hospitality, but we can't stay here. How do we get off this island?

There was no humor in the island kahuna's response. "There is no way off ka nai'a mokuaina. E komo mai. You are now part of our ohana."

***

Walking along the sand, through the jungle, in and out of the open areas of the little village, Chase walked at a brisk pace. Haley gamely kept up, but her persistent headache and aching body made exertion a chore.

"You're not buying into this, are you?"

---

[10] Adopt

The tone indicated he would think her crazy if she accepted the wild claims of Holokai. She approached the question reasonably. "It sounds unbelievable, but we're here. I don't see any cars or hotels or telephone lines or cell towers." With her splitting noggin a magic paradise sounded pretty good. As long as they had beds where she could take a nice long nap. "What if it's really an isolated island paradise?"

"It can't be!"

They toured the fishing beach and other sections of the small knot of civilization. Chase said he sensed the island was small, but complimented it was well proportioned with gardens, trees and an outstanding shallow bay perfect for spear fishing. Several times they talked with one of the numerous fishermen, or one of the women cooking or weaving. They spoke in Hawaiian. She could not converse in Hawaiian -- only translate a few key words absorbed in her years in the Islands. Chase could communicate with no problem and did, giving her aside translations.

The exploration stopped near some black lava rocks breaking up the blue of the ocean and the golden tan of the unblemished sand. The sun did not break through the clouds, because it was far down toward the horizon, but the glow of reflected light shimmered orange and copper, the bank of clouds in the east edged with rainbows.

Nearby, a long hut nestled under some trees set back from the shore, but still on the beach. The side mats were rolled up to allow the breeze to sweep through the house. The sand floor was neat and cleared, sleeping mats rolled and stacked in a corner. Kana and Amelia came to escort them over to the hut where an older man and woman and three teen-aged children greeted them with understandable, if heavily accented English.

Haley gave a slight bow. "Aloha."

"We can understand English," the man assured. "E komo mai."

Pleased they had someone more receptive and communicative than Holokai on the island, she observed the family and surroundings, absorbing everything.

"I am Moe Kauka. My ohana. Wife, Malia, daughters Nani, Noe, and Kam."

The children disappeared around a grove of trees and brought back trays filled with various chunks of fruit and vegetables and raw fish and other goodies that she recognized for the most part. The adults gathered around in a circle and ate from a crudely fashioned bowls made of half of a huge coconut shells. Haley savored the poke; cubed, marinated raw fish mixed with crisp seaweed. The freshest and best she had ever eaten! The fish was so moist and tender it crumbled in her hand, and the fruit sweet and fresh.

Bursting to ask more questions, as she knew Chase was, by silent agreement they remained quiet and allowed the social rituals to be observed. Traditional talk story – storytelling – by the villagers commenced as they sat in the sand, the flickering torches casting dancing, golden rays over they assembled gathering.

It was perfection. Haley thought she understood that concept in her mundane and uneventful life in San Diego. Now, she really did understand it. Far from the tourist lanes of Hawaii, they had stumbled into a private cove of purity and flawless wonder. She didn't care about going back to her hotel. She had found Kana, knew he was safe, and had the comfort of new and old friends in this cocoon of splendor. Pu'uhonua. Refuge. She never thought she needed one, but now that she found it, part of her never wanted to leave.

294

Holokai appeared from the folds of the jungle and offered further explanations. "We fulfill roles in this closed society. Amelia is our guardian. Hagoth, the connecting thread to the island, passed down from generations."

Hagoth – Kana – was their connecting thread? Haley worked that around her mind while she ate.

Chase stopped the narrative, asking the leader to go back to the beginning. How did this tribe of travelers get onto a remote island with no connection to the outside world? How did they stay hidden?

Holokai related that many years before, there were native Hawaiians unhappy after King Kamehameha died and the favorite Queen abolished the old gods. The Hawaiians were mistreated by the encroachment of Westerners to their idyllic paradise. As the years past, the monarchy power crumbled, the power usurped by malihini seeking the throne. Finally the queen was deposed. It was time to move on. As their ancient ancestors had before them, a small band struck out in their canoes."

"Hagoth," Haley supplied. "I read the log," she told Kana. "Your ancestor was on the Pacific Star and traveled here. Well, not here, toward Kauai."

"Yes," Kana confirmed. "They had canoes and supplies and wanted to start fresh."

Holokai added, "They were looking for pu'uhonua."

Kana nodded with approval. "They believed."

"The seas were unkind and the voyage was rough," Holokai continued. "After a mighty struggle they lost sight of Kauai. A storm carried them through black ocean and sky. Dolphins led them through to the sun. To the calm waters of this pu'uhonua. Here they built a new culture, free of Westerners, free of the ancient kapu and

295

ali'i, or royal society. "This was a new world for a free people. Protecting and preserving an unspoiled world, hiding from intruders."

"The perpetual cloud ring keeps the island from being detected," Amelia added.

Moe talked eloquently of the old times, of the strict caste system that had been abolished by Kamehameha's queen, and how, for a time, there was a displacement of the Hawaiian culture. New ways overtaking the old. Gods were abolished and a new period of confusion covered the islands. Then came Westerners, and the people adopted their ways, until many haole proved treacherous.

So rich, profound and passionate were these stories that it seemed as if Moe had lived through those years. He was a born storyteller. Talk-story she corrected. It was becoming easy to think in Hawaiian. Chase commented on that, and Moe and the Kahuna exchanged significant glances. .

"The time was right to follow the nature of our ancestors," Holokai intoned reverently. "They had traveled the seas and stopped here in Hawaii. The art of building long canoes and voyaging was lost. Until this small group of travelers decided it was time to leave the old and start our own culture anew."

The mysterious storm that cloaked the island opened to these voyagers. Dolphins led them to this hidden refuge in the mist; brought them to the sanctuary island and from then on was known as Dolphin Island. The playful creatures of the sea became the local mauka – the personal gods. With diligence and hard work, the new pioneers prospered in their new settlement.

Over a century later it was still paradise-raw. They had planted gardens and taro fields and rice patties. They raised animals and cultivated the native fruits. The original voyagers brought little of the modern, Western culture with them, and these descendants relied on the skills handed down from generations of pure Polynesians.

Moe commented he often heard the planes in the distance. Sometimes boats shipwrecked on the coral reef. Occasionally items from the modern civilization washed ashore. Rarely, the dolphins brought people -- castaways -- shipwrecked. Those few were adopted into the ohana.

"You will tell us more of your world?" The oldest daughter of Moe, named Nani, was exceedingly interested in both Chase and Haley. Throughout the evening, the girl, who seemed in her early teens, stared at her. Haley could feel it even when she did not catch the girl in the act. "There is much to learn beyond our shores."

"Not now, Nani," her father ordered and returned to a conversation with Chase.

As with the other villagers, Nani was beautiful in a natural and innocent charm Haley had never seen in such abundance as on this isolated island. Long dark hair, silken and exotic, hallmarked the women and girls.

During the talk-story, Nani made sure the malihini were well attended and fed. She inched her way over to sit next to Haley. When the girl stroked her hair, she resisted the urge to flinch.

Calmly, she turned to the girl and smiled. "What is it?"

"Your hair is like sunlight." She smiled, continuing to brush at the wavy, sandy tone that had turned blond with the salty water and the sun-drenched days. At least on this island no one considered her perpetually casual state sloppy. "And your eyes are colored from the stormy sky."

The distinctive Wyndham blue/gray eyes and thick, blond hair and pale Celtic-Saxon skin were certainly unusual here. This was probably the first time the islanders had seen anyone with her Aryan characteristics. Amelia, the only other haole here, was gray-haired and brown eyed, not much of a contrast to the norm.

After Moe and Holokai were finished with the stories, tentative questions came from the shy, but intrigued Nani. The young woman's extreme curiosity made it clear she wanted to know everything about the big world outside her shores. As Haley suspected, tales of the outside world soon drew her into the conversation. All in the Kauka hut hung on every word as Chase and she described Honolulu and Hawaii.

Then it was time to answer some of their questions.

"How did you find this place, Kana?" Chase asked his grandfather.

Kana deferred the response to Holokai, who explained a kahuna of the Hagoth ohana, handed down for generations, had been established as a connection between the two cultures. The Dolphin Islanders, as they thought of themselves, would never be cut off from the rest of their race. They were wise enough to know, though, that revealing the secret to others would ruin the hidden treasure and expose it to the elements that were eroding their homeland.

Here, a kahuna was the ruler of all who lived in peace and harmony. It truly qualified as a magical place where nature interacted with man, plants, and animals on a near perfect level. No sickness or rapid aging; simple lives with a technology sufficient to support them.

Chase shook his head and laughed with incredulity. "Come on," he denied. "This isn't some supernatural alternate dimension or something. People do not live in harmony because they are separated from the mainland. Our own history shows us that."

"Impatient," Kana shook his head and shushed him. "Let him finish the story."

Holokai came to sit on a rock near Chase. "It is true; our people are a violent race just like all the others on this planet. Our forefathers soon learned, however, when there was discord or disagreement here, the natural elements responded in kind. Fresh water, food, mild weather, would flee." The big, but gentle man believed the fantastic tale, his sincerity ringing with conviction through the now hushed crowd. "There is a connection here in this pu'uhonua, between the inner man and the world that he shares. We live in peace because we are part of the tranquility. In every sense of the meaning, this is perfection."

Every myth had a grain of truth, her parents had drilled into her, and every legend had an element of fact. Was she unbalanced from the recent upheavals in her life to even think these campfire tales could be true?

Shaking his head, it was obvious the cop did not buy the wild story.

"Bali Hai – pu'uhonua -- exists," Amelia assured them adamantly. "I am living proof." With quiet intensity, she related, "I came here in Nineteen Forty-four. Dying. I was chasing down a Japanese mini-sub that was trying to sneak into Hawaiian waters. We blew each other to pieces and the dolphins rescued me. My counterpart managed to find shore and he terrorized the people here before I took him out. These people wouldn't harm him even at the danger of losing their own lives. So I killed him."

Holokai fondly stood behind the older woman and clapped strong, big hands on her shoulders. "She suffered for the good of others."

Kana reached over and slapped the veteran on the knee. "She was healed. In reward, our aikane was allowed to come and go just as I have done for many years. Then I learned Sam Simon was spending a lot of money to find out about the legend. He must know the secret. Teo has been researching it, too. I always wondered if he became a friend of Kamala's to get to me."

"How could Teo know that you were connected to Dolphin Island?" Chase wondered.

"Teo comes from an old ohana, too. Legends are passed down in every ohana."

"Healing?" Haley asked, still incredulous about that element of the fantastic story.

"Immortality. Simon is wrong, of course. All life must run its natural path, even here," Amelia sighed.

The pronouncement seemed ominous, in counterpoint to the pleasant happiness of the gathered audience. When Haley asked what that meant, it was the old spy who responded.

"I'm dying," Hunter replied without regret. "It will take me little time and a great deal of pain if I stray away from this enchanted isle. If I stay here, I will live years, perhaps even be healed."

The impending death of her friend was a blow, but it was diminished with the sincere belief of two elderly people she respected and trusted, that they accepted magic! The supernatural bit was hard to swallow, harking her back to her parents and their endless New Age mantra of cure-alls and meditation rituals. But if it was true, then this was what everyone in the world had dreamed of for thousands of years. Since Adam's fall. Near immortality with perfect health, in a tropical Eden, in perfect paradise.

It was the society that activists like Teo and Kamala fought to rebuild. It was what many of her contemporaries hoped to reestablish. The irony was astounding!

"You will now be part of our ohana," Holokai smiled at them. "You are part of us. You will live here, raise your children, and stay here forever."

"No," Chase refuted.

Haley felt the blush fly up her face and was too stunned to reply.

It was an embarrassed Chase who responded for both of them. "We're not married. And we're not going to disappear and – and – raise children!"

Too overwhelmed to take it all in, Haley shook her head. It was a whole lot to accept. Perfect paradise. She wanted to believe. For the sake of her friend, she wanted to think there was magic to save a precious life. Kana and Amelia had the faith to think this was real. She wanted that, too. And Chase wanted to reject the gift!

The kahuna of the island moved closer, towering over them. "You can not return to the world beyond. No one can leave once you know our secret. The danger is too great for the world to know –"

"Kana left. Amelia left –"

"As part of the Holokai link. Amelia was one of us through her blood sacrifice for us. You are malihini who have come here and been accepted for shelter and survival. Kana and our dolphins, Makani Hou and Kahana, have accepted you within the sacred boundaries of ka'na'ia mokuaina. You can not leave."

The detective bore a glare into his grandfather. "You know we can't stay." Staring at her, he almost smiled. "Okay, I'm speaking for myself. Haley is more than capable of giving her own opinion. I have responsibilities and a life back home. So do you. And I think I know you well enough that I know your answer."

Regretting the necessity of their practical response, she nodded, sadly admitting to Holokai that, "He's right. This is paradise beyond description." No bills, no worries, no literal headache. On the other hand, no family, or new books, or driving in her car . . . . "We can't stay forever," she responded.

The leader, Holokai countenance grave, his eyes solemn, his deep voice intoned, "It is the needs of the island that are considered, not yours. You must stay. There is no choice." He walked away without looking back.

Chase came to his feet to object.

Kana also stood and tempered his grandson's reaction. "Keoni, please, no argument. There is no dissention here, only peace."

"Not any more, tutukane. He can't keep us here against our will."

"Amelia and I are not bound as you are. For now, it is my choice to stay as I please, mo'opuna kane."

"You can't keep us here." Chase seemed to be reading her mind again.

"You must stay, my mo'opuna kane. As must you, Haley." He smiled fondly at her.

Walking back to the hut he would share with Kana, Keoni was contemplatively silent. It was a lot to ponder, and Haley was wrapped up in her own reverie, still trying to juggle the reality of pu'uhonua with the crazy world beyond the magic border of the cloud barrier.

The two young people dropped back and she stayed close to Chase, speaking in a low voice. "Do you believe we can go back?"

"Yes. I hope. We must."

He stopped at a chunky point on the shore where the craggy lava spilled into the sandy grains of sand, where fresh, frothy waves kissed the crab-filled rocks. In the meager, quarter-moonlight, he stared out to sea for a time, then sat on the lava, staring at her.

"Right."

She wanted to believe. Her early years were peppered with the slamming pain of knowing that Peter Pan, Tinkerbell and Santa Claus were all myths, too. She had distanced herself from those fairytales long ago – from her parent's dreams of chasing down Atlantis and mystic powers. Why had it been so hard to believe in what her parents thought was real? Because it was their fantasy, not hers. In rebellion she turned her back on what they wanted her to think.

"I'm not hearing a lot of conviction."

She was just so tired. She sighed. "Wouldn't it be nice if it was true?"

"I've grown up with these old legends for as long as I can remember." Irritated, he explained, "Hawaiians long for an uncomplicated past, but that was a brutal, primitive time in our history. So they dream of a paradise where everything is great. I don't blame them but I can't believe it. I never have."

"Paradise and perfection are overrated."

"Really?" He seemed to leap on that thread as if he wanted to believe her.

"Really. What matters are the people you love. Isn't that your own personal paradise? What are flawless beaches and unspoiled beauty without the people who matter most?"

"Exactly," he agreed.

"So you're willing to give up all this for crime and danger?" she flung back at him. "I would think you have better reasons to stay here than I do."

"In the eye of the beholder," he countered. "I make a difference in my job." Smirking, he shrugged, "Besides, what would my brother and his wife do if I never showed up again?" Sobering, he shook his head. "You're right. The people we care about, aside from Kana, are back there." For a time he was thoughtful. "Maybe we can hitch a ride on a sympathetic dolphin."

"Maybe."

She laughed, looking forward to another swim with their sea helpers. She could do that tomorrow. It would give her something to look forward to while they figured out how to cope with life in Lemuria. "But while we're here, I'm going to soak up the culture like you've been telling me to do."

With slow nods, he considered her intentions. "Then it will be time well spent I guess. But only temporary."

***

They sat in silent contemplation as the warm, frothy waves of the evening tide washed against their feet. The sand was coarse and comforting on their bare feet. The placid lap of waves echoed in her ears and offered a soothing peace. With the empty beach and sky surrounding them it made it seem they were the only people on the planet. Staring out at the dark ocean, the brilliant, silvery stars twinkling like spotlights in the sky, she felt close to the whole universe. With no city lights to interfere with observation, the far-distant points of light felt close and dazzling, undiminished by the pale glow of the quarter moon. On the horizon, the billowy, dark indigo of the storm cloud barrier obscured the horizon, the curving stars, and any land that might be at the other side of the water.

Chase told her that he thought they roughly faced Oahu from this beach. She wondered what her friends, and enemies, were doing. Gar and Skye and Amy were far away. Teo and the rest of Hawaii might as well be in another dimension, oblivious to the Eden so close.

Treasure hunters, mystics; the desperate, the spiritually lost, the seekers, of centuries, had looked for Shangri-La. Bali-Hai. Perfection. Could this really be the enchanted realm of wonder, or just a safe harbor for fugitives afraid to live in a world where their race had been closed out? Holokai's people were right to keep this precious secret safe. What would happen if the public knew about this perfection? Developers, tour agencies, TV crews – instant ruin.

Chase joined her at the study of the stars. Playfully, he splashed water on her legs with his feet. "All of the sensory input of Robinson Crusoe. And all of the imprisonment."

As if taunting them, the familiar pair of dolphins cavorted in the bay. Was it their guardian dolphins Makani Hou and Kahana? She asked Chase to translate their names, and he said they meant New Wind and Turning Point. Ironic, the two cetaceans that brought them here, saved their lives, were so appropriately named. Yes, a new wind had come into their lives, two paths that had taken an amazing turning point courtesy of two dolphins. They brought the couple here to a refuge with no exit.

The creatures started to troll along the curving coastline, their sketchy lines arching in the pale, flickering light of the torches lining the beach. She followed, strolling along the beach, watching the dark, misty reef for the cavorting, flipping shapes.

***

Sleeping on the stiff lauhala grass mat was surprisingly easy. She was exhausted and when the sun shone through the slats of the bamboo mat on the east side of her hut, she was amazed the night was over already. Clean, tapa-pattered cloth was left folded in her hut and she tied the wrap-around sarong-type dress around her in the fashion of the women on the island. The change would give her a chance to wash her shorts and torn t-shirt.

When she emerged, she spotted Keoni in a revealing lava-lava wrap around cloth like the men wore here, and she again appreciated his appealing, good looks. The style was free and luxurious, adding to the exhilaration of the island experience. Beyond anything available at a resort, she was living a beachcombers dream. Paradise in its most elemental and natural form.

Breakfast was simple; fruits and fish. She stuck to the fruit, wandering around watching the women weave mats. Chase joined her and nibbled at some pineapple, mentioning he was going to talk to Kana again about them leaving.

"Teo is probably already causing more trouble in Honolulu. I don't want him to get away with this!"

Grabbing another handful of fruit, Keoni disappeared into the jungle. When he returned scowling she was forewarned of failure. "No luck?" she questioned when he plopped down in the sand.

"No luck. I tried to get Amelia to tell me where her boat is anchored, but she won't confess."

Chin in hand, she momentarily shared his depression, but the gloom did not last. They were sitting here in an unspoiled paradise. Tourists would kill to experience this for a few hours. While it seemed a prison to Haley and Keoni that this was their prison, it was, in reality, an Eden.

Moe joined them and asked if they wanted to go fishing.

Chase agreed to the fishing foray out in the bay. Haley was asked if she wanted to join, but politely refused. As much as she desired to scout out the reefs, the island and landmarks that would be useful if Chase and she tried to leave the enchanted pu'uhonua, her body, however, was still sore. A day of paddling a canoe or pulling in fishing nets was not going to help the sore muscles.

Standing on the shore, she was intrigued to see the women of the village join the canoe party. The women served as the front paddlers and navigators for the fishing expedition. The women also did the gathering of food because of their high level of skills with remembering spatial paths and landmarks with great skill. The men work at pulling in the nets and building and plowing because of their upper body strength. The society, like the mythical properties of the island, had perfect harmony for the roles – the differences -- of men and women. Women's libbers would be so mad that this worked perfectly.

When Amelia and Kana arrived, they sat cross-legged in the sand to scrape coconut shells into utensils and bowls. The kahuna was a storyteller at heart and easily slipped into legends of the old gods. Haley learned that Maui was a god responsible for slowing the sun so his mother could accomplish her work. She already knew of Pele, the fire goddess who lived in volcanoes in the Big Island. As they worked she learned there was a whole family of Pele's, with the usual tragedies that befell mythical beings.

The day slipped away with more entertainment than she would have derived from reading her favorite mysteries. This was learning from a master of tales – living within the story – surrounded by the trees and sand and beaches that were much like the Hawaii when gods and immortals walked the sunny land. She had missed this kind of tutoring all these years, and reveled in the education now. Even Chase eased from his impatience to listen and enjoy the words of a master kahuna.

When Chase returned, he confessed, "Fishing is hard work! I used to think I was in pretty good shape. Chasing down criminals is not the same as net fishing and paddling an outrigger."

"Different muscle groups." Smiling despite her attempt to be causal, she had to add, "Anyway, from what I can see you're in excellent shape."

He cleared his throat in a charming display of modesty. "You're very generous. And you look pretty good as a native yourself. Uh – back to business. I got a chance to checkout the reef and the bay."

The report thrilled her with encouragement. "Ah, still the cop."

"Yeah. It would be hard for two of us, but I think we could row out past the reef and get away. If we can get a hold of an outrigger."

"You were just in one."

"They wouldn't let me see where they keep them."

"Ah, a mystery."

Laughing at her triumphant tone, he agreed. "Yeah. And I know two people who are pretty good at solving mysteries."

When they strolled back to the village they noted Holokai was in a heated discussion with Moe and a few other men. Wandering over to Kana, Chase asked what was happening.

"Some food is missing from the store hut," the elder responded thoughtfully. "They think an animal is sneaking into camp. Holokai wants us to stand watch tonight."

Creeped out at the thought of predators of any kind, Haley stayed close to Chase the rest of the afternoon.

In the evening, after dinner, she joined the policeman at the beach. Long, shared moments of silence stretched into hours. The view of the sky streaked with twilight, and the ocean's dark waves lapping to shore, made it seem beyond perfection. A normal state for this island that was magical, for no other reason, than its pristine beauty.

"So what's the plan?

After a few thoughtful moments, he considered, "We can search for Amelia's boat. Or we can find where they hide the outriggers."

"I'd feel safer in the boat."

His expression twisted with discomfort. "That would be stealing. I can't do that. Besides, it would strand Kana and Amelia here."

"Amelia wants to stay."

"Kana will come back." His expression darkened.

Startling them both, Nani suddenly emerged from the tree line. "You cannot leave."

"We have to," Chase insisted.

"We promise to keep it a secret and not divulge the location of pu'uhonua. We don't even know it!" Haley realized, but the girl was not appeased. Her face was unbelievably sad. "We could even come back," was a final balm. Warily, he asked if she knew where the canoes were kept.

In a whisper, she said. "They do not want malihini to know."

Haley tried to sound neutral. "Can you show us where? It will be a secret."

She shook her head. "Only a few know. Only Kana and Amelia allowed to leave."

"They want to keep all of you here? Don't you ever want to leave?" she asked, feeling a little bit like the Serpent in the Garden of Eden. She was relieved when Nani shook her head in adamant denial.

"Keep the malihini here. You can not leave. No one can know the secret of Ka nai'a mokuaina. Kahuna says evil people will come. The evil that came to our people in the islands will come here if anyone knows. Ka nai'a mist protect us. Ka nai'a protect us." Her gaze was almost adoring. "You are special. Makani Hou and Kahana would only bring here greatest of spirit."

Uncomfortable with the admiration, she let Keoni do the rest of the talking, and she focused on the content of the message. Nani really believed they were led here by the dolphins. Unfortunately, Nani was probably right about the sinister conspiracy under the surface of paradise. No wonder this place was undiscovered. No accidental visitor ever left to report its existence. The islanders were concealing the canoes. For protection or secrecy? Maybe malihini – newcomers -- could navigate the treacherous reef, as well as the natives but the kahuna in charge felt threatened by that possibility and did not want anyone to leave. Almost laughing at her government conspiracy angle, she would not discount it out of hand.

"Nani, what if we found one of the canoes?"

Her eyes widened with alarm. "No. Kapu."

"Forbidden," Keoni reminded Haley.

"I understand they are kapu," Haley persisted, "but we need to leave. We need to get back to our own lives. People are worried about us.""

A stubborn resolve swept across Nani's face, easily read. She was not used to deception, or hiding her feelings. "I can not help. You must stay. You are ohana now."

"You stay here." Nani held out her hand. "For you."

Haley opened her hand, Keoni did likewise, and the girl dropped dark brown bracelets into their palms.

"Coconut band. For my ohana. You are ohana."

The tiny beads were made of small coconut shell pieces, looped with hemp. In the center two small, carved dolphins separated the beads. She took them from the two newcomers and tied them around their wrists.

"Mahalo, Nani. We appreciate this very much."

Her face brightened and she smiled. "You will stay?"

Keoni answered for them. "We can't. I'm very sorry, but we can't."

Her joy crumbled like a sand castle under the assault of the waves. She spun around and ran into the jungle, quickly disappearing into the dark curtain of foliage.

With a sinking heart Haley realized he had just pushed away their only ally, who did not want them to exit. They had become her friends and opened up a world of possibilities. They walked down the beach and she asked him if he intended to break the kapu.

The detective smirked. "You're not afraid of the ancient gods are you?"

She admitted she didn't know the punishment from the old gods for breaking a kapu, but she did know she wanted to go back home. "Breaking a kapu doesn't sound easy, though," she pointed out.

"It's probably not," he scoffed, "but I guess we're going to find out. As soon as we can figure out where the canoes are kept."

Trying not to sound too skeptical, she wondered. "So you think you can get us past the reef?" She would prefer the stability of Amelia's solid boat as a means of escape, but didn't want to push Chase and his ethics about the legality and ethics of filching her vessel.

"Kana travels between islands all the time. He's in good shape, but he's an old guy. I can do it, no problem."

"Kana probably comes and goes in Amelia's boat," she pointed out.

His scowl was proof she should not have stepped on his macho image.

They strolled down the beach to the usual outcropping of rock to stare out at the black, rolling sea. Low moonlight from the reflection beyond the clouds gave a silvery sheen to the waves. While her friend launched up and paced, she watched the tide and the surf on the reef. In the misty moonlight the dolphins played, as if taunting them.

"The canoes have to be somewhere nearby. Convenient for the fishermen. And, of course, on a sloping, smooth beach for easy access to the waves."

"Of course."

"Does your sarcasm denote your doubts in my abilities?"

"Your detective abilities? No, I've already mentioned you're a super detective," she assured honestly. "What worries me is the reef.

312

And I'm enough of an Irish descendant to be superstitious about breaking a kapu."

"I didn't know the Irish had kapu."

"They have everything you can imagine on the superstition front and then some."

He sat next to her and took her hand in his. "I would never do anything to harm you, trust me about that."

There was no hesitation. "I do. I mean – right."

Smirking at her turn of phrase, he tossed a nod toward the bay. "I've studied the reef. When I was out there fishing today I took note of the direction they went out, their methods, and the placement of the rocks, the currents, and the wave action. I surf, I've been on outrigger teams, and I know my way around in the ocean. I'm confident I can get us out to sea and on the way to Kauai or whatever is the nearest civilized island. I also think I can find the canoes. They would have to be away from the worst of the rocky shore and highest coral of the bay. Maybe around this cove on the other side of these hills."

"We could try that beach where we washed up. Remember we passed a cove where you said it was a canoe launch."

"Yeah. That would be a good place to start."

***

Well after dark, when the fires died to glowing ashes, and the moonlight had faded to a thin smolder far beyond the thick storm clouds, Haley met Keoni in back of his grass shack. Dressed in the more practical togs they wore when shipwrecked, they traveled in silence, sometimes holding hands as they coursed through the thick, close jungle, they searched for canoe tracks. She fought to not appear squeamish about the buzzing insects, the squishy creatures underfoot that she never really saw, the creepy noises all around them.

As they skirted one of the outer hut areas they heard stern, raised voices. They stopped, crouching low. After several moments of argument in Hawaiian the discussion stopped.

Chase turned and whispered in her ear. "More crime on the island! Supplies have been stolen. It sounds like we might be the suspects!"

"Great," Haley moaned.

"It's possible there is another outsider on the island."

It took a moment of staring at his solemn face to catch his meaning. "Teo?"

"Yeah."

They had no idea what had happened to the demented kahuna. Was it possible the murderer and kidnapper had found pu'uhonua after all? According to Holokai's beliefs, the dolphin gods would not allow evil people to come here. There had been the Japanese warrior in World War Two, but Amelia had eliminated him. By the providence of the island's aumakua – god? What if Holokai and his followers were wrong? Bad guys might be able to slip in here – the serpents in paradise. If that was true, then there was more than a thief loose on the island, there was a hidden killer lurking in the jungles of these trusting, simple and unprotected people!

A noise on their right abruptly brought silence. In the dim light they made out a lumbering boar trotting across a cross trail. The ugly animal stopped and sniffed in their direction, his curved tusks gleaming in the patchy reflection of the torches. They froze, not breathing or moving, staring at their foe. Wild boars could be deadly

314

and often attacked humans. The fishing party was not armed as hunters; they possessed little protection from the threat.

Moe, Holokai and Kana were in the lead of the single-file party. Suddenly, Moe jumped forward, waving his torch and stabbing it toward the boar. The fat animal flinched away, but crashing through the underbrush beside them, another wild pig threw itself at the impulsive man. The heavy beast ploughed Moe to the ground In a defensive distraction, then trod across his shoulder to run off into the jungle.

Holokai and Keoni helped the man to his feet, Moe wincing in a hiss of pain. "AHHHH!."

A string of Hawaiian words shot out from between the teeth of the injured young man, and Haley felt she was probably better off not knowing what they all meant. She brought the torch closer.

Carefully checking the right shoulder where Nani held onto his arm, Chase shook his head in sympathy. "You're bleeding. That boar must have torn your shoulder. "Let's get him back to the village."

The men closed in to assist the wounded man, while Kana led the way with the torches. As she tried to retrace the steps through the matted ferns encroaching on the narrow trail, Kana directed them in some new twists and turns that he said would make the trip quicker. When they reached the village, the women and Holokai gathered, taking charge of Moe and carrying him to Holokai's hut.

"That's a bad wound," the policeman commented to no one in particular.

Amelia arrived and looked on as several revered and older men of the camp, along with Kana, slipped into the hut.

315

Once the fervor died down, Chase guided Haley by her elbow and escorted her to the rocks in the bay that they had come to adopt as their favorite observation post by the sea. Glancing around after they were seated, he leaned close and quietly commented on the unusual route back to the huts.

"I noticed that, too," she whispered, wondering why they were keeping their voices so low. Suspicion was mutating, she guessed. Since deciding to revolt and try to escape the island, they were overly cautious and probably paranoid. "It was quicker than the trails we took over to that side of the island."

"It was. I also noticed the paths were well worn. I think it bears looking into."

"It was dark. I couldn't find my way back there."

"I can. Especially since I left a trail of breadcrumbs for us to follow."

"What?" she scoffed.

"Figuratively speaking. I was doing less helping than the others and managed to lag behind a little and drop torn leaves on the trail. With a little careful inspection, I think we can retrace our steps."

"Hey that is – akamai -- yes?"

"Yeah -- akamai -- clever. You're learning."

***

The moon became a subdued spotlight filtered through the palms as they observed the activity. The hidden detectives watched several natives carrying torches, tramping along a path through the jungle. Chase and Wyndham followed, the officer whispering that the group must be traveling to the secret cache of canoes to do some night fishing.

Haley wondered if they were stumbling onto kapu land. No one mentioned restrictions, so she warily kept going. Following the broken leaves had been a hit and miss idea, but they were now at the spot where the fishing party had veered off when the boar attack occurred. The new trail now was unknown and each step was taken with wary consideration in this uncertain territory, ascending ever higher in elevation. Keoni made a walking stick with an end sharp enough to be used as crude weapon, a crude defense against a vicious, wild creature. Embarking into the unknown left them vulnerable and without aid should anything dire happen.

Not long into the trek they heard low, quiet voices not far away. Keoni grabbed her and melted into the foliage, crouched low and hardly breathing beneath the thick ferns. It seemed like forever, but was probably only a few moments of waiting. Through the slits in the leaves Haley watched as Holokai and Kana walked past them on the trail. The two men spoke Hawaiian in stern tones, their pace methodical, but steady. As soon as they were out of range Chase relaxed, but did not release his hold on her.

"Tremors in the Force," he whispered in her ear. Scowling in confusion, he continued the pleasantly intimate conversation, his warm breath comforting in the tense hiding space. "The two kahunas know that something is up. They are searching . . . ."

"So the force is powerful but not perfect?" she whispered back. "Why didn't they find us?"

"I don't know." He shook his head slowly.

His face was close and she was beginning to read the subtleties of his expressions. He was perplexed. In contrast, she was afraid they were going to be caught. It was ridiculous to fear her friend Kana, but she felt trepidation of Holokai. What would the stern kahuna do to them if they were discovered trying to escape? What could he do? It wasn't like there was any violence that would come down on them. It was the disapproval of people she respected that she feared.

After they felt it was safe, they emerged from the cover. With a mutual nod of mute agreement, they plunged ahead. The tinted tropical moon was mostly faded through the thick jungle matting overhead, and made it light enough to catch the trail, but dark enough for them to conceal themselves should the need for camouflage arise. As they trekked, they passed waterfalls and huge patches of bamboo and fruit groves, attesting to the amazing natural wonder of the island.

Even in the cooling night the dense jungle was dark, steamy, and humid - a cloying entity surrounding them on all sides. Birds and bugs chirped as they traversed the raw territory. Creatures bit at their exposed skin as they trampled and stumbled through the deep forest cautiously, quickly, but as quietly as possible. As the moonlight waned only errant silver glow penetrated through the thick canopy of trees above, their search more challenging by the low light.

Keoni had assured her he knew the jungles of Hawaii, but not this one specifically. As close as possible, Haley followed the detective along the narrow trail, not admitting to the creeping anxiety inherent with their quest. They had to find the canoes and escape, of course, but obviously the job would not be easy.

The imprisonment was a bittersweet confinement, with magical and amazing events, good experiences with wonderful people, crowding their days and nights. It was the lack of freedom, the lack of choice, which drove them to search for a way out, a way back home. In the restriction and separation, home, with all its faults, seemed all the more sweet for the longing.

They came to the edge of a cliff that Keoni called a pali, and stared down at a pristine, silver-waved bay shimmering under the moonlight. Far below, she thrilled that there were dolphins frolicking in the surf. Her companion tapped her, gesturing to the bay.

"Ka nai'a," he whispered, and the acknowledgement of their familiar rescuers brought a comforting smile to his face.

Sharing the pleasure at seeing their cetacean friends, she watched the creatures in the shimmering night swim. They had both grown fond of the playing dolphins and she thought she could hear their singing on the wind.

"Do you hear that?"

She tried to tune out the gentle wash of tide and the errant notes of dolphin calls, and focus on what else he might be catching. "Something, yeah. What is it?"

"Water. A lot of rushing water."

Yes. Now that he mentioned it she could define the subtle rush of noise as flowing water. Not the surf crashing in rhythmic predictability, but something else Excited, he took her hand and dashed quickly along the thin path, and she realized -- a waterfall! The escalating roar of water was from a waterfall!

The trail ended at an old stonewall. She peered through the darkness into a clearing beyond the stones. The pale moonlight cast the ruins in ominous and eerie shadows of gray and black. Partially formed masks of anger seemed to leer out at them from the deep shadows.

"A heiau. Ancient temple," Keoni explained in a respectful hush. "There are archeological sites everywhere on the islands. Old, primal. Kapu." He patted the top of the wall almost reverently. "Pu'uhonua -- refuge." He peered into the darkness beyond the sacred site. "Waterfall."

The wind, or perhaps an intruder, rustled the brush and they scrambled over the stacked stones and into the center of the heiau. The grounds seemed in disrepair and aged from erosion of wind and water, but still possessing a powerful aura that commanded respect and reverence to this holy place. Not a religious or spiritually sensitive person, even she tuned into some kind of other world power here on this sacred ground. There was also a sense of safety and protection here. Spirits as old as the land must dwell on this spot, she imagined, and on some deep level, she knew they were safe here. Not intruders, but welcome visitors. Pu'uhonua. Refuge.

After several reverent moments of study, Keoni circled in an ever-widening path toward the mountain wall next to the waterfall. Then suddenly he slid behind the flowing sheet of crystal liquid, back into the darkest, shadowed recesses, completely disappearing from the sacred ground.

Haley, standing behind the stone altar in the center, became chilled with spooky wariness. In the filtered moonlight, she could see shapes of moai and tiki – formidable carved stone and wood sentinels who guarded the kapu area. It was her imagination that tricked her eyes into thinking the inanimate objects were moving. About to call out for her friend, she gasped a quiet sigh of relief when he reappeared from behind the waterfall.

In a whispered conference, Keoni speculated that judging from the rush of the ocean breakers, the back of the heiau must be built along the cliff's edge. More protection against enemies. And if this was a refuge like the well known one at Honaunau Bay, then it had to be difficult to breach – offering significant protection to those seeking asylum. The old gods had made their choices well for cities of refuge. Not just anyone could be granted absolution from angry ali'i or akua – royalty or god. Those seeking protection had to be worthy of the shelter.

The wind rose again, blowing leaves, flowers and bits of debris around them. Momentarily, the wind was so stiff it seemed to shift the waterfall, the tricky moonlight dancing strange and mysterious shadows across the glistening, dark face of the cascading water.

"Come on," Chase urged, and led her behind the altar to a rocky trail up the mountain toward the lip of the waterfall.

They moved quietly, slowly, sliding circumspectly along the rocks and dirt until they reached a precipice with the waterfall on the other side. He pulled Haley, with arms around her waist for the last few feet, edging them close to the water. Staring up at the falls, she thought she saw shapes -- figures -- maybe just a trick of the light. Chills coursed her skin. Uneasy, she turned back to scan the night for any threat, but the guarding moai -- stone idols -- and tiki were still motionless, inanimate objects. Only her imagination was playing tricks with her vision.

The wind rose again in an eerie crescendo of bluster and song. It seemed as if ancient voices called to them from the surf below and the trees nearby.

"Do you hear something?" He almost laughed. "Music?"

A spiritual mele, he called it -- a hymn. Ancient chant melting with the wind. Inexplicably, she heard them, too! Incomprehensible words and tones mingled with the mighty crashing music of the waterfall. The coconut band burned her skin, and from Chase's reaction his did, too. As if drawn by unearthly powers, they moved forward. As if the primeval gods were beckoning them -- chanting their way to refuge?

Heiau. Pu'uhonua -- refuge. Sacred ground.

Drawing near to the falls, she saw the shapes she had seen were not imagined, but real. Moai -- stone ki'i gods, inserted on the ledge of the waterfall. The sighting solidified the insane ideas touching his soul in a way he could not describe or even understand.

"Take a deep breath," he whispered into her ear.

Her skin chilled from the refreshing tingle of anticipation and wonder, along with the silvery droplets of water misting around them. Washed with the feeling they hovered on the doorstep of something magical and amazing, she stepped closer to him. Literally they took the plunge as he grabbed her waist with a tight grip, he dragged them both under the waterfall. Emerging drenched and exhilarated, they opened their eyes to find a hidden grotto behind the powerful stream of water.

"Wow," Chase breathed out in awe.

Breathlessly incredulous, she shook her head at the sight, leaning against the wet walls of lava indented into the mountain. It was like something Indiana Jones would discover! Above them, slit-skylights opened to the starry sky, filtering pale illumination from the moon. Behind them, through the narrow aperture, they could only see the wall of moving liquid plunging from on high to depths far below. It was a solid curtain of mist-wreathed water that served as a screen. Before them, a close opening blossomed into darkness a few feet into the secret cave.

"How did you know?"

He shook his head, seeming as confused and astonished as she felt. "I don't know. Instinct, I guess. It's crazy, but the chanting and singing, it seemed to come from here, didn't it?"

"I couldn't tell." Unable to help herself, she stifled a giggle. "The back side of water."

"What?"

"Just a joke from *Disneyland*."

"*Disneyland*?"

"Ever been?"

"Yeah, a long time ago."

"*Jungle Cruise*. Weaving along the river the boat takes you under Schweitzer Falls and the back side of water." He nodded slowly. "Right. It's all in the timing."

"And I guess I don't have it?" She was never good at telling jokes.

"Sorry, no."

Still holding her, both became aware of the contact at the same instant and released the other, backing away slightly, but not too far. She peered into the blackness ahead. Was the flickering light from the waterfall playing tricks with her sight again, or did she see shadows dancing against the murky unknown beyond?

Stepping away from the wall, Chase edged forward. "Want to go exploring?"

"Not especially." Dark, dank, closed, venturing forward did not appeal to her in the least. The situation was perfect for some governess trapped in an exotic plot and a handsome duke or earl. It was not so exciting, dripping in the drafty enclosure. Was that really a flow of air through the cave? "Do you feel the draft?"

"Yes. That means there is more than one way in and out of here."

Voices, this time distinct, alerted them, and they peered through the water to see bobbing lights approaching. It looked like a winding Chinese dragon flitting in a curve around the grounds of the heiau. Men carrying torches, she realized.

"Kana and Holokai." Nervously, he cleared his throat. "I hope."

"You hope?"

"Yeah, cause if they're not our mortal friends they're night walkers."

"Who?"

"Ghostly travelers who come in the night to claim souls. Good thing there's a back door," he snapped, "because someone is coming and I don't think they should find us here."

"Why?" she wondered, knowing he was right without any explanation.

Grabbing her hand, he moved quickly, but carefully, their hands sliding across the disgustingly slimy walls as they made their way past a huge grotto. Indefinable shapes indicated large stones in the cavern, and the pale light from the entrance suggested it was almost like a meeting place with a flat altar-like stone at one end.

"Heiau. Sacred ground and all that. I don't remember all the old legends from tutukane, but I know that intruding on something this important will not be taken lightly. We're already on the outs with this crowd, we shouldn't get caught here."

Out of plain logical principle that sounded like sound advice. "Then we better find the rear exit."

The splash of light and water from the entrance indicated the game was up and the travelers had arrived. Ducking into a wedge at the back of the cave, Keoni nodded toward the back of the cavern. It looked like a second tunnel. Quickly, jogging along the wall curve, they dashed into the tunnel and flattened themselves against the rock as the torch line entered the front of the hollow. Her nerves screamed for them to leave, but he held her hand fast, his cop curiosity getting the better of him, and her fear of the dark and the unknown was keeping her from fleeing out the back channel.

In the torchlight there was no question that the men were who entered the cavern. Holokai was in the lead, his tall image unmistakable, his torch high as a living symbol of his leadership and honored place in society. Behind him several men carried Moe's limp form and laid him on the stone altar. Holokai and Moe and several others gathered around the wounded man.

Haley held her breath, afraid she would be the spectator of some kind of grisly ritual. Did the Hawaiians ever practice human sacrifice? There had never been cannibals here, right? What was their custom of wounded or imperfect inhabitants? She had seen no one sick or lame, she recalled. Was this their answer? Purify society by eliminating the damaged?

From under the altar, in a small compartment closed in by a perfectly fitting slab, Holokai withdrew plants that he ground in a mortar and added water from a trickle running out of the stone wall. The gathered onlookers formed a circle and softly chanted. A few more words were uttered by Holokai; then he helped Moe sit up. Then the party helped Moe back through the waterfall, and disappeared. Soon, their flickering lights no longer dotted and danced in the mottled view from this side of the water.

Chase still held her, and she had no intention of moving. She had read too many books and seen too many movies where the people in hiding reveal themselves too quickly and the person they were hiding from was waiting just around the corner. No rush. Best to let the happy trail of medicine men get far away.

Tugging at her hand, he pointed behind them, down the tunnel they had not yet explored. Not sure which would be the best choice, she decided to trust in his instincts again and followed him.

The men stood in a ring, eerily lit by the flickering torch light. They chanted over the recumbent figure of Moe, who was stretched out along a slab of stone. After a time they finished their prayer and gathered the wounded man, marching out with him in their arms. The closeness, the danger, the fumes and smoke made her head light. It was hot and hard to breathe.

"What was that?"

"Ancient magic. Spiritual healing. I don't know," he admitted in amazement. "I don't believe it, but we saw it."

"Was it even real?" she wondered, still numb at the things they had beheld.

"Power of positive thinking," he insisted. "Moe was still hurt."

"It – looked -- real."

"It's a trick, Haley! The kahuna enhances his power and his hold over the people by showing them this kind of sleight-of-hand magic! I can't believe you were taken in!"

"Well I didn't see any mirrors."

"Your dealing in fiction has affected you."

She remained silent, stung by his rebukes and still feeling distorted.

He stopped on the beach and moved close to her. "We better keep this between ourselves," he confided in a low tone. "And not mention anything about this from this point on. Not unless we know we're alone."

"Agreed." She had been thinking similar guidelines. Best to not let anyone how much they knew about the island secrets. Kana and Amelia, she did not expect any threats from them, but they were on the inside track here. What would they think of the nocturnal skulking around to steal canoes, and spying on private rituals? "My lips are sealed."

He stared at her for a moment, slowing giving a nod.

"Kind of makes me feel like Nancy Drew and Joe Hardy out on a date."

Dispelling the intensity of the night, Keoni laughed softly. "It was fun, Nancy, let's do it again," he whispered and added a wink. With that, he turned and hurried back down toward the beach.

Haley hoped Keoni knew where they were going. Generally, she thought they were headed in the right direction, and hoped this beach connected with familiar strands they could recognize. It would be embarrassing if Holokai sent out a search party for them. What would he think? What would Kana and Amelia think? What would be obvious, probably, she considered, feeling a blush rise from her neck to her forehead. Two young people out late on a romantic island on an isolated beach . . . .

Flickering firelight cast eerie glows on the sand around the curve in the shore. Muted voices contributed to the confirmation that they approached the village. Chase no sooner whispered in her ear to assure their cover stories were matching, when Holokai emerged from the jungle. His expression denoted nothing close to romantic speculation about the couple. Rather, he seemed as angry as an avenging god. Torch held high, the native's wrath made his face a mask of righteous anger. She felt Chase tense for an attack from the muscled leader. The big Hawaiian's eyes burned with fury.

"Where have you been?"

"Out. Walking the beach," Chase snapped back instantly, "as if it's any of your business."

Wyndham clutched onto his hand with both of hers. "It was your idea that we stay here and get together," she told him. "How can we do that if we don't get to know each other first? You know we're just friends, don't you?"

The dark, narrowed eyes scanned her face, as if searching for subterfuge. He did the same of Chase. "You should stay in your huts," he barked. "It is late. Early fishing tomorrow."

"Right." Tentatively, he gave her a quick peck on the cheek. "Night, Miss Drew. See you in the morning."

"Night."

Under the watchful eye of Holokai and Keoni, she retired to her hut. Settling in on her straw mat, she listened as the village closed down for the night. Long after the fire died and the voices ceased, she stared out the open window in the shack, studying the amazingly bright, silver, twinkling stars blinking in the velvety, midnight-indigo sky.

In quiet moments like this, her mind swirled with the incomprehension of the wild ride her life had taken. Tonight was Wednesday. It had been a week today that her adventure of a lifetime had started in San Diego. Since then she had witnessed magic and the aftermath of murder. Unbelievable.

***

The next day they were watched carefully. Haley and Keoni waited out the surveillance, playing at courting lovers, while scouting and preparing. Under the guise of gathering food, or observing the fishing in the bay, they covertly stockpiled gourds and dried fruit for their eventually sea journey. They hoped to find the fishing canoes, but he would be happy with Amelia's boat as a means of escape.

Chase related that ancient Polynesians navigated by waves, currents and stars. Modern outrigger paddlers did not use such skills, but he knew enough to gamble on his sketchy course plotting. Stealing the vessel was unethical, but under the circumstances, Keoni felt justified in borrowing it as a means of rescuing them from the island. Later they would figure out a way to get the boat back here to Amelia.

That was assuming Teo had not landed on the island in an effort to discover the magic he believed was harbored here. If he had found this refuge, then he had done an excellent job of hiding out. There had been no thefts – that she knew of – for a few days Maybe they had been wrong in suspecting him of the stolen goods.

When she was invited to gather bananas from a new grove, Haley jumped at the chance to explore a new area. For the first time she traveled legitimately toward the windward hills in the direction of the sacred cave, near the canoe cove. The path taken this time was not familiar, but occasionally they would crest on the trail, curving out to observe the ocean, and she recognized a cove or a rocky point that was familiar from the nocturnal excursion of a few nights before. Trailing along, but a little behind the main group, she did a double take at one turn when she noted what she thought was a boat – no --

wreckage from a boat? It was hard to tell from this distance of what would be a block or so if they were in the city, but to her it looked like a boat. Amelia's boat? No, it didn't look quite the same as the pictures, but it was difficult to tell from the distance and break up of the wreckage. When Nani started rattling off some sour-toned comments, Haley pulled her attention back to her companions.

"What did you say?'

Malia supplied, "My daughter complains." Nani looked at her and she shrugged. The woman switched to English. "Bananas are running away! Some little menehune is stealing them!"

It seemed that the common pile at the edge of the grove had diminished by several bunches.

"Menehune?"

"Little people. "

Little people? Like Leprechauns?"

Nani continued the explanation. "Menehune supposed to live in Kauai, but maybe they come here. During the night, do magic. Maybe they come here," she huffed, shaking her head and calling to a few of the other women to gather the remaining fruit. "I will go find bananas."

"Don't be long," Melia told her and started after the other women who had already disappeared along the trail toward the village.

Haley told the younger girl, "I'll come with you. No one should be alone in the jungle if there's some kind of animal stealing things."

"No animal, I tell you - Menehune."

The difficult to follow trail of broken leaves and branches coursed erratically through the matted forest like that of a racing animal. Monkey? Monkeys weren't native to these islands, right?

330

She would have to find out. What else could it be? Haley was nervous tracking through the wilderness with only Nani at her side, but the young woman was determined and angry enough to be a match to any wild primate.

What was great about the journey was that several times they weaved out to the edge of the pali and got a great view of the ocean. At one point they dipped downhill to a lovely cove, and Haley spotted Amelia Hunter' boat, the Pacific Star beached up high by the tree line! The beautiful boat, intact! Their means of escape! Only about a half hour out of the village! She was sure she could find her way back here. Nani was so angry she did not take notice of the slip, apparently, because she just charged on in search of the Menehune.

The interior brush crackled and rustled and Haley held onto Nani's shoulders, forcing her to stop. When nothing came out to attack them, they waited. Silence. Slowly, Nani moved forward and parted a bush of thick ferns. There were some of the bananas on the ground and some peels! They must have just missed the thief! Nani triumphantly grabbed the goods and tromped back the way they came. Haley studied the scene of the crime for a moment, wondering what they had interrupted. What animal peels bananas? The human kind.

When they reached the village Keoni dashed over to her. "Where is Malia?"

Malia. Moe's wife. Nani's mother. Gasping, she didn't know what to say. "We were out gathering fruit, but she was coming back ahead of us."

"I know. The other women said they lost track of her and thought she went back to walk with you and Nani."

"Not likely that she is lost." She gulped. "Teo?"

"That's my first thought," he admitted tightly. "Why would he kidnap a woman from the village?"

"Information? He was all obsessed about the secrets of this island. Did you tell Holokai?"

"Yes, but he still refused to believe a bad guy could discover their island and break the magic spell that protects them," he scoffed.

"We have to find him. If any of these men go up against Teo, they'll be slaughtered."

His lip twitched. "And we won't? Teo took my service revolver! He's got a weapon of his own! We are unarmed!"

"So what do we do?"

"We join the search party."

Following behind the trail of torch-bearing searchers, Chase took Haley by the hand and veered off when she indicated this was the path taken to gather food earlier in the day. In the reflected moonlight finding the trail was easy initially. As they coursed through the jungle with stealth and caution, it became more difficult to find landmarks. She wished she would have remembered Chase's clever leaf-folding trick, but it had not occurred to her today. Without a torch, and with only meager, reflected moonlight, the trek was slow.

"Why are we separating from the group?" she whispered when they were a safe distance away from the bulk of the group.

The glow of the fire sticks gradually disappeared in the dense jungle. "This is the first time today we've had a chance to search for Amelia's boat. If Teo is shipwrecked on this island, he has to be looking for an escape just like us."

"Sure. Once he has the secret to the power of the island he will want to use it in his world. What good would such a gift be here at

332

the end of the universe? He'd want to go back where he has power and enjoy the magic in his own realm, to further his cause."

"Exactly."

When they broke out of the thick undergrowth to the sea cliffs, however, the venture became much easier. She remembered the wreckage was around a curve, and she thought they sloped down toward the beach. She groaned aloud when the trail came to an end at a rocky promontory not far above the crashing ocean.

"This is a little point that probably spills into the sea. Tricky sailing if the canoes are near here. Hmm." The frown was clear in the tone. "Wreckage means this could be a dangerous area. Not encouraging."

It was all too reminiscent of Gilligan's Island for her taste

Curving around a bend in the trail, they were suddenly in sight of a deeper cove notched in the shoreline. The wreckage was on the outside lip of the inlet. Deeper toward the beach, just below their hilltop viewpoint, rested the coveted outriggers. After long nights reconnoitering, they finally found the hidden fleet! Six canoes lay beached on a stretch of sand at a southeast tip of land. Thrilled, they hugged each other, Chase lifting her off her feet in exultation.

"We did it!" He laughed in glee. "Won't be long now!"

Too conflicted to respond, she shook her head. "We still have to find Teo."

"I know. Let's have a look at the boat."

Calming, he grew silent, studying the cove and the vessels. He guessed the direction of the island, the tides, the reef, in relation to this location. Then he discussed the course they would have to take to reach Kauai. It was just a guess. The reef here looked deeper than near the village, and the surf broke at a better angle. It would be tough paddling just two of them against the waves, but he thought they could handle the tough job. There were two sizes and weights of canoes. Two small craft were light enough for them to handle. The large ones would require a trained crew of six muscled and skilled men. The only thing that really concerned them was the dark storm always hovering – seemingly circling the island like an enclosure. If they became disoriented in the clouds, they could lose all sense of direction and be lost completely.

Leading the way down the rocks, Keoni scrambled down to sea level and studied the landscape. In the dim light his attention snagged on an anomaly to the left and he pointed down the beach. She thought she saw the outline of something protruding from the surf. He motioned for her to follow as he jumped down to the sand. Not until she was right at the splintered wood and broken bow did she see the partial name still visible on the wrecked boat.

"The Ocean Island," she gasped, reading the name on the stern of the wreckage. "Sam's boat! Teo did shipwreck!"

"So right my dear!" the growl shouted behind her. Before she could turn, one arm was grabbed and twisted up behind her back, while a strong arm trapped her neck in a vice-like chokehold. "Don't try anything, cop, or I'll twist her neck right off."

Chase had spun around to face them. Panicked that the crazed Sam Simon held her life in her hands, she strained to breathe. Knowing she was close to passing out, sickened at him pressing his face against the side of her head, she fought to achieve a measure of calm to save her life.

"Take it easy," Chase warned both of them. "I'm not armed. Stay cool, Simon. No need to panic."

He tightened his grip until she yelped at what seemed like her last breath was squeezed out of her. "Who's panicked? I'm perfectly calm. I think you two love birds are having the anxiety attack."

"Pretty brilliant plan," Chase conceded tightly. "Teo attacked us and made us think he had thrown you overboard. You were in it together."

"Smart cop, a lot smarter than that oaf Teo. He thought I was financing his political dreams."

So the big kahuna was dead? If Sam killed Teo, maybe he killed Carrie and Kai, too? Fighting to breathe as he choked her air off, she knew she was in no position to argue.

"So we have you to thank for the recent thefts in the village?"

"Yes, such a cozy little Shangri La. You could spare the food while I was searching. I was wondering how to find the secret caves and suddenly here you are to be my tour guides."

"What did you do with Malia?" Chase demanded.

"The lovely native? She was no use to me," Simon scoffed. "Spoke only Hawaiian. Useless language. She served well as a distraction. I tied her to a tree not far from the village. While everyone is following her trail, you two will lead me to the sacred caves."

"What are you talking about?" She tried to claw at his arm with her free hand, but the attack was met with a yank on her throat, closing off her air entirely. Head swimming, she released her fingernails from his arm, and the pressure eased. "What secret caves?"

"Don't play dumb. This is Dolphin Island! Magic! There is a pyramid cave in the center of the island. It is the source of power and energy for the whole earth! I've been watching. I know it's real."

His voice was tight and elevated with excitement and madness. "I saw that islander was injured and the next day he was healed after a trek in the jungle. I've been trying to recreate the path, but now I don't have to do that. You'll do it for me."

Chase shook his head. "You're crazy —"

His hold shifted and she felt something cold and hard press against her neck.

Simon's voice hissed, "Maybe. But I'm armed and you're not. I know what I saw. I've been hunting for years. Spending millions on research and divers and archeologists. Imagine my surprise when your foolish old grandfather and this little upstart bookseller stumbled onto the truth!"

"The logs."

"Yes. The old mariners knew about this place. It took a long time to find the coordinates. And I still didn't get it exactly right, but that storm actually did me a favor. I shipwrecked on a reef and managed to raft ashore on some of the wreckage."

So much for the idea that the dolphins saved only the righteous. Maybe they were too distracted saving Keoni and her to notice a serpent had run aground on their island.

"Now you take me there or she dies. Simple trade. My immortality for your girlfriend."

"And after that?" the detective wondered.

"I'll have the most important secret in the history of the world. I will be immortal. I will have all the power in the world. If you're lucky, I might let you live to amuse me as my slaves. Who knows?"

His hold tightened and she felt faint, hardly gasping, working on breathing shallowly and not panicking.

"You'll have to let her go --

"No deal. I know both of you went out that night with the others. You lead and we'll follow."

Twisting to look at him for a moment, she could read the hatred of the criminal. This close his mania and intent madness was terrifying. She turned to her ally for reassurance, which he supplied with a wink. An instant later Keoni's expression slid back to cold anger when he stared at Simon. "All right. Come on."

Her head swimming, they stumbled down the trail for a few minutes. When it became clear they could not travel through the jungle so closely yoked, Simon released the chokehold, but kept her arm twisted behind her back and the gun at her ear, in uncompromising control.

She didn't know if Chase was leading them in the right direction or not. She remained tensed for a sudden move on her friend's part to rescue her. After too long a time tramping in the jungle, she realized the stalling, the long trek in the wilderness, was the plan. Either the officer had something in mind, or he was wearing Simon down and hoping to come up with a plot. Maybe he had just forgotten where the cave was located. She was sure she could never find it again on her own, maybe Keoni was having the same problem. No, the terrain was looking familiar and there were not that many places they could circle around forever on this rock. They were close, she was sure, now.

Coming around a fern laden intersection of paths, the trio all halted when they heard the low-rush wind whistling loudly from somewhere above them. Simon yanked her to a stop.

"Hear that? Like wind blowing through a tunnel!"

"It's a waterfall!" she corrected.

"Yes! Caves are frequently hidden behind waterfalls! How clever of the ancients! The sacred cave is there, isn't it?" He didn't wait for a reply. "Let's go!" he commanded with a hard shove.

Haley would not look at Keoni, afraid it would give away that they were near the slope leading up to the lava cave. Stumbling ahead, Simon pushed her, commanding Keoni ahead, until they found the small trail leading uphill. Ordering them forward, they hiked up into the craggy rocks, Simon discerning the indistinct footpath with the old stone heiau now visible.

"There!" he shouted and drove her ahead. "It's one of their old temples!"

Think fast. Think fast. They – she -- could not allow this cretin to enter the sacred cave and discover the secret of Dolphin Island! It would be allowing the serpent into Eden! Think! Stop him! She blasted herself. As he shoved her up on the beginning of the trail, she stopped resisting. Then she sent an obvious glare, with narrowed eyes, to Chase.

"Okay, okay, you figured it out!" she snapped at Simon, trying to pull away from his grasp. "Just let me go. I'll take you up to the stupid cave!" She managed to gain freedom, and instead of fighting, she voluntarily started ascending the crusty lava mixed with red volcanic dirt.

"Hold it!" Simon shouted.

Frozen in place, she held her breath. Was the reverse psychology working? Did he fall for her misdirection? Should she push, or not? If he was undecided, too forceful of a presentation could ruin her scheme. Never very good at poker, she was depending on a monumental ruse, to a certified nut case, to shake him off the real trail. Hoping she could stall, she could buy Chase time to think

338

of a plan, or for Holokai and the cavalry to arrive. The latter being far fetched since the kahuna or Kana had no idea they had been out here exploring. Their whole purpose had been one of secrecy and concealment! They had been too good at that.

"Hey, I'm going up there," she decided, taking the risk of shoving him to react to her actions.

Simon stopped her with striking her arm. "Not so fast!

She looked down at his left hand – the one that held the gun. Predominantly left-handed. Haley stared at their captor, feeling stupid that she had that little piece of evidence in the back of her mind all along and never made the final connection. Left handed.

Another pivotal moment of life and death. Push him or remain passive? She sensed, from his agitation and the wild look in his eyes, that he was getting desperate, more desperate, so her choice was to ease back. Comply, but not capitulate.

"Sure, Sam. You're the one with the weapon."

Gulping back an involuntary gasp, she dared a quick dart of her eyes to Chase. Did he get the clue in her slip of the tongue? Gun! Weapon! They couldn't risk trying to grab the revolver from this maniac, but they might be able to goad him into shooting at something. A gunshot on this island would attract a lot of attention and bring her innocent friends into danger. Holokai, Kana, and especially Amelia, would know what to do. There would be safety in numbers. And they knew this island; it was their home. They really could be the cavalry if she played this right.

Without looking at Chase now, she stared at the thick forest to their left, just beyond the rocky trail. She gave her head a quick nod, then looked away. From the corner of her eye, she noted Sam turn in that direction.

"What are you looking at?" he snarled, grabbing her by the hair and yanking her around to face the jungle, with him hiding behind, using her as his shield. "Who's there? Come out now!" He pushed her up the jungle trail. She stumbled, hitting her head on the lava stone edging the path. "Go!"

With him pushing and holding onto her wrist, it was a tough ascent up the dirt path toward the waterfall. She winced as they crossed into sacred ground. Passing the old, worn lava stone, every step a little closer to the betrayal of this island, and the people, who believed in the miracles of Dolphin Island.

As they reached the narrow, wet, slippery trail, she came to a decision. This was treacherous footing and her last chance to prevent Sam from stealing the power of this island. Did she believe in it? Apparently so. She was about to risk her life to preserve the secret that the Hagoth ohana had protected for generations.

"No, run!" she screamed and at the risk of losing a fist full of mane, she ducked to the right. "We won't take him to the cave!"

Instead of being startled and trying to grapple with her, Sam spun to dash into the waterfall. Grabbing his arm, she twisted back, hoping Keoni was there to catch her. Thanks to the physics of wet dirt and rocks under their feet Sam plunged into the water, and the force of the mighty falls propelled his body back. Gravity and panic worked against him. He released his hold on Haley to reach out to the rocks for purchase. Instead he grabbed onto streaming liquid. His body continued its descent, tumbling like a rag doll into the stream of the powerful water.

Afraid she was about to follow his drop, she gasped when a strong arm wrapped around her waist and pulled her back. Keoni leaned on the solid rock of the mountain and she leaned on him, gasping for breath. When she felt steady enough to move again, she turned around and hugged him tightly.

In a final show of theatrics, the madman fired blind, shooting into the jungle as he dropped. Birds cackled in panic and took flight, some of them flooding out of the brush into their faces.

"You okay?"

She nodded, still breathing hard.

"Let's get you out of here."

Still gripping onto her, he guided them down the slippery dirt and rocks. As they stepped into the heiau, he slid to an abrupt halt. Looking up, she gasped at the sight of Teo standing there like an avenging god. Jeans torn, chest bare, his livid face burned hatred.

"You're alive!" she hardly breathed.

She had jumped to the conclusion that Sam had killed his competitor. The double cross had been in the works she guessed. Glancing quickly at his hands, she saw they were balled into fists. No weapon. Good. Did a guy that size really need any against two unarmed people much smaller and not nearly as strong?

Chase moved over and pushed her onto a stone ledge.

"Simon is dead," Teo growled. "You next. Nothin' gonna stand in my way now. I gonna get you, traitor. Haole in brown skin." He spat on the ground in contempt.

"Bring it on," Chase challenged, stepping clear of Haley. "You pretend to be the big kahuna for the people and all you want is power for yourself. You're no better than Sam Simon. He used you –"

"Shut up!" Teo advanced, growling and flexing his fists.

"He wanted power. That's all you're interested in, Teo. You're a fake! You're nothing more than a greedy thug!"

Keoni in mortal, hand-to-hand combat with this behemoth! The cop didn't have a chance! In her friend, though, she saw the muscles tensed and the face contorted in a feral anger that matched Teo's.

They circled each other like two wary tigers assessing their foe. Teo lunged and Chase leaped around to jump on his back. They twisted until Teo flipped the cop into the dirt and then fell on him, trying to strangle him or break his neck.

Keoni maneuvered out of the grasp and scrambled away, pausing to check on her for an instant. Teo picked up a sharp stone from the ground and came at the detective, slashing the rock like a blade as he tried to snag his opponent.

Heart in her throat, she raced over, snatching up a hefty lava chunk to smack Teo in the head. She struck the blow and the monstrous kahuna flung out an arm like an enraged gorilla.

The bash knocked the wind out of her and she plunged into the stonewall, faint from lack of air, her head pounding from another blow. Keoni used the momentum to drive them both into the side of the mountain. She peaked over the edge and was shocked to see no sign of the men!

Slowly crawling on her knees she closed the distance, picking up a rock along the way, she raced down, slipping and sliding, into the waterfall and through to the inside of the sacred cave.

"Keoni!" she yelled in panic.

Only hesitating a moment, she raced through the intense shower of spray and icy water and into the dark, close interior of the cavern. It took a moment for her eyes to adjust to the blackness. Hearing was the first sense that sharpened. The labored breathing and grunts from up ahead clued her to where the two men had gone. Able to discern the rocky floor, she rushed ahead, her hands steadying her uneven stumbling toward the center.

Stepping into the sacred room with the glowing stones, she screamed as Teo lunged from the shadows and grabbed her by the throat. His face bloody, his eyes unfocused, he seemed more dead than alive.

The lava rock in her hand came up and smashed into his skull. She did not turn her head to see the result, but felt the splatter of liquid, saw from her periphery vision the splash of red flying toward her. Then the hold on her neck relaxed and he collapsed to the earth.

Stunned, she backed away, stumbling into Chase. He gently took the rock from her hand and held her in his arms. The quaking was not the ground, but her, she realized. She kept her head against Chase's chest, too revolted to check to make sure Teo was really dead this time. She was going to let the professional take over now.

"Is he dead?"

"He is. Now don't worry about that now. He's not going to hurt you. Just relax. Are you all right?"

"That depends."

"On what?"

"If you or the island are quaking."

Laughing, his hold around her tightening. "It's all right, I promise."

***

Haley sat beside Chase, clutching his hand. It was a comfortable silence, companionable, as if between friends who had known each other for years. Living through a life and death crisis did that to people, she had heard. She never expected to experience such drama herself, but in the aftermath of several near-death terrors it seemed – right.

Sitting on their favorite beach, watching the perfect waves wash onto the unbelievably beautiful sand, ringed by tall palms and blue sky, she could believe in magic. It seemed more than skill that brought them through their recent adventures. Was it divine intervention?

"Do you think we were saved by the magic of Dolphin Island?"

"Magic? How about the ancient Hawaiian gods?" He smirked. "You're not buying into the magic of the island, are you?"

Clearly he was still a skeptic. "What about Amelia?" she refuted, not firm enough in her faith, in what she had come to understand about the eternal youth and health. To the reasonable, modern mind, it did sound crazy.

"Good living and positive thinking, I told you."

"And Teo and Sam being killed before they could hurt the island? Poetic justice from the protected land?"

"Carelessness on the part of the crazed criminals," he countered. "Magic –"

"I think it more like the bump on your head."

She felt the bump that had lost most of its swelling but still made the side of her head tender to the touch. The fights with Teo and Sam had aggravated the constant headache she had lived with for days. "Kana and Amelia believe it."

"So does Holokai. You're fiction-talking again. Maybe you should write fiction instead of selling it." In a gentler tone he admitted, "Dolphin Island has made me rethink a few things about my heritage. Kamala has some good ideas, she just goes about them

344

the wrong way. But magic? I think it was old fashioned police work beating the bad guys."

That he was willing to bridge the gap between his sister-in-law and himself was encouraging. This experience had changed their perceptions about Hawaii and the definition of paradise.

"I'm seeing things a little differently now. Like you."

Maybe this secret paradise was enchanted after all if Dolphin Island could change hearts and perceptions.

***

When the late afternoon sun burned the surface of the ocean with glittering fire, kissing the waves with rainbow sprays and fluffy whitecaps, a canoe was pushed from the sand into the water. The villagers gathered, placing leis and kisses on the departing couple. Even Holokai hugged Haley and Keoni in sentimental aloha and wished them well until they met again. Amelia was the last to hug them, and her tears brought Haley's watering eyes to a tender flood of emotion.

"I'm staying," the elderly woman announced with a radiant smile. "You know I've been sick." It was not a question. "This is where I have health and happiness and all I need." She kissed Keoni on the cheek. "I will think of you often."

"I'll never forget you," Haley responded, hugging her tight, regretting she would not have more time to hear fabulous stories of the old days and tales of outrageous adventures. Just more time to be with this amazing woman.

"No you won't." Amelia laughed. "Like poor Sam, I'm going to be lost at sea and declared dead."

Chase, Kana and Haley would sail back to Honolulu with a solid cover story. Chase would give the theory that Sam Simon and Teo concocted an insane plot to murder Kana, Carrie, Kai and Amelia to own a prized book. Then they kidnapped Kana, Haley and Keoni, took them out on the open ocean to find a secret cove where Amelia kept the valued book. Teo, Sam and Amelia left the others stranded. They never saw the activist, millionaire or ex-spy again.

It was a loose and weak story, but it covered most of the facts and mysteries. Chase disliked creating such fiction to excuse murder and kidnapping, but he had little choice in order to protect the secret of the island.

Amelia continued. "My attorney is prepared. He knows I've been ill and has told me numerous times I should not sail at my age." Impishly, she delivered, "With the threat of murder from known killers like Teo and Sam, my fate will be sealed." She dramatically placed the back of her hand on her forehead. "And so in a few months you will receive the bulk of my estate, my dear friend."

"What?" Haley gasped.

"You'll get the estate and enough money to live more than comfortably the rest of your life. I hope you do use it to open a mystery shop in the islands." She cast a meaningful glance at Keoni. "You might like to stay. Besides, you're also going to be my dog Hoku's keeper and she deserves to have you there to take care of her."

Too stunned to know how to reply, Haley shook her head in astonishment, while Keoni chuckled. Insisting they needed to catch the tide, Kana urged them to the shoreline. Pushing the canoe into the water, they waved when the villagers started singing a poignant song that was melodious and heartbreaking in its purity and beauty. It had to be a song of farewell, a gift of aloha as they left Bali Hai.

"I will never forget you. Mahalo," she called to them, then turned away to wipe the tears from her eyes. "Aloha."

Kana paddled with Haley and Keoni, angling into the surf to dodge the most powerful crest of the breakers. When she glanced back, the natives were still waving. Then she had to focus on fighting the mighty ocean and finally clearing the reef and following the curve of the island.

Before her arms fell off from the exertion, they reached the far, secluded harbor where Amelia's boat, the Hokukai, was anchored, Exhausted, they pushed the canoe onto the sand then swam out to board the boat. Settling down on a cushioned deck bench, Haley watched the island recede as the vessel sailed into the rolling waves and entered the dark, tumultuous clouds rimming the horizon.

Two grey forms exploded out of the ocean. Kahana and Makani Hou! They leaped in arcs in front of the bow and she was cheered that the friends followed them.

Rain pelted them and soon they were drenched, cold and she was disoriented. Waves threw the boat like driftwood and she hung on while Kana worked to keep them on course. When she turned to search for their ocean friends, she was disappointed to see the dolphins were gone.

The storm eased; the rain tapered away; and they soon cleared the dark clouds. As they watched, the mist bank cleared to reveal the enchanted tropical island beyond just for a moment. "There –" Before the sentence was complete, the island disappeared before their eyes. And the mist returned. She fingered the coconut bracelet on her wrist and the amulet around her neck. "Aloha, Dolphin Island."

EPILOGUE

I think San Diego is going to seem pretty
dull after all this.

Haley's motions were slow as she packed her suitcase. It was hard to leave. After calling her family yesterday to let them know she was alive and well, she was happy to hear there were no more mysterious break-ins or intrigues concerning her ohana or her store. The police in San Diego considered the case open, but probably the work of local kids. She was going to let that remain a mystery, feeling less attention on the incident and the log book was a good way to protect the truth.

There were so many other things to attend to it was mind-boggling. Her day and night had been consumed with legalities. The cover story was simple and had been accepted at face value. Who was going to dispute the logical and reputable word of a kahuna and a cop? There was enough eyewitness evidence and conjecture to nail Teo and Simon as murderers, kidnappers and crazed, obsessive collectors. The search for the fugitives and Amelia remained open, but the media was already discussing the ex-spy in the past tense.

If Haley had read all this craziness in the final chapters of a mystery novel, she would have never believed the end. In reality, though, the denouement was filled with enough coincidence, circumstantial evidence and witness veracity, to satisfy the police.

There had been meetings with Amelia's attorney and the closing up of her estate until everything could be settled. Following would be a waiting period before the missing could be declared dead. Meanwhile, Hoku was reportedly happy in her new, if temporary digs, with the Chase ohana. Haley would take possession of the dog when she returned.

The knock at the door startled her, and she dug in her pocket for a few bucks to tip the porter. She drew in a surprised breath at seeing Keoni in the hallway.

"Thought I could drive you to the airport. When will you be back to open your new bookstore?" he wondered, the wind whipping through the convertible with refreshing tugs.

"I need to settle things at home, of course."

"Sure."

"Then when I come back I'll need some local advice about a productive neighborhood, and some good help. Maybe some of your relatives would be willing to give me a hand?"

He smiled, a devastating gesture with dimples and white, straight teeth that she thought she would never tire seeing. "I think that can be arranged."

Her stomach did little flip-flops of delight. "Great."

Pulling up at the departure gate for her airline, he tugged the bag out of the back seat and stood with her at the curb. Dropping the luggage, he lifted his sunglasses so she could see his dark eyes, then he took her hand. "It's going to be pretty quiet around here without you."

"I think San Diego is going to seem pretty dull after all this," she admitted, not brave enough to tell him how much she was going to miss him.

"Yeah, same here." He cleared his throat. "I've grown pretty attached to you." From out of his shirt pocket, he removed a small parcel wrapped in colorful paper. "Here's a little aloha gift for you. A kind of memento of our – uh – adventures."

Touched and embarrassed, she took it in both hands and stared at it for longer than necessary to hide the deep emotions coursing through her heart and soul. This parting was tougher than she had expected, and the thoughtful present only enhanced the confusion, regret and sadness of the moment.

"I didn't get anything for you," she admitted with chagrin.

"You can bring me back something from San Diego." His bright tone gave the encounter an upbeat lift.

"I will." Carefully opening the Hawaiian print paper, she drew in a breath of surprise at the charming silver watch adorned with blue dolphins along the band. "Oh, Keoni. It's wonderful. Beautiful." The emotions surged at the backs of her eyes and she laughed to ward off a sentimental sob. "Kahana and Makani Hou." She would always wear this treasured watch along with her coconut band from Dolphin Island and her enchanting dolphin amulet. They would ever remind her of an unforgettable, magic refuge close to her heart.

"You'll think of them often," he predicted. "When you check the time, you will always remember a timeless place."

She gave him a tight hug that lasted longer than was socially acceptable for friends, probably. Fitting, since what they had shared at the charmed edge of the known world qualified them for some kind of relationship that was also indefinable right now.

Not so many days ago she thought she understood and knew perfection. Having found it for real, she readjusted her definitions. In the real world now, she might be able to find it again, in this plane of existence. At least she would be on the path searching for it now. It might be right here in Hawaii.

"I will."

"And I'm glad I won't have to really say aloha to you." He gave a last squeeze to the hug, showing no sign of wanting to release her. "I'm glad you're coming back."

Thrilled at the attitude, she nervously confessed, "I feel the same."

"Soon?"

"Soon."

Then he took her chin in his hand and tilted her face up to his. And kissed her!

***

Almost ten days after she left her home and her routine life in San Diego, Haley drove straight from the airport to her store at the harbor. It all looked the same, nothing had significantly changed on the freeway or in the coastal town, or at the quaint shopping center, but she saw everything differently now. She had changed, and her perception of life had correspondingly followed.

Edging into her crowded shop was like a homecoming in a sitcom. Amy, Skye and Gar were all behind the counter, and the store was so stuffed with people she could hardly work her way through the main aisle. When she made her way to the cash register, it was anticlimactic because her friend and relatives did not even notice her in the crush of customers.

Nacho, the Golden/Lab mix, snaked around the corner of the counter and nuzzled her whining for attention and she complied. "Some welcome. Thanks for remembering who I am, boy. I'm remembering you in my will."

"Hey, cuz, get over here and help!" Gar yelled. "We're swamped."

Amy and Skye looked up from behind the counter and gave her a wave. "Nice tan." Skye smiled. "Good to have you back."

"We've got more customers than books." Amy laughed as she gestured around. "About time you showed up."

"Yeah, aloha to you, too, my ohana and aikane," she smirked as she started bagging several books purchased by the elderly tourist at the counter. "Family and friends," she translated.

"Cool, cuz, still on Hawaiian time."

"Thought you were going to stay there," Amy nudged her. "Money and a good looking cop, you shouldn't have come back."

"I have to settle everything here. By that time, Amelia's estate will be cleared and we can start looking for a shop over there. I can't leave all my treasures on this side of the Pacific," she protested.

"I want to get a look at this cop," Amy told her.

Not sure, she appreciated the brush off, Haley knew from their tone they were only teasing her. "Listen, Gar, I want to check out that log after we close. It's still in a safe place?"

"Safe as can be," her cousin promised.

He turned around and pushed Nacho aside from the dog bed cushion that was behind the counter. Between the bedding and the basket, he pulled a plastic bag and unwrapped a beautiful, leather bound journal with the scrimshaw carving of an old sailing ship. It was much like the Pacific Star painting in Amelia's study.

"You hid it in Nacho's bed?"

"Who would think to look for it there?"

Whom indeed. Not Sam, certainly, who had burglarized her shop and home, Kana's and Amelia's to find the treasure that would take him to a magic island.

Considering the crazy adventures of the past fortnight, it all seemed fitting that the missing link ended up as a pillow for the dog. More irony and poetic justice than she could deal with right now. She'd save it for the next chapter in her life – Hawaii.

PAU

Printed in the United States
153601LV00007B/14/P

9 781615 841509